Surely he had heard wrong. The child couldn't have said what Charlie thought he did, could he...

Jonathan rested his cheek on Charlie's chest, his head facing the foot of the bed. The child's warmth penetrated Charlie's shirt, his hair smelling of baby shampoo. Their first conversation—the moment was magical. A slender thread was knitting their bond. The child spoke, his little voice barely audible. "I miss Gram, too."

Charlie stroked the little guy's head, barely touching its silky strands.

Then Jonathan uttered a few shocking words. Charlie was sure he'd misunderstood, but something in the child's trembling confession told him otherwise. Charlie was terrified of breaking the spell by asking him to repeat what he'd said, but he could not resist.

"Jonathan. Look at me." The child didn't move. "Please. I didn't catch what you said, and I want to know what's troubling you. Perhaps I can help."

Before Charlie could process a suitable follow-up, Jonathan eased from the bed and, without looking back, trudged from the room.

Stunned, Charlie raised himself onto his elbow. He waited. Nothing. Jonathan did not return.

Charlie could have sworn that Jonathan said, "I killed Gram."

He glanced toward Bill Kelly, but the old man appeared to be sound asleep. Charlie lowered his head back onto the pillow, attempting to process the fragile implication of what he'd just heard. Surely, he had misunderstood. How could a small child—

And yet—what could he make of such a confession? He hadn't a clue.

Vietnam vet and VA hospice patient, Charlie Alderfer, has survived a medical catastrophe, only to discover that he faces three final battles—an inoperable aneurysm lurks in his chest; a mute and despondent five-year-old visitor harbors a terrible secret and needs compassionate help; and a nocturnal intruder is murdering Charlie's roommates, one by one. When Charlie reports that they did not die of natural causes, no one believes him, labeling him *confused*. But when the five-year-old boy finally tells Charlie his secret, the former soldier quickly realizes that the death of this boy's grandmother and the death of the terminally ill roommates could be related. Is there really a serial killer roaming the halls of VA hospices, preying on defenseless old veterans? And if so, how can Charlie stop him? Using himself as bait, Charlie faces certain death, but if there's one thing he learned in the army, it's that "freedom isn't free."

KUDOS for *The Dying Hour*

In *The Dying Hour* by Nancy A. Hughes, Charlie Alderfer is a patient in a VA hospice center recovering from surgery on an aneurism. As Charlie's terminally ill roommates start dying, one by one, Charlie happens to witness one's murder and quickly realizes that what he saw was not a dream. His roommates did not die of natural causes as everyone thinks they did. But when Charlie tells his doctor about it, he suddenly starts being sedated and given some kind of strange drugs. But Charlie is no fool. He palms the pills, instead of swallowing them, and sends them off to a private lab, discovering that the pills are lethal. When he confronts the doctor, and they begin to investigate, all hell breaks loose. Armed with an eye-witness in the form of a five-year-old boy who watched his grandmother's murder, Charlie is determined to stop this killer from preying on defenseless elderly patients. The story is a page turner and Hughes's character development is superb. The plot is strong with enough twists and turns to keep you biting your nails all the way through. ~ *Taylor Jones, Reviewer*

The Dying Hour by Nancy Hughes is the story of a man and a little boy, both of whom witness separate murders by what appears to be the same serial killer. Five-year-old Jonathan hid in the closet when the Angel of Death came to take his gram to heaven, but instead of taking her, the angel left her dead on the floor, and poor little Jonathan thinks it's his fault that the angel didn't take her to heaven. Charlie Alderfer is a patient at the same VA hospice where Jonathan's grandpa is patient, and Charlie also witnesses a visit from the angel of death, this time to Charlie's roommate, but Charlie is old enough to know that the killer is no angel. Piecing together what he remembers from the night his roommate died and what Jonathan tells him about his gram's death, Charlie sets a trap for the killer, using himself as bait. Now all he has to do is survive. *The Dying Hour* combines a heart-warming story of family pride and honor with a suspense-filled murder mystery that keeps you on your toes, and the edge of your seat, from beginning to end.

ACKNOWLEDGEMENTS

My heartfelt thanks to the men and women of our us Armed Forces who unselfishly defend our freedom and our nation. *The Dying Hour*, while a work of fiction, honestly portrays the angels of our VA's hospices who serve our veterans and their families with skill, dignity, and grace during their final journey. I am particular grateful to the staff of the Lebanon PA VAMC Hospice Unit for allowing me into their world, particularly Scott T. Shreve, D.O, Director of Hospice and Palliative Care, his staff, and volunteers.

The following professionals shared their expertise and technical knowledge: Forensic Pathologist Neil A. Hoffman, M.D.; John F. Gilbertson, R.R.T., VAMC; Detective Sergeant Brian Lefevre, Criminal Investigation Section, DVA Police Criminal Investigation Section; and Angel Cabrera, Criminal Investigator, retired, Reading, Pennsylvania, Police Department.

Writers need wind beneath their sails. Polly C. Brockway encouraged, praised, coaxed, and cajoled me to keep writing, while critiquing thousands of pages. Barbara Ann Hughes patently applied her decades of early-childhood-education knowledge to authenticate my troubled five-year-old character. Margaret Funk, Linda Meyer, Connie Fegley, Mary Ellen Richards, Pam Young, and Phyllis Halterman spent precious hours critiquing copy and providing invaluable assistance. Bless you!

My novel would have languished in obscurity without the Mystery Writers of America's New York chapter. Through their friendship, programs, and encouragement my knowledge expanded exponentially. A shared journey is never lonely. Special thanks to Richie Narvaez and Sheila J. Levine, Esq.

My publisher, Black Opal Books, breathed life into my novel with professional insight and a sharp eye to detail. Special thanks to my editor, Lauri Wellington, and Black Opal professionals: editors, Reyana and Faith, and artist Jack Jackson for my cover.

The Dying Hour

Nancy A. Hughes

[signature: Nancy A. Hughes]

A Black Opal Books Publication

Black Opal Books

BECAUSE SOME STORIES JUST HAVE TO BE TOLD

GENRE: MYSTERY-DETECTIVE/THRILLER/WOMEN'S FICTION

THE DYING HOUR
Copyright © 2016 by Nancy A. Hughes
Cover Design by Jackson Cover Designs
All cover art copyright © 2016
All Rights Reserved
Print ISBN: 978-1-626945-43-2

First Publication: OCTOBER 2016

Published by Black Opal Books **http://www.blackopalbooks.com**

DEDICATION

For Bill, Lori, and Dan
Without my family, nothing would mean anything.

Prologue

Autumn, 2008:

Through the fire door's reinforced glass, the intruder studied the ceiling's dome mirror mounted across the hall. As anticipated, the VA's hospice corridor was empty at this time of night. With the heavy door cracked and secured with one foot, the stranger disabled the latch by securing it with duct tape. The intruder then slipped into the first hospice room and approached the only occupied bed. A frail patient, the chosen target, twitched as if in troubled dreams. *Good*, the intruder thought, *he's still here*. A quick glance at the clock confirmed that the time—three a.m.— was perfect. Withdrawing a vial from a backpack, the stranger removed its protective cap and pierced the seal with a skinny syringe. The needle sucked to the appropriate level. Then, with a touch from experienced fingers, the intruder expelled a few drops. That brought a smile—an air bubble wouldn't matter, but might risk the desired effect. Besides, one should never get sloppy.

At the stranger's touch, the patient's eyes fluttered open and squinted at the tiny light that probed his failing eyes. In a voice that was no longer strong nor commanding, the patient whispered, "Are you an angel?"

The intruder grinned, pleased that fabricating a plausible lie would not be required. "I am."

"Have you come to take me?"

"I have."

The patient drew a shallow breath, his head slipping sidewise on his pillow. Drawing another ragged breath, he closed his eyes, as if prepared for release. With a latex-gloved hand, the intruder grasped the man's withered arm and shook it gently. Bones. He was nothing but bones encased in what felt like a dry cell-thin membrane. The patient's eyelids stuttered open again.

The intruder risked a little more volume, lest the patient not follow the instruction that would provide the stranger with a powerful thrill. "Look! You must look at me. Focus on my eyes. Then I'll take you where you've been longing to go."

The patient did as the "angel" told him to do.

After selecting the appropriate IV line, the stranger delivered the precise measure needed to send the old soldier on his final mission. The patient locked eyes with his savior, staring, unblinking, at the angel of death. The intruder felt a whoosh of adrenalin and watched as that last spark of life faded.

When it was over, the stranger silently gathered all trace of the visit, slipped unnoticed into the hall, removed the duct tape that enabled escape, descended the stairwell, and vanished into the night.

୧୬୧୬

Across Town:

"Jonathan! Don't touch that! Never touch Gram's equipment!"

Jonathan jerked his hand from the shiny dial, fearing that it might shock him.

"You want to kill her? Gram could die if you mess up her stuff."

Jonathan's mother continued to scold him. He looked fearfully from his mother to his beloved old Gram. He dropped his gaze to the floor, clutching his hands behind his back.

The old woman's eyes flickered open. Her left hand that had lain limp on the bed made a small circular motion, beckoning him to her side. A crooked smile formed on her blue lips. Jonathan's mother rolled her eyes then grudgingly consented for him to get closer. Shyly, he inched toward her face. Gram mouthed *I love you* through the side of her mouth that still worked. He grinned in relief.

Jonathan's mother interrupted with a jerk of her head. "That's enough. Go outside. Or go play with your toys. Gram needs to rest."

Reluctantly, he backed from their presence to escape the sights, sounds, and smells he did not understand. He felt scared and alone.

As he trudged toward the door, a sharp rap interrupted his thoughts. "Get that, will you?" Jonathan's mother called after him. He tugged the door open.

A lady in a white uniform grinned down at him. "Master Jonathan! Just seeing my favorite five-year-old brightens my day. Are your folks home?"

Just hearing *Master* added to his name made him feel special, even though he didn't know why she always said it.

Jonathan stepped back and made room for Gram's favorite nurse. It tickled him that Mrs. White always wore white clothes. He grasped the hand that she held out to him and led her into their old dining room. Now it was used for Gram's special bed.

Jonathan's mom scowled at the calendar on which was scribbled Gram's stuff. "We weren't expecting you until tomorrow."

"I'll be on vacation, but I didn't want to leave without telling your mom and dad. The Visiting Nurses will be sending a substitute. May I speak to your parents, please?"

When Mom nodded, Mrs. White approached the bed.

Grandpa rose from the chair where he always sat beside Gram.

"Good afternoon, Mr. Murdock."

"It's Robert!"

"Of course. Thank you, Robert." Then Mrs. White turned to Gram and patted her hand. Gram smiled with her eyes the way she did for special people.

"I'll be away for a week, but a substitute will visit. I've told her all about you, and she knows just what to do. She's very experienced and anxious to meet you."

"No men. None of those male nurses!"

Mrs. White turned to Grandpa. "Of course not, Mr. Murdock—ah, Robert. Everyone at the VNA knows Mrs. Murdock's preferences. Your instructions will always be honored."

"Will she have the key? Someone's always here, but just in case…"

"Your house key is in the packet I bring to the house." She held up a fat folder with folds on the bottom that was tied at the top with string that made an eight. She unwound the string, reached in and produced a tiny blue envelope. She slid the key onto her hand. She lowered her hand to show Jonathan too. "She'll bring this folder with her."

Jonathan's mom cleared her throat. He hated when she did that while glaring at him. "Perhaps you could remind Jonathan that he shouldn't touch Gram's equipment?"

Mrs. White stooped to his level. "You know that, right?" she said softly. Even her eyes smiled at him. Standing, she patted his head, just once, like she did whenever she told him what a great helper he was.

"I'll see myself out."

As soon as the door closed, Jonathan's mom frowned at him. Mrs. White's magic was gone. He scurried outside.

Out back, he sank onto the cracked cement stoop that abutted his mom and grandparents' house. A loose piece of blistered paint drifted onto his shoe. A chilly wind swirled fallen leaves and chased a torn plastic bag across the scrap of neglected backyard. He shivered. Scrunching his knees to his chest and, rocking slightly, he buried his face in his hands and wept for Gram.

As the chill from the concrete seeped through his jeans, he shivered uncontrollably, yet was unable to move from the spot. In time, long shadows inched past his toes toward the fence as the daylight retreated. Why he hadn't heard the approaching footsteps, he didn't know, but magically his grandfather appeared by his side. The big man sat down with a grunt.

With his arm around Jonathan's shoulder, he snuggled the child against him. His coveralls smelled faintly of gasoline, his enormous rough hand covering Jonathan's shoulder with its warmth.

"She didn't mean nothing, boy." He paused for a minute. "Your mom's…well, upset. Not at you. She worries too much about your gram. She works too hard, trying to keep your gram here at home. Doesn't get enough sleep."

Jonathan stole a look at Grandpa who seemed to be watching the clouds. "I didn't mean—"

"Well, of course you didn't."

"I just wanted to help."

"You can. You are. Just by keeping her company, talking to her, letting her know that you love her. That's a lot. But, son, I want you to remember something very important." He paused. "Look at me."

Jonathan peered up at Grandpa, whose face appeared dark against the bright sky.

"Don't ever forget how much Gram loved—loves you. Try to remember the good times you had. Because nobody's ever completely gone as long as someone remembers and cares. You got that?"

"Is she going to die?"

"Not today. Or even tomorrow. Doc says not for some time. But we all go to heaven when God calls our name. And someday we'll all be together in heaven, just like Jesus promised. We just need to believe. Do you understand?"

Jonathan nodded his head to make Grandpa feel better, even though he did not understand.

Chapter 1

July 2009, Ten Months Later:

Charlie Alderfer struggled from the clutches of oblivion, having no sense of time or location. When he finally was able to form coherent thoughts, it struck him. This was not heaven. He had not passed through a tunnel. There was no light and no music. No loved ones to beckon him into the Kingdom. He was still here, but just where was *here*?

Without his glasses, he could identify nothing beyond blurry colors. The smell was distinctive—disinfectant with a trace of something unpleasant. He appeared to be in a hospital bed, and yet not. This wasn't an emergency or recovery room. No medical professionals bustled about. The lighting was dim.

Too weak to struggle further, he gave up and let himself drift.

Back, back, his dreams slipped to that special summer, decades ago. Hot and perfect for swimming, chores all completed. He stood on the bank of Aquasicla Creek, looking for her. And there she was! Seventeen. Tiny. Prettier than anything he could have imagined. Surrounded by multiple friends. So sweet, everyone wanted to claim her as their girl or best friend. Again, they begged her to show how she did it—swim and chew gum at the same time. She obliged, face in and out of the water, rhythmically breathing without choking.

Demonstration finished, she stood in the four-foot deep water, and blew a pink bubble. Everyone laughed and clapped with delight. When she looked up and caught sight of him, the newcomer, she beckoned for him to join them. And he was drawn into her circle. That was one of her charms—being inclusive. Ever widening her circle to include everyone. He had strained to catch her name. Emma? Yes! That was it.

Emma. Now, in his dream that fast-forwarded decades, he was swimming toward her, but wasn't able to reach her ever-receding outstretched hand. Her smile—that beautiful smile...

Charlie awoke with a start. Instinctively, he attempted to reposition himself, but his arms would not cooperate. He tried harder, but his muscles quavered in protest, forcing him to abandon the effort. The expression, weak as a kitten, popped into his mind. Groping to rub his stiff arms, he realized he was tethered by plastic tubing secured with white tape. He struggled to grasp his strange surroundings. This place was so quiet—no bleeping or whooshing or electronic pings.

Suddenly a woman appeared by his bed rail. "Mr. Alderfer? I see you're awake. So glad you decided to join us. I'll let the doctor know you're awake."

Squinting, he brought into focus a dark-skinned woman dressed in bright garments. "Where am I?" His voice came out as a croak he hardly recognized, words forced through a throat unaccustomed to speaking.

"You're at the VA." Her voice betrayed a French accent with traces of Jamaica and Creole. She enunciated her query with soft, measured words. "Are you in pain?"

He squirmed, his muscles and joints screaming in protest. He managed a nod.

"We can give you something for that. We want you to be comfortable. That's our specialty 'round here."

As she waddled toward a dark rectangle that must be a doorway, Charlie looked around. Bright orange and brown fabric circled an area on the opposite side of the room. And he could hear snoring off to his right. Brilliant light spilled through a wall of windows beyond the snoring, which meant Charlie must occupy a bed by the door. Wherever he was, his room appeared to be a ward of some kind. Where did she say?

The woman reappeared accompanied by a man dressed in white. Charlie croaked answers to questions, aware of warm hands and cold metal. When the man was finished, the woman took over. "We find pills easier to swallow if taken with a little applesauce. Do you think you can manage that?" When he nodded yes, she slipped the cold spoon into his mouth. With fierce concentration, he swallowed, allowing the tiny pill to slip down his throat.

"Water? May I have a drink?"

"We'll need to evaluate whether it needs to be thickened." To his puzzled expression she added, "You've been hydrated through an IV for some time. We need to make sure you don't choke on thin liquids."

"Please. Let me try..."

He half expected her to offer a straw or a sippy cup, like the ones his grandbabies used. But after cranking his bed to a more upright position, she held a hard plastic cup with a jutting extension. With fierce concentration, he sipped, relishing the liquid as if he'd been crawling through the desert for days. It tasted incredibly good. But his tongue snagged over rough lips, which felt like sloughed-off snakeskin.

"My mouth, my lips. They're cracked. And peeling."

"Let's try this." From the nightstand, she picked up what looked to Charlie like a small pink bouquet in a paper cup. She selected one, the end of which resembled a square of bubble gum stuck on a lollypop stick. She ripped off its crinkly covering. "Open your mouth just a little," she said, then gently swabbed his dry lips. He could make out a smile on red lips. He licked his and nodded his gratitude. "Staff is aware of your status," she said. "We'll have your evaluation updated. That includes what you can eat and drink."

"What day is today?"

"Why, it's Tuesday."

Tuesday! Charlie thought hard. My God! I've been out for five days. He glanced around helplessly. "Glasses. Could you please look for my glasses?"

She opened the drawer in his nightstand and located a pair of bifocals. She disappeared briefly, and from some-where nearby he heard running water. "These were filthy—that's better," she said as she glided them gently onto his face. Her hands felt smooth, cool and soft, her manner un-hurried.

Instantly, she came into focus. "Thanks," he mur-mured, and the nurse grinned with satisfaction. Then she bustled through the black hole that he now could see was the door to the hall.

He studied his new environment. Through the opening in the multi-colored curtain on the opposite wall, he could see a tiny gaunt man with an apricot-colored face. He slept in a fetal position, enveloped in a sea of immaculate white sheets. To Charlie's right, in the bed by the window, a heavy-set man in navy sweats had awakened. He was watching a sports channel on a tiny TV that was suspended close to his face. He looked over when he noticed that Char-lie was staring at him. He grinned. "Good morning."

Charlie projected his voice, which took utmost effort. "Where did that nurse say I was?"

"The VA. The Veteran's Association Medical Center." He chuckled and made a sweeping motion with a hand from which plastic tubes were secured with white tape. "And this here is the last stop on the train."

⋰⋱

Soothed by the pain pill, Charlie slept, all frantic

thoughts and raw prickles replaced by disjointed dreams. In twilight sleep, he saw a little boy, hovering near the foot of his bed. Eyes big, watching him. Jimmy! It had to be little Jimmy, exactly as Charlie remembered his brother. He had been only five when they had lost him. The doctor had sworn his heart had been perfect when he was born—before he contracted the measles. Now Jimmy's mop of nearly white hair floated in slow motion as he swiveled his head. Why had Jimmy, not his Emma, his parents, or grandparents, been sent to escort him into the Kingdom?

Charlie tried to wrench himself from the bed to follow the child. Bright lights intensified the white sea around him, preventing Charlie from seeing where his brother had gone. Again, he tried moving, sure that he'd float, but his body failed to respond. Jimmy disappeared through the dark space. Why had he come if not to lead him? Charlie felt himself slipping back into the sleep from which he had stirred. As it enveloped him, he was struck by the sensation of *clean*—the smell of strong disinfectant. Why was he stuck here, so *in between*? Exhausted, he gave up the struggle for cohesive thought.

༄ঞৎঞ

That night, a dream that was quite realistic interrupted his sleep. The movement of air. The sensation of someone pausing, as if to study him, and then moving on, leaving a familiar smell that he couldn't quite place. Then a voice— melodious—that was barely a whisper somewhere beyond Charlie's bed. Soft and low, someone was uttering priestly incantations. Not exactly like praying but something about *angels* and *taking you where you are longing to go*. Bewildered, he listened, but there were no further words, just the essence of someone. Rustlings and murmurs. Footsteps departing. Then silence.

A new dream transported Charlie back to his Emma. Still young and so beautiful, and their two little girls, beckoning to him. His ladies wore sundresses in fresh springtime colors and carried their old picnic hamper. The harder he tried to catch up with his ladies, the more the distance stretched like worn elastic until they were mere dots on a field of wild flowers.

A commotion, coming from somewhere nearby, brought Charlie back to the present. Dim lights flickered on the opposite wall above the jaundiced patient's bed. A woman with something black draped around her neck slid Charlie's privacy curtain around his bed. Stuttering on its track, its squeak awakened him further. Shortly he heard another curtain moving near the window.

"What's happening?" a gruff voice demanded.

"It's all right, Mr. D. Go back to sleep."

"He's gone, isn't he?"

Charlie strained to hear her reply, but the ringing of sleep in his ears seemed especially loud, and the woman soothed in barely a whisper. In time, the curtain at the end of his bed whooshed in a current of air. From the opening where the curtain didn't quite reach the wall, Charlie glimpsed a horizontal American flag floating out of the room. The lights were extinguished, the room cocooned in silence and shadows again.

Suddenly Charlie was wide awake. And scared. As scared as any moment he'd experienced since leaving Vietnam. It wasn't death itself that he feared—it was the process. And, at that very moment, he knew that he was not destined to transition smoothly.

☙❧

Charlie awoke to daylight striking his face. A cheerful soul was pulling back his curtain. "Mr. Alderfer, good morning. Sir! Glad you've decided to join us. Been kind of boring, talking to myself. I'm Mike, your first-shift nurse. Hope you can stand morning people. If not, you're still stuck with me." He elevated the head of Charlie's bed so that Charlie didn't have to look over his nose to see him. "How did you sleep?"

"I thought I was dead." Charlie processed the man. Not too tall, fair, slender, maybe forty, with closely cropped hair and steady blue eyes behind metal-rim glasses. "I had strange dreams. People coming and going. And I dreamed about my family who've been gone many years. Like my little brother, Jimmy. My brothers and I used to carry him everywhere. My daughters both got vaccinated, thank God." He tried to remember the impression. "The dreams were so real. Could it be the pain pill she gave me?"

Over Mike's shoulder, Charlie caught a glimpse of the now-vacant bed. The curtain was retracted way back to the wall, the bed stripped to its burgundy vinyl mattress. Disinfectant scent lingered.

Mike noticed his stare. "Mr. Jones passed away during the night."

"Oh! That's too bad."

"He was ready. Each morning he would say to me, 'Oh, dear, why am I still here? Why doesn't He take me? I'm ready to go. I keep praying.'"

"I never heard him made a sound. He wasn't in pain?"

"We're expert at keeping our patients comfortable without drugging them senseless. Here, it's about the quality of passing from this world to the next." He nodded, apparently satisfied with what sounded to Charlie like a corporate sound bite.

Mike snapped on a cheerful face and blue vinyl gloves. "We have a routine, you and I, that you probably don't remember. That's okay. It's normal. However, for now I'll have to listen to your complaints. That's fine, as long as you don't bash the Marines. Got that?"

Charlie couldn't help smiling. *Semper fi yourself.*

"First, we'll take your vitals, get you washed, shaved, and into fresh pajamas. I want you looking spiffy when the white coats arrive."

"Coats?"

"Your team—the doctor, support staff, physical and occupational therapists, social worker, psychologist, clergy if you choose, and so on. Residents, medical students, and nurses in training also rotate through here. Each team visits one-fourth of our patients a week, but our doctor and staff are on duty twenty-four seven. There are three nurses for every four patients on this ward. And first shift, you get me."

"When can I go home?" Charlie asked in what sounded even to him like a pitiful voice.

Mike's flinch was barely perceptible, but Charlie had been watching his face. "Dr. Szish will discuss your prognosis with you. I don't have the details, and besides, I'm not permitted to speak for the docs."

ભ્રભ્ર

It didn't take long for Charlie to realize the depth and degradation to which he had sunk. The catheter, the Depends, the mouths full of pills he needed to swallow to free himself from the IV. The nurse had been professional, assuring him of his credentials that ranged from medical to parental experience. But, in the end, the result was the same—the previously strong, healthy, active young retiree was reduced to being a grownup in diapers. Grateful as he was for the compassionate care, the humiliation was crushing.

Mike finished Charlie's morning routine and moved on to attend his next patient. Before Charlie had time to contemplate his situation, a tall, slender man who looked vaguely familiar arrived at his bedside. *Dr. Szish* was embroidered in blue script above the left breast pocket of his white lab coat. "Mr. Alderfer? Good morning, Sir. I'm your physician. How are you feeling?"

Unlike other medical professionals Charlie had known in the past, Dr. Szish did not seem to be in a hurry. He actually wanted an answer. With Charlie's permission, he repositioned the bed to enable the men to speak face to face. He pulled up a chair and, settling in, crossed his lanky legs that ended in spit-shined tassel loafers. His thinning black hair was slicked to one side in a futile attempt to combat curls, and his voice had a quiet, even cadence. It was his smile, however, that dominated his flawless face.

Charlie couldn't help smiling. "I'm okay. Glad to still be here. I think."

Dr. Szish's smile broadened. "We need to talk about many things—your medical condition, your concerns, your needs."

Charlie's bravado, what little he'd mustered, collapsed in the kind doctor's presence. What was it that made a person hang tough in the presence of battle, evil, or meanness, yet be completely undone by genuine kindness? Tears threatened, but Charlie succeeded in blinking them back. The doctor seemed not to notice.

"I'm so confused, and worried, and disoriented. What happened to me? And where is it all going? Please—help me understand."

"I believe in telling the truth. Is that acceptable?"

"Just give it to me straight. What I can't handle is not knowing. The fear of that other shoe falling. I'm no stranger to suffering and death."

"Okay. What do you remember about your emergency?"

"Very little." Charlie's recollections were sketchy at best. "I'd watered the roses and positioned the lawn chair to watch for that first star. The phone rang—it's in the kitchen—and I hurried to catch it before the fifth ring. Then, this incredible, searing pain. The phone clattered away—I was yelling, I think. Then people erupting into the house and snatches of being in an ER. A helicopter ride, then a hospital somewhere. Fragments of dreams I can't remember, except that they were frightening and weird. I could hear muffled voices, but couldn't make out what they were saying.

Nothing more specific until I woke up in here. It's all a big blur."

"Sometimes it's better not to remember. According to our records, you were transported first to a local ER, then grasping the gravity of your situation, to a regional trauma center. There, you had major surgery. They had to restart your heart twice. Ultimately, you were brought to the VA."

"What kind of surgery? For what?"

"You had a ruptured aneurysm. Because the paramedics responded so quickly, the ER stabilized you rapidly and air lifted you to a facility that could handle your needs, you had a shot at survival."

"A ruptured aneurysm? Where?" Charlie ran his hand through his thatch of white hair, but it seemed undisturbed.

The doctor pressed his own solar plexus with his fist. "Here."

Charlie gazed down at his own chest, as if he could see through his pajamas. "How did I end up at the VA?"

The doctor paused momentarily. "In spite of the surgeons' best efforts, you weren't expected to live. Twenty-four hours passed, but you hung on. That turned into thirty-six, forty-eight, and so on. Still, you didn't regain consciousness. They expected to lose you at any time. You were stable and able to breathe on your own, but the prognosis was grim. Finally, you were transported here, where we specialize in comfort and a dignified transition."

"A dignified transition? Where? A rehab? Home?"

Strange, the things you notice at the most inappropriate times, Charlie thought, distracted by the doctor's smooth, flawless skin. Had it not been for a few wrinkles, the man could have been in his mid-twenties. Charlie's eyes stuck on this contradiction while his mind tried to absorb what he was saying.

"This is the VA's Hospice Center."

Charlie jolted. "Hospice? That's what this is? But isn't that for cancer patients who are near death? Am I going to die?"

The doctor smiled. "We're all going to die, hopefully later than sooner. Our patients range from those who are actively dying to those whose expectancy is six months or less. You have surprised us. You're pretty tough. Your heart keeps on pumping, you have good lungs and no other major medical problems." He looked at a chart. "Your blood pressure's low normal, cholesterol numbers are great, you aren't diabetic, and you aren't overweight. Your challenge centered on that one condition and complications from this and past surgeries."

"So, what caused it—my war injuries?"

"I see from your records that you were shot in the gut. That you had major abdominal surgery. And prior to that you had both your appendix and your gall bladder removed, but at different times."

Charlie nodded. "And ten years ago, I had what they called a 'dissected aorta.' They rushed me to the ER from work, and operated on me immediately."

"May I have a look?" When Charlie nodded agreement, Doctor Szish lifted Charlie's pajama top and scrutinized his torso. Charlie took the opportunity to inspect the new scars himself. His abdomen was a maze of crisscrossing lines that reminded him of a railroad junction. Oddly, even the new scars looked old, his recent surgery completely healed. The doctor nodded approvingly.

"I'm confused. If everything's healed, why am I in here?"

"You mean in Hospice?"

"Yeah."

"Your incisions appear to have healed very nicely. Having been out of it for so long, you missed the agony of early recovery. That was a blessing. But you still have a long way to go."

Charlie frowned at the new scars that were merely pink lines. "I'm surprised that I healed so quickly. If this is Wednesday, and my attack was last Thursday…"

The doctor rested a hand on his arm. "Charlie. Your attack was on a Thursday, that's true. But that was five weeks ago. You've been with us a rather long time."

"Five weeks! Oh my god. My girls must be frantic."

"Everyone was very concerned, but we've keep your daughters informed. Both have been here twice, and are planning to return."

Charlie flopped his head with such vigor that it ground a dent in his pillow. "But they live so far away. Georgia and California. And they have their own lives. Jobs. Husbands. Children. What a hardship this must be for them."

"They're not complaining. Your daughters are truly amazing people."

Charlie rocked his head back and forth. "Then I guess I can't just go home without letting them know."

Dr. Szish laughed. "Well, hardly!"

"So what happens now? As soon as I get my strength back, can I go home?"

The doctor sighed and shook his head.

"What?"

"The surgeons repaired the ruptured aneurysm. That was successful. An aneurysm forms as a result of a weakness in the lining of the artery wall. Like a thin spot in a balloon. Just like a balloon, it can burst under pressure if it gets too thin. Some people have small aneurysms they don't ever know about—they live and die *with* them and not *of* them." He paused, a little too long.

"O—kay…"

"The challenge ahead of you now is that there's another aneurysm. The surgeon's primary function was saving your life—repairing what had ruptured." Again, the doctor indicated its location on his own chest. "The remaining aneurysm is located in a dangerous position. Going after it then would have been fatal. I'm sorry. They said it was inoperable."

Charlie was stunned. "I'm a ticking bomb? It could rupture any minute?"

"Let's not get ahead of ourselves. When you're strong

enough, further studies can be done. In the meantime, you need rehabilitation. We'll take precautions. For instance..." He lifted the hem of Charlie's pajama top again and pointed to the surgical scars. "You can never, ever do abdominal exercises again. Those muscles have been sliced and diced too many times. When you're ready to be up and around, and especially when you go to physical therapy, you'll need to wear a wide protective belt to support your abdominal muscles."

"Like the pro wrestlers and body builders wear?"

"Exactly. One will be made specifically for you."

"But what if—"

"Let's focus on the positive. Our professionals will be keeping you busy, evaluating everything from your ability to swallow to how soon physical therapy can begin. Everyone here is rooting for you."

"But you said this is Hospice—"

"The VA's Hospice offers patients and their loved ones comfort and the highest quality of life when illness is life limiting or cannot be cured. Our veterans are very sick people. We aren't doing surgery, chemo, or experimental treatment—just the ultimate possible accommodations for comfort and a painless transition. And we accommodate families as well. We have twenty-four hour visiting with no age restriction. Even pets are welcome—"

Charlie interrupted him. "Please answer my question. About that other aneurysm? Is it going to blow any minute? *Am* I in danger of dying right now?"

"We certainly hope not. We do, occasionally, have patients who graduate and go home. Yours is an unusual case."

"Then shouldn't I be on a regular ward? Or transferred to a rehab facility?"

"I believe the level of care that you'll receive here will make all the difference in your recuperation, especially if that other aneurysm becomes problematic. The ER and surgical suites are right in this building.

"But if I'm not going to die within your timeframe—"

Dr. Szish placed a reassuring hand on Charlie's arm. He hesitated. Charlie waited.

"You were badly wounded in the service of our country," the doctor finally said. "Your recent surgery was complicated as a result. You have paid in advance for the best care available. All our veterans deserve nothing less. Besides, the staff has grown rather fond of you." He grinned at Charlie. "We're keeping you. And I will personally verify that this facility is appropriate. Now—any other questions and concerns I can answer?"

"That handful of pills. Can we get rid of whatever is making me groggy? Giving me weird dreams?"

"Sure. I'll enter that order into our computer. But— now listen, this is important—I *will* prescribe something for pain if you need it. Recovery isn't always a straight line. If you feel overwhelmed by depression, anxiety, or insomnia, we want to know about that too. Tell us before pain gets intolerable. Whatever you need will have our attention. You just have to tell us. Don't say you're fine if you're not. Speak up. No matter's too small."

"I'm so hungry."

Dr. Szish grinned. "Dietary will be around later today. In the meantime, we'll raid our kitchen for something appropriate."

After he left, Charlie stole a peek at his belly and felt a wave of gratitude for once again dodging a bullet. Gradually, he calmed from the information overload. Unlike Mr. Jones, the man with the apricot face, he was still here and didn't have to break the news to his daughters. But he still didn't understand his prognosis. He squirmed, wondering just how much movement was safe. Later. He'd ask more questions later. Three nurses for every four patients? He located the call button, comforted that he could summon one at the first hint of disaster.

Chapter 2

Although no sound had roused him, Charlie felt watched. He had fallen asleep with his glasses perched on the end of his nose while trying to watch CNN on his tiny, suspended TV. His efforts at reorienting himself to a fast-changing world had worked better than a serious sedative.

What was different? Suddenly Charlie noticed a small blond boy who had slipped into the room on little cat feet. By his height, the lad must have been four or five. The child stared straight ahead at Charlie's neighbor by the window, whose name he had learned was Vincent DePasquali. Charlie lay perfectly still, struck by another mystery solved. Jimmy! Charlie's little brother who had died all those decades ago—the resemblance to this little boy was uncanny, although Charlie's recollection was limited to his own childhood memories and old family photos. This lad had a slight little body and home-barbered hair that lifted with static electricity. Who was this child?

Charlie watched. For once, Mr. DePasquali's circular curtain was fully open. The big man wiggled his left index finger coaxingly while rummaging in something that crinkled like cellophane. Then he dangled a silver object, suspended by a small strip of paper that glistened in a shaft of sunlight. Again, his roommate beckoned to the boy. When the child hesitated, DePasquali swung the object in a small circular motion while charming the boy with a grandfather's smile. Charlie repositioned his glasses to watch.

"Come on—come get it." The boy's face brightened as he slipped toward the bed. "I saved this one just for you," DePasquali said. "Don't tell now. It's our little secret. Go ahead."

The child plucked the proffered silver object from the man's paw of a hand and grinned.

"It's okay. You may eat it."

The child unwrapped the treat and popped it whole into his mouth. The man then extended his hand into which the boy placed the wrapper. Obviously, this routine wasn't new.

The boy suddenly jerked his head to attention. Charlie hadn't heard anything of particular importance, but evidently the youngster had. As quickly as he had appeared, he bolted from the room without saying a word.

"Cute little boy. Is he your grandson?" Charlie asked.

"No idea who he is, but I'm working on it. He's here every day." Grinning, he held up the cellophane bag. "Hershey's Kisses. Sold by the bag down in the canteen. Had my family fetch it for me. With kids, you gotta have the right bait."

Charlie thought hard, trying to reconstruct the fleeting dream into which he had worked the silent little visitor. It hadn't been Jimmy at all. Just something his groggy brain had dredged from the past. He'd never told his parents how deeply and unendingly he had grieved for his brother. They were upset enough. Now he realized that if he had to die, at least he would have Jimmy waiting for him.

DePasquali had been talking, and Charlie, embarrassed, asked him to repeat. "My family's Italian, and if you know Italians, we've got this food thing. The family thinks they can cure me with pasta. You won't believe the stuff they bring in." He smoothed his hand down his distended belly. "Can't eat it, though. It's the cancer."

"Isn't there anything they can do for you?"

"Nothing worked. After the last round of torture, I said

'enough.' When they offered to keep me comfortable here, I jumped at the chance. This wonderful stuff they pump into my veins—do you have any idea what the street value would be?" He chuckled, enjoying his joke. "Nobody cares if I get addicted because this is my last stop on the train."

"I'm so sorry."

"Don't be. It's been a great ride. And besides, I'm not done having fun. Best guesstimate, I could hang around until Christmas, and it's only September."

Charlie felt panic edge into his chest, the killer aneurysm poised to explode. He desperately needed to change the subject. "The little boy—what have you learned about him?"

"The only way he could be here is attached to somebody's family who's visiting a patient. You know, we have twenty-four hour visitation here. Staff wouldn't bring in a child—at least not every day and not while on duty." He exhaled and took a few halting breaths, his attention focused somewhere beyond the end of his bed. DePasquali shook his head. "Strangest thing about that child. He never speaks. Not one word. Give a kid your undivided attention, and you can't shut him up. But not him."

"How long has he been visiting you?"

"A couple of weeks. And I've never heard him say anything. Maybe he's deaf or mute or disabled somehow."

"Have you asked the staff?"

"Tried. But everyone's spooked about privacy issues. That HIPPA nonsense. Well, maybe some of it's necessary, but it's gotten out of hand."

"Has anyone ever come looking for him?"

DePasquali shook his head. "Kid must have radar. He becomes aware of something, then splits."

"I doubt that he's deaf. After he ate the candy, something caught his attention. Then he bolted. No, I'd bet that whatever his problem, it isn't his ears. He looked scared."

"Uh oh. It's the coats."

Before Charlie could question the comment, it became

obvious. At least eight professionals, mostly in white coats, trooped into the room. Bearing clipboards and kindly expressions, they formed a semicircle around Charlie's bed. With his permission, someone adjusted its height while someone else drew his privacy curtain, enveloping them in a colorful tent. *If they talk among themselves as if I'm some specimen, as if I'm not here—*

Instead, all eyes and smiles were on him. One by one, they introduced themselves by specialty and gave a brief rundown on how they would help. That they said *would*, and not *could* was not lost on him.

ℯↄℯↄ

After hours of mindless television repeats and feeble attempts at reading a magazine, Charlie mind came to attention. What DePasquali had said about addiction—did that apply to him too? He would ask, no beg, to be taken off all drugs, especially the ones that muddled his mind. He could tolerate pain, and he'd never had trouble sleeping. And that little brown pill, that so-called stool softener—that he blamed for his not having time to transition from Depends to the bathroom. At one point, he had been grateful for even the smallest service that kept him clean, comfortable, and free of sore skin. No matter the gender, or the constant reminder about professionalism, Charlie's sharper mind felt humiliated and degraded. Just how close was that bathroom door anyway? Ten feet? Twelve?

A second shift nurse, going off at eleven, approached his bedrail. "Still can't sleep? Your chart says you may have something if you feel you need it."

Charlie shook his head. "Reveille starts around here at six in the morning. I'd feel like a zombie the rest of the day."

"My point exactly. Tomorrow night could go better. How about half or one quarter dose?"

Charlie relented. "Okay. Just enough to take off the edge. My mind won't stop churning."

Perhaps it was psychological. Or sleep was long overdue, but within fifteen minutes Charlie stirred, realizing he had started to dream. He was in his daughter Susan's cozy rancher in suburban San Diego. She had been standing at her new stainless stove, stirring her latest version of chili. She looked so much like her mother, but unlike his Emma, had a feisty disposition when provoked. Susan was telling him…what? He turned on his side, tucking his blanket under his chin. He returned his mind to Susan's happy home. By now, he knew it was okay to ignore any commotion that fragile roommates required. He likened it to being in church, or an airplane with a fretful baby, about whom he had no responsibility or need to respond.

While floating from vision to vision, he became aware of squeaking footsteps. They drifted past him toward Vincent DePasquali. Night nurse, he thought, but noticed an unusual scent left in the person's wake. Not perfume. Not even feminine, but not manly aftershave or deodorant soap. Something oily. It was…what? In time, whomever he was sensing drifted beyond him. He was far too groggy to open his eyes. The visitor was saying something about *taking you where you've been longing to go*. The voice, as in a previous dream, was vaguely familiar. Not Mike. Not Dr. Szish. Charlie drifted back to his dreams.

✂✄✂✄

An ordinary evening—that's how Charlie would always remember it. He and DePasquali had fallen into a compatible routine, like old army buddies. DePasquali kept Charlie enthralled and in stitches, sometimes near tears with colorful tales of his childhood escapades in New York's Little Italy.

Charlie could picture it and felt intimately attracted to

his family and mischievous dozens of cousins with musical names.

When second shift nurses began their duties at three that afternoon, Charlie had felt at peace. While he didn't see daily progress, he recognized the difference time was making. And he had finally made some real progress on the PT machines. His muscles ached, but it *was* muscle, not bone, joint, incision, or arthritis. Tear down to build up, only stronger. And he made a conscious decision that denying the existence of that lurking aneurysm meant good mental health.

Charlie and DePasquali had said their good nights, De-Pasquali having received his meds right on time. Charlie knew the routine and never summoned staff for nonessentials while the meds were being dispensed. Managing pain was job one, and even a brief delay could mean the difference between comfort and agony. You could set your watch by the routine that superseded almost everything else short of a fire. In no time, DePasquali had been snoring.

With increased activity, and wrapped in the caring cocoon that was Hospice, Charlie usually slept soundly. Staff had located just the right pillows and adjusted his bed to perfection. Folded neatly at the foot of the bed a handmade quilt, appliquéd with American flags, stars and stripes on a white field edged in navy, waited for him in case he got cold. A VFW auxiliary had presented the quilt onto which was embroidered a simple message: *Thank you for defending our country and our freedom.* Charlie had gulped back emotional tears when the three women appeared in his room, their gift wrapped in white tissue paper. That evening, the quilt covered Charlie's long legs and feet, which were always too cold. The corner containing the message was positioned against the bedrail within easy reach. As second shift glided through their quality-of-life duties, his sleepy mind could usually ignore any commotion that didn't involve him. Night shift transitioned onto duty by eleven.

He began trusting that he might be lucky. Get well

enough to graduate and leave Hospice under his own power. A small, unintentional slip that a nurse had made while arranging his quilt gave him hope. She had said, "When you go home, you can take the quilt with you." Until then, he hadn't dared hope that his ride on the train would be a round trip. She had said *when*, and not *if*.

That night he slept with the peace of the angels, even dreaming of one. The angel in his dream was male with a silky, reassuring voice that uttered otherworldly incantations. Charlie didn't stir until a familiar hand touched his shoulder.

"Rise and shine," Mike said. Sunshine flooded the room. Charlie's stomach growled. Lots to do, he thought, as he ticked through his mental check list for Thursday's routine. Breakfast, his favorite meal. Shower day. Mike would position him on a chair, and allow him to soap and shampoo himself while enjoying as much warm water as he pleased. He'd wear his new sweats and sneakers and go to PT before lunch. As Mike prepared to help him out of bed and position him at his walker for the few steps to the bathroom, Charlie jolted. DePasquali was gone. His bed had been stripped to its heavy vinyl structure. His medical paraphernalia also was missing. What remained were his personal possessions, books and framed pictures, that lined the deep windowsill.

Mike was prepared. "Mr. DePasquali passed away during the night sometime after his daughter went back to New York. The family had tried to keep a vigil, but felt he'd be okay for a while. He just slipped away."

"But—but he was doing so well. Why, just yesterday he wanted his family to wheel him outside. The gorgeous weather here in the country exhilarated him. Made him feel wonderful—so unlike the gritty New York of his childhood. He was so full of plans. And he was talking about Hospice's Christmas party. That's three months away."

Mike nodded. "He did have a good day. He wanted a taste of ice cream, even though he knew he couldn't swallow it. That last burst of energy isn't uncommon when death is near. We had one old guy—he was ninety-five—who hadn't been out of bed in a year. All of a sudden, he wanted to go out. It was a perfect spring day. He loved every second of the adventure, as he called it. The next day he was gone."

"But Christmas—"

"We celebrate Christmas several times a year. No need to wait."

"But he seemed, so, robust for someone who was that close to death."

"He just talked a good game—that was his personality. But he was a very sick man."

Charlie tried to remember. A fleeting memory registered, which hinted at something unsettling. "That must have been what weaved itself into my dream. Not an angel but a male nurse checking on him."

"When was that?"

"No idea. But the hall lights were dim."

Mike frowned. "Couldn't be staff. Third shift in Hospice are women."

"In my dream, the angel wore white. He was tall. And big. In my dream, I tried speaking to him, but my mouth wouldn't work."

"Sure sounds as if you were dreaming. Did you take a sleep aid?"

"Just enough to help me relax. I'd been so wired. At home, sometimes I'd dream that I'd stayed awake all night, but this wasn't like that. An angel-like person came into the room. I'm certain of that. And he wore white."

Mike shrugged. "A late family visitor perhaps. They didn't like leaving him alone. They're afraid he'll need something and be too weak to ring the call button. And they didn't want him dying alone. Still, they couldn't keep a twenty-four vigil for months on end. Maybe he had a friend or relative who works on another floor. Stopped by on break or after second shift to check up on him. Sometimes people just come to pray."

Charlie sighed. "Yeah, that sounds reasonable and would account for my impression of praying." Mike didn't seem to be in a hurry. "When did he pass?"

"I heard it was around three. The dying hour."

"The dying hour?"

"Night-shift nurses describe a phenomenon whereby terminal patients tend to die around three in the morning, perhaps after making one last attempt to turn over. It's uncanny. No explanation. But observed often enough to become folklore."

"He's going to be missed by that little blond boy. Do you know who he is? The one who visited Mr. D. every day? I understand that HIPPA privacy stuff, but a child that age couldn't be a veteran. So what's the harm?"

Mike grinned. "Army or navy maybe, but definitely not a marine. Seriously, I don't think there's any harm in saying he comes in with his mother. She sits, all day, every day with her father. His room's down the hall."

"Is the child free to wander?"

Mike took a deep breath and exhaled slowly. "Just between us?"

"Sure. Of course."

"My sense is that the child has nowhere else to go. If his mother feels she needs to be here and there's no one to babysit him, staff doesn't appear to object. But I'm guessing. I don't know if there's a hard and fast rule about children. If there is, they're cutting the family some slack. Besides, the boy is a sweetheart. We never see him running around, getting into things, making noise or a nuisance of himself. He wouldn't have come into this room if Mr. D. hadn't coaxed him."

"What does he do all day?"

"Just slips around. Watches out the dayroom windows. Colors—he's quite an artist for such a young child. He looks at picture books. TV. He's like a little ghost. If he weren't so obedient and quiet, someone would have objected by now."

"How long has he been coming?"

Mike pursed his lips, eyes narrowed in thought. "His grandfather was admitted shortly after you came. No, make that two weeks after. Something like that. I didn't notice him at first. The gentleman wasn't my patient. And we'd had an unusually high turnover rate—patients here for two to four days. We were overwhelmed. And that patient didn't need constant attention."

"Why? What's wrong?"

"Heart." Involuntarily, Mike grimaced. "I wasn't supposed to say that. If the family wants to tell you about their situation or his diagnosis, that's one thing. But we are forbidden. For example, if a patient is admitted and he happens to be my neighbor, I can't go home and tell the others on our street that he's here. Even a minister, who visits a parishioner from his own congregation, cannot announce it in church without permission. I could be fired for what I just said."

Charlie chuckled. "Said? Huh? Don't hear very well..." He smiled, remembering a new VA joke shared with him by another patient from the Skilled Nursing ward. "One of the old guys waiting his turn in PT told me he had the honkers disease. I said, 'What's that?' and the guy made a noise like a goose: 'Huh? Huh? Huh?' He proceeded to tell me that staff labeled him as *confused*. 'I'm not confused. I'm deaf! Damn hearing aid is worthless for nerve deafness. So I pretend to know what they're talking about. Half the time, what I say doesn't make any sense. At least to them. We old guys call it the honkers' disease.'"

Mike smiled then refocused. "Mr. D's family will be coming in shortly to collect his personal possessions. The timing will be good for you—a shower, PT, and so on. And, if you're not too tired, Escort can bring you back to the dayroom. They're running movies on the big-screen TV after lunch. That will give the family time and some privacy."

"Do you think they'd let me have the bag of Hershey's Kisses? A certain little boy might appreciate them. Of course I could send to the canteen for my own..."

"I'm sure they'd be happy to leave them."

Mike helped Charlie out of bed, positioned him at his walker, then released the hand brake. With one hand on Charlie's back and another prepared to redirect the walker, Mike accompanied Charlie into the bathroom. He sat. All that water and fresh stuff he ate produced results effortlessly. Never, ever again would he take anything this fundamental for granted.

ⱺↃⱺↃ

Charlie was expecting, yet at the same time dreading, the little boy's next appearance. Mr. D, as he'd heard everyone refer to Vincent DePasquali, was gone. Perhaps the lad had one of those dissociative conditions or was incapable of feelings, empathy or loss. Or maybe he was too young to grasp the concept of death. Could he simply be shy? Or traumatized by some unknown person, place or event?

That afternoon, most patients were napping during that lull that followed the flurry of morning appointments, rounds, lunch, and meds. The ward beyond Charlie's door was very quiet. He settled for an old *Law & Order* rerun and became drowsy himself. Perhaps it was Charlie's sixth sense that sparked his attention. He opened his eyes. The little blond boy had materialized at the foot of his bed, staring at Mr. D's stripped bed. He turned to Charlie. Without words, he seemed to be asking the inevitable question.

"Mr. D isn't here," Charlie said. "I'm sorry to say that he won't be back."

The boy stared hard at the naked bed where his friend used to be. Then he looked back at Charlie. He waited. Perhaps, Charlie thought, he really is deaf. Responds to vibrations or his own inner signals. His little face seemed to be searching. Finally, he turned to leave.

"Wait!" Charlie called after him, a little too loudly. The boy jumped. *Ah ha!* Charlie thought. *He can hear.* "I'd love it if you would visit with me. I'll even find out where Mr. D. got the chocolate. I don't have many visitors, and it gets kind of lonely. I'd like it if you would stop in."

The youngster stared. Although he looked less afraid, his gaze dropped to his sneakers. Charlie noticed that even though they were too big, the toes were worn into holes. His elasticized jeans, rolled to a cuff, were patched at the knees, and his tee shirt was stained. The clothes, like the child, however, were clean. By the creases, he noticed, his shirt had been pressed.

The boy turned, as if to leave then stopped and turned imploring eyes to Charlie. Then, wordlessly, he held up both hands in supplication, as if to ask, "Where'd he go?"

Charlie, though taken aback, decided to chance an explanation. After thinking a moment, he took a deep breath while considering just the right words. He could lie and say Mr. D. had gone home or to another hospital, but that wasn't right. Children needed to trust what grownups told them. How to explain? With his daughters, the lesson had been gradual. The bird that broke its neck crashing into their picture window. The countless little critters that rotated through their small animal cages. Their garden funerals. The neighbor's cat that got hit in the road. Their grandparents' passing. Baby steps into the cycle of life. They'd gone to Sunday school since they were toddlers. By the time they were seven, his little girls were fully grounded in faith, knowing that Jesus would be there for them. What could this little guy's background be?

"Mr. D was a very sick man. He suffered a lot. But now, that's all over. Mr. D has gone to heaven to live with God and Jesus and all his family who died and went to heaven before him. In heaven, there is no pain. No suffering. Only God's love."

The child scrunched his face, as if not comprehending. Then he stooped to look under the bed.

"He's not here. His soul is in heaven," Charlie repeated. "He's through with his earthly body. He'll get a glorious new body. One that's never sick or in pain—" *No, that's too complicated. Way too abstract.* He started again. "He told me that his worn-out body will be taken to church. His family will have a lovely church service for him. They will be sad, but they know that they'll see him again in heaven when their time comes."

The child looked downright anguished. Then, in the tiniest voice, he whispered. "But—where is he *now*?" He wanted specifics.

Startled, Charlie groped for the right words. "Well, I haven't seen the place exactly, but from what I hear the hospital has a special room in the basement where caring people will place his old, worn-out body in a fancy box for its last journey. Then a big shiny car, with people dressed in their best clothes, will take his old body to wherever the family will have his church service. His family, from all over the country, will come to his service. There will be flowers, music, and lots of praying. They'll take turns telling stories about him. They'll laugh and they'll cry. But they'll be glad that he was part of their lives. When the service is over, the family and friends will take his old body to a place where it will rest forever. But Mr. D won't be in that body. He'll be in heaven."

Charlie was terrified that he'd said it all wrong. Babbled too much. But the boy looked less worried. Charlie continued. "He was your friend. I know that you'll miss him. But if you'll come visit me, I'll be your friend too." That brought a tentative smile. "Would you like that?"

The boy nodded slightly.

"More than anything, he wanted to know your name. Do you think you could share that with me?"

Charlie waited. Silence. He resisted the urge to fill it with words he didn't have. Just when he was about to give up and fill the void with "That's okay," the child opened his mouth.

"Jonathan," he whispered.

Charlie couldn't help grinning. "Jonathan! Why, I had a brother named John. We called him Johnny."

"My Gram called me Johnny. She died." Bottomless sorrow transformed his face.

"I'm so sorry." So this child *was* acquainted with death. With that kind of loss. He groped for something meaningful to say. "Your grandma and Mr. D will have something to talk about in heaven. They can talk about you!"

Jonathan started to cry soundlessly. Tears seemed to spurt off his long dark lashes before trickling down his chubby cheeks. The light had gone out. That dear little child. For a few precious seconds, his spirit had opened. And he had spoken. But the window had closed. Jonathan wiped his face on the back of his sleeve. Charlie longed to gather him into a hug and comfort him. But he was too slow. Head hung, the child turned to go.

"Jonathan? Please wait. There's something else I'd like to tell you about Mr. D. He was my friend, too."

Jonathan turned his head slightly but stared at the floor.

"Mr. D said many times how special he thought you are. How he enjoyed your visits. You made his days here very happy."

Charlie took off his glasses to wipe his own eyes. When he replaced them and focused, Jonathan was gone.

ৎৡৎৡ

In a working class neighborhood of identical ranchers, Elsabet Bentz admitted the prospective health-care aide into her home.

He jutted a huge hand for her to shake. "Ben Tothero, ma'am," he said. "Saw your ad. Thought I could help."

She took a deep breath and began rattling through the well-practiced summary of her dilemma to this man, her last possibility for help. "My husband can't walk anymore. And I can't lift him." Unconsciously, she wrung her hands, as if rubbing in too much lotion. That she was desperate was evident, in spite of her efforts to hide it. She loved her husband to distraction, had since they had been high school sweethearts. She never, in a million years, would pray that his suffering would end in death. What she and everyone who knew him wanted, prayed for unceasingly, was a cure.

"Mr. Tothero, I—"

"Call me Ben," he said with an easy smile. "What are you, four feet ten or eleven? Of course, you can't lift a man."

"My husband wasn't that old when he was first diagnosed. The paralysis crept up him, bit by bit, and robbed him of feeling. At first, it was numb feet and an occasional fall, which forced him to go to the doctor for tests. When physical therapy failed, there were more tests and finally the MS diagnosis."

"Did he try that injection therapy? Interferon something-or-other?"

"We prayed that would help. It's been a miracle for many, but it did nothing for him. With a cane, then a walker, and finally a wheelchair, he continued working as a locksmith. A handicap van with hand controls replaced his Ford F150. We installed a ramp in place of our beautiful front garden. We widened our interior doors and replaced toilets with handicap versions. Handrails everywhere helped. You'll see a track in the ceiling over his bed for an electric lift with a sling. That helps him move from wheelchair to bed and vice versa.

"He's such a proud man. When his inability to manage stairs made serving his clients impossible, he found an administrative desk job through his network of friends and business associates."

"Is he at work now?"

She shook her head. "The numbness spread up his body. Now he can't feel anything below his navel. One day, while I was at work, he fell in the bathroom and lay wedged between the toilet and wall until I got home five hours later. I was unable to extricate him—had to call the paramedics. He was so humiliated. At that point, he made the tough decision to check himself into a skilled nursing facility. He was too disabled for independent living. While there, he became semi-bedridden."

Should she tell him how their insurance ran out and their savings hemorrhaged? She just couldn't. "This is his idea," Elsabet told Ben Tothero, the complete stranger. "He insists he'll be okay here at home with hired muscle. Someone to get him up, help him dress, and get him into his wheelchair. See, if he falls, he's like a bug on its back. I've put a special chair in the shower. If my helper can get him in and turn on the water, he can bathe himself. Everything works above his belly. Since he has all his marbles, he can tell you himself what he needs. In the evening, we need to do everything in reverse."

"That has got to be a terrible financial drain on your family, him being as young as you say. How people can possibly plan for this? Whew! The medical-business industry is going to make everyone destitute. Sorry, ma'am. Just a pet peeve of mine. I've seen too much of this kind of thing."

Elsabet forced her reservations aside in light of her dwindled options. "I'll be honest with you. Several people have turned me down because I can't pay what a nursing job would. And I might need to summon help at odd times. I can't afford to call nine-one-one because he's taken a spill."

She noted the man's physical attributes surreptitiously. He was huge, but not fat. Six feet, maybe six-one, big shoulders and chest that tapered to his waist. Perhaps the man was a gym rat or did weight training at home. Obviously, he could easily help with her husband's care—that is, if he would. She tried to ignore his faint oily scent. And that he felt *off*—something her intuition just couldn't decipher. Otherwise, he was perfect.

And what other choice did she have?

Warily she continued to question Ben. "Another thing that worries me," she said, trying to sound nonchalant. "Injuries from falls. What if they think I'm abusing him? Even if he insists that's not the case, they might not believe us. Patient abuse gets lots of press. They could say that he was at my mercy."

Ben threw back his head and laughed merrily. "You? That's a good one. I wouldn't worry about that. You're way too small."

She couldn't help noticing how handsome he was. Beautiful green eyes, teeth that betrayed a pricey orthodontist, and full lips too perfectly shaped for a man. Acne scared skin and a deep wrinkle that bisected his low jutting brows corrected that impression, however, making him look rugged. He was bald, although she couldn't tell why—shaving or simply his genes. When she spoke, she noticed he turned his head slightly. Ah, a hearing aid, the tiniest kind, yet he seemed to miss nothing. Age? She couldn't pin that down within fifteen years. No wedding ring, earrings, or visible tattoos—whether gang, prison, or just guy stuff. Her excellent olfactory nerve again picked up his unusual scent.

"Would you mind telling me what you do when you're not helping patients like mine?"

"I'm a mechanic. Work out of my place in the country. I specialize in vintage and antique cars, doing routine maintenance, repairs, and restoration. Since I'm the boss, I can choose my own hours. That includes helping folks who need some assistance. It's what the Bible says we're supposed to be doing, right? Like the old lady whose toilet wouldn't stop leaking. Took twenty minutes to spot the problem and fix it. She paid for the part and insisted on paying me with stuff that she baked."

"Do you have any family?"

"Did."

That she decided not to pursue. "Where did you study medical assistance?"

"Well, first off, there's nothing medical about what I do. Like you said, what forces many folks into institutions is that they can't walk or attend to their personal needs unassisted. And the family, especially the wives, aren't strong enough to lift them. That I can do. Provide muscle. But I don't do injections or procedures, you understand."

"And you're so strong because…"

"Lady, do you have any idea how much engines weigh? When do you want me to start?"

She relaxed. "Right away, if you can. If we wait any longer, he'll try to get himself out of bed. I brought him home yesterday. We've done the best we could retrofitting the house. He can pull himself up with the bar that hangs from the track. He thinks he can push his legs over the edge, but if he leans forward too much—" She paused, gulped her anxiety, and switched gears. "The mattress is lowered to the same height as his wheelchair."

She resumed ringing her hands. Becoming aware she was ticking, she thrust them into her pockets. "I'm afraid his arms will get weak, and he'll go down like a ton of bricks. And then there's the bathroom…"

"Why don't I meet him? You introduce me, then leave us to talk man to man. Guys have things they just can't say in front of their women."

After leaving the bedroom, Elsabet killed time wiping the kitchen counter that didn't need cleaning. The men's first encounter stretched endlessly. She heard the murmur of voices, the sound of the shower, some spontaneous laughter. In time, the bedroom door opened, and her husband wheeled himself into the kitchen. His hair looked freshly washed, and he was dressed in clean sweats, socks, and his LL Bean moose hide mocs.

"This guy has a vintage Morgan!" He grinned at his new helper. They exchanged smiles like old buddies. "Mother, can we keep him?"

The men laughed easily. She managed a smile.

"That's up to him," Elsabet said, turning to Ben. "And we need to talk about wages."

The guy smiled broadly, resting his hand on her husband's shoulder. "He already told me what he can pay. That works for me. I'm not short of cash, and I enjoy helping people. One thing—and I hope you won't take this wrong— no paper trail. I get paid in folding green. You know, to cover my gas and, shall we say, expenses?"

A tiny voice niggled somewhere in her brain. Was she one hundred percent sure that this guy was honest? That he wouldn't rob her blind the minute she took off for work? Or relaxed her vigilance? Should she lock up the few valuables that she hadn't sold? In her desperation, she hadn't even thought about asking for references.

"One more thing," Ben added. "I prefer to find my own clients. So, if you don't mind, please don't give my name to your friends. You know. Demand being what it is. I don't have time to field all the inquiries."

"Well. Sure. Okay. I understand." Elsabet felt her stomach squeeze into a strangled ball. There wasn't time to check him out further, and she supposed she could research the man after the fact. But would he quit if he found that she had?

Glancing at her watch, she pushed those reservations out of her mind. If this worked out, the guy would be perfect. And using him would buy her time to research benefits she might have missed. Paying in cash happened all the time, right? That wasteful government wasn't helping her one bit. All her family had ever done was pay, pay, and pay. Besides, her helper's relationship with the IRS was none of her business. And she wouldn't need him enough hours to trigger social security issues. If asked, she was to say he was a volunteer whose expenses she covered. And that was incredibly cheaper than anything else her exhaustive research had yielded.

"Would you be okay with letting me have a key to the

house? That's much safer than leaving it unlocked. And only an idiot would hide a key outside. That's thief bait."

"Um…I'd need to have a spare made. In the meantime,
I'll be here in the morning when you arrive." She shook his
hand, hoping that by doing so, she wasn't sealing their fate.

Chapter 3

As Charlie waited for his escort to arrive, he reaffirmed his decision to focus on a positive outcome while refusing to acknowledge his ticking bomb. Denial, he had decided, was essential for his peace of mind. Every minute of every day was a gift, which he could invest in blessings or in despair. What would Charlie's fallen Vietnam buddies give for even one of his past forty years? Three hundred sixty-five times forty...

He pulled his attention to Friday's activities with fresh appreciation. The chatty volunteer from Dietary would visit with next week's menus, and Optometry had sent word that his new bifocals were ready. First, however, was PT. Or was it OT? He couldn't keep the acronyms straight, but he loved the experience. The therapists had the unending patience to charm even the crankiest patient. Charlie was making friends with residents from Skilled Nursing and short-timers from various medical units. They urged him to visit as soon as he was allowed off his own ward. One fellow had whispered details about how to apply for a motorized wheelchair, but warned that he'd need to pass a driver's exam. And he wasn't kidding.

Charlie's glance lit on Vincent DePasquali's bed, which now was crisply made for the next Hospice patient. A drycleaner's bag encased a patriotic quilt similar to Charlie's. Sadly, he realized it had been Mr. D's, who could not take it home. His reflection was jolted by an approaching male voice, belting out "What A Friend We Have In Jesus."

As the uniformed escort bounced into his room, Charlie acknowledged that this guy had to be the jolliest man on the planet. An official name badge clipped to his collar bore his likeness and identified him as *Zeke Something-or-other*, the surname being too long and complicated for Charlie to decipher. Cleanly shaven from his chin to the back of his neck, his entire head shined like an object d'art. Gold-rimmed glasses would have given him a scholarly look, had it not been for his impish expression. Dressed in khakis and a navy Escort shirt, he oozed exuberance. "Mr. A! Are you ready for the exercise chamber of horrors? For a small fee, I'll take you to McDonalds instead. Just kidding! Need help with those sneaks? A quick pit stop? A dancing girl for your lap?"

Charlie could only imagine the exasperation his former teachers must have felt as this happy soul entertained the whole class. He'd heard, however, that inside every navy escort jacket was a veteran in the final stages of rehab. Having progressed to this level of trust, Zeke would soon graduate to a halfway house and a job on the outside. The temptations would be vast, and the challenges to stay healthy and employed monumental, but the success rate of this VA program was impressive. And people like Mr. Bounce-Bounce-Bounce were obviously high on the prospect of living life clean, sober, and drug-free.

Even though the VA was a governmental entity and therefore forbid overt evangelism, Zeke let everyone know that Jesus, his personal savior, had bought his redemption from a despicable life. And he never shied away from telling complete strangers how lucky he was to escape the clutches of drugs. Charlie, the product of ultra-conservative country Protestants that quietly let the minister lead all the prayers, vacillated between annoyance and guilt. He had to keep reminding himself that there were many different pathways to God.

If this guy's route worked for him, and he could help others, well, amen.

With a flourish, Zeke whisked an escort wheelchair to the side of Charlie's bed and unfolded it. He flipped the footrests out of the way then locked the wheel brake. "Your chariot awaits, my good man." Skillfully he maneuvered Charlie into the seat, anticipating just how much help to provide. Footrests flipped back into position, he guided Charlie's feet onto them and released the brakes. "Onward!" he said and started for the door.

"Zeke? Could you hold up a minute?" They stopped. "I'm curious about something. A little boy, looks to be about five, had been visiting Mr. D. Do you have any idea who he is?"

Zeke abandoned the handles and coming around to the front of the wheelchair, squatting to Charlie's eye level. "Poor little kid. I feel so sorry for him. Would love to take him on rounds. We all would. We sneak him piggy-back rides when nobody's looking."

"Why do you have to be so careful not to be seen?"

"You kidding? Drop the kid and the family will sue our asses and the VA into the next century. He's related to an old man down the hall on the right. We'll pass the room on the way to the elevator."

"Do you think we could stop on our way? Just for a minute? I don't want to be late for PT, and I know you have other patients to escort. But if I could just introduce myself to the family…"

"No! You don't want to go there. The mother—" He lowered his voice to a whisper. "Jesus, forgive me for being judgmental, but she is a bitch. If anyone tries to approach that little kid, she goes off. She wants no part of *no one*." He hung his head and closed his eyes. "Lord, forgive me. 'Vengeance is mine, I will repay, says the Lord.'" He looked up and grinned. "Romans 14:19."

Charlie nodded, resigned to making an alternate plan. "Well, maybe we could just glide by slowly. Let me glance into the room. If the child's there, give him a smile or a wave. That is, if Mom isn't looking."

"We can do that."

Zeke not only sauntered down the hall at an extremely slow pace, but managed to stop outside the room in question. "How'd we miss that? You're going to trip on that shoe," Zeke said, sounding genuinely concerned. Parking Charlie's wheelchair exactly in front of the door, he bent to improve upon the situation. "And your sock is all twisted."

Charlie grinned, suspecting that Zeke had unfastened the Velcro before leaving the room.

At first, Charlie gave Zeke's ministrations his undivided attention, and only after a few moments, glanced at the name on the door. Slipped into the space provided for names, he read *Murdock*. No first name appeared. That made sense to Charlie who had been largely unsuccessful in getting all but his most intimate providers to address him as anything other than Mr. Alderfer or sir. Respect for the veterans was of paramount importance, down to the tiniest detail.

Nonchalantly, Charlie glanced about the single-occupancy room. An elderly man with a halo of silvery hair slept upright, propped on mounded pillows. An oxygen camula was affixed to his nose, its line disappearing into the equipment behind his bed. A leather recliner was angled beside the bed on the left. An upholstered visitor's chair with oak arm rests sat perpendicular to the foot of the bed. Nobody occupied the chairs.

"That's good," Charlie indicated to Zeke, who resumed his position to continue their journey to the elevator bank.

When a whiff of exotic fragrance permeated the air, Charlie signaled Zeke to stop for a moment. He sniffed. What was that heavenly scent? Such a departure from the antiseptic smells that he tried to ignore. Floral. But which one? His wife Emma would have known...

A woman whom he'd never seen before was engaging two nurses in animated conversation. Leaning her left elbow on the elevated counter, she punctuated her comments with a manicured finger. She was very tall, but small boned, with blonde hair anchored with a tortoise barrette at the nape of her neck. Unlike staff, she wore business attire—a raspberry suit and high heels. Charlie couldn't help but notice that her short skirt revealed perfect legs when she leaned over the counter to hand the head nurse a bundle of papers.

He swiveled and mouthed to Zeke, "Who is she?"

With that, the woman turned, sizing them up. Her features, lovely as a Botticelli Madonna, contrasted sharply with her hostile expression. She impaled Zeke with icy eyes. Even from a distance, Charlie could feel her ice-pick glare.

Zeke dropped his gaze to the floor. "Later," he murmured as he resumed their mission. Feeling chastised, Charlie averted his eyes, focusing on his lap until they had passed her and turned left toward the elevators.

"That," Zeke said, "is our mystery woman. Get in line, man. She's got all the guys plotting and scheming. Word is, she works in the business office, IT, HR—some back office job. One of the guys thinks she's a temp. She hasn't been around very long or we would have noticed. Hey! You're a nice guy—single, tall and good looking with all that hair. Maybe she'd go for a mature fella, rather than a young stud. You've got class, education—"

Charlie shook his head and batted his hand at the air, letting Zeke's words drift away. Single. He hated that word. He wore the status of widower like a badge of honor. Emma—she was a beauty, and so tiny he had to stoop to put his chin on her head. She'd hop onto the step stool, hold out her arms, and say "Hug?" In spite of his height, their beautiful daughters barely hit average. Susan wanted, with all her adolescent heart and soul, to be a ballerina, but by thirteen was entirely too well endowed. And Jeannette, who longed to be a fashion model, was much too short. If only Emma could see their daughters now—one a gifted teacher and one a leading scientist—Maybe she could.

Charlie gave one last thought to the object of Zeke's matchmaking effort. Emma would have suggested that the lady wasn't hostile but simply shy, preoccupied, sad, or having a bad day. That being too beautiful could be a curse. Men would be afraid to approach her or would pursue her like a trophy. Women would be jealous and mean, and the business world would not take her seriously. Emma was oblivious to human nature's dark side. The elevator whooshed open, its occupants saving Charlie from more of Zeke's schemes.

Zeke pushed the down button. When finally alone, Charlie's thoughts turned to the boy and the old man. He asked, "Murdock—any idea about his first name?"

"Don't know if I'm allowed to say that it's Robert."

⌐⌐⌐

Jonathan wandered the long Hospice corridors, oblivious to the familiar surroundings and caring adults who said kind words. Peeking into his grandfather's room, he saw that Grandpa was sleeping. He did that most of the time. Jonathan didn't go into the room. He walked farther until he came to the small family lounge. There he found his mother asleep, her feet propped on the coffee table, a magazine upside down on her chest. He continued past a room where patients in elongated wheelchairs were watching a musical program, some surrounded by people in regular clothes. Everywhere, nurses were coaxing very sick patients with pudding in small paper cups. Beyond the first nurses' station, he turned to the right, down a short corridor that ended in the largest activity room. People sat at square tables, playing games. One family was doing a puzzle with millions of pieces. An old lady had just baked cookies. His mouth watered.

"Have one." Jonathan jumped. "Here, have several." The woman, who must be a grandmother, mounded three warm chocolate chip cookies onto a napkin. "Want milk with that?" She opened the fridge and pulled out a carton. "Growing boys need lots of milk." She poured some into a flowered paper cup. "Help yourself to more cookies, if you're mom says it's okay." She gathered her purse and umbrella and scurried down the hall, accepting thanks from the staff who were always saying how much they appreciated volunteers.

Jonathan went to the window and set his cup on the sill then devoured the cookies in between sips. From this favorite window, he scanned the beautiful grounds and the country beyond the curving driveways. At this height, five floors up, he imagined that he was a bird. He would soar high above the farmers' fields, away from the hospital and all its bad smells. Heaven—how high did Gram say that was? He watched the sky as the last rain clouds skittered away in a stiff breeze. Streamers of sunshine beamed through a hole in the clouds. It looked as if someone was looking for him. Was Gram up there somewhere? He hoped that she could not see him down here. He had not meant to hurt her. He was just trying to help. He should have told Mr. D. sooner. Now Mr. D. had gone somewhere else. What was it that man in Mr. D's room said? That Mr. D. was down in the basement?

Something blue caught Jonathan's attention. Several patient rooms were in the short corridor that connected the activity room with the main hall. A dark haired woman in a brown uniform was pushing a large cart into the hall. Jonathan could see it was heaped with colored stuff. The woman called to someone in another patient's room. "I'll run this laundry down to the basement on my way out."

She parked the cart in an alcove and entered the activity room. "Break time!" she sing-songed. "Cookies! My, aren't we lucky?" Jonathan recognized her immediately as someone whom he saw every day. "Are they good?" she asked him. Jonathan bobbed his head. "Mmmmm! And she made us fresh coffee."

The lady plucked a mug from the cupboard, filled it, and sank into a chair at the table. As she turned her attention to a magazine with pictures of people's faces on the cover, Jonathan slipped out of the room. Spotting the blue cart with its mountains of laundry, he looked both ways. He flattened himself against the back wall of the alcove where no one could see him. He lifted what he recognized were many pajamas, just like the ones Mr. D. wore. Grasping the cart by its sturdy rim, he somersaulted into it, then buried himself in its depth. Snuggled into its soft warmth, he waited. In time, soothed by the milk and warm cookies, he fell asleep.

Movement startled Jonathan awake. Concealed in the large laundry cart, he remained very still. Hearing the chatter and phone conversations off to the right, he knew they were passing the nurses' station. He was getting a ride down the main corridor. Momentarily he recognized the whoosh of the glass doors that opened magically, beyond which lay the elevators he and Mom rode every day. Instead of approaching the elevators, the cart continued on its trajectory, as if toward his grandfather's room. However, it stopped abruptly, made a sharp turn, and then stopped again. Keys jingled. An elevator door whooshed open.

"Done for the day?" someone leaving the elevator said to his unknown driver.

"Just have to make this linen run down to the basement." Bump, bump. They were inside. Keys jingling again, followed by the unmistakable motion of the descending elevator. After the doors opened again and his driver pushed out the cart, Jonathan became completely disoriented. The wheels protested as they hit many bumps. Doors opened and closed with swinging crashes. He could hear machines, clanks and bumps, getting louder, then softer as they proceeded. Finally they stopped.

"Just leave it over there. I'll get it later," somebody said. The voice was not familiar. Jonathan waited for what seemed like a very long time and finally peeked out from under the pajamas. The room was enormous, like a huge garage. Not pretty like upstairs. Giant washers and dryers lined the wall, like where his mom took their clothes when their washer broke down. The place smelled like clothes-washing soap. If Mr. D. had been taken somewhere in the basement, he must be someplace else. Jonathan had to find him. Maybe he wasn't too late. Mr. D. couldn't be in the basement *and* in heaven. Maybe he could still tell him his terrible secret.

Scanning the room, he quickly realized he was alone. Maybe everyone had gone home. How long had he napped? There were no windows and no way to tell if it was still daytime. Where, oh where was he? If only he could find Mr. D. He'd know what to do. Abandoning the linen cart, Jonathan looked for a door. A huge metal one looked like a good choice. He pushed. Nothing happened. He pushed harder, putting his shoulder into the effort. His worn sneakers slipped on the smooth concrete floor. Again, nothing. Panicked, he yanked at the knob. To his surprise, it swung inward easily when he happened to twist and pull at the same time. He peered out. A long, dimly lit corridor looked like a tunnel, its walls tiled like a bathroom, only with bigger squares. The floor was made of bricks. Overhead, huge pipes that looked like overgrown spaghetti hung as far as he could see. Among them hung big wheels and other contraptions.

His footsteps and even his breath seemed to echo as he crept down the broad tunnel. He came upon another pair of metal doors. Twisting the knob, he pushed. When the door wouldn't budge, he twisted and pushed harder. From somewhere down the tunnel, loud footsteps echoed. Jonathan panicked. Only a monster could make that much noise. Desperately, he worked at the knob. The door relented an inch at a time. Not enough to let him squeeze through, he kept pushing, enlarging the crack. Cold air and a strong, pungent smell smacked his face. Bracing his feet and pushing with both hands, he expanded the opening just wide enough to wiggle into the room.

Once inside, the door crashed behind him. Then he saw it. A lumpy object on a shiny table, covered in a sheet. And feet. Bluish feet stuck out from under the sheet. Petrified, he whirled to regain the door and escape, but rough hands grabbed his shoulders. It was too late.

ↄ⁓ↄ⁓

Susan Alderfer McHugh, Charlie's oldest daughter, was hopelessly lost. She thought she had understood the volunteer's directions at the information desk, but realized she'd been too impatient and distracted to remember the details. Her flight from San Diego had been cancelled, the next one available wasn't nonstop and her rental car reservation had gone missing. Rectifying that was a major hassle. Instead of arriving by ten, it was now after six in the evening.

As she approached yet one more junction in the endless maze of building-connecting corridors, she came face to face with a stern looking woman in a maintenance uniform. She clutched a small boy by his upper arm, and she was half marching, half towing him toward a sign that read *Police*. The child, who looked the same age as Susan's kindergarteners, was petrified, crying and struggling. Susan didn't think. She reacted.

"What are you doing to that child?" she demanded. "You're hurting him. Can't you see that he's terrified?"

The woman scowled. "I found this kid in an area that's restricted even to some of our staff. He won't tell me who he is or what he was doing there. I'm going to let our police sort it out." With that the child thrashed harder, escalating his attempt to escape. Tears spurted off his thick lashes and splashed on the tiles. He howled like a wounded animal.

"Hold on a minute. As a teacher, I know that the way you're restraining him borders on abuse. If you don't stop immediately, I'll call nine-one-one. Let the state police sort this out. How's that going to sit with the VA's director and reputation?" The women glared at each other. Relenting, Susan broke eye contact first and softened her approach. "Let me try talking to him."

Ignoring the other woman's fuming protests, Susan stooped to the child's level. "If you'll stop struggling for a minute, I'll try to help you. My name is Miss Susan. I'm a teacher. I know lots of little boys just your age. Can you tell me your name?"

The child stopped resisting, but volunteered nothing. Susan continued to gaze into his beautiful little face.

"It's okay to be scared. Nobody wants to hurt you. We just want to find out where you belong. Did you come to the hospital with your family? Or do you live in the neighborhood?"

Nothing.

"Well, I have an idea." She pointed up to a box at the ceiling. "See that?" All three looked up. "I'm thinking the hospital has a PA system. Someone could send a message all over the hospital to tell your family where you are. Why don't we walk together down this hall and ask a nice policeman how—"

That brought an immediate response as the youngster howled, shook his head no, and stamped his feet. "Okay. Then we won't go to the police. We'll think of something else." She waited until the boy calmed a little. She looked up at the woman who towered over her from her crouched position. "Maybe he'll let me walk him down to the information desk in the lobby. I passed volunteers there. They should know how to page his parents."

The employee shook her head. "They've gone home by now. Best bet would be the nurses' desk on an inpatient ward. That's the building at the end of the complex."

Susan focused on the child's face again. "Why don't we find a nurse or a doctor who knows how to help kids who get lost? Maybe we could find some food along the way. I don't know about you, but I'm really hungry." The child didn't agree, but didn't mount a fresh protest either.

The employee jabbed her hand on her hip and poked a finger toward Susan. "Now just a minute. I have no idea who you are. If I turn him over to you, I'd hate to think how many procedures I'd be violating. How do I know that you're not some kidnapper or pervert?"

If Susan hadn't been a teacher, she might have been insulted, but she knew better. Some of the most innocent-looking people in the world did terrible things to children. She opened her purse and dug out her wallet. "Here. That's my California driver's license. And here's an ID from the school where I work. Two credit cards, a library card—oh, and here's my airline boarding pass. I just flew in to see my father. He's in Hospice."

The mention of Hospice had a soothing effect on the employee. "Well, I don't know—"

"I'll give you my cell phone number. You can call me and I'll let you know our progress. If you have a number, I'll call you, if you prefer."

The woman sighed. "Okay. But if my supervisor finds out, I'll get fired. If I didn't have to pick up my own kids, I wouldn't even consider…"

"Please. But before I go, fill me in on where you found him. His parents are sure to ask."

                                    ෴

Much to Susan's surprise, the child took her hand without resistance. An employee exiting a room whose door read Information Technology directed her through the corridors to a central location. She had sorted and discarded several options to orient herself then simply asked where there might be a restaurant. That brought a snicker and directions to a place referred to as the canteen. As they hiked what felt like a quarter mile of corridors, Susan spotted a sign that read Food Court. It dawned on her that the child seemed to pick up the pace and was, in fact, leading her instead of the other way around.

Sure enough, as they came to the Food Court, he veered toward the entry. Immediately, she smelled the food. Her stomach grumbled.

Her various attempts at drawing the boy into conversation had yielded nothing. He remained mute and was no help in locating his family. *Food*, she thought. *Food might soften him up.* She stooped, gently touching the child's face. He looked in her eyes. "Are you hungry too?" To her delight, he nodded his head yes.

Working their way through the cafeteria line, she chose a chef salad, pie, and ice tea for herself while he pointed to the hot dog, macaroni, and fries. Milk, she decided, was a must. She paid for their food and selected a remote corner booth. The position of the child's bench would make it impossible for him to bolt around her. She quickly realized that wouldn't happen as he gave the meal his undivided attention. He devoured the hotdog, roll, macaroni, every fry, and the last drop of milk. When he looked longingly at her cherry pie, she passed that to him as well.

After they finished, she gazed at him benignly. He had calmed down so completely that she felt it was safe to try again. "It's time for us to find your family. I'm guessing that you know your way around here, just a little. Am I right?" The boy looked down at the table. "That's okay. In fact, that's great. Do you think you can lead me to your family? I suppose we could ask for some help—"

At the latter suggestion, the boy's eyes widened with fear. Much to her amazement, he grabbed their tray and headed for the trash can. He pushed their waste paper through the slot and then, on tiptoe, jockeyed the empty tray onto the space provided. Either the kid ate fast food often or he came here a lot. Reaching back for her hand, he tugged her toward the corridor and turned in the opposite direction from which they had come.

A map on the wall indicated that this was the way to

the inpatient building. Ultimately, they came to a break in the one-story connecting corridor. A quick left placed them in front of an elevator bank. One opened, they got in, and, without hesitation, the boy pushed a button. Even as they exited and needed to choose their direction—twice—the child didn't hesitate.

Susan peered down the hall and immediately realized that she was in Hospice, the very ward where she'd had previously visited her father. Now, if the child just knew which room—

It dawned on her that the entire hospital should have been looking for him. She hesitated, pulling back into the elevator alcove. Surely, someone should have approached her. And she should have heard a lost child announcement over the PA.

Where the woman came from, Susan didn't notice, but she pounced as swiftly as any lioness on prey. "What are you doing with my child!" A demand, not a question. She turned back to the boy. "Jonathan, you get back to the room. Immediately! Go!"

With frightening fury, she backed Susan into the wall across from the elevators. Horrified, Susan looked for help, but they were separated from the functional corridors.

"Answer me! I demand to know what you doing with my boy! Where did you take him? I should—" The woman stepped forward, fists clinched.

Susan, only five feet four, still towered over the scrawny woman, yet she felt totally unprepared to defend herself. The woman was junkyard dog tough, her skinny body contrasting her rough demeanor. Susan bet that she learned her bravado brawling with brothers. What came to Susan's rescue was her own temper. Her father always said it would get her into trouble one day, and she'd spent a lifetime cultivating gentility. Now something snapped.

Hands on her hips she stomped into the woman's personal space. "How dare you accuse me, when you're the one who can't keep track of your own little boy? How old is he anyway? Four? Five?" She didn't wait for an answer. "Do you know where they found him? In the morgue. The morgue! Do you know where that is? A good mile from here, underground, through a labyrinth of corridors. Machinery. Plumbing. Heating systems." She was guessing at the dangerous mechanicals, but was unable to stop herself. "The individual who found him was about to turn him over to the police. I'm sure they would have called Children's Services, and you'd have had a tough time explaining how such a small child ended up in harm's way. And would they have even known how to find you?

"When I met him, he was being escorted to the VA's police station. You son was terrified. Totally freaked. What's that all about? Do you have a history of domestic violence? Do police break up fights at your house routinely? And he was starving! He tucked away enough food in the canteen to satisfy a ditch digger. And you have the audacity to confront me? As a teacher, I've seen bad parenting, neglected and abused children, but this—do you even know how far he had to wander to end up in the *morgue*?"

A woman, whose badge identified her as a nursing supervisor, rounded the corner. "Is there a problem here?"

Susan gathered her professional presence and voice. "Not at all. I believe we're done chatting."

With that, she turned and stalked down the hall in search of her father, heart hammering, whole body sweating. Rethinking, she detoured into a bathroom and locked herself in a stall to calm down.

Chapter 4

Susan was exhausted when she finally entered her father's room. One look at his delighted face, however, swept the unpleasant encounter out of her mind.

"Surprise, Daddy!"

"Oh, my dear angel! What are you doing here? You're supposed to be at a conference in Sacramento. Oh my, that was a ruse, wasn't it?"

"If I'd told you I was coming, you'd have done everything in your power to tell me it wasn't necessary. Know what I think? You're a fraud! You look absolutely wonderful." She bent to kiss his florid cheek and ruffle his perfect thatch of white hair.

"It's the quality care. Do you know they have three nurses for every four patients in Hospice? I'm scared to death they'll kick me out. As a former roommate told me, this train doesn't schedule round trips."

"Is that a possibility? Making you leave?"

"I don't think so. My team has quite a program worked out for me, and they're tough. True, I'm getting stronger and regaining muscle tone that I lost. Each day in bed requires three days of rehab.

"Susan, they're into the quality of my life as long as it lasts. And I plan to make the most of it. I can eat whatever I can handle—there's no special diet. I can have visitors, participate in a bunch of activities, and even go to some off-campus events. It's like being at college without taking classes."

"There's got to be a down side—"

"Yeah, honey, there's a problem. That's one reason why they're keeping me. Have they leveled with you about my medical condition?"

She sighed. "About the other—you know…"

"They told me that they won't kid me. My prognosis is 'iffy.' As I understand it, the other aneurysm could blow any time. Or not. They won't speculate. I think it's too close to my heart or some vital organ. If I get really healthy, maybe there's something that they can do. Or I can just wait and see. Would you and your sister like to flip a coin for the Corvette? I don't think I'll ever drive it again. I don't want the responsibility for harming other people. Unless, of course, they can fix me."

"One thing at a time, Dad. You just keep healing."

"My new friends in Hospice keep dying, but I've met guys on other floors who are pretty sharp but can't live on their own. Diabetic amputees, war wounded patients, MS patients, heart, strokes, and the like. As a Vietnam vet, I'm considered a youngster. Imagine. We're having a good time swapping war stories, playing Bingo, going to chapel—"

Charlie looked at his watch. "I assume you'll stay at the house. Before Jeannette returned to Atlanta, she and my neighbor arranged for a woman to clean as needed. The neighbor's son is mowing the grass. The fridge is empty, but my car's in the garage, keys on the hook. Why don't you turn in your rental and use the Buick or the Vet?"

Susan grinned. "If I know my little sister, Jeannette will have everything ship-shape, complete with lists on the counter." She looked at her watch. "What time are they kicking me out?"

"They aren't. Twenty-four seven, remember? But I am. By the way, if you're hungry there's what they call a food court downstairs. Guys here call it the canteen."

Susan suddenly remembered her previous experience

and recounted it in detail. When she finished, she realized he had a strange look on his face."

"That little boy must be our Jonathan. His grandfather's a patient on this floor. My gut tells me there's quite a story there. Even though Jonathan came to see my old roommate for a couple weeks, Mr. D. couldn't get him to talk. We assumed he was mute or brain damaged or something."

"Something's not normal," she said, describing his terror at the mention of the police.

"I've heard, from a reliable source who must not be quoted, that the family has a 'situation' that's been in the newspapers. Privacy issues prohibit staff from saying anything about it."

Susan shrugged. "Might explain the boy's behavior. Do you know the family's name?"

"The patient is Robert Murdock. The boy's name is Jonathan. He probably has a different last name, ditto the mother who accosted you. She would be Murdock's daughter. She might go by a husband's name. Wait. I remember. The name's Kepley. If you could find anything out, maybe that would help me communicate with him. Something is troubling him deeply. Perhaps I could help."

"I'll Google the name. See if anything pops."

Charlie laughed.

"What?" Susan asked.

"I was just thinking about your confrontation with Jonathan's mother. I feel sorry for her, taking you on. For all your dignity, education, and professionalism, you're like your grandmother, not your mother—a lioness when it comes to protecting little children."

"Yeah. Pity the stork keeps missing our house."

❧❧❧

Susan slipped the key into the lock of her childhood

home. With the same old combination jiggle and turn, the tumbler relented. Funny, she thought. In California, she had a deadbolt and a security system. In this rural community, people rarely locked their doors unless they were traveling. The joke was that locks were good for keeping the wind from blowing doors open in the event of a storm.

She stepped into the sprawling rancher's living room, the familiar sense of loss grabbing her gut. A lamp on a timer glowed in the corner, just as it had when she was a teen. It would go off at 12:05, shortly after her Cinderella license expired for the night. She'd know she was in trouble if she turned onto their block and did not see the glow in the window. How she would pray that the bulb had burned out. It never had, yet her parents never scolded their responsible daughter.

She flipped on multiple lights to diminish the sad tricks her imagination played. Momentarily her mother would skim down the hall from their bedroom to greet her. She would be wearing her housecoat, a special gift from her father. She had hated the confines of her professional wardrobe, especially underwear straps. She would ditch her street clothes the minute that dinner was finished. The house was exactly as her mother had left it, kept by her dad like a shrine. It looked as if Mom would return any moment from work, shopping, or tending her garden. The only concession her father had made was to part with her clothes. Mom had insisted that women in need should have them after she didn't need them anymore. The housecoat, however, still hung in their closet.

Susan remembered one remarkable evening that symbolized her father's capacity to comfort her. A year before her mother's death, Susan had been summoned from college. Her mother had collapsed and been rushed to the hospital. As Susan drove home, tears nearly blinding her nighttime vision, she panicked over things left unsaid to her mother. Childish things she'd never confessed, gratitude for her patience during adolescence, love that she had failed to put into words. By the time she got home, visiting hours were over. She was distraught. Bursting into the house, the first thing she said to her dad wasn't a greeting. "Is she going to die?"

With a gentle smile, her dad had said in his even, quiet voice, "I don't think so. Not now." He was standing in the kitchen, still dressed in his trademark spiffy clothes, his shock of graying hair neatly combed. What he said next did more to soothe her than anything else he could have come up with. He pointed to the basket that sat on the cabinet beside the phone. "Would you like a banana?"

She had stared at the basket that sat between the phone and a hurricane lamp. *A banana? He's offering me a banana? How serious could this emergency be if he wants me to have a banana?* "A glass of sherry, perhaps," he had continued. "And a few crackers?" As if an afterthought he added, "We'll see your mother in the morning. She was better when I left and doesn't want you to worry. She's concerned that I make sure you have enough blankets. We're supposed to bring her the stuff that she put on a list. It's on the dining room table."

Fifteen years. Where had the time gone? Susan was so busy with her own life across the country, yet she could not possibly face the prospect of losing her dad. In her heart, no matter her location, *home* would always be here. She could even delude herself into thinking that included Mom. The phone rang.

"About time you showed up," her sister Jeannette started without any greeting. "Details. I want details. And how did Dad look?" They talked for an hour and finally hung up.

෯෯෯

Susan smiled, remembering the plaques she and Jeannette had designed and installed on their old bedroom doors the year after their mother's passing. DAD'S B and B. The girls had given their father an ultimatum. The shrine stops at these doors. That first day they had divided their childhood stuff into three categories: pitch, pack, or take home. Piles were boxed. Gone were the burlap-covered bulletin boards from which hung dry corsages and high school mementos. Childish furniture was moved to the basement to be advertised in the Merchandiser. Adult-size mattresses and daybeds with trundle pullouts for little grandchildren were delivered. The walls were attacked with colors other than pink that coordinated with new curtains and coverlets.

Charlie was pressed into the adventure, cajoled into accepting that their childhood was over and wouldn't return. One wall in each room was devoted to photos that he selected. They spent two days matting, framing, and hanging his favorites. Charlie proclaimed that his B and B was now perfect, and that out-of-town families had better show up. Often.

Now, from the closet, Susan withdrew a collapsible luggage stand, set it in the corner, and opened her bag. She unearthed her cosmetics, laptop, and prescription meds from her carryon. Before adjusting the privacy blinds, she scanned the old neighborhood. Beyond the rural acre lots with the houses enjoying a substantial setback, she could still identify the neighbors' activities. Early-to-beds' houses were dark while other bedrooms glowed bluish light. Old Mr. Greer, the neighborhood night owl, could be seen in silhouette behind his sheer curtain, reading a book.

Susan sighed. Of course, Jeannette was right. A retirement home would kill Dad as surely as an arterial explosion. His roots were as deep as that hundred-year oak that the developer had wisely spared. Perhaps live-in help. The lower level apartment was handicap accessible.

Susan stripped off her pantsuit and stepped into the Jack and Jill bathroom that connected the sisters' bedrooms. She luxuriated in the hot water, lathering bath gel and shampoo until all trace of her transcontinental challenge circled the drain.

As she toweled, she made mental lists. On top: Resist turning Dad into her child. Only then, with her brain sufficiently warmed and feeling as if she had minimal control, did she remember Robert Murdock. Hair wrapped turban-like and snuggled into the terrycloth robe that she kept in the closet, she trotted barefoot to the opposite side of the house. In her parents' bedroom wing, a small spare room that abutted the living room wall served as her father's office. This might have been Mom's sewing or hobby room, but she hadn't been the crafty type. Her love was the garden. All that stuff was still in the garage, except for her books that lined the top shelf.

Flipping on the computer, Susan half expected her practical sister to have discontinued the Internet service. She watched its machinations as she absently toweled her hair. The evening was more humid than warm, but the scent of approaching rain meant uncomfortable sleeping. Retracing her steps, she studied the thermostat and set the AC. By the time she returned, the PC was ready. She double-clicked the Internet icon. Much to her relief, it opened. She Googled Robert Murdock then waited. She blinked. Rising from her chair, her towel slipped unnoticed to the floor. There were dozens of entries. Could they all be *her* Robert Murdock? A few quick clicks answered that question. They were.

Opening one desk drawer after another, she rummaged for a telephone directory. Not finding one, she Googled the newspaper's name. That produced a directory and phone numbers that ultimately led her to Archives. She grabbed the phone. Dialed. Connected with a man who either had the time or the patience to talk with a lady. "How can I get copies of all the articles you've published on the Robert Murdock case?" she asked him. She waited impatiently while he checked billing records.

"Since your household subscribes, just go to our website. Following the prompts, enter the account number that's on your bill, then search for the articles listed by subject or the reporter who covered the story."

In no time, Susan found what she needed. Transfixed, she absorbed the unfolding drama with growing alarm. What had her father stumbled into? Was he inserting himself into a dangerous situation? She'd been too absorbed to notice that her feet had fallen asleep until she lurched for the printer. Forcing herself to be calm, she arranged the articles sequentially to share with her dad.

ℰ୬ℰ୬

Early sunshine played on Charlie's wall, his waking thought being of Susan. Guiltily, he felt better just knowing that she was in town. He imagined her making good use of Dad's B and B. Clever girls—easing him into a better reality. They'd been right. Now, instead of mourning the departure of his little girls, he would picture them as grown women. And the trundle beds held the promise of visiting grandchildren.

With the school year over and a free place to stay, Susan wouldn't be too inconvenienced by her visit. Of course, there was Susan's hand-wringing husband who would rather have driven her cross-country than let her fly alone. An old-fashioned guy. Yeah, that suited Charlie just fine.

Since Charlie had all his marbles, thank you God, and all his legal stuff was in order, he and his daughter could have a real visit. The toughest part had been which of his girls should have power of attorney, AKA that pull-the-plug thing. He could only imagine how frantic they must have been, his being carted away, then air lifted, the surgery, and not expected to live. All the waiting and not knowing. Days that morphed into weeks. And Jeannette, his youngest, who lived in Atlanta, had a full-time career and two little children. Emergencies were an equal-opportunity affliction. He was more determined than ever to live a long, healthy life, if only to postpone their inevitable pain. If, among his carefully crafted personal business, there were any details he'd missed, he would tackle that the minute he got home. So many ifs—

"Charlie! You're not supposed to get out of bed alone!" Mike's bark was appropriate. "You could have waited a little while longer, or rung for assistance."

One of these days, if he pushed independence too hard, Charlie's newfound privileges could go poof. More seriously, what if he fell? An MS patient on another floor had warned him what would come next. Even if he could scramble undetected to a walker, chair, or his bed, someone always found out. Then he would be off to X-ray. Lots of poking and prodding. Lies to fabricate about how easily his older skin bruised. Myriad forms to fill out. Doctors to convince that he was okay. And staff that might get into trouble. Hell, a fall could even bring the suits from the executive office. A social worker. An attorney. He shuddered.

"Sorry, Mike. My mind was elsewhere. After sixty-eight years of getting around on my own, its reflexive."

Mike's attempt at maintaining a scowl dissolved into a grin. He chuckled.

A jumble of hushed voices approached Charlie's door. With polished skill, two EMTs, trailed by two Hospice staffers, guided a gurney into the room. "Say hello to Mr. Kelly," one of them said to Charlie and Mike. The ancient man smiled and waved in slow motion, like a monarch acknowledging his subjects. Even from the distance of half the room, Charlie could see the brightest blue eyes, pinkest skin, and snowiest hair that he'd ever observed on a man. He looked positively angelic and wore a permanent smile.

Mr. Kelly appeared to be feather light as the EMTs gently lifted and positioned him onto the bed. In response to every question about his comfort, he said, "That's fine." "That's perfect." "That's good."

Charlie tried not to stare, but couldn't help noticing that Mr. Kelly was accompanied by paraphernalia. One EMT disconnected a portable oxygen tank and placed it back on the gurney.

The other brought a line from behind the bed then adjusted the nosepiece for his patient.

"Thank you," Mr. Kelly whispered, forcing volume from ancient vocal cords. "Every little bit helps."

Mike turned to Charlie. "Why don't we rocket through your morning routine? Shortly, there will be lots of newcomer activity, and you can miss the whole thing. Perhaps you'd like your breakfast in the dayroom. Catch *The Today Show* while you eat."

Charlie nodded toward his new roommate. "Did I get all this attention when they first brought me in?"

"More. Only you couldn't talk back."

☙☙

After demolishing his breakfast and doing PT, Charlie had fallen asleep. As he awoke, he was startled to find Jonathan was peering at him. Having given up that the boy would ever return, especially after the uproar he'd caused getting lost, Charlie had tried to put him out of his mind. That hadn't worked. Jonathan had crept in unnoticed and stood at the foot of his bed. His profiled face turned toward Bill Kelly who was sound asleep.

"Hey, Jonathan. I'm so happy you came to see me. I was afraid you'd forgotten about me." The child had nothing to say—only continued staring at Charlie's new roommate. "That's Mr. Kelly. He arrived early this morning." With that, Kelly opened his eyes and turned his head toward the two with a radiant smile. Charlie thought that he either truly loved people or that was simply his natural expression. Perhaps he was senile or, at his advanced age, was just missing the point. Mr. Kelly raised his forearm, as if his elbow were attached to the bed, and gave Jonathan his regal wave.

The boy looked back at Charlie as if for an explanation. "I'm told he's a World War II veteran who served under one of our greatest generals, George Patton. No doubt he'll have some remarkable stories to tell."

Jonathan continued to stare, then touched his own nose.

"That plastic thing?" Jonathan nodded. "When we breathe in, our lungs take oxygen out of the air for our bodies to use. We all do it. Breathe in, then breathe out the stuff in the air that our bodies can't use. When someone's body can't get enough oxygen out of the air, a little extra can be added. See Mr. Kelly's little nose clip? It's attached to a long tube. If you follow the tube with your eyes, you'll see it's attached to the wall behind his bed. Behind the wall, where we can't see, is a pipe that goes to a big oxygen tank. Well, maybe it's not a tank. I've never seen it, but that's the idea. The doctor knows just how much oxygen to send Mr. Kelly."

Charlie lifted the hem of his pillowcase and extracted an item that he'd been hiding. He dangled it by its thin strip of paper, allowing the teardrop-shaped silver object to swing in a circle. "Look what I found. Do you know a certain little boy who would like to have this?" Jonathan grinned. "Well, come get it."

Shyly, the boy inched toward the bed. He extended his hand. Charlie placed the Hershey's Kiss into his pudgy little palm. "Go ahead. You can eat it," Charlie quoted Mr. D. Just as Jonathan was unpeeling the wrapper, he glanced over at Mr. Kelly. Horror overtook his face, and the Kiss fell to the floor. Charlie jerked to follow his stare, hardly knowing what to expect. Had his roommate convulsed, started to choke or vomit? Mr. Kelly was lying, relaxed in his bed, holding the nosepiece of his oxygen equipment. Jonathan's face bled pure terror, as he scrambled and stumbled out of the room.

Charlie tried to call after him, but the child was long gone. Cautiously, he slipped off the side of his bed and, grasping his walker, released the wheel brake. With prudent caution but maximum speed, he pushed himself toward the door. He scanned the corridor to its vanishing point, but found no trace of the boy. Carefully, he retreated and wheeled the walker toward his new roommate. Fine plastic tubing, intended to hold the nosepiece in place, had slipped off his roommate's ear.

"Do you need some help with that thing? Or can I page the nurse?"

"Nah. Darned thing irritates my ears and nose. Sometimes I just need to give it a rest."

Charlie was perplexed. Why would something so innocuous spook Jonathan? If his grandfather was dying, surely the child was familiar with oxygen equipment.

Charlie parked the walker and sat on the edge of his mattress, noting what he'd accomplished. He had hustled himself out of bed and beat it to the door, without his muscles screaming for mercy. His exercise regime was working. Still, he vowed to pester for a motorized chair so that he could get around even faster. Staff was resisting, however, citing that motorized chairs promoted dependency, not stronger muscles. For now, though, he wanted what all guys lusted after—speed.

ຕແຕ

Susan always was a quick study, Charlie thought, as his daughter wheeled him to the opposite end of the ward, down a lesser corridor, and into a beautiful little lounge. It was tastefully furnished with an upholstered love seat, matching traditional wingback chairs, a cherry bookshelf, and end tables. Floor-length gauze curtains, dense flat-napped wall-to-wall carpet, and brass lamps with low-watt bulbs completed the cozy visitors' escape. From its size, Susan guessed that once it had been a single-occupancy patient's room. Two similar rooms, strategically placed out of the way, were furnished with single beds instead of the love seat. Family members, Charlie had learned, could grab a night's sleep while keeping an end-of-life vigil.

Susan locked her father's wheels and guided him into one of the wingbacks that offered back support. His tall frame and very long arms fit the chair perfectly while enabling him to reach whatever Susan would give him. He sighed contentedly. "You can't imagine how stiff I get, being either in bed or in a wheelchair. This is delightful."

Susan opened her bulging satchel from which she extracted a pile of paper. She placed them, face down, in two piles and positioned herself near the corner of the loveseat. She began her presentation. "This should explain a lot about Jonathan and his mother. I've put the articles in chronological order, the earliest on top."

She handed him the first story and kept quiet while he read it. Dated the previous year, it simply reported the death of a local woman and the relevant circumstances. Responding to a nine-one-one call from local long-time resident Robert Murdock, the EMTs and police found Murdock's wife, Clara Murdock, age seventy-nine, unresponsive on their dining room floor. The room had been equipped as an in-home hospital room. Efforts to revive her were unsuccessful. The medical examiner, summoned to the house, pronounced her at 3:45 p.m.

According to a follow-up article, an innocuous postscript, Murdock was quoted as saying he found his wife on the floor. He assumed she had tried to get out of bed and had fallen, perhaps striking her head. Frail and bedridden for over a year, she should not have tried to get up unassisted. There had been no indication that she might try. When he shook her shoulder gently and kept calling her name, he was unable to get her attention. He tried unsuccessfully to get a pulse. She did not seem to be breathing, so he tried CPR. Getting nowhere with that, he called nine-one-one. He would have called minutes sooner, but he was afraid to stop trying CPR. While waiting for them to arrive, which took only a few minutes, he tried mouth to mouth, giving up only when the EMTs replaced him. They quickly realized she had expired.

"So," Charlie summarized. "The wife was an invalid being cared for at home by an elderly husband. That's sad. And strange that he agreed to be interviewed, like he needed to defend himself." He reread the article, contemplating it for a moment. He shrugged. "Must have been a slow press day—nothing blowing up or burning down."

Susan handed him the third article. "It's a standard obituary, but it identifies Jonathan." Charlie read the particulars, which contained the usual stuff. Her last address; whose daughter she had been, now deceased; her education, blue-collar jobs, volunteer and church work. He paused when he reached the survivors' names. "Here we go. '...predeceased by a son in a motorcycle accident, survived by a daughter, Jade (Murdock) Kepley, and grandson Jonathan Kepley...'" He looked up. "That's our little visitor." Charlie scanned to the last paragraph. "That's interesting. In spite of Mrs. Murdock's charitable involvement it says here, that in lieu of flowers, donations can be made to an account at a local bank."

"A scholarship fund?"

"Unlikely. I'm guessing it's to help the family pay funeral and final expenses."

Charlie skimmed the next article that Susan handed to him. It was short and matter-of-fact. Because Clara Murdock had died at home without a medical professional present, the coroner needed to establish the cause and manner of death. The *cause* was broken ribs that had punctured both her heart and her lungs. A contributing factor was a head injury that caused bleeding in her brain. The *manner* of death was *undetermined*.

The fifth article raised Charlie's eyebrows. "Is this for real? The authorities are investigating the so-called manner of Clara Murdock's death? Isn't it obvious that she died accidentally or of natural causes? Is it still okay to say *old age*?"

"Evidently not. Sounds like they're thinking it was suspicious. Read on."

The next article contained specifics from the autopsy that must have raised a red flag: numerous older, healed fractures; malnutrition and trace amounts of panduronium in her system. The latter could have been related to recent surgery—if she'd had any, which she had not.

"Here's where things take a dramatic turn." She handed her father the next article.

The thirty-six-point headline screamed: *HUSBAND QUESTIONED IN ELDERLY WIFE'S DEATH.* What followed was an account of what detectives referenced as suspicious circumstances surrounding the death of Clara Murdock, seventy-nine. Previously published accounts repeated Robert Murdock's explanation of what had happened. He sounded like a frantic husband with no medical training trying desperately to revive his unresponsive invalid wife.

The investigation was prompted by discrepancies found at the scene and in the coroner's report. A search warrant was obtained and served for the Murdock residence. A CSI team processed the house. No details of findings, if any, were made available.

Robert Murdock was quoted as saying that maybe his attempts at CPR were too vigorous. After all, she did have osteoporosis and had been bedridden since a stroke the previous year. He didn't know how she managed to get out of bed, although her paralysis was only on one side and, in his words, "she still had all her marbles." She could talk and seemed to understand. And she had never tried to get out of bed and into her wheelchair unattended. Lately, she had been confined to her bed.

According to the article, Murdock became agitated when questioned about the head injury. Other drugs found in her system were prescription, and everyone who cared for her took great care with the dosage.

To avoid confusion or duplication, a written chart had been kept and initialed by every person who administered her meds. Nurses paid by Robert Murdock handled the oxygen tanks and the administration of any IV drugs as needed.

If she had anything inappropriate in her blood, he couldn't explain it.

Ultimately, he demanded that the detectives leave his house. They had returned later with the search warrant. However, Clara Murdock's bedroom had been stripped, the hospital bed and all her medical equipment removed. A professional team that specialized in infectious disease control had sanitized the room.

"What's next? Surely they couldn't believe—" Charlie gasped. "Oh my god. This, I did not expect."

Chapter 5

The bold headline summed up the story: Quickly Charlie scanned the details.

MAN CHARGED IN WIFE'S DEATH.

Police today arrested Robert Murdock, seventy-five, in connection with the death of his wife, Clara Murdock, seventy-nine. He has been charged with first-degree murder. Papers filed by the district attorney's office contend that Robert Murdock struck his wife repeatedly then crushed her chest as she lay on the floor.

The article ticked off an assortment of secondary charges. Details of the coroner's report included what should have been a fatal level of Panduronium, the inference being that, had the head and chest injury not been fatal, the drug would have killed her. The implication was that the husband became impatient or did not trust the drug to do the job for him. Perhaps she fought back. The motive was attributed to the financial drain and constant demand of caring for an elderly, dependent invalid. The hasty removal of medical equipment, specifics not included, was noted as relevant.

A quote from the district attorney followed. "Old, frail, ill people should be safe in their own homes. If Robert

Murdock was at the end of his rope, resources were available to him, from the Agency on Aging to myriad country and state services. We intend to prosecute Clara Murdock's murder vigorously. In death, she deserves the dignity and justice she did not receive in life. This prosecution is a message that, in this county, we will not tolerate the abuse of our weakest citizens."

Robert Murdock's "legendary" temper was illustrated with a previously reported altercation at Clara Murdock's nursing home. A neighbor, who spoke on condition of anonymity, described him as "combustible—a man known for his outrageous temper, shouting, and neglecting his reclusive wife."

Charlie snorted. "Everyone wants to be the bride at the wedding or the corpse at the funeral. The media should insist on revealing their names. That would prevent vicious gossip and force 'em to be honest. Susan, what's this about a previous altercation?"

"I did find articles that predates those about Clara Murdock's death. Seems the man has quite a temper. Here you go."

Charlie read the articles, which Susan had kept separate from those about Clara's death. The police had been summoned to a nursing home where Clara was being rehabbed after a stroke. According to the administrator, Murdock became offensive over, in Murdock's words, "mistreatment of his wife." The incident escalated into a shouting match. When Murdock threw a punch that bloodied and broke the administrator's nose, the police were called.

A follow-up article cleared the nursing home of any wrongdoing. Seemed Murdock had expected a nurse to stay with his wife twenty-four/seven, although unwilling or unable to pay for private duty nursing. In exchange for not filing assault charges, Murdock agreed to take his wife elsewhere. Finding other facilities suddenly *filled to capacity* or *with waiting lists* and Clara not qualifying for the county home, Murdock took his wife home. There he cared for her with the help of his daughter and nursing aides.

"So—Clara Murdock was a patient in an economical, but well-run nursing home until the husband mixed it up with the staff and ended up being cared for at home. That's tragic."

"Stay tuned," Susan said. "Read on."

"That explains how someone in her state of health was at home with only an elderly husband to care for her twenty-four/seven. I was still in my forties when your mother first because ill. But I was strong as an ox and quite capable of lifting a ninety-pound woman. But today? I couldn't do it now. How old did they say he was?"

Susan glanced through other clippings. "Says here he was seventy-five, which made him three or four years younger. Even so—"

"What else do you have there?"

Susan tidied her stack that she'd arranged beside her and kept in order after Charlie had read them. The rest remained face up on her lap.

"They released him?" he asked incredulously, staring at a headline that read, *Indicted Murderer Suspect Foils Bail Hearing.*

"Not what you'd think. A famous Philadelphia lawyer, who specializes in age-related abuse, appeared to represent Robert Murdock, replacing the public defender. According to this article, he contends that because of his age and local roots, and with no living relatives out of state, he wasn't a flight risk. Also, he was running out of money. The attorney demanded that his client be released ROR—on his own recognizance. More interesting, however, was his diatribe that the whole case was about the district attorney's upcoming election and his need for a 'sexy issue.' The lawyer's most compelling sound bite was his frequent reference 'old Mr. Murdock and his own fragile health.' Meaning he couldn't possibly have lifted his wife—whom he said was a large woman—out of bed and caused that level of injury."

The article continued. According to the clever journalist's wording, before the judge could stop rolling his eyes, Robert Murdock crashed to the floor, an apparent heart-attack victim. Paramedics rushed in, paddles were used to restart his heart, and the victim was carted away in an ambulance to the local hospital's emergency room.

Charlie sucked in a breath then read and reread the article in detail. He shook his head. "That hearing must have been a circus. Do you suppose there's a shred of truth in any of this?"

"I'm glad I won't have to sit on that jury. It screams lack of probable cause. Everything can be explained logically. Except for that drug they found in her system that didn't belong there."

Charlie contemplated the entire situation in silence for several minutes then raised a finger to punctuate a thought. "Let's consider the larger picture as it relates to Jonathan. Put yourself in the daughter's place. What did you say her name was?"

Susan riffled to the obituary. "Jade. Jade Kepley. That must be her married name."

"Yeah, her. If she didn't have any doubts that her mother died as her father described, she must be outraged and mad at the world. And poor little Jonathan. Jade must be so brittle that any little thing could set her off. Maybe that's why she lashed out at you and it also explains her absentmindedness about Jonathan's whereabouts. You gave her an excuse to vent, although she probably felt justified at the time."

"Dad, even if the grandfather is guilty as sin, that shouldn't wreck Jonathan's life. No wonder he's traumatized. How could he possibly miss being a witness to at least part of this drama, even if he doesn't understand what's at stake? If you're hoping to help, aren't you afraid of making things worse? You're not a child psychologist."

Charlie, ignoring her comment, pointed to the papers that remained on Susan's lap. "What else do you have there?"

Susan picked up the remaining clippings and handed them to her father. Charlie identified them as letters to the editor. While one decried the unfairness of trying a case in the press and another expounded on the crushing demands put on family caregivers, several others shrieked around one central theme: What goes around, comes around.

"I guess that explains what Robert Murdock is doing here at in the VA's Hospice ward."

"Someone here, who doesn't want to be quoted, did tell me that he's a heart patient. I guess he isn't expected to live more than six months, much less stand trial. The DA would be stupid to wheel him into a courtroom on a gurney, oxygen mask over his face with a monitor beep-beep-beeping. How fast would you vote that DA out of office?"

Charlie squirmed, arched his back, then ran his hands up and down his spine.

"Dad, let's get you back to your room. Hunching over this stuff must be a strain. How about a little nap?"

"I am a bit weary. But Susan? Let's keep these articles out of sight. They're ballistic about privacy issues around here. If everyone doesn't already know the Murdock family tragedy, I don't want them to learn it from us." He frowned, head down, not looking at anything in particular. "If I could find out what really happened—you don't suppose the child knows…"

෴

Susan nibbled a guest meal while her father attacked his lunch in the large, cheery dayroom. She marveled at the variety and number of small portions that made up his meal. Not a great fan of her own cooking, she found her sandwich more than adequate. Her dad, she noticed from the checks on the menu slip that accompanied his tray, had ordered nearly every available item. Finishing every scrap, he declared it "most satisfactory."

Interesting—in a setting like this—how mealtime becomes the highlight of the day.

Finally, he pulled off his clothing protector, an overgrown terrycloth bib, that the staff had velcroed behind his neck. "Better to just let them do it," he chuckled. "Some of these guys don't have great muscle control and appreciate not having to wear their lunch all afternoon. It's kind of a joke. Everyone says they don't need a bib, but they go along so that others don't feel conspicuous. Trying to spoon soup over big bellies with shaky hands is hard. And some have trouble finding their mouths."

Susan had not failed to notice that at each of the other three card tables a staff member was either helping a patient eat, was chatting with him, or simply holding their hand. Most patients, however, ate or were fed in their rooms. "Dad, is being here depressing?"

"Not really, hon. It's a beautiful place. Every staff member wants to work here—could probably make more money elsewhere. It's a religious commitment for many of them. And, if you listen, nobody's shrieking in pain, but they aren't drugged senseless either. They find the balance. It's real quality care. And the appreciation for the veterans' contribution to our freedom is everywhere.

"There's two young guys in private rooms down the hall—can't be forty years old—both with terminal cancer. One of them can operate a motorized wheel chair, and the other inches around with a walker. They get together and spend hours playing a computerized medieval resource management game. One guy brought his own laptop, and someone from Information Technology scrounged another, and hooked them both to the Internet. They keep in touch with family and friends all over the country. Watch TV together. Escorts take them for wheelchair walks around the campus.

"If a patient is actively dying, a nurse holds his hand, strokes his forehead, reads to him, whatever the patient finds comforting. Really, it's humbling to watch them help families cope. So, depressing? It's inspiring. Everyone who works here is committed. Being rich is not just about money."

"Dad—you look so much better. You're obviously not in immediate danger. If they want to discharge you, have you considered where you'd like to live?"

"You mean, a nursing home? Assisted living? Before I do that, I think I'd try for the floor above us. That's Skilled Nursing. But if I don't need that level of care…" He thought a minute. "Perhaps, something temporary. A step down in between the hospital and going home.

"Jeannette and I have been talking—"

"Oh boy. Here it comes. And the answer is 'no.'"

"Hear me out, Dad. Both in Atlanta and in San Diego, we have plenty of room. Jeannette and her husband purposely built the house with a grandparent suite on the first floor, and there's just Doug and me in California. That is, until you can be on your own. Unless you'd rather stay permanently." She perked up intentionally. "You could come and go as you please."

"Sweetie, that's awfully kind of you both. But I cannot, I will not, live on the fringe of my daughters' lives. I want to go home, even if it means having professional help." He reached across the small round table and covered Susan's small hand with his own. "You and Jeannette must get your minds around my reality. In all probability, some day that other aneurysm is going to blow, and that will be it. Next time, there won't be months languishing in a hospital, steady recovery, and a victorious roll out the door. It might be tomorrow. It might be next year. Or maybe in ten. I have no regrets, other than wanting to dance at my grandchildren's weddings. And who knows—I may do that yet. You do understand. Oh, come on. I didn't mean to make you cry. We just need to deal with reality. 'If you're going to steer your little boat through the rapids, you have to look for the rocks.'"

"Who said that?"

"I did. Now, if we're finished with lunch, let's go back to my room. I'm tired enough to need a rest, and you need a break. Go shopping. Enjoy this great weather. Go spy on my neighbors."

Susan laughed. "Okay, Dad. But we're not finished with this discussion."

"Are too."

❦❦❦

Charlie had never been one for napping. He could sleep for all eternity, so why waste time now? In the here-and-now, he did not want to miss anything. Even speed naps weren't his bag. He would need an hour to fall asleep and two more to fully awake up. The morning's visit, however, had left him exhausted. Maybe he'd just stretch out—close his eyes and relax. Just for a few minutes—

"Need anything else?" Mike had delivered and collected Charlie from his bathroom. In addition to addressing his other needs, Charlie had insisted on brushing his teeth. His mother, God love her soul, had been determined that her children would have good teeth. Nothing was eaten in their pre-fluoride household without her intonation, "go brush your teeth." Candy was permitted at Halloween and Easter, but even then in minuscule amounts. He would die with his own teeth, and later than sooner. A crown here, a root canal there, a dozen unavoidable fillings, none of which he counted. He was on track.

He grinned at himself in the mirror, feeling more like himself every day. The in-house barber had done justice to his thick, straight, white hair. Men were jealous. Women called him cute. Cute! Huh! That was for babies and little girls.

"Just help me onto the bed. I need to rest my legs. Gotta stay sharp to keep up with my kid. She and her sister are cooking up plans for my future. I may be in for a fight."

Mike smiled as he maneuvered Charlie's legs closer to the center of the bed and flipped the end of the quilt onto his legs. He grasped that unless Charlie was in between sheets, this didn't really count as being in bed. That was for sick people and little kids, he had said. This was more like being in a lounge chair.

"Say, Charlie. If a single room becomes available, would you be interested? Several of them have leather recliners. In the past, patients' families have brought them in and, when the patient passed away shortly thereafter, offered to leave them. The VA bought others. You might be more comfortable there."

Charlie glanced in Bill Kelly's direction. "No, I enjoy having company. And, if Bill needs something and can't manage the call button, perhaps I can help. Thanks anyway." Mike flipped him a wave and hurried out to attend other patients.

Charlie had no sooner closed his eyes then approaching sleep spread its warmth. He felt as if he had completed a strenuous double shift or a Saturday spading Emma's garden. A familiar hum rose in his ears, drowning all the ward's other sounds. He slept.

By the time something nudged him awake, lengthening shadows had spilled onto his quilt. He opened his eyes. Jonathan stood at the foot of the bed. Charlie grinned broadly and beckoned the child to come closer as he fiddled with the buttons to elevate his bed. "I'm so glad to see you. You make every day happier."

Jonathan glanced tentatively toward Bill Kelly. "Mr. Kelly? You're worried about Mr. Kelly? He's just taking a nap. He's really, really good at that."

Jonathan smiled shyly.

"I'm awake," Bill Kelly's weak voice belied his bright eyes and big smile.

"Jonathan, Mr. Kelly has something to explain to you—about his oxygen equipment. I mean, that plastic thing he wears in his nose that's attached to the tube. He can't talk very loud. Why don't you go over by his bed? Make it easy for him."

At first, Jonathan remained rooted to the spot, occasionally moving his glance from one man to the other. "When you get back, I'll have something for you." Jonathan brightened. As if struggling with imaginary demons, he edged within a yard of Bill Kelly's bedrail.

"The last time you were here, I did something that I believe frightened you. Or maybe you were just worried," Bill said. He paused a moment to catch his breath. "Now don't worry, I won't pull it out again."

Jonathan looked skeptical, scrunching his eyebrows, but said nothing.

Bill paused for a minute. "Wait. Hard to talk and breathe sometimes." Jonathan remained by his side. Bill's chest rose and fell rapidly at first, then slowed. Several moments passed. "That's better. Now, they can't stick the end of the tube up my nose. Right? That would be silly and it wouldn't work. So they attach the tube to this little nosepiece. I don't need a lot of extra oxygen—just a little. If you could feel what comes out, you'd think it was air. Sometimes I take out the nosepiece because my nose gets itchy. Or it runs. I put the nosepiece back after I've rubbed my nose or blown it. Now—if I take it out, for just a minute, you won't be frightened, okay?"

Jonathan scowled. Bill continued. "The nosepiece is held in place by these tiny plastic pieces that hook around my ears." He unhooked the one closest to Jonathan. "That's okay. I don't have to take it off if that scares you. I just wanted to show you that it's safe. okay?"

Jonathan nodded slightly.

Kelly slipped the nosepiece out and held it a few inches from his face. "I can't let you touch it because it's germy, but if you hold your finger, just a little bit away from the holes, maybe you can feel it."

Jonathan's little face convulsed in fear as he shook his face in alarm.

"Okay." Kelly put the nosepiece back in position. "Maybe some other time. I just wanted to show you."

Charlie had unearthed a Hershey's Kiss from his bed-side table. Perched on the edge of his bed, feet dangling, he was prepared to present it to his brave little friend. Jonathan, however, turned abruptly and dashed out of the room.

"Thanks, Bill. That was great. Even I understood."

"That kid is terrified of something."

"And I'm going to make it my mission to find out what that is."

☙☙☙

Charlie anticipated physical therapy with pleasure. He knew it was helping. One day in bed, they kept reinforcing, meant three days of hard work to regain what he had lost. At first, in his bed, the only weights he had lifted were his own arms. Up and down. Up and down. They felt like twenty-five pound weights. Then, seated on the side of his bed, the therapist flexed his legs at the knee. Up down, up down.

When he graduated to the small weight room, he hefted one-pound hand weights while seated in an armless chair. That was increased to two-pounders. Similar weights were strapped to his ankles. More up and more down. Slowly, he graduated to greater resistance. The weights were racked on a wooden pyramid, from lightest on top, with numbers etched on their ends. Each increment was painted a different color. Charlie compared his progress to ascending a rainbow, the pot of gold—the prize—being his independence. He thrust aside images of that hidden demon lurking somewhere in his chest, poised to rupture if he twisted too far. Hefted too much. Dared to dream.

Once his muscles got comfortable and the routine got easy or boring, he progressed to the machines. From wheelchair to walker to the black vinyl seat, Charlie mastered the motions under the watchful eye and skilled hands of the therapist. Charlie felt safe wearing his wide leather belt that supported his abdominal muscles.

As days became weeks, he made progress on the machines. Upper back, shoulders, biceps and triceps, seated leg curl, leg extension, leg press—he learned to adjust the resistance and number of repetitions by pressing yellow buttons at the end of black bars. No need to pick up heavy plates, as in his previous gym. This equipment was ideally suited for recovering patients.

While there, he made friends with residents from other wards, particularly Skilled Nursing. The goal of one army veteran, an MS patient, was just to maintain his upper body strength as long as possible. Charlie was awed by his jolly attitude, his refusal to complain or rail about his fate. Instead, he kept everyone enthralled, recounting his misadventures as an air traffic controller. While the veterans waited their turns on the machines, they discussed CNN's morning news, swapped war stories, argued politics, bragged about grandkids, and expounded upon their spiritual journeys.

Room numbers were exchanged as were the times and places of the next Bingo marathon, a special bus outing, or a favorite gospel group that had scheduled a concert. How seductive it might have been for Charlie to slip into this easy comradery without forcing himself through the rigors of recovery. These friends were entrenched for the duration, but he dare not give up or give in.

Charlie was brought back to the moment when Zeke, his escort, arrived at his door. "You ready to rock 'n' roll?"

Charlie grimaced, wondering how many more times he could bear to hear that expression.

"Oh, come on! It's not that bad. You know that you love being worked to death. Oops. Bad choice of words." Zeke snickered, enjoying the expression. Even Hospice had its own private jokes, as long as Staff didn't hear. "Are you ready? I am way early. Could come back in thirty minutes, or you could hang with the guys down at PT."

An idea formed. "Do I have time to stop at a room down the hall? I can meet you at the elevator in half an hour."

"That's cool. I'll let the desk know the plan. They get cranky if we get too creative with the schedule. We'd both be in big trouble if we went AWOL."

As soon as Zeke disappeared around the corner, Charlie wheeled himself into the hall. He envied the fellows who could tootle around in those motorized chairs, but his request *was* denied as counterproductive. His arms needed exercise, and his legs were not helpless. He glided then stopped to peer into Robert Murdock's private room. It was deep and narrow, the head of his bed abutting the exterior wall. To the bed's left, a tall window probably overlooked the parklike expanse of manicured grounds. The mini-blinds, however, were closed, obscuring what should be a magnificent view of the rolling countryside. The gloom produced by one forty-watt bulb was depressing.

Charlie rolled toward the doorway, halting beside the propped-open door. He had intended to knock. Instead, he said "Knock, knock" softly. If Mr. Murdock were sleeping, Charlie didn't want to disturb him. The man's eyes were open, however.

"Hi. I'm Charlie from down the hall. We haven't met yet. Just thought I'd drop in and say hello."

When the man smiled weakly, Charlie felt braver.

"May I come in? I don't want to disturb you if you're resting."

"Sure." All but a whisper.

Charlie started the familiar dialog that prefaced all conversation when vet met vet at the VA. "So. What branch of the military were you in?"

"Army. Korea."

"Really? Nam here." Charlie did the math. If Murdock was seventy-five years old, he must have been one of the last to serve there. Perhaps an advisor. Or maybe he was a career man—a lifer as they were called—and served multiple tours. They could swap stories some other time. Charlie was on a mission.

"Say. Didn't I see a cute little kid come into this room? My roommates and I have been trying to figure out who he is. Can't tell you how much a child brightens things up around here. My two grandchildren live in Atlanta and I don't get to see them very often. You know, parents have jobs, kids have school, and airfare's expensive. We borrow our friends' grandchildren whenever we can."

The man smiled. Charlie couldn't help but compare Murdock's condition to that of Bill Kelly. The latter was in much better shape while being two decades older. If Charlie and Bill Kelly were both lucky, they'd be around for the real Christmas. *Funny how quickly you get attached.* He refocused his attention.

Murdock nodded. "He's my grandson. Comes in every day with my daughter." He paused to catch his breath then continued. "She's real protective. Won't leave him with neighbors or strangers. Says they're real mean. Doesn't trust them. Can't say that I blame her. So many neglect their own kids..." He faded off, turning his face toward the wall.

"How old is your grandson?"

The old man turned his head, brightening. "Five." Then the light faded. "I missed his birthday, being sick." A pause. "And all." A slight turn of his face, a tear glistening on his cheek. He didn't say more.

"This seems like a great place for a child to visit, the way the staff welcomes families and guests. I've overheard how everyone loves your grandson. They all say he's so well behaved. Your daughter's doing a great job."

Murdock refocused on Charlie, a wide smile brightening his translucent face.

Charlie forged ahead. "Something I've been wondering. When I was a child, unfamiliar places and strangers scared me. How does your grandson react to such things? Does being here make him uneasy? Is he afraid of something?"

Charlie nearly leapt from his chair when an angry voice boomed from behind him. "What the hell are you doing in here? Who gave you permission to barge into this room and bother my father? Didn't you read the signs on the door? Get out! Now!"

Charlie's heart doubled its rate, adrenaline plunging him into flight mode. Immediately, he grasped the wheels of his chairs, but in trying to flee, he crashed into the woman who was now making disparaging curses about his parentage. "I'm sorry. So sorry. I didn't mean any harm—"

The woman jumped out of his way. "Just get out! Leave my family alone."

"Yes'm." Heart pounding, head focused on the tile floor that preceded him, Charlie rolled down the hall. He half expected angry personnel to pop from various doors to read him the riot act since the irate woman's words must have traveled all over the ward. A sign on the door? He'd missed that entirely. But as he approached the nurses' station, none of the nurses paid any attention to him. No one even looked up. Charlie glanced at the wall clock. His escort, Zeke, was not scheduled to meet him for another twenty minutes. He cleared his throat.

The man at the desk covered the phone's mouthpiece and whispered, "You looking for Zeke? He said to tell you he'd be in the kitchenette. Probably grabbing a cup of our *black death*." He winked conspiratorially.

Charlie located Zeke without difficulty. "Take your time with that coffee. My mission failed miserably."

⚬⚬⚬

Even a great workout spiced with the companionship failed to elevate Charlie's low spirits. He could not shake it off. All he had been trying to do, he kept telling himself, was to learn something, anything that might shed some light on Jonathan's problems. The child was more than sad or depressed. Something awful had penetrated his spirit. Charlie didn't need to be a shrink to know that. So why wasn't anyone tending to Jonathan's needs? Had he been evaluated? Was he seeing a therapist? If not, what was the grace period beyond which he'd fall through the cracks from which he could not be extricated? And now Charlie had made an enemy of the mother.

Declining an offer to join his buddies to watch a vintage movie in the auditorium, he asked Zeke to take him back to his room. That morning, Mike had lowered his bed to rump level, enabling him to get himself in and out unassisted. Such progress should have made him euphoric. But it didn't. Zeke, the eternal mother hen, insisted on supporting his arm as Charlie completed the maneuver. And he endured one more of Zeke's lectures on the importance of properly setting the wheel brakes.

"You okay?" Zeke concluded.

"Sure. I'm fine. Just a little tired from my workout." Given the number of times he'd been asked that same question, Charlie chided himself to either snap out of it or punch up his act. The last thing he wanted was for the medical folks to insist on this pill or that. He knew what was weighing him down and just wanted some privacy.

"How was PT?" Bill Kelly inquired. His eyes were closed, but he had missed nothing.

Charlie made a decision. "Bill, can I trust you?"

"Absolutely. What's up? Is it our little friend?"

"I got caught snooping." Bill laughed merrily, which made Charlie smile. Then he gave Bill the executive summary of what he had learned from the newspapers.

When he finished, Bill sighed. "I sort of remember something like that. Last fall, right? It was on the news just before I got sick this last time. I was short of breath. A friend drove me to the ER. Hectic night—big traffic pileup. Lots of victims. I ended up watching the news while I waited. As I recall, a man was arrested, supposedly for killing his wife. I remember thinking that was unusual, given his age. An old guy like him would be more likely to smother her with a pillow."

"The husband is Jonathan's grandfather. He's right down the hall."

"Explains a lot."

"I tried to talk to the grandfather. I was attempting to find out what's eating Jonathan when his mother caught me. What a tiger! She was livid. Ordered me out. That's twice now for my family. If that mother puts Susan and me together—I just hope she doesn't take it out on the child. Or complain to our administrator. I doubt we'll be seeing that little guy any time soon. I was just trying to help. Sometimes that's worse than doing nothing."

Bill smiled. "That kind of heart problem never killed anyone." He sighed, slipping his covers up to his chin and nesting himself in his favorite position facing the wall. Charlie knew what that meant—enough talk and exertion. He needed to nap.

Perhaps he was too tired as well. He'd overdone it, depression being the penalty phase. Charlie plumped his pillow and adjusted his quilt, his eyes falling on the beautifully embroidered inscription. *Thank you for defending our country and our freedom.* That, more than any ugly words, brought tears to his eyes. What would Emma have done? She never, ever took anything the wrong way. She was incapable of seeing flaws in others, which had only made him more protective. She projected emotional safety, and people instinctively knew she would keep their secrets and not be judgmental.

In middle age, she was an expansion of the teenager who had befriended him. Everyone wanted to be her best friend. And she had chosen him. Sometimes he thought, in spite of his girls, he'd never adjust. That he was stuck in a bottomless void. Fifteen years had gone by in a blink. His memories were crystal as if she'd been here just yesterday. He turned to the wall and buried his face in his pillow, a tear narrowly missed his ear. *Stop it! Be a man!*

Susan had brought in his favorite picture, not a professional portrait, but a framed candid. A magnificent coral sunset that was sinking into the ocean, back dropping Emma, Susan, and Jeannette who were attempting to launch a brilliant purple kite. A brisk wind jumbled their hair and clothes, sticking Emma's voile coverup against her slim body. That fall came the first diagnosis, supposedly caught in plenty of time. Strange how his life was divided in two—what came before, and what came after. He never said it out loud, but he reckoned time in that way. *What year did that happen? Let's see. That was X many years after that day in September. That would make it 19xx or 20xx.*

How Jonathan had crept to his side undetected, Charlie couldn't explain. The child's approach had hit neither Charlie's radar nor his excellent foxlike ears. He felt the small hand on his arm and turned bloodshot eyes to meet his. Jonathan face was a mere foot from his, blue eyes filled with compassion. Charlie hastily wiped his face on his sleeve.

"Why are you sad?" the child whispered.

Slowly Charlie extended his hand and gently stroked the boy's silky head. "My wife died a long time ago. Now she's in heaven with God and Jesus, just like Mr. D and your grandma. But I still miss her, sometimes so much that I simply can't stand it. It makes me so sad. I was just thinking about her and wishing she were here. How she would have loved to meet you."

Jonathan rested his cheek on Charlie's chest, his head facing the foot of the bed. The child's warmth penetrated Charlie's shirt, his hair smelling of baby shampoo. Their first conversation—the moment was magical. A slender thread was knitting their bond. The child spoke, his little voice barely audible. "I miss Gram, too."

Charlie stroked the little guy's head, barely touching its silky strands.

Then Jonathan uttered a few shocking words. Charlie was sure he'd misunderstood, but something in the child's trembling confession told him otherwise. Charlie was terrified of breaking the spell by asking him to repeat what he'd said, but he could not resist.

Chapter 6

Jonathan. Look at me." The child didn't move. "Please. I didn't catch what you said, and I want to know what's troubling you. Perhaps I can help."

Before Charlie could process a suitable follow-up, Jonathan eased from the bed and, without looking back, trudged from the room. Stunned, Charlie raised himself onto his elbow. He waited. Nothing. Jonathan did not return.

Charlie could have sworn that Jonathan said, "I killed Gram."

He glanced toward Bill Kelly, but the old man appeared to be sound asleep. Charlie lowered his head back onto the pillow, attempting to process the fragile implication of what he'd just heard. Surely, he had misunderstood. How could a small child—

And yet—what could he make of such a confession? He hadn't a clue.

❦

Since Charlie's arrival, days had edged into weeks. Bit by bit, it seeped into Charlie's consciousness that his progress had slowed to a crawl. Propelled by his initial euphoria at just being alive then followed by his determination to regain his faculties, he now felt stuck on some kind of plateau. He thought he should be going home, but none of the professionals seemed to entertain the same thought. They smiled at his ideas. They hedged. If he pushed, they suggested one more goal. Then another. They didn't insult his intelligence or act condescending, but Charlie grasped that they'd heard it too many times. Sometimes new Hospice patients, who had been struggling elsewhere or on their own, improved with round-the-clock care, fine-tuned medication, and proper nutrition. No doubt, staff had learned how to respond by attending objection clinics. The doctor hinted at Charlie's inability to re-enter Hospice if his return home was *unsuccessful*. He didn't need them to elaborate. Elsewhere he might not receive the same quality of care that had fast-forwarded his recovery. Wait. Be patient. Ha! Not his long suit.

To himself, Charlie appeared healthy and energetic as he moved around his room, now with a walker except for journeying throughout the complex. The contraption had a built-in seat in case he become tired or needed a break. He pretended that he was at home. Thanks in part to enormous concentration and his recovered arm strength, he never came close to falling. He lacked his fellow residents' grogginess and energy depletion to such a degree that he felt guilty, powering himself around the halls in his wheelchair. That guilt intensified when he visited friends in Skilled Nursing. Barring the unforeseen, they would not leave the VA by the front door. He caught himself feeling impatient when trying to traverse the halls at a clip, only to get hung up in traffic behind frail patients who could only inch along.

Susan, ultimately, would have to go home. Summer had morphed into August. As they traversed the sidewalks that circled the buildings or luxuriated on a bench beneath the old maples, the air began to smell different. Cicadas screamed their raucous message—summer was waning. A visitor reported that first red leaf on her black gum tree, which she swore signified an early fall.

Weeks of excellent care, however, had proved hugely beneficial for Charlie's roommate, Bill Kelly. With a portable oxygen tank strapped to his chair and an Escort for transport, he participated in Bingo, had lunch in the day-room, and went to Chapel for Mass. He brightened every-one's day. Family, the closest of whom resided in Mary-land, were so pleased with his progress that they began scouting neighborhood facilities that also provided skilled nursing—just in case. They wanted their dear man to come home. And who could blame them?

In spite of the privacy curtains that the white coats drew around patients, Charlie's fox-like ears missed nothing of Bill's medical progress. The competition was on between the two roommates—who would graduate first? Guilt cast its pall when Charlie acknowledged his selfish disappoint-ment that his friend would be leaving. This wasn't college. This wasn't the army. New friendships here, at this stage in life, were compressed into tiny segments. Charlie needed to get out of here—to surround himself with young, healthy people. To see traffic zip by, watch teenagers' antics, wait in line at the grocery, look at the endless junk in K-Mart. Even hinting at this sadness might be viewed as depression. The last thing he wanted was medication. He valued a sharp mind, above everything else, and kept his thoughts to him-self.

One day, Charlie's impatience got a reality check. Now allowed off the ward, as long as he got staff permission and informed them of his destination, he had wheeled himself to the ground floor canteen. Maneuvering around clumps of people without hurting anyone was more of a challenge than he had anticipated, although people graciously helped him or simply got out of the way. After a bite, he chose fresh air for dessert. Seated in a small courtyard near the main doors, he watched people coming and going from the vast parking lot to the main lobby of the outpatient building. He noticed their gait, the bounce in their steps, the ease with which someone doubled back to retrieve a forgotten item from the depth of his car.

He guessed they were here to keep routine appoint-

ments or visit someone. Most were retirement age, some
looking a lot older than he did.

Whatever brought them to the VA wasn't hindering
their mobility. Even with his walker, he could win any foot-
race in Hospice or even Skilled Nursing. But on the outside? In the real world? He watched an old lady help her
husband direct his walker from the main door to a waiting
car at the curb, its four-ways blinking. It must have taken
five minutes to successfully maneuver him into the front
seat. She fiddled with the walker until it collapsed then
gratefully accepted a volunteer's offer to stow it in the trunk
of her car. Wow. That old guy moved faster than he could.
Yeah. Charlie got it. He wasn't ready.

The only way he could cover great distances would be
in a motorized chair. A fresh breeze riffled his hair, ratchet-
ing his longing for independence. His home. Her garden.
The clean country air. Even the cow barns when the wind
changed direction. Charlie's determination redoubled. Within his restrictions, he'd push himself to become stronger.
More agile. Driving, he admitted, was out of the question.
He'd never do that again. He'd hire a service to get to a grocery. And he'd ask the physical therapist if they couldn't
push his workouts a little bit harder.

For the first time, he admitted a basic truism: the only
way to regain his freedom was to deal with that second aneurysm. A plan formed. Do some research. Have all those
tests. Go for it, unless it meant certain death. He'd never
been much of a gambler, but he'd study the odds. And yeah,
he'd have genetic testing to see if his family was at risk.
Determined, he muscled his wheelchair back through the
labyrinth of corridors that led to his ward.

℮∕ℑℯ∕ℑ

"There you are! I'm so glad to see you."
Charlie felt both overjoyed and relieved that the little

guy had shown up. He reached into his bedside table drawer and fumbled with the cellophane bag. He grasped two Hershey's Kisses by their paper, but managed to drop one on the floor. Jonathan followed its trajectory and pointed to where it had landed.

"Can you help us out here?" The boy scrambled to retrieve the errant Kiss. "Go ahead. That one's for you." Charlie unwrapped one for himself and popped it into his mouth. Jonathan stared.

"He didn't eat them," Jonathan said.

"Mr. D? That's because Mr. D's stomach was very sick. He couldn't eat chocolate."

Jonathan dropped his gaze and seemed to swallow a lump in his throat along with the Kiss. He looked so shattered that Charlie just couldn't stand it. The child's troubles seemed to run so much deeper than the death of a friend who, Charlie acknowledged, Jonathan had known for just a short time. He looked fearfully across the room.

"Are you afraid you might have caught what he had?"

Jonathan looked surprised by that idea and shook his head.

"But things can be scary, right?"

Jonathan looked up without disagreeing.

"When I was a little guy—not any older than you are—lots of things scared me. Like stuff I did not understand. A branch fell on our roof one time. I was scared the whole tree would fall and squash us flat. So I was afraid of the wind. I couldn't tell the grownups that I was afraid."

"Why?"

"I thought that I had to be brave. That my father would be disappointed if I weren't brave. He thought little boys should act like small grownups. That's what parents thought way back then. I tried very hard to please him."

"But why?"

"Because I loved my parents. There were six of us kids in my family. The grownups worked very hard and didn't have much time to play with us. I thought that if I did every-

thing right, that would make them happier. Our family
didn't have much money. Nobody did. As a grownup myself now, I realize that what I was noticing was they were
worried. They never talked about their problems, but I could
tell something was wrong. So I kept my problems to myself
too."

"Did you tell the other kids?"

"No. I was afraid they'd laugh at me. Do you know
what scared me the most?"

He shook his head.

"Spiders. I was terrified of spiders. I know now that
most spiders are harmless. In fact, they eat a lot of bad bugs
in our houses and gardens. But back then, oh boy!"

Charlie's mind transported him through time to his
childhood home. "We had this huge dining room with a
great big oak table and lots of chairs. The house was old
then—an ancient farmhouse. It had a big living room, big
kitchen, and that dining room. There were bedrooms upstairs.

"My grandmother lived with us. She kept her sewing
machine in a corner of the dining room. When she made
clothes or mended, she'd use that big table to lay out her
fabric. She had a treadle sewing machine. Do you know
what that is?"

Jonathan scowled and gave a slight headshake.

"It didn't plug into the wall. It wasn't electric. It had a
foot pedal that you pumped with your foot. That made the
needle go up and down to sew the fabric. I was never, ever
to touch that machine, but I played with the foot pedal when
no one was around."

"Where'd they go?"

"Outside to work in the garden. Or hang out the wash.
Or hunt for food. If my father didn't hunt, we wouldn't have
meat on the table. Anyway, I'd get under the sewing machine and pump the foot pedal with my hands—get it pumping real fast. I'd pretend the sound was a great big truck engine and that I was driving someplace exciting.

"One day I got into big trouble." He paused for effect.

"What happened?"

"I almost got caught. There I was, pumping away. I suppose I was making truck noises too. Then I heard the screen door in the kitchen slam. Oh, boy. I pressed on the pedal to make it stop quickly, climbed over it, and scurried into the corner behind it. There was a big basket of mending beside the machine, so I tried to make myself very small. My plan was to escape as soon as my mother went back outside. But Mother stayed in the kitchen, right on the other side of the wall. Then I saw it. This humungous spider! Big! Black! Scary! And I imagined that it was looking at me. It must have been sleeping in that very corner. Or maybe in the mending basket. At any rate, I'd disturbed him. I bet he was very angry. He must have been staring at me with his big red eyes and planning to eat me."

The child's own eyes grew large with anticipation. Charlie had his undivided attention.

"What did you do?" Jonathan whispered.

"I sat very still. I was terrified. It was the scariest thing that had ever happened to me. I couldn't call for help or scramble away because then I'd be in trouble for being there in the first place. They had warned me over and over. The moving parts of the sewing machine could crush little fingers. I was just as afraid of being caught as anything that spider could do. It was huge."

Charlie cupped his hands together as if he were holding a baseball.

"It got closer and closer. I had to make a decision—to face my fear. Face that spider. Defend myself, however I could. I watched and waited. My heart was beating so hard that I was sure my mother would hear it. It looked for a minute like the spider would pass me. But it rolled right up against my leg." He paused, long enough to make Jonathan squirm. "Do you know what happened next?"

Jonathan's face appeared franticly empathetic as he shook his head.

"I reached out to flick it away. Squash it if I had to, praying it wouldn't devour my hand. The second I touched it I made a discovery. It wasn't a spider at all! It was a ball of black sewing thread. A loose bundle that my grandmother must have torn from something that she had been sewing. It was a crinkled ball that only looked like a spider. I couldn't believe my eyes."

Jonathan grinned.

"So you see, Jonathan, sometimes it's better to face our fears. Long before that day, I should have told my parents about things that scared me. They would have listened and helped me understand. Because things aren't always what we think they are. My folks would have taught me how to be safe around spiders."

"Are you still scared of spiders?"

"No. Now I know that most spiders are our friends. But I also know that some of them bite. And I recognize different types by looking at them. Those that bite are protecting themselves. I respect them for that. But I don't touch them."

"What do you do when one gets in your house?"

"I trap it under a drinking glass. Slide a paper between the glass and the floor. Carry it—glass, paper, and all—outside, remove the paper, and shake the glass. I say, 'Goodbye, little spider. Go eat some bad bugs. But don't come back in the house.'"

The child grinned.

Neither said anything for a few peaceful moments as Charlie let time provide a transition.

"Jonathan, you can trust me. If there's something that's scary, you can trust me. I won't laugh or tell you it's silly. And I can keep secrets. Do you understand what I'm saying?"

"Yeah."

"Why don't you take a turn? Tell me a story. Is there something you'd like to tell me about?"

Jonathan shook his head.

಄ೂ಄ೂ

Charlie loved the end of the day. With most housekeeping chores and repairs completed, non-medical staff had gone home. Throughout the ward a blessed hush settled. Dinner was over, and since it was too early to sleep, he and Bill passed the time swapping stories. And Bill was a natural entertainer.

"Were you really a cook in Patton's army?" Charlie asked.

"Yep. Let me tell you, that was a challenge. We were marching through France toward the Rhine, the goal being to advance into Germany. Those huge transport planes you had in Nam? There was nothing like that. We supplemented whatever the supply trucks could provide with what we could scrounge from the land."

"Did the French citizens help? After all, you were liberating them."

"If they could. But those few who hadn't fled or been killed had less than we did."

"You seem awfully young to have been in World War II. Did you lie about your age?"

"Didn't need to. I was seventeen and had a skill that was needed. I could cook. My mother was a baker. Even during the depression, folks had to eat. She supplied diners and lunch counters with rolls, bread, and pies—whatever baked goods they needed. Sometimes they'd pay her with yesterday's leftovers. Customers shared their food coupons. My dad hunted for rabbit, squirrel, groundhog, and pheasant—now there was a treat. You had to chew carefully—buckshot, you know."

Charlie remembered that well from his grandparents' day. "Did you help your mom with the baking?"

"Let me tell you, she did not tolerate waste—either time or ingredients. I didn't get to play with the dough. By the time I was eight, I could roll a perfect circle with only eight turns. She was real picky—rolling out dough that was shaped like South America or even Australia was unacceptable. Re-rolling wasn't an option either because that made the pastry tough. Giving her customers excellent service was practically a religion to her. And she was right. That's how she kept our bills paid."

He grinned, again transported back to his mother's kitchen. "Her pies were delicious. The pastry so flaky. The recipe was simple. Two cups flour, one cup shortening, minus two tablespoons, one teaspoon salt, one third cup of water. She made me measure until I could do it by feel. Her dough started out wet and a little bit greasy, but she floured the wooden table heavily, divided the dough into three balls, and then patted each into a half-inch perfect circle. Floured the rolling pin, stroked the dough with minimal swipes—to twelve o'clock, back to six o'clock—and repeat it. Then pick up the dough, reflour the table, then flip it, and turn it one quarter. Roll out and roll back. Lift, flip, flour, do it again. In four turns, she had a perfect circle. With three balls, she'd line three pans. Got a whole lot of mileage out of that recipe.

"She taught me to make bread and rolls, weighing the ingredients on an old metal scale. Today, they fetch a big price at flea markets. If she could see how people decorate their homes with those old contraptions." He shook his head, grinning.

"And you cooked for Patton?"

"Two of us cooked for our unit. We had a Ford F-150 converted to a cook truck. During the day, we'd advance. Then in the evening, we'd set up and cook while the troops dug trenches for the night. Lot of folks don't know we lost soldiers in those trenches. See, the tanks, guns, and so on were at the rear. They'd bring the tanks forward at night. That's how we advanced. And not seeing exactly where everyone was, the tanks might stop over a trench. The exhaust would gas 'em. The other cook and I, we'd take our wool blanket and roll ourselves together under the cook truck. There, we were warm and safe."

"How did you find food on the land?"

"We'd send out a scout." Bill started to chuckle. "Oh! My favorite story. It was the winter of forty-four. Bitter cold, ground frozen, snowy. Our scout came back to camp all excited. Someone had butchered and hung a steer in a barn, he said. The farm was deserted. We didn't care if it was a steer, cow, or a bull. We headed out to the barn. Sure enough, there it was. And I had fifty, sixty hungry soldiers to feed. Even under those circumstances, however, the army had rules. We had to summon the guy who could bless the carcass with that purple stamp.

"Well, he came, took one look at our prize, and said, 'That's a horse!' I said, 'Not if you say that it's beef.' We sort of looked at each other for a minute, then he got this sly smile on his face. He pulls out his stamp, and whoomp! We had beef.

"We hauled it to camp, carved it up, and served roast that evening. The guys chewed and chewed and chewed. Afterward, one of them came up to me and mumbled, 'You don't have to admit it—but that was horse, right?'"

He grinned, remembering, as if it had happened yesterday. "Next day, we cut more meat into tiny little pieces and stewed it to death with wild onions. And the guys said that it was the best beef stew they'd ever tasted."

Charlie couldn't stop laughing. He wiped his eyes. "I hope you wrote down your stories for your family."

"Ah." Bill batted his hand. "They've heard them so many times. It's the grandkids that are the most interested. One of them won a prize in school for a story he wrote. Sorry—I talk too much. It's been over sixty years, and so much has happened since, but the memories are as vivid as yesterday's."

"Please. Go on."

"I didn't see it myself, but one of the guys in our unit swore on the Bible that it was true. Said he saw it with his own eyes. We finally got to the river that separated France from Germany. General Patton—he wasn't one to hide at the rear. He led the troops to the bridge. Now, the bridge could have been rigged with explosives or disabled in some way to make it collapse under our weight. Anyway, the general motioned for us to stay back. And he strode out onto the bridge and stopped at the middle. Then he undid his fly and peed in the river. It was what you call symbolic of his incredible distain for the enemy. Then he buttoned himself up and motioned for the troops to follow him across the bridge."

"He could have been blown up—"

"That was the point—he wouldn't let his troops do anything he wouldn't do himself."

"Do you think that really happened?"

"Our men swore they saw it with their own eyes. That famous movie, *Patton*? It felt off to me. Whatever Patton did, no matter how it seemed, was for the cause and the men."

"What about the French people. How did they treat you?"

"You'd think we were gods. Their gratitude was overwhelming. And humbling. The French were so gracious. Little kids came running to see us. One little girl clutched a bunch of dandelions and gave them to me. Now that brought tears to my eyes. Did you see the movie, *The Longest Day*? Red Button's character gets hung up in the church steeple after they parachuted off target? That was a true story. To this day, the French have a dummy hung from that steeple in honor of the real GI. When the parachute wears out, they hang a new one. A buddy who had been in the 101st Airborne Division and made that jump himself brought back pictures from their fiftieth reunion."

Charlie made a mental note to watch both movies again. "I thought the French didn't like us."

"Even when foreigners hate our government, they love our people. And they make the distinction. It's a strange thing—nations win wars, but soldiers who survive just get to go home. I've never known it to be any different."

"What about Christmas? What was that like?"

"One Christmas Day we arrived in a tiny country village that was deserted. Buildings destroyed. Houses burned. We assumed that it had been bombed, but when or by whom, we couldn't tell. There was this one house with no roof, and just one wall left standing with a window frame still in place. On the sill was a small statue of an angel. That felt like a sign. A Christmas angel in the middle of all that destruction. I realized nobody would be returning for her because the whole town was gone. So I took her with me. Still, I felt guilty. Knowing more or less where we were, I tried for years to locate survivors." He shrugged. "That went nowhere."

"So where is it now?"

Bill pointed at a small white figurine on his windowsill. "She's makes every move with me. A reminder of how lucky I was to return with all my parts and to never forget the sacrifice made by our troops. Freedom isn't free." He grinned. "Yeah, you're a veteran. You know that."

Charlie nodded, having seen that exact quotation in various corridors, accompanied by framed photos of immortalized sacrifice. Pearl. Iwo Jima.

"And I pray for the family, wherever they are, living or dead. Hell does not adequately describe war. That winter we were marching through snow. One guy's feet were so cold he hadn't realized his boot had come off and got stuck in the ice. We couldn't find it." He grew quiet.

Charlie didn't ask what happened to his foot—and maybe his leg.

A perky young second shift aide rolled a cart into their room. "How about a snack?"

"My dear, we could have used those goodies in France."

&sc&

Charlie glanced at Bill Kelly's sleeping form. He'd been downright excited by the array of brochures his family had brought him. From what Charlie gathered, his team had met with Bill and his family that afternoon to discuss his prognosis. Barring the unforeseen, his life expectancy was extended. The winning facility, located in Maryland, was fifteen minutes from his family. Beautiful and new, he could afford it. The facility was structured as a nonprofit and had every level of care, from independent living to assisted living to skilled nursing. He could lock in a rate. Moreover, old friends of Bill's family resided there. Assuming Bill's application was accepted, the VA's Patient Advocate would coordinate a smooth transition. Charlie swore that Bill even slept with a smile on his face.

Bill's son had raised a practical concern with the medical team. Should they postpone their family's vacation? They badly needed a break. The airline tickets were non-refundable as were various deposits. And the trip had been planned for over a year. If the son completed Bill's application for the retirement village, the three-week processing period would dovetail nicely with their trip. By the time they came home, it should be a done deal. The exciting bonus was Bill's stabilized health, the family being cautiously optimistic that he could go on several years. After all, his father had lived to 103. The son would wrap up pressing business in Maryland and put wheels in motion. He would, however, return the following Saturday for a brief visit before they left for the Grand Canyon.

Just before dinner, Bill's son had cornered the Hospice doctor in the hall and tried to pin him down. Charlie couldn't help overhearing their conversation.

"Are you very sure he's in no immediate danger?"

Charlie imagined the doctor's serene face.

"There are no guarantees. If we try, patients will make liars of us every time, so we don't make promises. As of the moment, however, your dad's doing well. He has responded nicely to his new meds, has regained some weight that he'd lost, and appears to be stronger. In short, he's in better shape now than when he arrived."

"Does that happen often?"

"No. Most of our Hospice patients are very sick people, many of whom are actively dying or shortly will be."

"So—it's okay to leave him alone for a week?"

"You'll have to make that decision. But I assure you, he's not alone. We'll take very good care of him. But if his condition should change, we'll get in touch immediately. Be sure to leave your itinerary and contact information with us. And of course you can call us any day, any time."

Now, hours later, Charlie glanced at the clock Susan had brought her sight-challenged father. Large red numbers glowed 9:30 p.m. He wasn't the least bit tired. Nothing on TV sounded attractive. He remembered seeing the new *National Geographic* in the dayroom and decided to venture down the hall. He'd prop up his feet in a comfortable recliner and read until he got sleepy. He'd grown rather fond of the over-the-calf socks with animal footprints on the soles that made slipping unlikely. A cane. Could he soon swap the walker for a cane? Probably not. One little slip and they'd have him back in his bed.

Choosing the walker instead of the wheelchair, he cautiously traversed the hall.

Much to his surprise, as he entered the room, he found Jonathan's mother curled up in the very recliner he had pictured for himself. Of course, there were others, but finding her here was a jolt. She looked as if she hadn't slept in days, her lank hair pulled severely into a ponytail, her face void of color. She wore a short-sleeved gray T-shirt and faded jeans. Flip-flops lay on the floor. Spotting him, she pulled herself upright and reached for her sandals.

"I'm sorry. I didn't mean to startle you. Please. Don't get up. Not on my account. You'll never know that I'm here. I'm just going to read that *National Geographic* over there until I get sleepy."

She stared at him so blankly that she appeared to be sleepwalking. Or sleep sitting. She said nothing.

Charlie decided to give it a try. "That dear little boy—Jonathan—he's yours, right? You're doing a great job. It's so nice to have a child around here. Everyone says he's a love."

Her face told him nothing.

"I'm sorry. I didn't mean to disturb you. I'll just pick up that magazine and take it back to my room." He pivoted, meaning to cross the room, not really focused on where he was going. Suddenly, he stepped on his right toes with his left heal and lost his balance. Frantically, he clutched for the walker's supports. A matter of seconds passed like slow motion. In a whoosh, he envisioned broken bones, angry staff, descending daughters, and going home a vanishing concept. Strong arms circled his chest, righting him. Shaking with fear, he grasped the walker.

"I've got you. You're okay. Over there. One step at a time." Gently but firmly Jonathan's mother maneuvered him into the chair where she'd sat.

He peered at her gratefully. "Thank you! We both could have landed in a heap. I'm sorry. I didn't mean—"

"Do you say that a lot? 'I'm sorry.' It's a bad habit. You haven't done anything wrong."

He knew he looked sheepish. "I just don't want to be a bother. Everyone—the staff, my daughters, the neighbors, the church—have been so kind, so helpful, have put in so many hours. It's just not my way. I'm no good at *taking*. People are so good."

He looked up in time to see her flinch, her eyes grow hard and cold. He realized that she had been crying. "You're lucky," she mumbled.

Charlie extended his hand. "I'm Charlie. Charlie Alderfer. I live down the hall, if that's what you call it. I keep forgetting this isn't an apartment."

She extended her hand, which was warm, rough, and surprisingly long-fingered for a small woman. "Jade

Kepley. My dad's down the hall. He's not doing well. It's his heart."

"My roommate's a heart patient too. They've taken such good care of him that he's going to graduate. Go to a retirement village near his family in Maryland. Maybe your dad will get better too.

"Huh!" Her face looked disgusted. "He's on borrowed time as it is. Those bastards, they've killed him, and the vultures are circling to pick whatever's left of his carcass."

"Is there anything that I can do?"

"There's nothing anybody can do. It's over. Or will be."

"I'm truly sorry. Well, if you'd just like to talk—I have daughters close to your age. They say I have good ears and a closed mouth."

"Thanks." An automatic response.

She wasn't taking him up on his offer, but she wasn't giving him the bum's rush either. Maybe she hadn't recognized him from the other day. "Hey, I'm sorry I yelled at you—the last time we met."

He feigned surprise. "You did? I don't remember."

"Yeah. You were talking to my dad."

Head drooped, he looked up sheepishly over his bifocals. "I shouldn't have intruded. There were signs posted outside his door. I hadn't noticed, and I should have. Patients are entitled to have their privacy respected. I didn't, and I'm sorry."

"There you go again with the 'I'm sorry.'"

"I'm—" He grinned and shook his head. "I'll have to work on that. Well, I'd better go back to my room. They're rousting me early."

"You okay to walk?"

"Long as I don't get tangled in my own feet."

"There's your problem. Raise your foot. No, the other one." She bent and tugged his sock into place. "Damn things don't have any heels. You have to be careful—keep them pulled up."

"I'll remember that." Grasping the walker, he rose as quickly as possible, hoping that he looked capable. "Thanks again." He headed toward the door.

"Wait. Your magazine." Catching up with him, she dropped the *National Geographic* into the walker's handle-bar bag.

He smiled appreciatively, his brain cranking fresh pos-sibilities.

Chapter 7

C harlie pulled the chain that provided enough illumination to read, but not enough to disturb Bill. His roommate, now curled and facing the window, was sound asleep. The retirement village's colorful brochure still lay on the quilt beside him. Charlie smiled. He must have been reading them, again before drifting off. His beautiful gift quilt would accompany him to his new home in Maryland.

Charlie reflected on Bill's philosophy of life through one of his stories:

"My grandfather lived to be ninety-nine and my father, over one hundred. So when I had my first heart attack at seventy-eight, I was appalled. No, make that insulted. At that point, I was counting on twenty-plus active years. Having survived the war, I thought of myself as invincible—a permanent person. I made what I though was a complete recovery. I tired a bit more easily, perhaps, but otherwise was no worse for wear. I did all the right medical stuff. Diet, exercise, took my pills right on schedule. Put it out of my mind. Then, at eighty-two, I had number two. Yet I kept going. By the time I ended up here many years later, I had made peace with my mortality. I've had an exceptional life, a wonderful family, traveled the world. Done all that stuff people promise themselves. And, as a practicing Catholic, was ready to join my wife in the Kingdom.

"As I started that last journey here in Hospice, I was resigned. Ready. It was okay. Until, that is, I started to feel better. Stronger. And the determination I felt at seventy-eight returned with a vengeance. That's the thing about human nature. The survival instinct is so strong. I'm back to feeling like a permanent person. Wouldn't it be something if I were—had always been—the only person in the world and everyone else was just props?"

A permanent person. Charlie grinned. George Burns, Bob Hope, those beautiful people on *The Today Show*'s hundred-plus birthday salutes. Their angelic faces smiling from the Smuckers jam labels. He'd like to be one himself.

An aide tiptoed in. "Mr. Alderfer? You have tests scheduled for first thing in the morning. Perhaps you should think about getting some sleep?"

"You're right." He set the *National Geographic* aside and pulled the light's chain. "I'll try. Good night."

Sleep did not come easily that night. All his life, he had dropped off the minute his head hit the pillow. Emma had claimed to be jealous, needing to turn her circles, as he had dubbed her nocturnal routine. Eyes tightly closed, he remembered those circles. When all else was finished, she needed to prowl. Have a small glass of milk. Read one more chapter in her mystery novel. Check tomorrow's weather before committing the newspaper to the recycling box. Circle the windows to make sure the neighbors were all okay. Once she had noted too many lights at an old couple's house. She'd thrown on her jacket and knocked on the door. Sure enough, they needed some help.

Charlie had been nearly dozing, but the memory of her crawling in beside him, cold feet and all, stabbed him with fresh loneliness. He sat up and reached for a tissue. Was he ever going to make peace with her loss? Perhaps this was why some people resisted forming relationships in the first place. Was it worth it? He blew his nose and lay back down. Yeah. Of course it was.

He tried again. This time he focused on Jonathan. What

was it he said? It sounded like "I killed my gram." That couldn't be right. He had laid his head on Charlie's chest, murmured so quietly with his head turned away. What else could he have meant? Charlie played with different sound combinations, but came up with nothing. Jonathan hadn't repeated it since that day. Charlie started to formulate a plan.

First, he had the advantage of knowing about Robert Murdock's legal and medical catastrophe. Perhaps Jade didn't know that Charlie knew. But surely she'd think that everyone did. After all, it had been in all the papers. He did read local papers, but not those from outside his county. And he hadn't known until Susan researched it. He made a decision to play dumb.

So—befriend Jade. Encourage her to let Jonathan visit. Coax the little guy to talk. To say it again. His tone had sounded so like a confession that it could be the root of his problems. Talk about a grotesque misunderstanding! He wondered if he was the only person Jonathan had chosen to talk to. Hospital personnel still said that he never spoke. Mentally, Charlie rebuked himself for such conceit. But still...

Charlie pulled his special quilt close to his chin and commanded himself to see with his mind while not thinking in words. Just look. Imagine a group of Amish ladies quilting. Like in the movie *Witness*. They were talking, laughing, and stitching while the men raised a barn. He pictured the enormous tree spreading its shade over the project that now warmed his body. He'd have to find out who his quilters were and thank them properly. There! He was thinking in words. Not good. He repositioned himself to try again.

He knew that he'd been asleep when he realized how warm, cozy, and totally at peace he'd become. Something had roused him to a near-conscious level. With the practice of many weeks, he dismissed the disturbance as nothing that he needed to know. What further roused him, though, was a strange smell. He had been dreaming that he was working in some kind of garage where there were oily substances he couldn't identify. It was faint and seemed to be moving around him. He opened the eye that wasn't buried in the pillow and squinted at the huge red numerals on his clock. Nearly three. He *had* been asleep.

Then he heard whispering and picked up on the words *angel* and *death*. What started as idle curiosity prompted him to high alert. With his right hand that lay between his face and his pillow, he dented the pillow to expose both his eyes. Without raising his head, he looked toward Bill Kelly. Bill was lying flat on his back, but from that distance without his glasses Charlie couldn't see if he was awake or asleep. Ministering to him was a very tall figure in white. Okay. A nurse, Charlie thought.

Yet, simultaneously, he remembered what Mike had said. All third shift nurses were women. It was a popular shift for families with small children. Men worked first shift, wives third, eliminating the need for daycare. Mom slept while the kids were in school, then they all had dinner and the evening together. He squinted without making any motion that would call attention to himself. His exceptional ears strained to catch what the nurse was saying, but the nurse's back remained turned. The man was mumbling words that resembled an incantation. Perhaps a prayer?

The person in white seemed to glide around the side of his roommate's bed. Charlie perceived motion, as if he were reaching for something over the bed. What was it? The only things he could remember were Bill's oxygen line and the contraption that suspended Bill's IV drip when it was in use. Ah. The person must be a tech of some kind, checking on Bill's equipment. Maybe a respiratory therapist. Of course. For patients who needed specialized care twenty-four/seven, there were professionals available or on call. Perhaps the oxygen equipment had malfunctioned. Or this was a routine adjustment. Or administration of meds.

Yet Charlie inexplicably panicked, his heart rate accelerating, pulsing in his neck and his ears. Why did this feel so wrong? Mr. Di! He remembered a male nurse checking on Mr. Di the night of his passing. That was when he had noticed that smell. He couldn't place it then either, but it was out of place and not the clean antiseptic smell of hospital products. Torn between feeling paranoid and having no reason for his niggling dread, Charlie lay motionless but on high alert. The man appeared to be bent over Bill amidst the rustling sound of his sheets. Soon, the man turned and moved toward Charlie. Quickly, Charlie squeezed his eyes shut. The nurse paused. Charlie could smell him, and his own sweat.

He held his breath then pretended to mumble as if in his sleep while preparing to scream or scuttle away. But abruptly the man turned, squeaking feet approaching the door. Through slit eyes, Charlie watched as long as he could without moving his head, eyeballs pulling until it was painful. It was impossible to see anything beyond the end of his bed, thus he lost the opportunity to see the man's face. Footfalls disappeared as he turned right and into the hall. The squeaky footsteps diminished. Charlie heard the fire door open and then shut. He waited, unmoving, until he was confident that the stranger was not returning. Propping himself up on one elbow, he studied Bill's sleeping form. He seemed okay, having resumed his favorite sleeping position on his right side, knees bent, pillow cockeyed, facing the wall. Charlie swore that he heard his faint snore.

Charlie chided his over-active imagination while acknowledging his ignorance of complicated, life-sustaining procedures that the medical staff quietly perform. He could never remember sleeping so lightly, except when Emma was hospitalized and following her death. In the morning, he'd ask Mike about the three a.m. visitor, just so he'd understand what to expect on subsequent nights. And he decided to cut out caffeine after lunch.

❧❧❧

"Go away. Just let me sleep a few minutes longer."

"Charlie. It's time." Charlie peered through pasty eyes that were immediately accosted by bright morning light. Momentarily, his brain was washed as clean as the sand at low tide. He knew where he was, but couldn't get his mind beyond his desire to return to his dream.

Mike persisted. "Wake up, Charlie. I have something to tell you."

Charlie dragged his stiff elbow into position to prop up his head. "What?"

"I'm afraid I have some bad news." He paused a moment for Charlie's attention. "Bill passed away during the night."

Charlie jerked to attention, wrenching his body toward the window. An orderly and a cleaning woman were dispatching Bill's bedding, disconnecting his equipment, and dumping his medical paraphernalia into a HAZMAT container. Outfitted in rubber gloves and yellow protective coveralls, they disinfected the naked burgundy vinyl mattress with strong-smelling liquid from squirt bottles.

"*What happened?*" Charlie gasped more than asked. "Last evening he was just fine. His heart condition was under control. He was ready to leave. Everyone said—"

Mike squeezed Charlie's arm gently. "Charlie—this *is* Hospice. True, Bill had rallied and seemed to be making positive progress. But he had a bad heart. No, that's not what I meant. The guy had a heart of pure gold. But it failed. His passing was inevitable."

"When did it happen? Who found him?"

"A nurse making final rounds early this morning, around six. She's very conscientious. Doesn't like to leave any surprises for the first shift that comes on at seven. Goes way beyond peeking at sleeping forms."

Charlie frowned, searching his fragmented memory. "I *felt* something was wrong. Damn it. I should have asked that nurse who was talking to him. Bill *seemed* okay. At least, he moved from his back to his side. The nurse was doing something with his IV. Or maybe his oxygen. I thought his equipment might have malfunctioned. I didn't look out for him. And I should have—"

Mike interrupted. "What nurse? What are you talking about?"

Charlie scrunched his eyes shut, thinking. "A male nurse. Very tall. Wearing white. He seemed to be having a conversation with Bill. I couldn't catch many words, but his tone was soothing. I caught the word *angel*. And *longing*. His voice was soothing, as if he were praying for Bill. You know, like interceding. I didn't want him to think he'd disturbed me, or that I was eavesdropping. So I pretended to be asleep. But something seemed off, to the point where I was afraid to let him know I was awake." He paused. "To be honest, I was scared. I should have done something. Rung for a nurse. But I froze."

Mike stooped to Charlie's eye level and lowered his voice to a whisper. "Don't repeat what you just told me to anyone else. Save the details until we're alone. Okay? What you're telling me doesn't make sense."

"In what way?" Charlie mouthed.

"As I told you before, we don't have any male nurses working third shift."

"Could it have been a technician? Like someone from Respiratory?"

Mike shook his head. "During third shift, including weekends, there's only one respiratory therapist on duty. Two employees cover that duty, but not at the same time. Had Bill been having trouble breathing, a nurse would have been the first responder. Depending upon the seriousness of the situation, the doctor, then the therapist, would have been paged. The sole therapist could have been occupied with a patient on another floor. If he'd thrown a code, a number of people would have descended immediately."

Charlie shook his head. "No alarm sounded—not then or throughout the rest of the night. What do the two respiratory therapists look like?"

"One hottie and one grandmother."

"Both female…"

"And short. Charlie—want my advice? For your own safety, keep this to yourself until I can check out everyone who was on duty last night."

"In the entire hospital? Is that possible?"

"I have friends in payroll and HR, but that will take time. First, I'll concentrate on this building. Expand the inquiry to other wards and support areas. Describe this person as well as you can."

"He was big, like I said. Not just tall, but big. At least, that's what his outline looked like. I wasn't wearing my glasses. When he left, I was aware of his footfalls because his shoes squeaked. I remember thinking he must be very tall because his stride, while not hurried, was long. He covered the room with very few steps."

"What else besides male, tall and big."

"Without my glasses, and in the dim light from the hall, I just got an impression. Caucasian. White clothes. Buzz-cut hair—light."

"Could he have been bald?"

Charlie closed his eyes, searching his memory. "Possibly. Without my glasses, smooth surfaces appear fuzzy. As the distance increases, so does the blur. Closest he came to me was ten or twelve feet. So yeah, he could have been bald."

"Was he carrying anything?"

"Some kind of bag, like a small white backpack. But it's just an impression. Could just have easily been a balled-up jacket."

"In August?" Charlie shrugged. "Did he stop by your bed?"

"Briefly. If he'd stayed more than a moment, I would have lost it and screamed."

"Why? That doesn't sound like something you'd do."

Charlie consciously unclenched his fists. "Something about him was frightening. He just creeped me out. Maybe because of the way that he smelled." He snapped his fingers and locked on Mike's eyes. "That was the trigger. I remembered that smell from before—in the dreams I had on the nights Mr. Jones and Vincent DePasquali passed away."

Mike glanced toward the window where employees were wrapping up Bill Kelly's medical effects. "Let's zip through your routine, then I'll do some checking."

Charlie nodded agreement. He tried not to look at the bed by the window because, if he did, he knew he would lose it.

☙❧☙

"Mr. Alderfer! Hey! What's with you this morning? Task at hand, man."

Sheepishly, Charlie snapped back into the moment. He must have been pulling slower and slower on the machine dedicated to strengthening his upper back. His eyes had been stuck, unseeing, on the far wall. "Sorry. Didn't mean to be a slacker. I was deep in thought."

"I'll say. Any lower and we'd have to send for a crane. Care to talk about what's on your mind?"

They were alone in the room. The physical therapist, always patient and compassionate, tempted Charlie to unburden himself of a different kind of weight. Remembering Mike's warning, however, he chose to invent a plausible lie. "I was thinking about the importance of balance. My mind wandered to an article I recently read in *National Geographic* about how the Grand Canyon was formed. My family and I rode burrows down to Phantom Ranch. Such surefooted buggers. I thought, all the way down, that they'd slip and we'd plunge to our death, but those creatures never missed a step. That's what I was thinking about."

"Life's like that, don't you think? We make plans and decisions on our best information but, in the end, some things are beyond our control. Speaking of control, if you're done with those reps, let's move on to your arms."

With the trainer's assistance, Charlie sat at the tricep machine and twisted the yellow buttons to adjust the resistance. An idea emerged. "Say. Have you ever worked here at night?"

"I've helped out second shift on the third floor when the nurse manager was desperate. It was, let me see, in '04. We had a terrible ice storm. People couldn't get into the VA, and some of us opted to help."

"So you've stayed overnight?"

"Yep. Round the clock. For two days." He chuckled. "It was kind of fun, like going to camp. A real bonding experience. Believe it or not, it boosted morale. Not only for us pulling together in a surreal situation but for those stuck at home who appreciated the effort."

"Then you've familiar with third shift?"

"Yeah. And I was here once for forty-eight hours straight when my grandpa was dying."

"Did you ever meet a male nurse who works third shift? A big guy?"

He shook his head slowly. "Nope. Can't say that I have."

"How about someone who'd wear a white uniform—perhaps from another building—who might work third shift?"

"No. But the VA's a big place. Even after fifteen years there are plenty of people I've never met. And there's always turnover. Why? Is it important?"

"No. I just thought I recognized someone from home. Guess my imagination's working overtime. Or I was dreaming. I've had disrupted sleep lately. Maybe I'm taking too many naps then sleeping too lightly at night."

Momentarily, Charlie worried that he'd triggered an alarm because the therapist began writing on Charlie's chart.

Abruptly the therapist looked up. "Pharmacy. Some pharmacists wear white."

"Are pharmacists at the VA around the clock?"

He scrunched his face in concentration. "I doubt it. But you can find out with a phone call."

"That's all right. I'm really not that curious."

The therapist's mind had returned to business. "Okay. Good job on those arms. Think we can add more weight the next time. Now let's up the challenge for the leg curls." He adjusted the yellow knob then smiled with satisfaction as Charlie gave his best effort.

ભળ

Shortly after first shift ended, Mike entered Charlie's room, having traded his uniform for chinos and a golf shirt. Mike positioned a wheelchair while Charlie hovered, anxious to go. En route to the elevators, Mike braked at the nurses' station. "You need this guy back anytime soon? We're going to the canteen for some R and R."

The charge nurse smiled. "Let me check—yep, his meds are current. Just let us know when you'll be back and if he'll miss dinner." She gave him a wink. "And don't get into trouble."

As they rounded the corner toward the elevators, Charlie beckoned to Mike. "Where are we going? And why?"

"To do a little recon. Roll past the offices and nonpublic areas. We'll look for someone who matches your description. Even if you don't spot him, point out someone similar."

Charlie's heart rate accelerated. He tried to ignore the throb in his ears and the blood pulsing through his neck. Was that the jugular? Or the carotid?

At first, the elevator was empty. He took slow, deep breaths and focused on a sign mounted above the elevator door. *Attention Employees: Discuss patient information in private areas only.* Charlie donned the baseball cap Susan had brought from California. Face partially hidden, he peered from beneath the scrunched brim. Doctors in meticulous coats and ties, OR personnel in blue scrubs, nurses of all sizes and shapes, residents, visitors, patients on foot, and others in wheelchairs—surreptitiously Charlie searched all their faces, their shapes, and their clothing. Was the killer among them?

Killer? Was he that sure?

Yeah. He was.

He willed himself to calm down. Scanning the tide of humanity traversing the corridors, he observed that half were women and children. Of the men, most were too short, frail, or disabled to be his nocturnal intruder. Eventually, they entered the canteen and selected a corner table with a clear view of the parking lot, outpatient lobby, and connecting corridors. They sipped cokes for an unproductive hour, watching employees on break come and go.

"Let's head past the business offices," Mike said, pulling an official-looking folder from the wheelchair's back pocket. "Here. Hold this. Glance inside from time to time, like you're checking information. We'll sweep the outpatient waiting rooms first."

Charlie peered into offices with dozens of functions, down corridors, and into waiting rooms. Veterans, whose caps represented every branch of the service, war, and conflict, waited at pharmacy windows for assistance. In business offices, some vets received immediate attention while others waited in lines that snaked into the hall. Escorts whisked patients in pajamas through connecting corridors toward signs that listed everything from Barber Shop to Prosthetics to Wheelchair Repairs. Everyone flattened themselves against walls as EMS teams sped by with gurneys toward the ER. Nobody seemed remotely curious about Charlie and Mike.

"Let's take a break. The chapel's this way. There are no services at this time of day. Unless individuals stop in to pray, we should have the place to ourselves."

Mike was correct—it was deserted. Grasping Mike's

hand, Charlie pried himself from his wheelchair and clutched the back of the pew, just in case. He eased to the farthest seat from the door and flopped onto the cushioned oak pew. It struck him that he should have been excited about his expanding mobility and the freedom that represented. But not today. Closing his eyes, he prayed for Emma, his roommates, departed family, and VA friends past and present. And he prayed for his daughters and grandbabies so far away.

As he waited for Mike to scope adjacent back offices where Charlie had no reason being, he studied the chapel. In the front right corner, a pair of menorahs flanked what looked like a little stage with a drawn purple curtain. It reminded him of a marionette stage with which his grade school class had staged productions. He'd have to ask someone about its meaning. On the chapel's side walls little oak cupboards probably concealed Stations of the Cross. An altar, back dropped with floor-to-ceiling purple fabric, stood against the front wall. The altar was vested with a green super-frontal and a white fair linen. Matching green brocade hangings adorned the pulpit and lectern.

The green of Pentecost, he realized, was the only reference to Christianity other than the descending doves incorporated into the stain glass windows. No cross, Catholic or Protestant, was in evidence. The clergy must bring out the appropriate icons for different services. Several huge floral arrangements sat on the step ascending to the altar. More fresh flowers spilled from vases that flanked it. Perhaps a memorial service was scheduled? Even stripped of specific symbolism, Charlie still felt the presence of God. The chapel was totally peaceful. Charlie relaxed and cleared his mind, convinced that he must do the right thing.

Mike returned. "I checked every office. Nada. And the chaplains must be making ward rounds. The only tall person was a gorgeous blonde. Thought I'd strike up a conversation—see if she knew our mystery man—but she was on the phone, listening and keyboarding at the same time. I knocked on the doorframe, but she glared at me—I mean daggers—then turned her back." He grinned stupidly, shaking his head.

Charlie jerked to attention, alarmed. "You weren't really going to tell her anything—"

"Of course not. Just inquire about a newer employee I was trying to locate. No explanation. Our person might have tried hitting on her or someone she knows."

Charlie sat up straighter. "Did she look like one of those magazine models? I may know whom you mean. She's been on our ward—has all the guys talking."

Mike frowned as his thoughts shifted focus. "She wore a white blouse. That got me thinking. Who else besides doctors and nurses wear white? Dentists, lab techs, pharmacists?"

Charlie shrugged. "If the chaplain returns should we include him in this conversation? Chaplains have to be confidential, right?"

"No idea what governmental rules might apply, especially if the chaplains are federal employees." He patted Charlie's arm. "If you'd like to talk with a chaplain, however, one would be happy to visit your room for a private conversation. Hey—you're looking weary. Had enough?"

"More frustrated than tired. My roommates keep dying, and I can't stop it." Charlie dropped his head, ashamed for feeling so needy. "Why do these deaths shock me so much? As you reminded me, this *is* Hospice."

Mike eyebrow-shrugged. "Maybe because being here wasn't your choice. To be part of the day-to-day drama. For staff who work Hospice—it's a calling that borders on religious commitment. Many of us rotated through Hospice during our training and became drawn to this particular specialty." He paused to correct himself. "Of course, there's death in other areas, but not as a concentration. We learn to focus on all aspects of transition, not just on death itself. But not on what lies beyond. As a governmental entity, the separation of church and state forbids us from evangelizing.

But if patients ask us to read the Bible or request a visit from clergy, we accommodate them. Staff, who end up feeling uncomfortable or unable to cope with Hospice, rotate out."

"But surely you get attached."

"Normally, it's not the same gut-wrenching experience as loosing family or loved ones. A degree of professional detachment is necessary for our mental health. Some patients stay with us briefly, and we're so busy tending to their needs that there's little opportunity to form friendships. But it's still rough when we lose patients who have been with us awhile. Our veterans are such great, interesting people who have lived through remarkable times. They've defended and ensured our freedom. And now we're losing the Great Generation, one at a time, with Korean Conflict and Vietnam veterans following behind them."

Charlie nodded, remembering his precious conversations with his roommates. Their time was so brief, yet he'd never forget them. He hoped their families had scribed all their stories. Most people think there will always be time. That's what he thought, and look what had happened to him.

"Did you learn anything about third shift personnel?" Charlie asked in barely a whisper. His voice seemed to echo from the vaulted wood ceiling. In spite of the solitude, he still felt a reverent presence.

"I confirmed what I said earlier. There are no male nurses on the third shift. In fact, there are no males at all from eleven to seven who remotely fit your description. Mostly, it's a women's world late at night."

"But there's got to be lots of men in the buildings. This complex is huge."

"Well, yeah, but none you'd be likely to find in white uniforms *and* at night *and* treating patients. Charlie, is it possible that you were dreaming?"

"Once, maybe twice. But three times? Sitting here alone—thinking—I'm positive I'm right. Let me back up a little. There's that smell. I've read that our earliest memories are sometimes triggered by smell. When I was a teenager, I pinpointed my earliest memory of anything when I got a whiff of almond oil. Something clicked. I asked my mother about it. She said, 'I had a bottle of almond-scented Jergens hand lotion when you were a toddler. I've never used it since.'

"When I first arrived in Hospice, Mr. Jones, that emaciated fellow in the third bed, passed away during the night. Newly aware of the hospital's sounds and smells, I was super-sensitive to everything. That night, I smelled something oily when a person moved past the foot of my bed to tend to him. It meant nothing to me at the time.

"The night that Vincent DePasquali passed away, I smelled it again. On someone ministering to him. The activity around me was like part of a dream in which my hospital bed was located in an automotive service center or a machine shop. And I heard a low voice say something about angels and death.

"Afterward, I rationalized what must have happened. I had been dreaming—you can dream about smells, right? I also dismissed what I'd witnessed as being unnatural—although I don't believe in supernatural stuff. Possibly a drug I'd been given caused hallucinations or a bad taste in my mouth.

"Last night I saw, smelled, and heard it again. Somebody *ministering* to Bill Kelly in the middle of the night. Again, I made out the words *angel* and *death*. It was barely a whisper, but I have incredible hearing. The audiologist says I hear everything I should and many things that I shouldn't. Fox ears, he joked. Mike, I believe it's possible that a serial killer is victimizing our ward."

Mike frowned in concentration. "Go on."

"On one hand, someone might feel obligated to hasten death. To put those without hope out of their misery. To be their angel. On the other hand, what about someone who enjoys killing people? Maybe he gets off on holding the power over life and death in his hands? What better place to find victims than in a hospital where lots of people are expected to die? When visitors are gone, no treatments are scheduled, and there is only minimal staff?" Mike had been silent while Charlie ruminated. "Mike, what are you thinking?"

"Can we exclude family members?"

"My roommates were unrelated."

"Right. Of course. Okay then—that smell. Can you be more specific?"

"I can't nail it down. It's like a name that's on the tip of my tongue."

Both men were quiet for a while, lost in their thoughts. Mike finally broke the silence with a sigh. "Well, let's see. Why don't we brainstorm plausible explanations? Suppose your angel is a legitimate visitor and these deaths are coincidental. Who could the visitor be? Someone who works in an industry where they'd wear white clothing? A person who stops by Hospice to pray for our patients?" He snapped his fingers. "Like a baker, who begins his day at, say, four in the morning and stops here first? Or a nurse who works at another hospital and visits here during third shift? Maybe a former Hospice employee."

Charlie frowned. "You'd think the building would be locked and secured during the night. That after-hour visitors would have to sign in. Can you check on that?"

"I can answer that now. After hours, everyone accesses the VA through the emergency entrance. Our police are on duty there twenty-four/seven. Visitors can't get beyond the waiting room—which isn't that big—unless the officer on duty buzzes them through to the corridor that connects to the complex. The corridor doglegs at the end of a hall and stops at another door where there's a camera. Beyond that door is our elevator bank—you know the one. Before passing through that door, however, the visitor must activate a button. A camera sends the image back to the police. If anything appears to be inappropriate, they can investigate or simply prohibit the door from opening."

Charlie thought for a moment. "Regardless of who our visitor might be or how innocent his motivation, do you think hospital security should get involved? Couldn't they look at surveillance tapes for that timeframe? And what about the staff? Don't they keep track of the comings and goings?"

"Night shift can be a challenge. With visiting hours over, no patient appointments, testing, or rounds, and with most patients sleeping, there are fewer employees on duty. They don't have eyes on the wards. If someone did have criminal intent, it wouldn't be difficult to slip around unde-tected. Or have an excuse at the ready. Or come in early and hide."

Charlie shivered, even though the chapel was warm.

"Where are you thinking of going with this?" Mike asked.

"I've got to tell someone."

"If you're convinced a crime's been committed, you'll need proof. And I doubt if any evidence remains. Both Mr. Jones and Mr. D. are long gone. And Bill Kelly's written instructions require his immediate cremation. He wanted his money for his grandkids' college fund, not for funeral ex-penses. He was very vocal about that. An urn and a mass. That's what he told me he'd put in writing."

"But he wasn't expected to pass so quickly. Wouldn't there be an autopsy?"

"No reason without a red flag. An old guy with conges-tive heart failure whose health had been slipping since two heart attacks dies in Hospice. Remember the guidelines—to qualify for Hospice the patient's death is anticipated within six months. Most happen sooner, sometimes within days."

"I still say they should do an autopsy. I'm in Hospice and I'm getting better."

"Your case is unique." Mike broke into a grin. "Truth is, you keep up our spirits because you represent hope." He took a deep breath and let it out slowly while shaking his head. A face that reflected the grim nature of their conversation replaced the casual smile. "So, Charlie, that brings us to your choices. As I see it, you could do nothing. Wait and see. If you're worried about your personal safety, ask to be transferred to another facility. Or demand protection from hospital security. Or share your suspicions with those in charge."

"I want to do the right thing for our patients in whatever way makes sense. Guess I'll start by talking to the head nurse and my doctor. If there's something bad going on, they deserve to know first. If they blow me off, I'll complain to the administration. Maybe talk to the families. Perhaps the police."

"Yes, you can do any or all of that. But, Charlie, you've got to anticipate their reaction. They could say you were dreaming or medicated. You could get labeled as *confused*. Hospitals have lots of older people who really are confused due to illness, injury, stroke, medications, et cetera. You can joke about the person who is a beer short of a six-pack, but how could you defend yourself against that? It wouldn't be the first time that a patient's complaints are ignored, covered up, or treated with drugs. Administrators run scared of lawsuits. Consider what a negative image could do to their stakeholders, even if proven unfounded."

"Stakeholders?"

"Anyone who has a stake in the hospital—patients, their families, staff and their families, the Fed, volunteers, fundraisers, regulators, politicians, neighbors, the military, the media... The administrators have good reason to resist what sounds like unfounded accusations. Unscrupulous administrators will bury patients' complaints to cover their butts."

"Surely that wouldn't happen here."

"Our VA is a well-run, respected institution. Patients and families rarely complain, and those that do, in my experience, are taken seriously."

"What about the Walter Reed flap?"

"Huge misconception. In the first place, Walter Reed is an army hospital, not a veteran's hospital. And it was slated for replacement before the Persian Gulf wars sucked up all the funds and exploded the patient count. So of course, they hadn't been making repairs. Would you repair a building that was scheduled for demolition?"

"So VA hospitals, ours included, are not army hospitals."

"Correct. Nevertheless, I can guarantee that you might have an uphill battle on your hands. Stir the pot too much and you might be considered too well to stay here. Or you could be dismissed as confused. That, on your records, might be difficult to remove."

At that, Charlie laughed. "I can picture myself, sitting at the curb in my wheelchair, ranting to the press that I was thrown out." He quickly lost interest in his joke. "If there's proof to be had and we act quickly enough, could we stall Bill Kelly's cremation pending the results of an autopsy?"

"Since you're not family, you don't have any standing. Reaching and convincing the family will be impossible since they're somewhere en route through the heartland. You know they went out west on vacation."

"The hospital has their contact information. I overheard that discussion. We should at least ask the question."

"Even the family might not be able to override Bill's wishes."

"What about his equipment? I'm sure I saw that man doing something to his equipment."

"Immediately after death, his entire environment was sanitized. That stuff is long gone."

Charlie took a deep breath and then exhaled. He thought for a moment, mind summarizing. "Okay. I hear you." He punctuated a decision by thumping the pew with his palm. "I've made a decision. I'll talk to the doctor and the head nurse first and ask them to speak with the family. I'll wait to talk to the police until the doctor gets back to me. Can I count on you, Mike, to swear that I'm not drugged or a nutcase?"

"Sure."

"No, wait. That's not fair to you. Instead, can I have a printout of my medical records that show that I'm not being given anything that would make me hallucinate?"

"I'll look into it."

"I've just got to do something. Thank you, so much, for listening to me. And for everything you do and have done. You are my hero."

Averting his face to conceal welling tears, Charlie reached for the back of the next pew and pulled himself to a standing position. He inched across the back of the chapel, then stepped toward his wheelchair. He stopped and swiveled toward Mike. "What if I'm right? Consider the worst-case scenario. Suppose there really is a serial medical murderer targeting the VA. Who will be next?"

"Even if nobody believes you, at least they should be on high alert."

Chapter 8

While on break the following morning, Mike dropped in on an old friend who had been in Human Resources since it was called Personnel. "Hear you're thinking of packing it in—leaving all this for a boring life of leisure." He held up both palms like a scale. "Sleeping in? Up before dawn. Fighting with new software? Playing games with the grands. Scurrying home to make dinner? Feasting on cruise ship cuisine…"

"Young man!" she started, as if unaware of Mike's graying crew cut. "You're just jealous! The old man and I are going to enjoy our retirement while we're still young." She bounced her ample rear on her chair, wiggling her fingers above her tight curls as if dancing the salsa. He laughed. "You're far from your beat," she noted. "What's up? Need a little inside scoop on the latest cute nurse?"

"No, ma'am! Not my style. Besides, Ginny would kill me. Just thought I'd stop by and—"

"How many years have I known your sorry ass? You've got something big on your mind. What's up?"

"I need a little general information."

"Shoot."

"What other types of male employees wear white uniforms, besides doctors and nurses?" She frowned, but didn't ask why as he ticked off the obvious. "And do we ever use temps, say for housekeeping? And if so, how are temporary employees hired? Can they walk in off the streets, apply, and then be hired? Or is it more complicated than that?"

"White uniforms. Well, anyone can wear white clothing, although it isn't exactly serviceable. But uniforms? Few female nurses wear white these days, most opting for something more cheerful. Supposed to be better for patient morale. When I started my career, back in the dark ages, it was white dresses, hose, shoes, and starched caps that bore the identification of the nursing school. How times have changed! Lab workers wear white coats. Pharmacists. Huh. I'd have to give that some thought."

She didn't add anything that Mike hadn't considered or that had *ah ha!* possibility. "What about temps?" he repeated. "Can they be hired off the street? Or does the VA use a temp agency?"

"No way. They have to jump through the same governmental hoops that full timers do, which includes verification of their credentials, criminal background checks, fingerprinting through the national database…"

"So everyone who works here has been scrutinized…"

"Yep. And since nine-eleven, security's even tighter. Why? Do you know somebody who wants part time work?"

Mike laughed, then grew serious. "Confidentially?" She raised her right hand, as if to swear. "We're trying to identify a visitor to Hospice who is a mystery man. He has made one of our patients uncomfortable, just by his presence. Nothing overtly inappropriate—the patient is just feeling spooked. A big fellow. Wears a white uniform. Has visited only at night to unrelated patients. Anyone who works here, past or present, who has passed through your doors ring a bell?"

Before he could finish his last sentence, she was already shaking her head. "Not a tinkle. My advice to your patient is to discuss his concerns with his doctor and/or nursing supervisor immediately. Even if this visitor has a legitimate reason to be there, your patient may need to be moved to another room, perhaps across from the nurses station, where he'd feel protected. Just because somebody works for the VA doesn't mean they can go anywhere and do whatever they want. If someone inappropriate is on the ward, it should not be your patient's problem. That's staff's responsibility."

"Okay. I'll follow up. One more thing. Is it possible for an employee to circumvent a criminal background and fingerprint check?"

"Well, sure. If they've never been arrested or fingerprinted. But don't forget, lots of innocent people are printed all the time. All our employees' and volunteers' prints are on file with the fed. Military and anyone who has ever needed security clearance. And, in the case of a crime, those who are printed to eliminate them.

"Where's all this going? Newborn babies?"

She shrugged. "Not my problem. I am ree-tirin! My old man and I will be boozin' and cruisin'…'" She cupped her hand over her mouth and leaned over her desk. "and chewin' and screwin'…"

Mike howled at the thought then snapped a look at his watch. "Gotta run."

"Mike? I won't repeat any of this, but if you need my help, you have five months, fourteen days, and six hours, give or take."

❧❧❧

Charlie tried to remember when he had felt so nervous and couldn't. He had asked Dr. Szish and the head nurse for a meeting, stating the urgency for which was of paramount importance. They agreed immediately. Now, as he wheeled his chair to the doctor's small private office, he began second guessing himself. He had agonized until his digestion was shot and sleep unattainable. But further worry trumped any negative results that this meeting might cause.

The professionals were already seated across a small

round table. All Charlie had to do was roll into the room and claim the empty half of the table. Ice cubes settled with a clink in a pitcher that dripped condensation onto a tray that held twelve-ounce glasses.

"May I?" Dr. Szish poured for the nurse then, like a gracious host, offered Charlie a glass. Amenities complete, Dr. Szish closed the door, cocooning the three in privacy. He smiled at Charlie like a valued friend. "Not claustrophobic, are you? My mother could never use a telephone booth, even if she left the door open and could see in every direction."

Charlie relaxed his white-knuckle grip on the chair's arms. Paranoia seemed out of place in the presence of these compassionate professionals. The pair looked at him with expectation. The floor was his. He cleared his throat and lifted his palms in supplication—a motion intended to make him seem calm. He started his well-rehearsed speech.

"I'm very concerned that you don't think that I've lost it, or that I'm drugged or imagining things. Or that I have a sleeping disorder. Rather than worry any longer, I have decided to share with you what I think is a vital concern. Or worse, a dangerous situation."

Dr. Szish nodded with one motion. "That's exactly why we are here, for you and for all our patients. We're not just about physical medicine. Whatever concerns you is important to us."

"I've thought and thought, until my brain's fried, about the right approach to this very troubling matter. Details first? Work up to the punch line? Or just give you the sound bite in one sentence."

"Why don't you start with the topic. Then we can piece the story together. Informally, but thoughtfully and thoroughly."

Charlie took a deep breath. He was aware of the air handler's hum and the intensity of the fluorescent lights. If he didn't get it out now, could he ever?

"Take your time…"

"I suspect—" he croaked slightly and paused. Cleared his throat. "I suspect that someone, other than our Hospice staff, has killed three of my former roommates." As he uttered the words, he studied their faces for any reaction. He couldn't help expelling a little sigh of relief. The nurse had taken a quick little breath then flicked a glance at the physician. Dr. Szish had frowned slightly. Otherwise straight faced, both looked concerned. Neither took their eyes from his face. Both remained calm.

"When did you first suspect something was wrong?" Dr. Szish asked.

Charlie guessed that the doctor would do all the talking. Neither took notes. In fact, the pair had brought nothing to the table except the pitcher and glasses. Charlie wasn't sure if that was problematic or not. Maybe they had excellent memories—after all, they had been capable of high-level education.

"The first incident didn't mean anything to me at the time. I had just regained consciousness, and a third patient was in a bed opposite mine."

"I remember that timeframe." Dr. Szish nodded to the nurse. "That was the last time we used any of those larger rooms for triple occupancy. We'd been very busy. Tell me what you observed that caused you concern."

Charlie relaxed. Encouraged by their undivided attention and their seeming to have all the time in the world, Charlie ticked through the chronology with surprising ease. At times, they interjected with questions to make sure they grasped what he meant. If they had misunderstood what he was saying, Charlie had ample opportunity to fine-tune his wording. When he paused to think about his phrasing, they didn't rush in to speed him along.

"To summarize, on three separate occasions, a large Caucasian male nurse with a distinct smell—" And here he made the dreaded quotes with his fingers. "—'*ministered*' to three of my roommates, incanting words about angels and death, immediately before their untimely passing. In Bill

Kelly's case, this nurse did something to his equipment. No one I've asked can identify that nurse or his purpose. I believe we have a stranger victimizing our patients who cannot protest. I am requesting that you investigate and alert security to a potential threat to our safety."

Silence. The head nurse looked at a grim-faced Dr. Szish for his reaction. From his expression, Charlie expected him to say hummm. And when he did, Charlie was unable to contain a smile.

"Well!" Dr. Szish finally broke the silence. "You've given us a weighty matter to investigate. We'll look into it right away." After transitioning into lighter inquiries about Charlie's well-being, he rose, held out his hand, and shook Charlie's. "Thank you. I appreciate the courage it took for you to bring this to our attention. Your safety, as well as your medical progress, is of paramount importance to us. You may not notice any activity, but I assure you, proper steps will be taken judiciously."

As Charlie wheeled himself back down the hall, he had to ask himself if he felt disappointed. The meeting was short. Almost too short, although they said all the right things. He'd been prepared for resistance, perhaps even an argument, a protracted—perhaps heated—fight. And denial. To be viewed as someone being critical and unappreciative of their outstanding institution, dedication, and attention to detail. Or someone with too much time on his hands and a vivid imagination. Instead, they had listened attentively, thanked him sincerely, and promised immediate attention. As Charlie wheeled himself back to his room, he felt enormous relief.

ℰᴈℰᴈ

"What's this?" Charlie asked that evening, pointing to the little green pill that lay in the small pleated paper cup a pretty, second-shift, weekend nurse's aide had handed him.

"It looks like one of our 'fussy tummy' pills. Since your digestion's acting up a little, it's just the ticket." She squinted at the pill, attempting to identify it by its imprinted number and nodded her head. "They're better than any ant-acid. Soothing. Taken with meals or your bedtime snack your belly will be a happy camper."

"If you're sure…"

"My personal doctor swears by them." She winked and whispered, "I keep a supply at home."

Charlie knocked back the pill and washed it down with a large gulp of water. Then he turned his attention to his bedtime snack. Chocolate pudding. He smiled, remembering how his Emma used to put a large marshmallow in the bottom of his daughters' animal mugs, then top it with the hot chocolate pudding. The melting marshmallow would bob to the surface, all sticky and luscious. He'd have to ask Jeannette, his youngest who lived in Atlanta, whether she remembered and made that treat for her two little boys.

As soon as he finished, he piloted his walker into the bathroom. Feeling sleepy, he sat. When finished, he steadied himself at the sink with one hand while brushing his teeth. By the time he was nearing his bed, he felt downright woozy. With fierce concentration, he got into bed and immediately fell into dreamless sleep.

Sometime in the middle of the night, a woman began elevating the head of his bed. He shook himself awake to follow what she was saying. Dutifully, he tipped the little green pill from the tiny white cup then accepted her help with some water. By the time his bed had motored back down, sleep was enveloping him once again.

"Good morning, Charlie"

He recognized the weekend nurse's alto singsong and squinted at her. His head ached and his muscles felt weak. With extreme effort, he made it through his bathroom pit stop, then inched back into his bed. "Please. Just let me sleep. I feel like I'm coming down with a bug."

"Can you eat a little breakfast? Dietary will be here any

minute with your tray." She popped her head into the hall, then returned. "Yep. They're rolling down the hall as I speak."

"I'll try. But my stomach..."

Momentarily he heard the familiar rumble of the meds cart, which stopped outside his room. "Mr. Alderfer?" An unfamiliar weekend employee wearing sterile gloves lifted Charlie's wrist and swiped the bar code on his hospital bracelet. Then she handed him a small white cup in which rested another tiny green pill, along with his usual vitamins. Without asking, she assisted him in tipping it into his mouth and guided a sturdy plastic cup. She tipped the extended lip toward his mouth and waited for him to take over. Like an obedient child, he did as she asked.

Charlie tried to eat breakfast, but found his English muffin too dry to swallow. He sampled scrambled eggs and managed the juice and a few sips of coffee. Barely touched, he pushed his bedside table away. By the time he opened his eyes again, the tray was gone and the table had been pushed to the end of his bed.

His head cleared a little. It was Saturday, he remembered, in spite of his fog. That meant no physical therapy or routine appointments. The murmur of visitors' voices and an occasional child's squeal meant working folks had more time to spend with their loved ones. He missed his family so badly it hurt. Why was that? Both daughters were fulfilling every expectation that he and Emma had envisioned for them. So why wasn't he happy with that? The distance— that had to be it.

He felt rotten. Depressed. Couldn't get the cobwebs out of his mind. He tried to analyze his situation, his memory finally lighting on the fussy tummy pills. Had he said anything to the doctor or nurse to make them believe he had indigestion? He had, blaming his nerves. In the rendition he had rehearsed, he may have referred to his stomach as *tied up in knots*. Had they misinterpreted that description? After all, that was just a figure of speech. Did they forget that he did not want to be drugged? Tranquilizers and their ilk had not been part of Friday's conversation.

The weekend nurse appeared at his side, bearing another little white cup. She swiped his bracelet then extended the cup. "I'd prefer ice water if it's no trouble," Charlie said. "And I can manage a regular cup. Here, I'll take that," he said, relieving her of the white pleated cup. The minute she turned her back to pour ice water from his thermal pitcher, he pretended to dump the pill in his mouth while capturing it in his hand instead. Casually, he slid his hand under the covers. She approached with his water, which he exchanged for the empty white cup. He thanked her and took a big swallow.

"Thanks again." She hurried on to her next patient.

The minute she was gone, he rummaged under the sheet, retrieving the pill. Glasses in place, he studied it. The pill had a tiny alphanumeric sequence stamped into its surface. It looked innocent enough, but clearly, it was bad stuff. He was tempted to flush it, but then had a better idea. He needed to find out just what it was. He pulled a small pouch from his bedside table drawer in which he kept his spare change. He dropped it in and shook the pouch slightly, which positioned the pill under the coins. Then he buried the pouch in the drawer.

At five that afternoon, again at bedtime, and sometime during the night, the pill taking procedure was repeated. Staff administered. Charlie stashed. He didn't even risk cheeking the pill, lest it begin dissolving on contact with his saliva. Early Sunday morning, he woke feeling fresh and alive to the sound of murmured voices in the hall. He practically sang good morning to the nurse and told her that he was starving.

Whispers in the hall caught his attention. He listened. Hard. Funny thing about whispers—they had that effect.

"What do you mean he's agitated?"

Immediately, Charlie buried his face in the pillow. When the nurse he suspected had been doing the talking came into the room and looked at him suspiciously, he changed his story. Then he repeated, as faithfully as he could remember, how he had acted the previous day. Tired. Groggy. Not hungry at all. Silently, he vowed to do something. Fast.

Charlie's request for an escort for chapel yielded an unexpected bonus. Zeke bubbled into the room, humming. "Don't you go home on the weekends?"

"Nah, I live here for now, they love me so much. Glad you've reconsidered my offer to take you to chapel."

Zeke waited patiently while Charlie transferred himself to the proffered wheelchair. "Can I ask you something without your telling anyone else?"

"Certainly, ma man."

"How can I speed an envelope to my daughter without anyone knowing? Like FedEx or US Mail. It doesn't matter. What matters is fast. I have cash for same-day delivery."

Zeke laughed. "For one scared moment there, I thought you wanted, shall we say, something recreational?"

Charlie couldn't help grinning at that picture.

"It's a legal matter that needs immediate attention. I don't want my personal business bantered about the ward, even in this good place."

"After the service, let's ask the chaplain if he can help."

Charlie rolled over to his bedside table, pulled open the drawer and extracted a number ten business envelope onto which he had written his daughter Jeannette's Atlanta address. He was sure she knew enough people at the CDC to get information.

⌀⌀⌀

Charlie's daughter picked up the phone on the third ring. "Something's happened, Jeannette. I'm praying that you'll take it seriously and not think I'm confused or have succumbed to paranoia." In the background, Charlie could hear the clamor of little children. Having just returned from Sunday school and church, Jeannette's preschoolers were cranky, hungry, and past due for naps. Her husband was handling the situation with his usual easy-breezy patience.

The background noise receded as Jeannette must have been walking from the kitchen to a remote part of their roomy Georgian-style house. "Dad. What is it?"

Having been through it enough times in his mind, Charlie now had an executive summary. Common sense told him, however, that if he told her that he suspected a serial killer was victimizing the VA, she and her sister would be on the next plane, obligations be damned.

"I thought I had left strict orders that I did not want to be tranquilized, given sleeping pills, or otherwise drugged beyond what was absolutely medically necessary. I had a complaint, which I thought was justified, and met with the doctor and head nurse. Almost immediately, they started giving me pills, supposedly to soothe my stomach. It knocked me out. After three doses, I started palming them, and, sure enough, my head got itself back together. You should get a same-day mailer immediately. Do you have a contact who can analyze them discretely?

"Why don't you just ask the doctor? Or I could. And Susan's a force to contend with."

"No! I don't want them to know that I know that they didn't believe me."

"You better explain."

He hesitated, collecting his thoughts.

"Dad? Are you there?"

"I thought—I think, that I witnessed someone harming one of the patients. What I requested was oversight. Or beefed up security. I suspect that what I got was labeled *confused* and that they are sedating me."

"Say the word, Dad, and we'll transfer you to Atlanta. There's an excellent VA hospital here."

"I hope I'm wrong. I don't want to make trouble unnecessarily for the VA. And I'm making great progress. You know that I want to go home. Once I leave the state—"

"Dad, we'll never force you into a lifestyle that doesn't fit. You're of sound mind and capable of making your own decisions."

Tears welled in Charlie's eyes. "Thank you, dear. Especially for the sound-mind part. Think about it. If everyone thought that my elevator didn't go all the way to the top, I'd be at their mercy. Old people can't defend themselves against that."

"Dad, you're not old."

"Thanks. Again."

"Are you sharing this with Susan? Or should I?"

"First things first. Let's just find out what's in those pills. This may be innocent enough, a miscommunication or an intolerance or allergy on my part. And the VA has been wonderful to me. I've had no other complaints to date."

಄಄಄

Charlie successfully palmed the next doses of the strange little pills, and somehow got through the night. Early the next morning, he was overjoyed to see Mike, knowing that he could trust him not to do anything hinkey. Instead of confessing what had transpired over the weekend, he followed his better judgment. Putting Mike in an *us versus them* position might jeopardize his career.

Oddly enough, nobody had shown up that morning to dispense anything other than vitamins. He ate a hearty breakfast, enjoyed his shower, and put on fresh clothes. He looked forward to the rigors of physical therapy. He was waiting for Escort Zeke to arrive and was reading the paper when the doctor appeared. His eyes snapped uncharacteristically with anger, transforming his trademark calm demeanor.

"I just got off the phone with your very angry daughter. She 'read me the riot act' about your being given a powerful anti-depressant that is in no way appropriate for your medical treatment. What did you tell her? And why didn't you ask me? If you had a problem with how we were handling your treatment, we would have dealt with it immediately. More to the point, I didn't order any such drug. You didn't need to call out the troops. Tell me—where did you get such an idea?"

With that, Charlie's phone rang. He held up his index finger to put the doctor figuratively on hold while he snatched the receiver. Jeannette disgorged a torrent of information much to Charlie's astonishment.

"Are they absolutely sure?"

"Even though it was stamped with a code, my friend analyzed and confirmed it," she said. "According to her, this should have been obvious to any pharmacist."

"And your friend would swear to it?"

"Yes. It's proper use is for severe mental disorders. She went as far as to say you could put her on your witness list if it comes to that."

Charlie focused on the grim-faced doctor. "The doctor's here. May I call you back later?"

"Of course. I love you, Dad."

"Okay. Love you too."

He took a deep breath, the interruption seeming to have sucked the energy from the doctor's desire to vent. When he started to repeat himself, Charlie bellowed, drowning him out. "This is not my imagination. I am not crazy. I am not confused. There is no earthly reason to give me anti-psychotic drugs. After two doses, I knew something was wrong, so I palmed several and sent them to my daughter in Atlanta. Her biochemist analyzed them." He poked his index finger into his left palm for emphasis. "The very same pills I was supposed to swallow. Did my daughter tell you what they were?"

The doctor stared, as if not quite grasping what he was hearing. "Charlie. Mr. Alderfer—believe me. I never ordered any such drug."

"Well, somebody did. She's faxing you the report. You can read it yourself."

"I promise you. I will personally get to the bottom of this. In the meantime, I'll order some blood work to see if there's anything lurking in your system that shouldn't be there."

"Good idea. But I'd prefer to have the work done by an outside lab so there's no conflict of interest."

"I understand. We can send to another hospital or lab of your choosing. And again, I'm very sorry. This has never happened here before." He strode quickly from the room. *A man wearing white.* Mentally Charlie bumped *pharmacist* to the top of his list. But what might they handle that smelled like oil?

He had a few minutes to analyze the confrontation and will himself to stop shaking before Zeke would show up with a wheelchair. Already Charlie felt bad for his rage. Did he believe the doctor? If he was lying he was an excellent actor. Perhaps his astonishment was genuine. Or was he shocked by Charlie's ability to neutralize their attempt to silence him so quickly? For the first time it occurred to him that more than one person might be involved.

"Good morning, my good fellow." Zeke sailed into the room with an Escort department wheel chair. "You ready to rock 'n' roll?"

"Thank you so much for helping me yesterday."

"I knew that once you got into the chapel that you would find Jesus."

Charlie grinned at the man who was on a mission to save his sorry soul. "The mailing. My daughter received it immediately. Can we keep it between us?"

"Keep what?" He slapped his thigh and laughed heartily. "I am the *soul* of discretion. You get it?"

രരെ

Charlie loathed confrontation. If there was unpleasantness brewing, he made a point of being somewhere else. When he and Emma felt grumpy, they simply left each other alone, after which they'd end up kidding each other and laughing. The outside world was so much more hostile, and helping others save face was not part of the American culture.

He felt trapped and paranoid as if everyone was staring at him. The staff undoubtedly had heard the ruckus, and they knew that something was up. What if Dr. Szish had torn through their ranks, demanding answers?

The more Charlie thought about the entire situation, the more upset he became. In the past, he would have jogged, chopped firewood, or shot a few baskets until he felt human again.

But his former life was fading inexorably into history with fresh limitations imposing their will. No sooner did he compensate for each problem that arose than a new batch showed up.

Physical therapy got him out of the ward for a while, then he ate lunch alone in his room. By mid-afternoon, he was lonely and bored. He rolled his wheelchair to the farthest dayroom in search of distraction. Jonathan's mother Jade stood at the window, hands splayed on the deep sill, staring at nothing. He halted, undecided about whether to advance or sneak a retreat. Too late. Aware of his presence, she turned.

For a beat, neither said anything. Jade relented first. "Hey."

"Hey, yourself." He set the brake. "How's it going?"

"Okay. I guess. You got no visitors either?"

"Friends from my church stopped by yesterday, but I think most are freaked because I'm in Hospice. I don't think they know what to say. 'How're you doing?' 'How are you feeling?' 'Get better soon' and so on. The usual clichés aren't appropriate. Perhaps I remind them of their own mortality."

"What about family? Do you have anyone?"

"I have daughters and grandkids, but they're all out of state."

"My dad and Jonathan—they're all that I have. You think you have friends, and then when bad stuff happens, they desert you. Nobody wants to come near you, as if it's contagious. More likely, they don't want to look guilty by association. Or they're afraid you'll ask them for money. If you're on top of the world, rich, or famous, everybody wants to be your best friend."

"I agree. And that's not fair."

"Thanks for all the nice things you said about Jonathan and how you thought I was a good mother. That meant a lot. It's not the kind of thing that I hear. I'm treated as if I'm trailer trash. That's not fair either. Some of my favorite people lived in trailers. They're not even called trailers anymore—they're *manufactured homes.*"

"I meant what I said about Jonathan. He's a dear little boy. And that doesn't happen by accident. It takes a lot of time, energy, patience, and love to raise such a great little guy."

"I feel so guilty about him."

"Come on. Sit down," Charlie coaxed, motioning to the leather sofa across from his wheelchair. "Let me show you what I've accomplished." He parallel parked the chair against the edge of the sofa, set the wheel brakes, kicked the footrests out of the way, and pushed himself up by the arm-rests to a standing position. He pivoted and, with his normal gait, approached the couch. He lowered himself deliberately rather than letting himself plop. "Thigh muscles!"

Jade grinned and gave him a little applause. "Here! Here!"

"Okay, Miss Jade. Tell me. Is guilt your favorite miserable feeling? Like my needing to apologize?"

"I have every reason. I'm neglecting Jonathan terribly. My family's situation has been overwhelming. And he's no trouble at all. Obedient. Doesn't get into mischief. So quiet that it's easy to overlook him. And I've rewarded him by ignoring him. Poor little fellow. I got a terrible wakeup call recently. He wandered off and got lost in the hospital complex, and I didn't even know he was gone. A total stranger found him and fed him. Somehow figured out where he belonged. I yelled at the woman because I thought she was kidnapping him. And here he'd been gone all that time. I'm so ashamed. I've dealt with mean, greedy people so long that I don't know how to be nice. The only way I know how to act is to fight. I should find her. Thank her. Apologize."

"I'll tell her and explain. I'm sure she's forgotten by now anyway."

Jade looked up in surprise. "You know who she is?"

"My feisty oldest daughter, Susan. A kindergarten teacher who can't seem to have one of her own. She gets, shall we say, a little carried away."

Jade couldn't help smiling. She stopped picking at a loose thread on her jeans that had started to fray then got serious again. "Everything that's happened—I should take Jonathan to a shrink. He doesn't talk. But when could I? And with what? The lawyers got all our money."

"He has said a little to me."

She jerked. "He did?" An anguished look overran her face. "He talks to *you*? And not his own mother? Why? And what did he say?"

"Not a whole lot. He told me his name."

"I haven't heard him say anything since my mom died. Everyone says that he'll talk when he's ready. They adored each other and he must miss her terribly. Then there's all that terrible business with my father—"

"I…ah…have read the newspaper articles. It must have been horrible."

"They made it sound like we were subhuman. They'd stick a microphone in your face and ask the most personal questions. Then they quote you, including swear words."

"It sounded like your dad got a raw deal. That everyone was trying to further their personal agendas.

"They've killed my dad, or they will shortly. He

doesn't have much time left. His heart's getting weaker, and his kidneys are failing."

"I am so sorry. If there's anything I can do—I'm pretty useless in here, but my girls say I'm a good listener. I had to be, living in a house with three ladies."

"And you heard Jonathan talk? How did you do that?"

"My former roommate, who was here before me, softened him up with Hershey's chocolate Kisses. He said that with kids you have to use the right bait. Evidently, Jonathan loves chocolate."

"My mom spoiled him, but I never did. Teeth, you know. Guess your roommate struck the right nerve."

"I hope that was okay. Jonathan seemed really troubled about something. Do you know if it's something specific?"

"He couldn't help hearing everything that went on. The house is quite small. It's a very long story."

"I have all afternoon."

Chapter 9

"My dad had a combustible temper—that's what my mom called it," Jade said. "But he was all bark and no bite. He never laid a hand on either of us. But could he yell! And as he got older, his nerve deafness got worse to the point where he couldn't hear himself, and he sounded downright ferocious. That prompted the neighbors to call the cops any number of times. Domestic disturbance, that's what they called it. Thing is, nobody ever documented any sign of violence.

"I was a typical rebellious teenager. Didn't like school, although I did well. It was too easy not to. As soon as I graduated, I hit the road. Hung out with some real low-lifes. Guess you could call it my bad-boy phase. Then I fell madly in love with a special guy. We got married, and I thought my life was just perfect. We didn't have any money—and he took off the minute I got pregnant. I found a ratty little apartment, shared babysitting duties with neighbors, and barely eeked out a living."

"Did your parents offer to help?"

"Sure. But I was too proud and, besides, they had been really old parents. I didn't think it was fair for them to have to help me. I'm sure you've heard all the stories about worthless young adults who return home and sponge off their parents. Our family situation should have been the other way around. I should have been helping them."

"So what happened?"

She gazed off into the room. "My mom had a small stroke. Dad opted for early retirement and took over the household routine. She could still do most things for herself—personal stuff and all—but he couldn't leave her alone. She'd put on the kettle and forget it. Try to cook and forget how. Couldn't read any more. Say goofy things. Wander off. Then she had another stroke. After the hospital and physical therapy, she went to a nursing home, supposedly to finish her therapy. That's a euphemism, you know. The implication of *finish*. With that kind of stroke, any progress she'd make beyond that first month would be minimal. No insurance covered prolonged care, but Dad and I knew that she couldn't come home.

"Dad got really, really angry with the nursing home staff and had it out with the director. In all fairness to Dad, they were supposed to provide a certain level of care. They lost her clothes and limited her to two Depends a day. Two! When we brought them in by the carton, they disappeared, as did any money we left for incidentals. She got bedsores and had a roommate who screamed night and day. I suspected somebody shorted her meds—probably sold them on the black market.

"Dad threatened to file a grievance with the outfit that accredits the place, even spoke with a former employee who claimed there was fraud—something about selling supplies and shorting prescription drugs. I tried to find her, but she had fallen off the grid. Probably scared. The newspapers got it all wrong. The director goaded Dad, even threw the first punch. You don't do that to Dad. He hit back. Broke the guy's nose. The nurse who 'witnessed' the altercation and 'verified his story' to keep her job was probably part of the conspiracy.

"Next thing I knew, Mom was kicked out. And that rat bastard director must have called every other nursing home in the state to blackball my family. So Dad took her home and tried to do everything for her. His own health took a beating. That's when he called me and asked me if I could move home and help. That was a godsend and face-saver because I wasn't making it on my own, anyway, and was spared the humiliation of asking for help. Dad set Mom up in the dining room, and that left the three little bedrooms for him, Jonathan, and me.

"We were doing okay until Mom died, and the police accused Dad of killing her. He couldn't explain how she got on the floor. Her covers, they insisted, were undisturbed and the bedrail was up. They charged that she couldn't have gotten over the rail and out of bed by herself. Not in her condition. His motive, they said, was money. That she was a burden that was bankrupting him."

"Where were you when she died?"

"At work. Jonathan was at a next-door neighbor's house. By the time I got home, the police and the coroner's van were at the house. Dad had tried unsuccessfully to do CPR. Next thing you know, the police were carting Dad off to jail.

"You know those attorney ads you see on TV? How they don't get paid until they get money for you? Well, that doesn't apply to criminal cases. If you have nothing, you get a public defender whose resources are so limited that your only option is to accept a plea. You've got to say under oath that you did the crime. Or you hire your own attorney. You pay him a fortune up front as a retainer. He whittles at that in twelve-minute increments. Call 'em on the phone, talk for one minute, or get stuck on hold, and they deduct increments. The retainer disappears in a flash."

"What about that big Philadelphia lawyer?"

"He never talked to any of us until that day in court when my dad had his heart attack. He was there for the show. Everyone was. All we have left is Dad's little house, and when he dies, that too will have to be sold. It's so sad. My parents bought that house when they were first married. He worked so hard and was so proud when he paid it off. Dad did every repair, all the plumbing and electrical work, painted every wall several times, inside and out. Dug every hole, planted each twig that grew into a tree. And now the lawyers are getting it all for doing nothing."

Charlie felt his whole body sag. "That's just awful. And Jonathan knows all about this."

"More is the pity. He's too young to understand the complexity, but there's no way to sugar coat what is obvious."

"Maybe that's okay. At least he's too young to be bitter."

"But I'm not. And I will hate every last one of those bastards until I can dance on their graves."

❡❡❡

In the next county, Elsabet Bentz took the small brown paper bag from its hiding place in her kitchen. Then she unearthed her largest purse. Unable to resist, she carefully unfolded the paper bag and peered at the eight-ounce drinking glass that lay in the bottom. Satisfied, she secured the bag's opening, affixed a paperclip and carefully lowered it into her purse.

Anxiety, guilt, and uncertainty plagued her as she collected her briefcase and transferred essentials from her small purse to the larger one. "I'm leaving now. You be okay?" she called to her homebound husband for the fifth time.

"Sure," he called from their bedroom. "Go. Ben will be here any minute. He's never late."

"I'm so sorry to have to leave early, but I can't avoid this early appointment. It's important. Got your cell phone?"

"Within easy reach."

"Now, don't hesitate—"

"I know! I know! I'll be fine. Get going, or you'll be late for your meeting."

Two weeks, without incident. Everything had gone perfectly well. So why was she squandering precious dollars on a private detective? She had lain awake beside her husband, night after night, knowing that every few hours she'd need to help roll him to a new position. Before Ben Tothero had joined them and before the nursing home, this had been as routine as giving a baby his three a.m. feedings, after which she'd go straight back to sleep. But now...

Elsabet backed her old Escort out of the driveway and headed in the opposite direction from the real estate office where she was employed. Finding a spot to parallel park, she got out while rehearsing her speech one more time.

The interior of Limerick Bureau of Investigation was hardly what she expected. The walls, while hung with plaques of appreciation from various police departments, were paneled with cheap material of an unidentifiable vintage. Worn industrial carpet divulged nary a clue as to its original color. The place smelled strongly of cleaning solution. Although earlier than eight a.m., several people already were waiting in mismatched metal chairs upholstered in vinyl.

She whispered her name to the receptionist and slunk to a seat, praying nobody would recognize her. No one even looked up. Before she had time to feign interest in a dog-eared *Readers Digest*, the receptionist summoned her to the desk. Papers to fill out—just like a dentist's office. And yes, of course they'd accept folding green.

"Go on back." The receptionist directed her through a closed door beyond her metal secretary's desk. Elsabet did.

Finding herself in a long narrow hall paneled with more of the same cheap material, she looked left then right at four closed doors. The one at the end of the hall jerked open. "Ms. Bentz? Right this way, please."

Elsabet couldn't help smiling. After all the PI and bounty hunter shows on TV, she hardly expected and was totally unprepared for the slight little man. Receding slicked unparted hair, black- rim glasses, clean shaven, white shirt, suspenders, nondescript brown dress slacks made of cheap fabric. When he rose to shake hands, she feared their collective short arms wouldn't reach over his desk. They shook fingertips.

John Limerick opened a folder. "So, Ms. Bentz, you have a concern about your new employee?"

Elsabet rattled through her well-rehearsed description and summary of the circumstances that had brought Ben Tothero to her home. Finally, she dug the paper bag out of her purse. "His fingerprints are visible, even to me. Could you possibly find out who he is?"

"You have reason to doubt his integrity?"

"I had to make a split-second decision whether to hire him. I was that desperate. He seems perfect for our needs. Too perfect. But when I tried to check his references after the fact, the phone numbers were disconnects. I've considered everything from witness protection to fugitive from justice. Or maybe he simply got fired and was embarrassed to tell me."

"What else?"

"That first day, he said he didn't do anything medical. He ticked off several examples, including injections. He presented himself as muscle for hire. I admit it—I snooped while he was helping my husband in the bathroom. I looked in his bag. Inside I saw hypodermic syringes sealed in plastic, and a little glass bottle. You know, the kind that nurses stick a needle into when they're going to give you a flu shot? But he had said he didn't do that kind of stuff."

"Could you read the label on the bottle?"

"It didn't mean anything to me. Something long that started with a P. Pan-something, I think. I didn't have time to copy the spelling—I heard him coming."

"Ms. Bentz—if you suspect this man of something, why not discharge him? Or go to the police?"

"With what? He hasn't done anything wrong. In fact, that's the first thing that made me suspicious. He was too good to be true. And you know what they say about that.

Besides, what if he is exactly as he claims? I'd be humiliated to have him find out I'd involved the police. Maybe I'd
get sued. We don't have very much left, but I have a job and
there's equity in the house."

"Do you want me to follow him? See what he's up to?
Do a backgrounder?"

"Just run the prints. See if he has a record, and if so, if
we're in danger. I don't care if he boosted cars as a teenager
or false-carded under age at a bar or has a dozen unpaid
traffic tickets. I don't even care if he's behind on his child
support. I need to know if he's dangerous."

"Anything else you might know about him? Place and
date of birth? Education? Previous addresses or employ-
ers?"

"I'm afraid I know nothing about his background. If
he's telling the truth, he's a skilled mechanic." She retrieved
a piece of paper and slid it across the desk. "That's what he
claims is his current address and that is a working phone
number. And the two references he gave that are disconnects, but the names may be legitimate. That's all I have."

John Limerick stood and offered his hand. "I'll get
right on it. I'll leave you a message that will instruct you to
call your doctor's office. Buy one of those prepaid phone
cards and use that, not your home or cell phone, to call me
back. Okay?"

Elsabet startled. "Isn't that a little bit paranoid?"

"Not really. Your employee could be a privacy freak or
ducking the settlement from a lawsuit. Don't worry. We'll
get what you need to protect your family."

"Oh! One more thing. He says that he works on vintage
cars. He has a strange smell about him—like kerosene. My
husband identified it as something he called *penetrating oil*.
It smells like gasoline, but it lingers. It's not a health issue.
He brings his own nailbrush and scrubs before he assists my
husband. Like they do on those doctor shows on TV? Then
he puts on latex gloves. He made a point of telling us repeatedly that he was more danger to my husband than vice

versa. You know, if he's coming down with a cold or the flu. I wonder if he was a doctor or nurse in a previous life. Someone who lost his license."

Limerick nodded approvingly. "We'll get on this today. In the meantime, try not to worry. Lots of people have perfectly innocent reasons to stay under the radar."

As Elsabet approached her car, she peered nervously about her. Ridiculous, she scolded herself. No one could possibly be interested in her.

Inside his office, John Limerick scowled at the collective information the woman had provided, which did not make him happy. If only she'd copied the name on that bottle. He snatched his cell and hit the speed dial to put his best operative in play.

ოახო

Dr. Szish and the head of Pharmacy convened in the latter's private office. The pharmacist had rolled an Rx cabinet into the room as a reference although that was overkill for the experienced doctor.

"Have you called in security? Reported this incident to anyone?" the pharmacist asked.

"First I needed more information. Lives and careers could be at stake. This could have been an honest mistake. Conversely, something premeditated and potentially lethal. Regardless, I need to prevent this from ever happening again. You know what they say—perception is reality. And we can't appear sloppy or inept, even if the event was totally innocent.

"Is your patient threatening to sue?"

"Not yet. This should go away. But it's a scary precedent that can't be shrugged off. Can we start by reviewing the procedure, then try to figure out what happened?"

"Sure." The pharmacist pried his bulky, white-garbed frame from his worn leather chair and approached the cabinet. "First, Pharmacy 101, with apologies for insulting your intelligence. On every ward, the doctors compute instructions for each patient, updating it as necessary. That information arrives on our secure back office computer for filling. I, or one of the other pharmacists, review the doctor's instructions and communicate them to a pharmacy tech."

"And that's a responsible position…"

"The tech? At least two years of professional training, then the VA's own background check, then orientation to our particular environment. Employee screening is required for everyone from the director down to entry-level novices. Our police fingerprint potential employees and send the prints to the fed, where they're checked and kept on file. That's vital because our narcotics cabinets can only be unlocked by touching a fingerprint pad. Besides checking references, a criminal background check is completed."

"Right," he nodded. So far, this was SOP. "But routine prescriptions—how could the wrong pills reach Mr. Alderfer?"

The pharmacist approached the demo cabinet and pulled out one of many tiny plastic drawers that was labeled with a fictitious patient's name and a barcode. From inside, he withdrew a pill sealed in cellophane. That too had a barcode. Then he lifted a hand-held scanner tethered to the top of the cabinet and motioned to the computer screen that sat to its left.

"With the scanner, I can cross-reference four things: the prescription you ordered as seen on the screen, the patient's barcode that's on his personal drawer, the barcode on his hospital bracelet, and the barcode on the med's packaging."

"And the pills come from…"

"In bulk via the VA's distribution system."

"What keeps a tech from swapping out pills? In Mr. Alderfer's case, I offered a mild sedative in case he felt overly anxious. That he declined. When he mentioned some gastric distress, I ordered a mild antacid similar to Tums but a little more appropriate for his situation. That's what somebody switched."

"Let's follow this little demo pill. These portable cabinets are loaded here in Pharmacy, one per ward, then wheeled to that nurses' station by a pharmacy tech. Upon arrival, he or she checks the contents against the computer again. Then, when meds are administered by the nurses, the patient's personal barcode and the med's barcode are compared against what's on his personal drawer and the computer screen."

"What about human error?"

"On very rare occasion that could happen—a mental lapse when loading the drawers—but in my experience it's always caught by so many checks and balances. Staff's pretty sharp, too. Being familiar with each patient's case, nurses spot anything that looks off and question it."

Dr. Szish frowned. "It sounds unlikely that this was unintentional. The patient would have consumed seven wrong pills, had he not caught the discrepancy himself. Any thoughts?"

The pharmacist sighed. "If the fed had the funding, we'd have robots to fill our prescriptions. But that would cost millions, plus the cost of renovating our buildings. Anytime you add humans to the mix, the potential for error is there. But—look at this." From an unlabeled drawer he withdrew two cellophane packages. Both were identical size—about 1.5 by 2 inches—and each contained a little green pill.

"If you look carefully, the colors and sizes appear to be identical. And neither has a stamped number. Were it not for the barcode, the untrained eye couldn't tell the difference." He held one up. "This is what Mr. Alderfer should have received. The other is what he got, and it's wrong."

"This one looks a tiny bit thicker."

"The big difference, of course, is the ingredients. One is what your staff nicknamed a 'fussy tummy pill' and the other a powerful antidepressant. I'm betting somebody deliberately switched them. Of course, without the wrappers, we can't confirm tampering. This scenario would require someone who is expert in our computers, prescription medicines, and has access to altering your orders. Or knows a way to open and reseal a cellophane bag undetected. The latter would be tricky."

"Do we agree that this happened internally?"

"Absolutely. The manufacturer would have neither the motive nor the ability. Different companies made these two pills. Either someone at my end switched the packages, or one of your weekend staffers made the substitution. Or some unknown person hacked into Pharmacy's computer. Our staff—without exception—has been with us for years. I've questioned the techs who service that ward and they appear innocent.

"We have surfaced one breech of procedure, however—an older employee whose tenure predates our computerization. Occasionally she forgets to log-off after working on records. Staff, who are very fond of her, routinely check her computer, remind her or log-off for her. I thought we had that problem fixed."

"Suppose an outsider got into your area. Perhaps after hours. Could they hack in?"

"I have no idea what's involved with hacking into computers. That isn't my field. Much more likely would be something simple. Your perp accesses the cabinet, opens the patient's drawer, and swaps the pills. That would only require knowledge of how to tamper with packaging—you know, the right solvent and glue. We're doing an inventory right now to see if the substituted pills came from our supplies. If so, there should be a few missing."

The pair fell silent for a moment. Suddenly the pharmacist came to life. "Hold on—suppose someone in Hospice accessed the entry you made—would anyone notice? Do you review your screens every day?"

"We do."

"Even if they changed it back, say over the weekend?"

The doctor shook his head. "I don't see how, but why don't we ask Information Technology if there is a trail—if you can change an entry, then revert to a previous entry?"

"Sure. Now, let me tell you what I've already done. I've asked our police to patrol our area after hours for any suspicious activity or unauthorized personnel. We're inspecting our inventory, including signs of tampering. When in doubt, we'll throw it out."

"And Hospice staff is on high alert. Should we go to the director?"

"Oh, geez! We can't possibly anticipate how this might get blown out of proportion. Let's gather facts quickly, then we must follow our protocol. Right after you called, I asked our police to update background checks in case any of my employees have been in trouble since coming onboard." The pharmacist rose and extended his hand. "We'll keep in touch. Oh, and by the way—your patient was extremely lucky that he didn't take all those pills. Depending upon his constitution, he could have died."

"And not suspecting foul play, there would have been no reason for an autopsy."

👁️✦👁️

The next day Charlie wheeled toward the large dayroom looking for Jade, who was not in her father's room. Overnight, he had tossed and turned, replaying every word she had said as she relived the horror her parents had endured. He was angry with himself for not conjuring a plan to relieve her situation. Everything she had said was outside his experience.

He glanced through the dayroom's double doors and, not seeing her immediately, rolled to the second pair at the far end of the hall. He spotted her seated at a card table with her back toward him. Jade had company, unlike the type Charlie had noticed visiting Hospice in the past. Most locals dressed in modest clothes that could have come from a big box chain store or the outlets. Women in jeans, chinos, sweater sets, or embellished tees or sweatshirts, guys wearing jeans, T-shirts, or flannel shirts ruled the day. This couple was different. Something felt off.

The visitors had pulled up card table chairs. They sat, like a molded unit, holding hands, facing Jade. The woman had one of those tri-color hairdos with an elegant cut that Susan joked cost the earth. A silk blouse with matching sweater, linen slacks, matching alligator bag and shoes. What his girls called major jewelry, rocks tastefully set in what must be real gold or platinum. The man looked as if he'd just stepped from the pages of GQ magazine. Clearly, they were nervous and looked out of place. A hospital experience for them would be a posh private clinic with a ministering hoard in attendance.

On impulse, Charlie rolled through the rows of card tables to where the three sat. He positioned himself to Jade's left, as if he were their fourth for bridge. "There you are. I've been looking for you." He nodded acknowledgement to the couple whom Jade did not introduce.

Jade smiled, looking him straight in the eyes. "The volunteer we were talking about put our fresh teabags and other refreshments in the cupboard." She pointed to the end of the room where Charlie had entered. "Sorry to keep everyone waiting. Go ahead with the tea. I'll just be a minute."

He caught her drift. *We won't start without you.* He nodded to her visitors and retreated. Back turned, he stifled a smile. She needed someone in her corner, someone she trusted, perhaps a witness, the reason unknown. That he could learn later if she wanted to talk. She trusted him and that felt good. He took his time easing himself out of his chair and balancing himself along the refreshment counter, going through the cupboards for teabags, a bowl, mugs, and plates. He waited, feigning interest in the microwave's panel, his ears drawing backward, like a primitive creature.

"Is there some place more private?" the man asked, eying two other families at Charlie's end of the room. A woman was helping her patient-husband complete a crossword puzzle. A young woman and man, who looked like siblings, flanked an old man who was prone in a recliner. Each held a hand while she murmured verses from Psalms. Keeping the vigil—Charlie knew the routine. That the scene could have been him did not escape him.

"This works for me," Jade said. "Staff needs to know where to find me. Why are you here?" Her voice was flat. Unfriendly. Just south of hostile.

"We've come about the child," the man said.

"He's not 'the child.' His name is Jonathan. And he's an adult who's going on six."

The couple exchanged wary glances.

"We'd like to do something for him. He *is* our grandson," the woman said.

"Oh, that's just terrific. You did everything in your power to break Jonathan's father and me up, didn't even see fit to come to our wedding. Your disapproval was caustic. How would my family have looked to your precious country club friends? What would they say? What if the press had shown up at the chapel? Shot pictures in my parents' back yard? We aren't trash and we didn't live in a trailer. But so what if we did? Nice people live there. They just don't have any money for mansions and servants and ski trips to the Alps."

The woman had dropped her gaze to her lacquered nails even before Jade got to the part about the wedding. Charlie felt the acid creep into his throat. Anger flushed his face red. In-laws. Very ostentatious, very rich in-laws.

The woman glanced at her husband who scowled back at her. "We've both have regretted this…ah…unfortunate misunderstanding many times. We'd like to make it up to you and the boy," she said.

"Jonathan. His name is Jonathan."

"Yes. Of course."

"What is it you want? Why are you here? And why now?"

The woman bent forward in her chair. "We didn't know Jonathan existed until we read your mother's obituary."

Jade scowled. "Oh, that's just lovely. Your son, my ex-husband, abandons us the minute he finds out I'm pregnant, and you think you can pretend you know nothing about him?"

"Ex?" the man asked. "Did you divorce him?"

"Well, duh! He just packed his bag and took off in the middle of the night. After three years with no word, I wasn't waiting around any longer. Where is he, anyway? And what did he use as his excuse? And don't try to tell me you had no idea what he was pulling."

Another exchange of covert glances. Finally, the mother relented, her shoulders sagging. "He showed up with a bag and his equipment, all excited about some big surprise. The surprise, he said, would have to wait until he returned. He said he had an unexpected opportunity for a photo shoot that had Pulitzer potential. The shoot was extremely confidential and potentially dangerous.

"He'd dreamed of being a photojournalist ever since he saw his first *National Geographic*. He wanted to travel to faraway places. Capture exotic worlds. Anything but being a bridal photographer, which is what he ended up being. He said this opportunity had big buck potential."

"Oh, yeah. How many times did you tell me—or were you screaming?—that marrying me ruined his life? Well, sounds like he got his wish. Went off to capture the world with his camera, wife and baby be damned."

"You don't understand. We never heard from him again either. And it's been six years."

Jade opened her mouth, but nothing came out. Mid-course adjusting, her expression said she was rethinking her next volley. "Wait a minute. You don't hear from your son, whom you'd flip on if he didn't phone you once a week, then didn't try to reach him for how many years?"

"We tried! First, we phoned. Your apartment—you blocked our numbers—his cell, his friends, his business, his clients. Everyone we could think of. We called hospitals, morgues, airlines, and rental car places. We hired private detectives who scoured in ever-widening circles. They finally traced him to Greece through a charter airline, on which he'd been a last-minute substitute passenger. Then nothing. We believed he was heading for the Middle East to shoot pictures of ordinary people in their bombed-out houses. He hated the Bush administration's crimes against humanity, as he called it. He wanted to expose that to the world."

A long pause lay like a pall over the room. Finally, the woman said, "We were late trying to trace him. By that time, any trail had gone cold. Our daughter Cindy—you remember Cindy?"

From Jade's reaction, Charlie knew that the mother-in law had just stepped into another minefield. "Yeah, I re-member the sister who called me a whore, refused to come to my bridal shower, or be a bridesmaid."

"Cindy was diagnosed with a brain tumor which, evi-dently had metastasized from her lungs. We were dumb-founded. At twenty-five, for Pete's sake. She'd led a very healthy lifestyle—a vegetarian who worked out. She didn't smoke, there's no family history, she wasn't exposed to chemicals that we know of. And then bang! It hit her. She quit her job and came home for treatment, but nothing helped. Six months later, she was gone."

Charlie couldn't stop the old saying, *what goes around*...from invading his mind.

The father tag teamed. "The time she came home to die coincided with when our son left for Greece. We were overwhelmed with Cindy's care. Time, which meant noth-ing, fused into one continuous passage. When we realized that death was imminent, we redoubled our effort to reach him. We couldn't."

Jade jumped into his pause. "You do realize, don't you,

that if either of your kids were available, neither of them would be with me right now? You hated me and poisoned our marriage. There is no way I want Jonathan near people like you."

"Please." the woman stated more than asked. "Let us help you. From what we've read—"

"Where's all this going? You think you can buy your way into my little boy's life? If I don't let you near him, which I don't intend to do, you'll go to court? Try to get custody? Or visiting rights? Use my family's tragedy as leverage?" She leapt to her feet. "Over my dead body. You can't reload your family with my child. Now get out! Leave us alone. You've had lots of practice so that should be easy."

The charge nurse popped her head into the room. "Is there a problem here?" she asked as if the TV had malfunctioned."

"I don't want these people anywhere near my family."

The nurse approached them and, in a soft, professional whisper said, "Sir. Ma'am. I think it would be a good idea if you visited some other time." Awkwardly the pair moved out of the room. Soon normal sounds and activity replaced the dead silence left in their wake.

Charlie rolled to the chair where Jade had flopped her spent body. Angry tears coursed down her pretty, thin face, her crossed arms hugging herself like a defiant child. He rose and, easing her to her feet, slung one arm around her, and pulled her into a hug. "It'll be okay. I promise."

"I meant what I said. If they try to get at my son—"

"That's not going to happen, Jade. That law about grandparents' rights was overturned. And you're a wonderful mother. If they try to pull anything, I'll go to court with you, I promise. I have the resources for one big nasty fight."

She cried harder and just couldn't stop the wracking sobs that shook her narrow shoulders. Finally, it lessened. "Is this ironic or what?" she blubbered. "The whole world was against us. People who were supposed to be family, friends, and neighbors. People we helped any number of times. Then no one would give me a job. They drove Dad over the edge, and now he's dying. The media, photographers, and complete strangers hounded me. But here in Hospice I'm surrounded with wonderful people. Patients and their families that I didn't even know, who are overwhelmed with their own tragedies—they stop to see how I am. Me. Not just Dad. Even though they know who we are. And there's you. Thank you so much."

Charlie fumbled unsuccessfully for a tissue to wipe his own eyes. Jade couldn't help laughing through her own tears as she passed one to him. "We're quite the pair, aren't we?"

"Yeah, we are. Say—Speaking of Jonathan—"

"My minister's wife thought I needed a break. And she's getting a rotation together to help at night. I've been so hard on everyone. I've failed to see that there are good people. I've had my back to the wall for so long that I've forgotten how to be civilized."

"How about that tea?"

"Hate the stuff. But I know where they stash the sodas in the kitchenette down the hall."

"Jade—there's something we must talk about. Jonathan may be ready to talk about whatever is bothering him. Is it okay if I pursue it? I'd like your permission. I don't want to harm him. Can you deal with whatever he might say? On top of everything else?"

Jade locked eyes with him as if for emphasis, then reaffirmed her consent. "You can't hurt children with love and concern. And that's your special gift. Go ahead."

Chapter 10

I'd never lie to you, Jonathan. In fact, I never lie to anyone. You can trust me to tell you the truth. Always. Do you understand? I know you're only five years old—"

Jonathan raised his head and frowned. "I'm almost six."

Charlie grinned. "Okay. Almost six. That's old enough to have a grown-up conversation with me, don't you think?"

The child studied Charlie's face with a quizzical expression then agreed with a nod.

"This is very important. I know you *think* that you killed your gram, but you didn't. There is no way a little guy like you would be able to do that."

Jonathan screwed up his face with a mixture of exasperation and disagreement, but Charlie shut down any argument the child could launch by blocking the air with his palm. "I want you to tell me exactly why you *think* that you killed her."

Jonathan stared. Nothing.

Okay. Try a different approach. "Tell me what happened that day. What was it like?"

Jonathan scrunched his face, shaking his hands, palms up, in supplication. He wailed, "I don't remember!"

Bad approach again. Charlie smacked himself mentally. Way too complicated. It had been too long since he'd reasoned with little children. Emma was much better at that.

He started anew. "That's okay. Maybe if you'd tell me *how* you killed her. Did you shoot Gram with your super-duper X-ray space gun?"

Startled, the little guy's eyes snapped to attention. He grinned. "Nooo."

"Then you must have clobbered her with a huge ice cream cone."

A giggle. "Nooo."

"You ran her over with a giant cement mixer."

"That's silly!"

"I know! You let King Kong, the giant ape who's bigger than the whole neighborhood, sit on her."

The child dissolved in giggles.

"Okay. I give up. How'd you do it?"

His face straightened, and he glanced toward the ceiling, eyes sweeping the tiles. The silence that followed nearly did Charlie in. Finally, Jonathan took a deep breath. Expelled it more as a sigh. "I touched that—that thing. You know."

"What thing?" The child shrugged. "What did it look like?" Jonathan's eyes swept the ceiling again. "Was it big like a TV or small like an egg?"

"Real small."

Charlie demonstrated with his thumb and index finger, holding them like a huge letter C. He held his hand within Jonathan's reach. The child squeezed the C together until the circle almost disappeared. That meant it was tiny.

"What color is this thing?" Jonathan looked puzzled. "Is it red?" Head shake. "Green?" Bigger shake no. "Sky-blue pink?"

Big grin. "No, silly. It doesn't have any color." He focused on his sneakers for a moment, then lit on Charlie's face. "Like Gram's tea kettle."

"Silver! Is it silver?" Charlie looked around for something metallic. "Like that bowl over there?"

"Yeah. Like that."

"Does this thing have a name?" The boy shrugged.

"Okay. We have a small metal object and you touched it. Did it make a terrible noise? Shoot sparks or something wet? Go bang? Blow up?"

"Nah. It just fell off."

"On the floor?" Head bob. "Did it smash, like glass or bounce like a ball?"

"It rolled. Under Gram's bed."

"So you crawled under the bed and retrieved it?"

A look of pure anguish took over his face, tears welling in his eyes and spilling down his cheeks. "I tried to fix it, but I couldn't remember where it goes. And Mommy said, 'Never touch Gram's stuff. That will kill her.'" He sobbed into his chubby hands.

"Jonathan." Charlie waited a moment then reached for a tissue. He patted the child's wet face. "Jonathan, it's okay. I promise you. If that thing that fell off was very important, an alarm would have sounded. Bells or beeps would have warned your family that something was wrong. Did you hear anything like that?"

Jonathan thought a minute, rolling his eyes back and forth across the ceiling. "No."

A long pause. "Did you hear anything at all?"

"Only that door. The one that slides and goes out back. It squeaks."

"There's a door in the room?"

"Yeah. We used to eat at a big table in there. But then Gram got sick. Gram came home from the hospital. Grandpa put the table in the basement. Some people brought in a bed. Like the one she had in the hospital."

Charlie tried to picture the room as Jade had described her parents' former dining room, but she had said nothing about a door, possibly glass patio sliders. "Are you sure the door squeaked? Could the noise have been a fan? Or an air conditioner?"

"Nooo!" the five-year old said, bobbing his hands, palm up, impatiently. "It squeaks when somebody pushes it open. Or when someone goes out."

"Who was it? Who came into or out of the room?"

"The angel. The one who came to get Gram. After I killed her."

Stunned, Charlie opened his mouth, but paused, unable to react to that statement. What on earth was the boy talking about? Mind racing, Charlie took a deep breath. He was terrified that he was pulling a too-slender thread and that it might break. "Why do you think there was an angel?"

"'Cause the angel said so."

"The angel spoke to you?"

"Nooo." Exasperated. Patience exhausted. "The angel told *Gram*."

"And you too? Did the angel speak to you?"

"No"

"Why not?"

The child hung his head. "Because I was hiding."

"Where were you hiding? Under the bed?"

Head shaking, eyes averted, he whispered, "In the closet. I hid in the closet. So the angel wouldn't see me. The angel would know what I did."

"Do you remember anything that she said to your gram?"

"He. It was a guy angel. He said he was the death angel. He said he'd come to take her to heaven."

"Are you sure that's what he said?"

"Yeah." A long pause. "'Cause he said it three times." Jonathan held up three fingers.

"In a row?"

Jonathan started to cry again. "I don't remember!"

Charlie was terrified to continue but afraid not to. This opportunity might not come again. He opened the bedside table drawer and pulled out the cellophane bag of Hershey's Kisses. Without a word, he lined several up in a row on the bed. "Go ahead. Take one. I'll have one too. We need a little break. Then we can talk some more about the angel."

With every ounce of his self-control and determination, Charlie forced himself to be quiet and patient. The child could bolt any minute. *With kids, you have to have the right bait.*

Finally, he approached Jonathan again, changing direction. "Did the angel have wings?"

Jonathan swallowed kiss number two and was eyeballing number three. "In a minute, son. Now, about those wings. Did he have any wings?"

"They must have been in his backpack. It was white."

"White? He wore white, like a robe? Or a Halloween costume?"

"Nooo! He wore pants. And a shirt. And shoes."

"What color were they?"

"White."

"Everything? All his clothes?"

Jonathan nodded in the affirmative.

"Is it possible that the angel was really a nurse checking up on your gram?"

"No! He said he was going to take Gram to heaven. He told her three times. At her bed. And then he picked her up. And then he put her on the floor. He looked at the closet. Then he looked at my gram. But he didn't take her. He just flew out the door."

Charlie was stunned. "Jonathan. This is very important. Before the angel put Gram on the floor, did he do anything to her?" Charlie dangled Hershey's Kiss number three just beyond the child's reach, then put a fourth on the bed. He waited a beat. "Jonathan, try to picture it. Up here." He tapped his own temple, then the child's, and waited for what felt like forever.

"He cut a piece of that thing." He held his hands six inches apart, which Charlie interpreted as length."

"What thing? Do you know what it's called?"

Before Charlie could press him further, Jonathan scurried across the room and looked, perplexed at the plate into which Bill Smith's oxygen tube had been attached. When he spotted tubing, coiled and hung from a bracket, he pointed at the stand. "Her oxygen line?" Charlie asked.

"No. There's this bag thing. It hangs. Then this other thing goes into her."

"A plastic tube? Like Mr. D had?" He bobbed his head. "He cut the tube?"

"Yeah. After he stuck it with something. *Then* he touched it a lot. Then he had some tube in his hand."

"Then what happened?"

"He put Gram on the floor. Gram just kept staring at him."

"Did she move? Say anything?"

"It was like she was stiff."

"Do you know what that something is called? That thing he stuck the tube with?"

He shrugged. "That doctor thing."

"Then you've seen it before?"

He groaned. "Yeah! I hate it. It hurts so bad. I got really, really, really sick. Mommy took me to the doctor. He stuck me in the butt with this really big thing. It was like that."

"And you saw all this? How could you see it? Were you still in the closet?"

"The door has little pieces of wood. There's a piece. Then there's nothing. A piece, and then nothing. I got down on the floor. I looked through the nothing places. I hid a very, very, very long time."

"Jonathan, where is the thing that rolled under Gram's bed? Where did you put it?"

He hung his head again, studying his sneakers. He wiggled his toes, seemingly transfixed by their movement.

Charlie had to force himself to be patient—to resist the temptation to wring out the facts. Yet he needed every possible detail. And he was so close. Evidently some little screw or small knob, probably inconsequential, had separated from some piece of equipment when Jonathan touched it. Perhaps it was part of the equipment swapped out by the medical supply people. Or something they dropped.

"It's okay. You can tell me. Nobody's going to be mad

at you because you've done nothing wrong. Accidents happen. They can't be helped. Jonathan, where did you put that little thing that rolled under Gram's bed?"

"In the trash—the one with the little white bag. The one where the angel put stuff—and that thing that got dropped."

"The tube? The angel put the tube in the waste paper basket?"

"Yeah. Something—" He started to cry again. "I had to walk around Gram. She was staring up at the ceiling. She wouldn't look at me. I was so scared."

"Where was the angel?"

"He flew away."

"When?"

"When I was in the closet."

Charlie slumped. That poor little kid. What he had seen would be upsetting enough for a grownup. And the evidence? All of this happened months ago. Household garbage would be in some landfill. Wait—surely, the police would have taken the bag and its contents.

"I needed my bear!" Jonathan hugged himself, as if crushing an imaginary teddy against his chest, swaying with it for comfort. He cried inconsolably, hiccupping, and wiping his nose on his sleeve. "I was scared someone would find out. Then Mommy would know I killed Gram. That Gram's not in heaven. It's all my fault. I miss her sooo much."

Jonathan smothered his face with his hands and sobbed as only a broken-hearted five-year-old could. Then he looked up imploringly at Charlie. "The angel wouldn't take her. He left her there on the floor. She's not with Mr. D. She's *not*. She's somewhere bad. It's all my fault. And they'll put me in jail."

Charlie scooped the brave little guy into his arms and held him tightly until his wracking subsided. "Jonathan, five-year old children do not go to jail. Ever. Believe me. Besides, you did nothing wrong. God has welcomed Gram into the kingdom. She was a very good person. And God loves kids, right now, every minute. He understands just how good you are and that you did not hurt your gram. I want you to try to understand something that's very grown up. Can you listen to me carefully?"

Jonathan lifted his drenched faced, sniffled, and wiped his eyes on his damp sleeve. He stared at Charlie.

"That angel was not an angel. He was a bad man in white clothes. He bothered your gram, even as she was dying. The police will find him and lock him up so he'll never hurt anyone again. Please believe me. I wouldn't lie to you. Ever. I promise."

Charlie pulled several more tissues from the box, dabbed Jonathan's wet face, then asked him if he knew how to blow. He did. "Let's go into my bathroom and wash our faces and hands." Charlie stiffened his arm and distracted Jonathan by letting him help him traverse the floor. He paused. "One more thing—did the angel see you?"

Jonathan thought a minute, then shrugged. "I was real quiet."

"Did you see his face?"

A long pause, then a little nod yes.

"Would you recognize him if you ever saw him again?"

"Rec? What?"

"Would you know him?"

A frightened nod yes.

"How would you recognize him?"

The child made a V with his index and middle finger and tapped his own face. "He had mean eyes and no hair."

c/o e/o

Charlie prayed he was doing the right thing to wait, suppressing the urge to shout to the world what he had just learned. He'd found the key to Jonathan's torment and, at the same time, a lead, however slim, to Clara Murdock's murderer. But in the end he had to separate facts from imagination and plan how to approach the matter judiciously. Mostly he needed to calm down.

He hoped what he'd learned had been correct, tempting as it was to question Jonathan further. But sooner, or later, the child would have to relate his story to all concerned—his mother, the authorities, and a child psychologist who had experience with this kind of trauma. Charlie feared that by restating what *he* understood the child had been saying, Charlie's verbalization might contaminate the boy's memory. What Jonathan had witnessed had to be pure.

If the circumstances surrounding Clara Murdock's death were exactly as Jonathan described, his grandfather was innocent. Furthermore, Jonathan, who had witnessed the crime, could be in grave danger. Could a five year old have remained completely inert? He doubted it.

The problem was three different issues—Jonathan's psychological health, the grandfather's legal case, and the killer himself. That each issue needed expert handling seemed obvious. Still, Jade needed to know first. Deserved to know. She'd been through so much, and for what? Would she freak out? Push the child over some critical edge? Charlie's gut feelings re-emphasized the depth of her love for her child. *The truth will set you free*—did that wisdom apply to children as young as five going on six? He had to risk it.

He shuddered, his heart doing extra thuds whenever he imagined the killer. The implication he had previously overlooked, in his preoccupation with Jonathan's confession, now horrified him. Jonathan quoted him as saying, "I'm the death angel." It dawned on Charlie that what he probably said was, "I am the angel of death." He didn't dare suggest that to Jonathan, however, because that might change his story.

Was it possible that this man, whoever he was, had actually entered through the patio door for the express purpose of murdering Clara Murdock? Charlie's mind spewed possibilities. How had he known she was there? Alone, even briefly? Incapable of summoning help? And accessible through a back door? Why hadn't the neighbors reported a stranger? Didn't Clara Murdock's equipment look different to the family? Charlie's imagination hit overdrive.

If the man in white did put Clara Murdock on the floor, did he think she was already dead? Why did he leave, unless he had no business being there in the first place? If his visit was official, then why not call nine-one-one? Perhaps he was a medical worker and for personal reasons, did not want to get involved. Maybe he had a past...

Enter Robert Murdock. According to the newspaper accounts, he swore that he'd found her on the floor, unresponsive. That corresponded with Jonathan's story and accounted for the bedrail being raised. Jonathan made no mention of his grandfather's presence or how or when he'd left the house. Murdock said he'd tried CPR, for which he had no training. He'd been afraid to give up the effort for even the minute it would take to run to the phone. None had been present in the former dining room, and the kitchen and bedroom phones were tethered landlines. He admitted he might have been too aggressive, which would account for her fragile ribs breaking. So many questions. An intruder made sense.

⊘⊘⊘

The child had finally trotted off, seemingly calmed, after Charlie distracted him with a games of Go Fish. He'd sit with his grandpa for a while, then have dinner with his mom in the canteen.

The minute Jonathan left, Charlie grabbed a tablet and pencil and sketched a two-column chart. In simple phrases, he listed precisely what Jonathan had said, then beside it, how he had said it, including his gestures. Leaving blank space between each notation, he inserted details as he reviewed the timeline. Rather than being left for later with a fuzzy overall impression, he concentrated on what Jonathan had said, including his own remarks. And he tried to faithfully reproduce Jonathan's specific choice of words.

Charlie thumped his forehead with the heel of his hand. Why hadn't he asked the child what became of the bag in the waste paper basket? No, that was silly. That wouldn't matter months later. Even if the bag hadn't been discarded immediately, anything injected into the line would have degraded by now. Flipping the paper, he started a list of unanswered questions. After reviewing everything that he'd written until his mind felt empty, he folded the paper into a small packet and slipped it into his pocket.

He paused. Thought. Something else was bothering him. A memory triggered by the child's story, which sounded vaguely familiar. A big man. All in white. Death angel. Angel of Death? No, it couldn't be—

Time crawled. The ward's evening routine was accomplished with pinpoint precision as staff distributed meds, snacks, and made final medical rounds. Soon curious ears would go home.

The familiar hush settled. Charlie longed for the lost companionship that his roommates' deaths had left. Strange, he thought. In the fifteen years since his Emma's death, he had grown comfortable with his own company. Their home cocooned him, and his daily routine kept him busy. He'd had part-time jobs, which gave him plenty of contact with people. That was the thing about sales—he could enjoy others without getting chummy. He and Emma had rarely done restaurants, and he quickly tired of takeout and deli. He had tackled home cooking, trying to duplicate her specialties. He ate all that leafy green stuff she'd promoted, including what he'd resisted. He tended her roses and even entered one perfect bloom in a local competition. Roses—now there was a time hog, but one that he welcomed. Best of all, the endless line of divorcees and singles, who tried to tempt him with casseroles and cleavage, had stopped.

If, make that when, he got out of here, he would reload his life with new friends, especially families with children. What had started as a desire to help little Jonathan was paying him back several fold with the pleasure of his company. Their eventual parting was a reality he could not yet face. When Jonathan's grandfather passed, and that might be soon, there would be no reason for Jade to bring Jonathan to the VA, unless—

The thought of Jonathan leaving the safety of the VA with a killer out there chilled Charlie. Did the killer know that a child had been watching? Would that thrill a sociopath? The killer should feel safe—why would anyone believe such a small child? If there were a way to protect the little fellow, Charlie would find it. And that meant unmasking the angel of death.

The clock finally clicked the anticipated time. Opting for his wheelchair instead of the walker, Charlie seated himself and disengaged the brakes. Silently he glided toward the day room. Jade wasn't there. He tried the kitchenette, thinking she might be having a snack. She wasn't there either. What if, of all nights, she had gone home? What if she couldn't get a sitter but couldn't bring him here either? Could the two of them be alone and vulnerable in the very home where Clara had died? Finally, he approached Murdock's room. The door was closed. He looked left; right, then eased the door open, just enough for a peek. Jade was curled, sound asleep, in the recliner. A red, white and blue afghan wrapped her slight form, the recliner's overstuffed arm supporting her head.

"Jade?" She didn't respond. He rolled a few feet into the room and tried again, but she was dead to the world. He hesitated, uncertain how to proceed then made a decision. Reaching behind him, he pushed the door shut, then wheeled all the way into the room, stopping parallel to the side of her chair. Gently he touched her arm, giving it a tiny shake. "Jade?"

She jerked to attention, focused on him, then shot a reflexive glance at her father. Satisfied that he was still breathing, she squinted at Charlie. "What's wrong?"

"I've got to talk to you. I've learned something important that could make all the difference in your family's life, depending upon how you handle the information. It's complicated, but very important. Can you come with me now? To one of the lounges where we can talk privately? I don't want anyone overhearing what I have to say, including your father."

"What is it?" Jade demanded. Fright, dread, panic—Charlie felt her emotions reflected in her face. "Jonathan! Has something happened to him? Has my minister tried to reach me? Why didn't someone come get me? Why—

Charlie touched her shoulder gently. "Jade. Please. Slow down. Nothing has happened to Jonathan. I'm sure he's okay. But I need to share with you what he said. Can we go down to the lounge?"

With one more furtive glance at her father, Jade rose and opened the door. "Sure. Let's go."

They traveled the short distance through connecting corridors in silence. The lounge was deserted, patients being in bed, their loved ones resting nearby or at home. Charlie chose a leather loveseat and motioned for her to sit next to him, where he wouldn't be overheard.

Groggy and disoriented, Jade blinked anxiously at him while rubbing her eyes. She shivered.

"Jade, I know what's bothering Jonathan. I had tried unsuccessfully with several approaches, but then, when I least expected it, he unburdened himself. I hardly expected what he had to say. Children can get such mistaken ideas."

Jade stared, huge eyes glued to his face. Charlie dug the folded yellow tablet paper out of his pocket. Its surface was smooth from excessive handling and beginning to split at the creases. He opened it with shaky hands. "I wrote everything down, as faithfully as I could remember how he said it." He cleared the catch from his throat. "His first utterance that caught my attention was one simple sentence. I thought he said, 'I killed my gram.' Since that day, I've tried to clarify his words without spooking him—to understand what he meant."

"But why? Why would he say such a thing?"

"He knew that touching his grandmother's equipment was forbidden and potentially dangerous, right? Evidently, he touched it anyway and some little object rolled onto the floor. He scrambled under her bed to retrieve it then couldn't remember where it belonged."

"And that coincided with her death? Oh, god. I was much too hard on that child. He was an easy target for my frustration. He—"

"Wait! That's not it at all. He was nearly caught by an intruder, whom he described as the 'death angel,' adult translation, I'm guessing to be, the 'angel of death.' He hid and watched a drama unfold that no little child should have witnessed."

Charlie detailed the sequence of her little boy's story, patiently trying to dilute the horror with a level, even voice, as if he were describing a work of fiction. He had no idea what her reaction might be. Would she jump up and yell, rant and rail, demand blood or justice from everyone involved? Instead, she stared, all color drained from her face, hand clamped over her mouth. Charlie panicked, fearing that she might pass out.

In a daze, she finally asked a practical question. "What happened next? I mean, after he told you his story?"

"Of course he cried, but then seemed relieved. As if confession had set something free. I had emphatically insisted there was no way he could be responsible. He seemed, well, calm. Perhaps not convinced, but unburdened. I distracted him with games and stories until he was ready to find you for dinner. Forgive me, Jade, for not coming to you immediately. I sensed he needed a break, and I needed to think." He took a deep breath and stopped talking.

Tears, following earlier tracks, dripped unheeded from her jaw. "My poor little angel," she whispered. "That sweet little child. What kind of monster am I? That he didn't feel he could come to me? To keep such a terrible secret bottled up inside him—"

"You *are* a wonderful mother. And that's why he couldn't tell. You've taught him right from wrong. That there are rules. Little kids aren't told not to play in the street when a truck's bearing down on them for the first time. They've heard it before, many times, when there were no trucks. Rules can be learned far before application is needed. How to be safe, follow instructions, and consider the welfare of others. But little kids make mistakes just as we do. He knew he'd been bad and, in his mind, that caused fatal consequences." Charlie groped to underscore his meaning. "Suppose he hadn't cared? Instead of hiding, he had come face to face with a killer?"

Jade clamped her head with both hands, raking her hair. "What if that monster really did see him? What if—" She jumped from the chair, ran toward her father's room while Charlie wheeled after her. She lunged for her jacket. "I've got to go, make sure my baby is safe."

"Jade, wait! Just hold up a minute. Let's make a plan."

She stopped struggling into her jacket to listen, shifting her weight in agitation from foot to foot.

"Let's call the police," Charlie said. "Insist that they watch the house or wherever Jonathan's staying. And tomorrow, let's get a detective involved."

"They won't give a rat's ass—"

Charlie held up his hand. "I understand. They've been awful to you in the past. But they've got to listen to me. I have absolutely no standing in what happened to your family and nothing to gain by telling my story. I'm a neutral witness. They cannot ignore me."

She expunged a heart-felt sigh. "All right. Bring 'em on. I'll do battle one more time. I'll battle forever to save my son."

"Does your minister's house have a security system?"

She calmed somewhat. "A pair of loyal Dobermen."

He extended his arms and she buried her face into his hug. Backing up, he rummaged in his pockets for tissues then gave them to her. "I know you're upset, and for that reason, be extra vigilant driving home. Keep your eyes on the road. Focus. Okay?" She nodded agreement then rushed toward the elevator.

ᖇᑎᖇᑎ

A complication. An unnecessary, self-indulgent complication. That's what the kid had become. What to do? Les pictured various scenarios that would rectify the situation—permanently—and drummed itchy fingers on the stolen black SUV's steering wheel while scoffing at the last traces of ambivalent feelings.

A scared-witless witness—Les savored the alliteration, tasting it with soulless pleasure. From personal observation, the killer knew that the kid couldn't talk, wouldn't talk. Or would he? Les's experience had only heightened the uptick in absolute power over life and death by shocking the little witness. But now, the kid was seen, coming and going with that old vet. Was that patient becoming a threat? Huh! He was perfect—Alone.

And now, might the kid speak? Even one utterance might breech the dam.

Les weighted the possibilities. A, who would believe a small kid if he did? And B, what if he was believed? Relocating again was just too much bother. And the opportunities here were seemingly endless. Especially if that back-office idiot kept forgetting to log-off after updating her records. She should bless Les for covering her transgressions after—of course—Les digested or changed what furthered the agenda. That employee would never know. And her supervisor? Clueless.

Les smiled, decision obvious, remembering the donkey that starved between two bales of hay because he couldn't make a decision. Pick and stick. Loose ends must be snipped.

Les maneuvered the black Explorer through the VA's parking lot maze, selecting a spot between two pickup trucks, and backed in to obscure the muddy license plate. Second and third shifts would be swapping slots shortly.

Les waited. Nodded. Dozed, just a moment, then bolted upright, head hitting the roof of the Explorer. Damn! How did the mother and her kid get into their car without being seen? Les had been wool gathering, succumbing to mind games, and giving free reign to imagination. But picturing, pre-living the tiniest detail with expert precision, was a necessary component of a successful outcome.

As the mother's old Caddie pulled from its spot, Les focused intently. Count the bodies. Driver, of course. The kid? Was he there? That damn car seat was simply too tall, its rigid back blocking any view of the boy. He had to be there—she toted him everywhere like designer luggage. The way movie stars dragged small dogs in satchels that cost more than some people's paychecks.

Les eased the Explorer from between the two trucks and followed the Caddie at a safe distance. Within ten miles, Les would resolve the witness problem—permanently.

Chapter 11

Jade gunned her dad's ancient car from the VA's visitor lot and aimed it toward home. Her mind ricocheted the horror of what her child had held in his mind—in his heart. Angrily, she swiped at tears, cursing herself for being so oblivious to Jonathan's plight. Why hadn't she realized how upset he had become? No trouble? Hell, she'd hardly noticed when he had stopped speaking. Where was her mind? Five-year-olds simply aren't mute. That he'd talk again when he was ready? Whose lame advice had that been?

Ignoring the speed limit, she pushed the old vehicle on-to the four-lane and tromped on the gas. It hiccupped then caught and grudgingly picked up momentum on the steep grade. Horrible mother. Despicable parent. What gave her the right to raise such a dear little person, letting his life plunge into despair? Not putting his needs before hers? Why had it taken a complete stranger to open her eyes? To save Jonathan from his own mother?

A tormenting thought crept into her mind. Had her ex in-laws been right? Would he be better off sequestered in their privileged world? No! No way! Not going there—

Jade couldn't pinpoint what flagged her attention, penetrating the anguish into which her mind wallowed. Per-haps it was her unconventional trajectory through back alley short cuts, reducing the distance by zigzagging through secondaries. Headlights she'd barely noticed before made every turn with her. What the hell! Testing the theory, she cut through a car wash that was closed for the night. The headlights slowed momentarily then followed, keeping their distance precisely. Terror shot straight through her gut as she confirmed that she was being followed. Flicking glances into the rearview, she registered—a black SUV, two hunched silhouettes. No, one—driver and the passenger's headrest. Cell phone—where was it! Buried in the purse that she'd carelessly tossed into the back seat.

"Damn it to hell!" she cursed, gunning her car toward the highway. The second she cleared the onramp, she forced it to eighty. The SUV kept pace, maintaining the distance. With the expert ability she'd learned as a teenager street dragging with the neighborhood boys, she exited onto a two lane then tromped the pedal to flee down the road. As she approached a traffic light that was already stale orange, she accelerated, buzzing the intersection, as it turned red above her. Fifty, sixty, seventy…

Gas—how much was left? The old Caddie's gauge had died long ago, and its powerful engine slurped gas the way tourists downed Margaritas. She coasted a bit to see if he too would slow down, but he closed the distance in seconds. Closer until all she could see was the windshield. Momentarily transported back in time, she waited until the split second he'd ram her then floored her machine. It rocketed forward, pressing her back in the seat, enveloping the SUV in filthy exhaust.

Red, blue, and white lights burst into her rearview. A cop! She'd be saved by the price of a ticket. She braked, drifting onto the berm as the SUV blew past her, the cop in pursuit. Riveted, she focused on the fleeing vehicle, confirming that it was a new black Ford Explorer. A glimpse of the license revealed a Pennsylvania plate that was briefly illuminated by the cop's headlights. In the split second her intense focus permitted, she caught the first letters and parts of four mud-splattered numerals.

The SUV squealed a hard right at the next intersection, the cop in close pursuit in a better-equipped Crown Victoria. Lights, sirens, all trace of both quickly receded into the night. Jade recited the letters and numbers, over and over, least she forget. Tempted as she was to sit and recoup, she shot a U-turn and backtracked to the highway, continuously flicking nervous glances into the rearview.

Her parents' sad little house, like the neighborhood around it, was a dark yet welcoming sight. She circled what was left of the lawn and, parking around back, rummaged for her house keys. While juggling her purse and various parcels, she dropped her keys in the overgrown weeds. Fearing the light, she crawled through the brush, patting for metal. Finally, she risked a tiny penlight and snatched at the errant keys, raking the mud with her nails.

Inside the house, she called her minister's wife and relished the sweet details of Jonathan's evening. He was just fine, the woman reassured Jade, and was now tucked in bed sound asleep. Jade had vowed to keep her evening's misadventure to herself. In the quietness of her family's home, however, she had begun rationalizing that it was an idiot getting his jollies by scaring her. Maybe from her rocket-like takeoffs the jerk identified what was under the hood—a machine lovingly fine-tuned by a mechanic's devotion to speed.

But responsibility trumped, and she detailed her precarious experience. "I'd feel terrible if I led trouble to you," she finished. "Should I call the police? Come and get Jonathan? Put distance between us?" She hoped she didn't sound too desperate for her friend to say no.

"I promise, we're fine. Tell you what—I'll turn on the downstairs motion detectors."

"What about the dogs?"

"I'll tell them to guard—park 'em at the top of the stairs by the boys' door. They're trained to identify breaking glass, windows being lifted, doors being jimmied. And of course they'll react to strangers. If they run downstairs, they'll set off the motion detectors. Besides the racket, no intruder in his right mind would stick around when confronted by a Doberman let alone two."

"This is asking so much—"

"Come on, Jade. You'd do it for me. Now, turn on your floods—lighting's a great deterrent—and get some sleep."

"Thought I'd turn on all the lights—"

"No! Fish in a bowl. Just the floods. Then pull all the curtains and shades."

"For a minister's wife, you're pretty paranoid."

"Before seminary, he was a uniformed police officer. Why don't you come over here?"

"I've gotta stay here in case Hospice calls. And I need stuff for tomorrow."

"Call. Or just come over. Whenever or whatever works."

"Thanks, Marge. I'll never forget this."

Weary, exhausted, unable to sort any further possibility of lurking danger, she flipped on the four-corner floodlights, tested every window and door lock, then drew all the curtains and shades. The floods penetrated the home's interior sufficiently for her to inch through the house. By the refrigerator's light, she found leftover ham spread and a half-quart of milk. Then she pulled a box of stale crackers and peanut butter from an overhead cupboard. Standing at the sink, she chewed and gulped as she thought about what she could use as a weapon. Knives? No—he'd turn that on her.

Threading her way through her father's garage, which was crammed waist-high with spare car parts and junk, she located his baseball bat in its customary spot. Too tired and afraid of being caught naked, she passed on a shower and opted instead to watch and wait in her father's recliner. With one hand firmly grasping the bat and the other supporting its opposite end, she settled.

Suddenly headlights pierced the drapery, but by the time she had scrambled to peer through a crack, the car had completed its maneuver and backed into the opposing driveway. She resettled, and another half hour passed. A scream! What was that? Again, she scrambled to peek out the window. A cat-skunk fight and, judging from the pungent odor that soon permeated every crack in the house, the skunk had won. Annoyed beyond reason by her paranoia, she forced her eyes closed. She slept dreamlessly until the bat clattered onto the scared hardwood floor the following morning.

ⅇ∕ঌⅇ∕ঌ

Jade had overslept in spite of her fears. Jolted awake by the noise and the sunlight that streamed through the flimsy curtains, she jumped from the recliner, her cramped muscles screaming in protest. Limping through the house while casting wary glances into each room, she threw herself into the shower. After five restorative minutes of hot water and lather, she invested two more blow drying her hair. Naked, she pawed through her dresser for what passed for clean laundry. Wash! She had to find time. Tugging on yesterday's jeans and throwing on a fresh tee, she shoved her feet into her sandals and grabbed her tote. From Jonathan's room she added fresh Batman jockeys, jeans, and a tee, pausing momentarily to absorb the wear on his second-hand clothes. The Goodwill—maybe she'd find him new clothes. Caring people often donated outfits on which still hung the original tags. Presents, she'd guessed, from distant grandparents, having forgotten how fast children grow.

"I'd buy you the sun, moon, and stars if I could afford it," she had once said to her son as they explored bargain bins.

"Mommy! Where would I put them? My closet's too small!" Remembering, she smiled. This morning, she'd take him to I-Hop for his favorite breakfast, after which they would hide at the VA.

Later, as the elevator stopped and opened onto Hos-

pice's floor, Jade reached for Jonathan's hand. He acquiesced, and the pair proceeded toward Robert Murdock's
room. Ever expecting the worst, in spite of no calls in the
night, Jade paused at the nurses' station. Having learned
that no change had occurred in her absence, she led Jonathan into his grandfather's room. The old man brightened at
the sight of his family. "Grandpa!" Jonathan shrieked,
throwing himself onto Murdock's bed and into his arms.

"Jonathan. Be careful," Jade began, but quickly responded to her father's nonverbal warning. Ruefully, she
recalled her similar admonishments when her mother was
still alive. She hated herself for the things she had said and
could not take back.

"Can I go say good morning to Mr. Charlie?"

"Sure. But if he's not in his room, check back with me
before going anywhere else."

"Sit, daughter. Newspaper's here, on the chair. How
about reading the sports page to me?"

Jade pulled the armchair closer to the bed. As she riffled past the National section and was about to bypass the
Local, a headline jumped off the page. *Police Officer Slain
in Routine Traffic Stop*. Beside the story, a little map
showed the exact location where the police cruiser had followed the black SUV that had tailed her for miles not
twelve hours ago. Speed reading the article, she realized the
time exactly matched her near rendezvous with—what? The
article ended with a plea for witnesses and a phone number.

"Jade, what's wrong?" Murdock asked as his daughter
jumped from her chair.

"Gotta make a call. Go somewhere that cell phones are
allowed."

"You can use this phone—Jade? Jade?"

∽∾∽

If anger had color, Charlie knew it to be red. But what

color was grudging acquiescence? It had to be gray. The detective's expression exuded it, as did his conservative suit and somber tie. Even his faded socks were an unremarkable sludge and his polished shoes betrayed wear and tear. None of the visuals, however, equaled his attitude. His face betrayed no reaction as he jotted the partial plate number Jade had recorded from the previous evening and phoned in response to the newspaper plea about the cop killing.

Charlie seized the opportunity to detail the new information about Clara Murdock's murder. That the detective was disinterested shocked Charlie. His conclusion? That this new information, considering the source, would be unreliable. Charlie watched Jade's face redden, as she received neither thanks nor satisfaction for the information they had just shared. Eyes narrowed, her expression said *screw you*. And to Charlie, *go figure*.

Charlie and Jade had met with him under an ancient maple tree's welcoming shade. Even at eleven in the morning, the grounds had warmed quickly, and a late summer scorcher was in the offing. The garden's serenity belied the serious nature of their meeting. The detective re-crossed his legs and glanced at his watch, making no effort to hide his impatience. When he pocketed his small spiral notebook and pen, his message clearly stated that anything further was inconsequential.

"Hey!" Charlie staccatoed, his imperative startling even himself. "Without notes, how can you discuss the facts with the DA? Or, having gone so far out on a limb to accuse Robert Murdock, that now you can't consider a different scenario? You're dismissing the source because it's one scared little boy, his angry mother, and a sympathetic veteran? Do you think Mr. Murdock's death will make this all go away?"

Charlie angled his wheelchair to face the bench where Jade and the detective sat on opposite ends, refusing eye contact with each other. The veteran's protruding feet would bump the detective's shins if he moved an iota. "Listen up!" Charlie barked in military fashion as he unfolded his cryptic notes on which he concentrated as if with fresh eyes. While a cardinal sang incongruously nearby, Charlie reiterated every detail that Jonathan had said. In the silence that followed, he scrutinized his notes for anything that he might have missed.

Concluding, he leveled the detective with narrowed eyes, anticipating the obvious objections. He added preemptively, "I have no vested interest in this matter. I am an accidental witness. Prior to landing in the VA, I never met any of these people. Never read about the Murdock case, never heard it discussed. I'm not bored. And I certainly am not confused!" He paused, palms up, in supplication.

The detective finally spoke, his voice steady, words measured, tone neutral. "Has it occurred to you that this little boy wants to believe what he told you? That his story is a product of an overactive imagination? Or that he made it up out of guilt for his actions? Or love for his grandfather? Or an idea he got from TV?"

"No, sir! I am a father who raised little children. This boy, only five, is much too young to construct such a complicated story. And there are details he couldn't possibly know unless he witnessed the scene unfold with his undivided attention. Such as how Mrs. Murdock got onto the floor without lowering the rails or disturbing the sheets. And what came next in logical order."

"Ms. Kepley, did you or anyone else discuss your mother's death or your father's...ah...situation in front of the boy?"

"Never! He's too little. I had to protect him, have all his life. If he understood the ugliness of it all, he could be scared for life. We don't have cable TV, and the news is off limits."

Charlie chuckled, breaking the tension. "Of course, your entire police machinery would look incompetent, unless, of course, you 'discover' the truth yourself." He grinned. "Murdock was innocent all along. But you can take credit for proving that. You and your fellow officers."

The detective reddened. "That's ridiculous! And hardly procedure. We go where the evidence takes us."

"To the wrong conclusion," Charlie snapped. "To one traumatized little boy and the imminent death of this woman's father. Nobody's blaming you personally. A clever sociopath outwitted everyone, only to be exposed by a five-year-old child."

The detective sighed, regaining his composure. "Okay. Let me discuss your version of the events with my supervisor. Ma'am, we'll need to interview your boy."

"And traumatize him further? Can't you just take Mr. Alderfer's statement?"

The detective shook his head. "That would be *hearsay*, which is not admissible in court. We have experts who know how to talk with young children in a non-threatening manner. You can meet our child psychologist first, and if you're comfortable with her, we'll proceed."

"So you believe us?" Charlie asked.

His demeanor revealed nothing. "I'll talk with my superiors."

"Make sure he or she grasps the implication of Jonathan's story. It's not just about the boy and the Murdocks. There's a killer out there, harming frail people who are incapable of defending themselves."

Charlie rolled backward to let the man rise. As the detective strode purposefully toward the parking lot, Charlie thought of unanswered questions. Did the grandmother address her killer by name? Did Jonathan hear anything else she said to the angel? Had there been strange cars in the neighborhood? Or strange noises, like equipment? Did the killer have scars or tattoos?

Jade offered to push Charlie's chair back to the ward, but Charlie declined. He needed to sit outside for a while and breathe the fresh air. On that particular day, he longed to distance himself from any trace scent of Hospice.

The morning's newspaper that someone had left folded

on the bench caught his eye. He'd read the local page first and of course, the comics. Retrieving it, he separated the sections. As he was about to set the local section aside, the lead story grabbed his attention: *Police Officer Slain During Routine Traffic Stop.* He scowled, read further, absorbing the scant details that had caught Jade's attention. A twenty-eight-year-old police officer was shot and killed while attempting to ticket a motorist for a moving violation around 9:30 the previous evening. The officer had approached the vehicle that had been pulled over on the berm after ascertaining that it had been reported stolen. The vehicle, a black SUV with dark-tinted glass, fled the scene before backup arrived. Further details were unavailable as of press time. An investigation is ongoing. Potential witnesses are asked to call…

૯⁄ᕱ૯⁄ᕱ

Elsabet Bentz hardly expected such prompt service from the Limerick Bureau of Investigations, but was relieved that she'd soon have some answers about the home health care provider whom she had hired without checking his references. Having been alerted by the code words, *call your doctor's office*, she fumbled with the prepaid phone card she'd been instructed to buy. John Limerick picked up the phone on the second ring. Sun blazed cruelly through the phone booth's dirty glass, forcing her to crack the door. No matter. No one was around to eavesdrop. She clamped the phone against her sweaty face while wiping her overheated forehead with an iced spring water bottle.

"Here's what we learned, Ms. Bentz. Benjamin Samuel Clark was born February 2, 1965, to Elsa Tothero Clark and Samuel Paul Clark in Columbus Ohio. He graduated from Ohio State University in 1987 with a bachelor's degree in biology, and from their College of Pharmacy in 1991. An Ohio pharmacy chain then employed him until 1997 at which time he was fired. He was caught 'shorting' narcotic prescriptions—twenty-eight pills instead of thirty—and keeping them for personal use. As a first-time offender, and with no evidence of selling, his attorney brokered a deal for probation and rehab. His family, who were prominent Columbus society, paid the legal expenses and hushed everything up with the proviso that he leave Ohio for places unknown to Columbus gentry.

"He stayed under the radar after that, re-emerging as Benjamin Tothero five years ago. Seems his father was a sports car enthusiast, which whetted his interest in vintage sports cars.

He studied to be an auto mechanic at a vocational technical school in New Jersey then turned up in your community a year later.

"An item of interest. His older brother appears to be the family's golden boy. Star athlete, honors graduate, medical school, and orthopedic residency, now in a posh private practice. You'd think smart parents would know better than to compare one child to another."

Elsabet had forgotten how hot and uncomfortable the phone booth had become. She opened the door farther to admit fresh air while her mind formed pictures of Ben's former life. "Is there any history of violent behavior?"

"No record of other arrests, convictions, nothing. Not that we know of."

"So he's clean?"

"Let's say as far as records go. But there are periods when he disappears."

"If you had to guess, what was he doing?"

"Perhaps he supported himself with odd jobs on a cash basis. He could get by on too little to need to file tax returns. Or he could have been out of the country. If you want my firm to investigate further, we could research his movements to fill in the blanks."

Elsabet sighed. "Let me get back to you about that."

"I understand. I'm sure you need to weigh the cost versus the benefit. We can work something out, if that's your concern. We also could provide a bodyguard, but dismissing him and hiring a nurse would probably be cheaper."

"I need to think." Unable to make a decision, she asked the obvious. "Should I confront him?"

"No! Don't do that."

She startled. "Why not?"

"If he has a criminal agenda, that could trigger…well, unwanted behavior. But that's a worst-case scenario, and forewarned is forearmed. If he'll do for the moment, that will buy time to discretely research a replacement. And, when you find the right person, have a believable excuse ready, such as a need for more advanced care."

"I wanted so badly for this to work."

"Well, it might just do that. Who knows—maybe someday he'll tell you his story. If he lies, you'll know it. Just don't ask leading questions. Humans have a tendency to fill in the gaps in conversation, so just let him run. As he learns to trust you and your husband, perhaps he'll open up."

"What about the drugs?"

"Two suggestions. Both of you should be alert for buzzed behavior. And check the quantities of your husband's meds."

As she drove to work, Elsabet admitted that she had another problem. Her husband knew nothing about John Limerick, and he was the one at Ben's mercy. She hadn't a clue what was best—quit her job and risk losing their home, take a second job and hire skilled care, or maintain the status quo. When did life get so tough? Did this guy have a hidden agenda? And what of his missing years?

More to the point—could he hurt her husband? She had to tell him—then let him decide.

Chapter 12

Charlie wanted to look as alert, professional, and competent as possible to project a believable impression, even though the child psychologist would not be interviewing him. From his metal closet, he chose red and green plaid trousers and a short-sleeved hunter green polo shirt, and matching green socks. Taking the metal grabber, with which he'd been practicing picking up dimes, he slipped the top edge of his sock between the pinchers. Extending the handle, he positioned the sock over his toes and wiggled them into the sock. Repositioning the grabber at the cuff, he yanked the sock into place. Perfect. He repeated the procedure with sock number two, then pushed into new black leather walking shoes. With the grabber, he velcroed each strap into place. Was he allowed to bend double at the waist to accomplish this task with his hands? He'd have to ask, but his inventive mind could almost hear his aneurysm protesting.

Jonathan and Jade showed up right on time. "You ready?" she asked.

"Let's motivate."

"What's that?" Jonathan asked. The adults grinned over his head.

Stepping briskly, Charlie glided his walker's wheels down the hall, hands near the brakes, just in case. Jonathan rested his hand on Charlie's right forearm, and the trio traversed the entire length of the hall in synchronized steps. They turned right and entered the dayroom. Sunlight spilled through the window-walls where Jonathan used to pretend he was a bird. He'd told Charlie he was too busy now.

The child psychologist was waiting for them. Dr. Kaye was short and plump with graying hair scooped into a bun. She radiated the aura of the kindergarten teacher that she had once been before her PhD and expanded profession. Now in private practice, she also consulted for the police. Charlie guessed she couldn't be much more than fifty. In his eyes, that made her a young lady.

A low table with several child-sized chairs had been set up for the meeting. Dr. Kaye sat on one side and invited Jonathan to sit at the adjacent end. He looked up at Charlie, as if for permission, and sat when Charlie smiled affirmatively.

"Should we stay?" Jade asked.

"Why don't you have a seat on that couch over there and ignore us. We'll see what works best." Dr. Kaye turned her attention to her little client. Without explanation, she set a large leather portfolio on the table. Set on its side, she opened the zipper. Jonathan watched.

"Guess what I have in my valise?" she began.

He shrugged, palms up, but watched intently as if something magical would spring from its depth.

"Da, da!" She extracted a huge box of new crayons and slit the perforations with her thumbnail. Positioning the box to face him, she flipped open the lid. His eyes widened at the sight of so many colors. While he eyeballed the possibilities, she took out an eleven-by-fourteen-inch piece of white construction paper and a roll of blue painter's tape. She positioned the paper in front of him and anchored its corners with the tape.

"There. Now the paper won't wiggle around. You can draw with any colors you like. Which one would you like to try first?"

His eyes slid up and down every row, finally lighting

on a bright yellow. With surprising care, he wiggled it out of the box. "Mommy says you have to be careful not to break big boy crayons so they last a long time. I like big boy crayons. The fat ones are too hard to use."

"Your mommy says you like to draw pictures that tell a story. Could you draw me a happy picture? Use any colors you wish."

He studied the ceiling, considering, then went to work. He seemed lost in thought, tongue clamped between his lips, absorbed in his creation. Finally, he looked up.

"That's beautiful," she said with genuine admiration in her voice. For such a little guy his attention span, detail, and use of color were excellent. "Who are these people?"

He pointed to the largest one, who dominated one third of the page. Her head was a huge circle compared to her body, outlined with silvery loops. A brilliant red smile connected her ears. Purple curlicues dangled from each lobe. "That's my gram."

"And her? Is that your mom?"

"No. That's me. I'm a boy." A smaller figure, also all head, had straight yellow lines where hair should be. His smile was equally broad, but his mouth was pale salmon.

Dr. Kaye pointed to the flat surface with legs—obviously a table—that was drawn with three different browns. A curved green line on its surface held large tan circles with smaller black dots. "And this is…"

He shot her a grin. "We're baking cookies. They're chocolate chip." He glanced over at his mom then cupped his hand to his mouth. "It's a secret. Gram saves some of the chocolate chips and I eat them. We play a game. She pretends she doesn't know there's some left. Then she looks in the bag. She says we must have used them all up." He put his hand over his mouth to stifle a giggle.

"That does sound happy."

His smile slipping away by degrees, he lowered his head. He picked at the paper sheath covering the last crayon that he'd used. "We can't bake cookies any more. She got sick. Then she died."

Dr. Kaye touched his hand with the softest flick. He raised his eyes. "Does that make you sad?"

He bobbed his head yes.

"Can you draw me a picture of what makes you sad? It's okay if you don't want to. That's a pretty hard thing for a five-year-old child."

"But I'm almost six." Jonathan was so still for a minute that the adults must have all shared the same thought: this is not going to work.

"How about a new piece of paper? If you'll draw me another picture..." Dr. Kaye paused for a minute to dig a Sharpie out of her bag. "I bet you'd like to use this box of crayons whenever I come to visit. And when we've drawn all our pictures, you may keep them. But for now..." She took the Sharpie, closed the crayon box and wrote the letter J. "Can you help me spell your name? Then I'll know which box is yours."

"J..."

She wrote as he dictated.

"O...N...A...H...A...N."

She left enough space in between. "Does that look right?"

He screwed up his face in concentration. "You forgot the one that looks like our roof."

"Where does it go?"

He pointed. She printed a T. "Like that?"

"Yeah!"

She taped a fresh piece of paper in front of him. "Do you think you can draw me a sad picture now?"

With a solemn face, he selected a gray crayon and drew an elongated U that nearly touched the bottom of the page. A small head attached to a small body lay horizontally across the base of the U. He drew dark gray, not silver, curls and huge blue circles for eyes and an upside down U for a mouth. Then he moved on to the other side of the page. In black, he drew a small head, a huge body, and huge feet.

Then he took a white crayon and scribbled all over the figure. The drawing had no hair, big red circles for eyes and an upside down U for a mouth.

"Wow. You're a wonderful artist. Can you tell me about your picture?"

"That's my gram. She's very sick."

"And who's this?"

He hesitated, as if frozen in place. Finally, he got down from his chair and approached Dr. Kaye shyly.

"It's okay, Jonathan. You can whisper it if you like." She bent to his level, cupping her ear with her hand.

His breath tickled as he hissed his secret. "That's the death angel."

"And you feel sad because your gram is sick, is that right?"

He shook his head no and started to cry. "He wouldn't take her to heaven. She was a good gram! Why wouldn't he take her? He said that he would."

"He said that?"

Jonathan shook his head in anguish. "He just said that he was the death angel. Three times." He held up three fingers, reaching, almost touching her face.

"When did he say that?"

"Before he stuck that thing in that...that...I don't know what it's called." He buried his face in his hands and sobbed.

"I know something that will make you happy. How would you like to keep this box of crayons? Right now. And..." She dug into her valise. "I brought you a sketch pad. You can keep that as well. And..." Another dip into her bag. "Your very own bag to keep everything in."

The bag was bright red with a Transformer trademark emblem appliquéd on the front.

Somewhere between the crayons and the sketchpad, Jonathan forgot all about being sad. Clutching his new treasures, he scurried over to show Jade his present, as if she didn't already know.

ᑕᔕᑐ

"So you believed him?" the detective asked Dr. Kaye as he debriefed her in detective's conference room.

"I do."

"Could he have been coached?"

"I didn't sense that. At his age, it's unlikely he could have memorized so many details. And he wasn't glancing at his mother or Mr. Alderfer to make sure he was saying it right."

The detective shrugged, unconvinced.

"Look at the pictures. In this happy scene, both heads are large, the people occupying most of the paper. Picturing himself in proportionate size to an adult, and with a large head, means he has good self-esteem. Look at the smiles. What bothers me is that he described this picture in the present tense. I wonder if he'd fully grasps what it means to be dead and that he'll never see his grandmother again.

"I think we're really lucky to get this much information. He could have drawn himself playing ball, or riding in a truck, or swimming. Quality time with his grandmother was the first happy thing that popped into his head. As for a sad picture, it could have been rain. Or a broken toy. Or himself sick in bed.

"Was he told in advance to be thinking about happy and sad things?"

"No. All he was told was that a kindergarten teacher was coming to draw pictures with him. He knows what kindergarten is because he'll be going this fall. I was prepared to have him draw more neutral pictures if he balked at happy and sad. I was practically holding my breath. Look at the detail! This curly line represents his grandmother's IV, complete with the bag. If the *stick* he drew, here, is a hypodermic needle, then this picture represents murder. He had to have seen it."

The detective studied the detail a minute. "The grandmother's eyes—he didn't draw them that big in the first picture. Does that mean anything?"

Dr. Kaye frowned in concentration. "Looks like she's watching him, as if he has her undivided attention. Maybe she's scared or can't blink."

"So she's awake. Not asleep, or in a coma."

"Or already dead."

"And all we've got is the story of a five-year old boy. I wish we had something more tangible."

"Ask that veteran—Charlie Alderfer—if he remembers anything else from Jonathan's original story."

കകക

Charlie's imagination was running wild. He knew it and couldn't control it. First, the suspicious death of his three former roommates, then Jonathan's eyewitness account. Was there a preponderance of medical murderers out there? Were there two people? Or was one serial killer victimizing their community? He dismissed the latter as unlikely—illogical. Unless…what if the killer saw Jonathan that day? And by now knew he came to the VA? Or was he already familiar with Hospice as a flush killing field? What Charlie needed was a stiff drink. He drew, instead, on old wisdom: *Put each problem in its separate compartment. Take them out, one at a time, when you are ready to deal with them.* He needed more information.

Mike's arrival relieved him from agonizing loneliness. Mike's calm, capable demeanor felt like cool lotion on a bad sunburn.

Charlie pounced on him without a preamble. "You attended my three former roommates. I'm puzzled about something that might shed some light. You've seen their records, right? Can *you* track and/or change their status, particularly their meds?"

"Changes originate with the doctors. They are the only ones who can enter those orders."

"What if the technician made a mistake—either intentionally or inadvertently?"

"That would be immediately obvious to the nurse who matches all barcodes before medicating the patient."

Charlie digested that for a moment, imaging the little green pill's odyssey through myriad checkpoints. "So—somebody had to enter bad information into the computer. And if it wasn't the doctor…"

Mike grimaced, shaking his head. "For that to occur, someone needed computer access to change or supplement the order somewhere between the doctor and the pharmacist. That someone would require pharmaceutical training and high-level computer skills."

"Wouldn't the doctor spot the change pretty quickly? The next time he checked?"

"That's point number two. Someone needed a window of opportunity to enter the order."

"Had this happened any time other than the weekend, would you have noticed something was wrong?"

"You? Of course. If not in the specific pill, in your reaction."

"But suppose my situation had changed…"

"When we go on duty, we talk with both charge nurses, going off and on duty, to update our knowledge. And we talk with the nurses assigned to our patients to learn what happened while we weren't here. Then we check the computers. Usually that information overlaps what we just heard, such as a change in their meds. We review their treatment particulars. However, in spite of excellent technology, it's from the people that we learn the nuances—that certain something that can feel different. Guess that's long-term exposure to dying. Sometimes it's what's not being said or something that's missing. Some patients, particularly the men, do not complain. They think whatever's happening to them is normal."

"And me? Would you have noticed?"

"You bet. I know how you feel about being sedated,

would have questioned any new meds, and known your behavior didn't fit your recovery. I'd want to know why."

Charlie digested that for a moment, feeling relieved by Mike's protectiveness. He focused on another puzzle. "To the best of your recollection, what did all three of my roommates have in common? I mean, besides qualifying for Hospice?"

"Two were army vets, one navy—no, marine or national guard."

"Um—Hometown? Duty stations?"

"No match there. They didn't even serve on the same continent. Vincent DePasquali was from New York City. Bill Kelly from Maryland. And your first roommate, Mr. Jones, who died shortly after you woke up, was a Pennsylvanian. Their hometowns and places of birth shared nothing in common. But there is something," Mike added. "None of these men had family who lived in this county. They resided too far away to make visiting easy. I mean, nobody came every day. And none ever stayed overnight at the hospital."

"They had different medical conditions—"

"And their ages varied greatly."

"Mike, could they have been together at one time? Could they have shared a similar experience that involved their killer? Given him a motive to kill all three?"

"If so, nothing comes to mind. And I'm sure it would have come up in conversation. Mr. Jones and Mr. DePasquali were Korean Conflict veterans. Mr. Jones, World War II. Mr. Jones served in Greenland. Mr. DePasquali never left the states."

"So, all they had in common was being veterans and having no family nearby. What about their medical records? Do they have any issues in common that would have been noted on the computer?"

Mike snapped his fingers. "Yeah. DNR—Do Not resuscitate."

"Which means..."

"If they code—stop breathing, have cardiac arrest—let

them go, don't interfere with the natural process. All three were terminal and did not want to be kept alive artificially. Mr. Jones and Mr. DePasquali were particularly adamant about that. While they were too religious to be suicidal, neither wanted to prolong the agony."

"Okay. No family nearby. DNR. What else? What about procedures? Did they have anything in common there?"

"Nothing unusual. There's oxygen for whoever needs it. And pain meds, of course. That's not the same thing as DNR though. That's about comfort, just like the treatments Mr. Jones got from the respiratory therapist."

"Would that be the guy who brought him the mask with the vapor?"

"Right. That's called a Nebulizer. The vapor opens restricted airways to facilitate breathing and loosen congestion. But, Charlie, that's typical for most of our patients at one time or another."

Charlie mulled that over for a minute. "How could a killer snuff these patients quickly and quietly? And why them? How would you do it?"

"Me? If I were a serial medical murderer, I'd inject their IV line."

"Which they all had?"

"They did at some point. See, if I were to inject a person inappropriately and foul play was suspected, the body would be searched for any unexplained puncture marks. If one were found, then the ME—the medical examiner—would order a toxicology screen to find out what's in the blood."

"And they don't check IV lines?"

"Not unless they suspect tampering."

"What happened to these men's IV lines?"

"Immediately after death and the body is removed, the entire area is sterilized, laundry is disinfected, and biological waste is committed to HAZMAT containers for safe disposal."

"I remember. In both Mr. Jones and Vincent's cases, their beds were stripped and the paraphernalia gone by the time I woke up. What else would these people have in common?"

"Me. Other personnel. Food. Supplies. Meds. Equipment..."

Charlie sighed. "But to go undetected. What would you do if you were determined to kill innocent strangers in a hospital setting?"

"Pick patients who were expected to die anyway. No audience or family keeping a continuous vigil. Inject their IV with too much medication of what they're already taking. Or an air bubble. Or something like succinycholine, which paralyzes all muscles and dissipates quickly."

"And nobody checks?"

"This is Hospice. All three of your roommates were expected to pass. Unless someone suspected foul play, there would be no reason to order an autopsy. Oh! Something else they had in common. Each had requested immediate cremation."

"That's pretty convenient. Say—is there any way someone could add that into a person's records to help cover a murderer's tracks?"

"You mean hack into the VA's records?" He shrugged. "I kind of doubt it. We've been on high alert and have undergone intensive re-training since someone lost a laptop at another VA. It contained patient records. No harm came of it that I know of, but the aftermath was intense."

"What about an employee?"

Mike raised his eyebrows and shrugged. "I guess. We do have computer specialists who work in IT—Information Technology. And there's a secure department where specialists with appropriate clearance manage computerized patient records. But those people are scrupulously screened, their work supervised, and their office doors are swipe-locked. It's possible that someone, besides the doctor, could have access. But, Charlie, that person's knowledge would have to be..." He held his hand as far as he could reach.

"Oh, brother. This is far more complicated than I imagined."

∽∾∽

A reverent hush cocooned the nocturnal ward. Jade settled into Charlie's guest chair for what had become their nightly chat. They talked about everything and nothing at all.

"How's your dad doing?"

"About the same. He's asleep. It's strange—my brain knows he's terminal and that death is inevitable, yet I keep hoping for intervention. That someone can treat him or that I'll simply wake up. That everything's been an elaborate nightmare and it's still this time last year." A nurse bustled by, responding to a nearby room where a patient's call light strobed in the hall. Then the corridor fell silent again.

"And our little guy?"

She nodded in the affirmative, face grim, but did not elaborate. "What's wrong, Charlie? You look awful. Did the doctors give you bad news?"

"Nothing like that. I'm wrestling with personal demons." He dropped his voice to barely a whisper, even though the other two beds were unoccupied. "And I have to make a decision—to choose the right course of action over what's easy. Then make a plan."

Jade scowled. "I don't like how that sounds."

"I don't want to scare you..."

"Come on, Charlie. I'm tough. Spit it out."

He took a deep breath. "I am convinced that a killer is working this very room. And, in fact, has struck three times." He let that sink in for a beat as Jade's eyes went to slits. "In addition to having several criteria in common, I believe this room is ideally located—it's the farthest room from the nurses' station and next to a stairwell that exits onto a small service lot. That would be empty at night. Easy in, easy out. I've made a decision. If there's a chance this madman might return, I've got to catch him."

"That's crazy! Why on earth would you attempt that? If you're afraid—"

Ignoring her, he plunged on. "The killer couldn't stumble in here blindly. I think he accesses the VA's computer to gather patient information. That would explain how my meds got altered. Maybe I was next on his list, but I foiled his plan."

"Who could do such a thing?"

"An employee, a temp, a vendor, or an outsource professional. Perhaps a hacker who figured out how to move about undetected. A visitor. A loner. A sociopath or someone with a grudge. The killer would have to be diabolically clever to have gone undetected."

"You've got to tell somebody."

He raised his eyebrows and nodded his head with sarcastic exaggeration. "And that has worked for me, how?"

She nodded, acknowledging the obvious. "I suppose we could rule out a terrorist. A terrorist wouldn't be interested in terminal patients. He would do something showy, like burn the place down or gas everyone."

Charlie couldn't help smiling at her use of *we*. He pressed on. "Okay. Let's assume we have a hacker—no, broaden that to anyone with unauthorized access to patient information. He targets terminal patients with the right credentials—no local family, an IV line that can be injected, DNR, and cremation orders. Bedridden, asleep, but conscious. Perhaps other qualities known only to the killer. And he has the capability of changing and reinstating orders."

"You mentioned location."

"That's the key that makes it doable. This room. Right here," Charlie said."

"But—speaking of keys, he'd need one to exit the ward. I can enter by way of the stairs, but need staff to let me back out. That prevents patients from 'wandering,' that is, escaping. He'd need to know, be that familiar, to disable the latch," Jade added.

"Wouldn't he have to know a lot about drugs to interpret patient records? And, if the patients' meds are listed, which ones are injectable?"

Jade snapped her fingers. "A pharmacist! Or someone with pharmaceutical training. That's it! Don't they wear white? Dad's nurses wear colorful garments. He appreciates that because his vision is poor and that helps him tell them apart. But pharmacists—Hold on, Charlie. Where are we going with this? I don't like—"

He held up his hand. "I know what you're thinking. There must be a dozen ways to extricate myself from harm's way. But he'd simply go elsewhere. Keep right on killing. Had it not been for my excellent hearing, he'd have gone undetected. In time, move on to other hospitals, other states. Haven't we heard that hundreds—maybe thousands—of unsolved murders are committed by a handful of serial killers?"

"You are serious, aren't you? This sounds heroic, an adventure, sure-fire cure for boredom while you're all safe and snug in this fortress. Knock! Knock! Reality Check. This could blow up in your face."

"This is not about being heroic. I've had days, weeks, to come to grips with my reality. There's a chance I'm not going to die in the foreseeable future. All my life I've taken pride in pulling my weight. Helped my parents with chores and younger siblings then served my country with pride. Worked hard, paid taxes, married, and raised a wonderful family. Served my church and community. Why? Because my dad always said, 'Service is the price we pay for our space on the planet.' *Taking*, for me, is a repulsive concept. When I leave this institution, I will need..." He groped for a word then choked on the thought. "...social services. There's no way to escape being a burden to my girls and society. Then suddenly this opportunity is dumped in my path. How can I not do what I can?"

"Charlie, by your physical description of this night stalker, you wouldn't stand a chance in a confrontation. Best case scenario, your death might generate publicity for tighter security. Picture this—he grapples with you, kills you, exits via that stairway, slips into the darkness, and vanishes before anyone finds you or identifies him."

"But if I sound the alarm, making a gigantic stink now, that would simply force him to go elsewhere, anywhere, and keep right on killing. I don't want that on my conscience. And don't forget about your father and Jonathan. Your father fits the criteria. *He* could be next."

She frowned. "You're thinking the killer would want to eliminate my dad as a potential witness? Dad wasn't home when Mom died. Besides, my mother's killer verses this maniac—the odds are against them being the same person..." Her voice drifted off. "Anyway, if I'm wrong, time's on the killer's side. Dad could check out any time."

"But Jonathan—how long would our little witness be safe? The challenge with using me as the bait is that I am not actively dying. I'm alert, a light sleeper, and fully capable of screaming for help. Perhaps he knows that."

"Bait?" Jade jumped from her perch. "You are serious!"

"I'll need to check my records. See if they state DNR."

"That's an awful idea. What if—"

"I do have a living will, but the wording says something like *no hope of recovery*; specifically, brain dead."

She frowned. "I suppose that might be enough."

"I've done some snooping. Every other patient has families that are keeping a vigil, mostly keeping irregular schedules. Occupancy is low at the moment. A handful of rooms at the far end of the ward are empty. Other patients have roommates who are alert or awake on and off over twenty-four hours. I'm an especially good target because I'm alone. No family or late-night visitors and I no longer need continuous monitoring. That leaves us with a big challenge: how do we make me an irresistible target?"

She sighed, absently twisting a small sapphire ring that she always wore. "Now I'm an accomplice?"

"I don't have an IV line," he added, feeling inspired. "I'd need an excuse to have one inserted."

"I could do that for you. I did lots of medical stuff for my mom, like drawing blood, injecting drugs, take BP, and checking her temperature. I even know how to use a defibrillator."

"So you could stick a line, say, in my arm and I could cover it up with a long-sleeved shirt except at night when nobody would see it. It would have to be in my left arm since they use my right arm to take my BP."

She laughed. "That's not going to work. You have to shower, change your clothes, wear short-sleeved gym clothes—you couldn't hide that from three shifts of nurses, although I suppose you could tell Mike."

"No! He can't know anything about this. That could jeopardize his entire career. Late in the evening, you could insert it, then I'd take it out first thing in the morning if the killer doesn't show up."

"No good. It could take days, maybe weeks for him to strike. You'd look bruised and battered in no time. Someone would spot that, and fast."

Charlie snapped his fingers. "Suppose you don't really insert it? Just tape it in place? Leave a length of tube visible with that end plug thing showing."

She grinned. "I like it! If he's able to sneak up on you, whatever he injects would be trapped in the line."

"Can you find some tape that doesn't leave marks the way adhesive tape does?"

"I've got just the thing."

"When can we start?"

"Not so fast, Charlie. Suppose he comes into your room. I assume you don't have a weapon. How do you plan to defend yourself, much less subdue him?"

"I need a gun. Do you know anyone who could get one for me?"

She laughed. "If you're serious, I'll make some inquiries—but it's got to be something nonlethal. But please, won't you consider a room by the nurses' station or another heart-to-heart with the doctor?"

He wasn't listening. "Oh! Find out if there are metal detectors at the hospital's entrances. And if I need a concealed carry permit to keep a weapon in here."

"All right. But don't get your hopes up." The smile disappeared from her face, and she lapsed into reflective silence. "You know, for the first time since Mom had her stroke, I feel empowered. It's been hell, not being able to do anything about wave after wave of injustice. Now, if this weren't so dangerous, it would be downright exciting. I feel forward momentum again."

"If I thought they'd believe me, I'd propose that the hospital bring in the police. Let professionals go under cover—literally—and set a trap." He shook his head in answer to what seemed obvious to him. "They don't believe me."

"You'll never know how hard I tried to convince the police that Dad would never hurt Mom. They were each other's whole life. The cops refused to pursue alternative theories." She batted her hand as if to repel a year of horrific images. "And Jonathan's just a bright little kid with an overactive imagination. They implied that Jonathan had the circumstances of Mom's death mixed up with watching our visiting home healthcare workers tend to her needs."

Charlie lifted his eyebrows. "What healthcare workers? What other people tended your mother?"

"There was the team from the medical supply company. They came in pairs, first to set up the bed and other paraphernalia and then to service her oxygen."

"What did they look like?"

"One of each. Rather young. Neither was very tall."

"Was there anyone else?"

"We used nursing aides from a service for her catheter and to bring fresh supplies. They taught me to catheterize her. It's not hard—you just have to be scrupulously clean to prevent infection."

"Did any of them resemble Jonathan's description of his death angel?"

"Mom would have freaked if we'd used a male nurse. We knew that without asking and insisted on women."

"And they could lift her?"

"Those gals were great. One couldn't have been much more than five-five. She works out at a gym. Teaches weight training. Besides, Mom's weight had dwindled to ninety-five pounds."

Charlie sighed then tried a fresh vein. "How did they get into the house?"

"One of us was always there—Dad or myself. We let them in."

"Did anyone have access to the house unescorted? Could someone have taken a key, copied it, then returned it unnoticed? People misplace keys all the time."

"House rule number one—keys go on the hooks in the kitchen. Besides, if Jonathan reported the incident faithfully, the killer came in through the sliding glass door. There is no key. It locks from the inside, and we wedge a wooden bar in the track at night or when we're away."

"But it was unlocked in the daytime?"

She nodded. "Well, sure."

"That still leaves unanswered questions. How did he know she was there? When could he count on her being alone? And how did he approach her undetected?"

Jade formed a T with her hands. "Back up. Hear what we're doing? We keep rolling these cases together. Know what I think? If it's the same killer, and he's transparent here at the hospital, it's just a matter of time until he spots my baby."

"Then you'll help me?"

Jade rubbed the back of her neck then stared out the window into the darkness. "If I can't stop you, okay. But, Charlie? Promise me you won't do anything rash until we work out a plan."

"Or else?"
"Just promise."

Chapter 13

The very next evening Jade returned to Charlie's room. Glancing nervously toward the hall, she reached into a large LL Bean tote.

Charlie strained his excellent ears. "Nobody's coming. What did you find?"

Gingerly she removed a stubby, cylindrical blue object. It looked innocent enough, but he instinctively knew it was some sort of gun. "What is it? And where did you get it?"

"Sorry. Can't say. No worries—it's not hot. Only on loan."

"What if we have to use it? Surely the police will ask questions."

She grinned. "I'll deal with that when the time comes. Besides, Charlie, if we manage to identify this bastard, after the way my family's been treated, I don't think they'll call me on something so minor. You any good with a gun?"

"Well, sure. I am a Vietnam veteran, although I haven't touched one in decades."

"Guess they didn't use stun guns, huh! I learned on the Internet that anyone can order stun guns, tasers, and self-defense nonlethal weapons. So I visited a local dealer who sent me to a creepy-looking character who owed him a favor."

"Did he ask questions?"

"Quite the opposite. He told me that more women would become victims of aggravated assault this year than heart attacks. He showed me stun guns, like you see on cop shows. They generate a high-voltage, low-amperage electrical charge. On the video, which shows the bad guy twitching on the pavement, you can see fine wires that extend from the gun to his body. Trouble is, you get only one shot. Then the wires must be repackaged."

"So your aim must be perfect."

"Every stun gun I considered has a red laser light to fine tune your aim. But yeah, you get just one shot. And for some, you need to be close enough to touch skin. That I do not recommend for obvious reasons. So I brought you this puppy instead."

She handed him the dark blue cylinder. A black handle was folded into place against the barrel. "It shoots up to five pepper-filled projectiles up to forty feet. Just aim the red light at the perp, fire, and it goes bang! He's hit with enough force to knock him back. The projectile's impact releases tear gas and pepper spray." She handed it to him. "Here. As long as the handle is folded against the barrel, it's locked. To unlock it and form the handle, pull it away from the barrel at a ninety-degree angle. When it clicks into position, it's armed and ready to fire."

He took it gingerly from her hand. "Try arming it."

He did, then refolded the handle. "If I keep it under the covers, it can't go off accidentally?"

"That's right. As long as the handle is locked."

"But—where to hide it? I'm in and out of the room all the time, there's staff, housekeeping…"

She rummaged in the tote again. "I've thought of that." She produced a large bible with a leather-like cover. "Charlie, you would just love this store! Check this out. Rather than pages, the interior is an empty box with a magnetic clasp to keep it from flopping open. It's sturdy and quite big enough to conceal a weapon."

Charlie tried it for size. It was perfect. "So, I could pretend to have fallen asleep reading. But what if some helpful soul tries to put it away for me?"

"Wouldn't happen. You won't really be sleeping. If a nurse comes in, you act as if you've awakened, and stow the book yourself. Staff would have to do serious snooping to find it."

"And if they do?"

"You don't need a concealed carry permit for this. I'm sure you could talk your way out if someone gives you a hard time. You did complain about security, right?"

"You've thought of everything. Except what happens after the stunned, pepper-and-tear-gassed killer stumbles into the hall. If I scream for security, how fast could they respond? Or would they assume I was crazy? Could he talk his way out, or escape? Or if armed, shoot lots of people?"

"If it's the same guy, as you suspect, he'll be armed with a lethal drug and not expecting resistance in Hospice. Maybe that's part of the thrill—the risk." She reached into her bottomless bag one more time. "And here…" She tossed him a gasmask. "Small room like this? After five shots, you've got to breathe! Hide this under the covers, too. I've made arrangements for Jonathan. I'll be nearby. And, between one and three a.m., I'll watch your back."

"Are you sure?"

"Hey! You got a better idea? If you're determined, and I can't stop you, I'm in."

"Jade?" She looked up. "An important detail that you've overlooked," he said. "Suppose something happens to you? What would become of Jonathan?"

"Nothing's going to happen to me!"

"But suppose—"

"I've named my minister and his wife as his legal guardians. They'd make sure he was well taken care of. And, having done that legally, nothing will happen. Bad stuff only happens when we're unprepared."

Charlie refrained from countering with the obvious contradictions.

ⁱⁿᵗ

Charlie drank an ocean of coffee and coke, praying he could stay awake that first night. Never one to take naps, especially in advance of needing sleep, he committed to an all-nighter. The next day, he'd catch up on sleep after Mike left at three, then nap after dinner. By eleven, he would be wired for night number two, and so on. Pumped and desperate to pounce, he tried not to think about how many nights this could take. He took a deep breath and another peek into his bible box.

With too much time and nothing to do, uninvited loneliness crept over him. Exactly when Jonathan and Jade had burrowed into his heart, he wasn't certain. But they had. They'd become family, and knowing he could not protect them percolated anxiety deep in his gut. Later that evening, she would be back, having taken her son to her safe place. The thought of them navigating dark streets alone terrified him. Jade was tough, or so it seemed, though he suspected that was veneer.

Charlie had protected Susan and Jeannette, as much by teaching avoidance as self-defense. A home in a safe, rural community; a close-knit church, family, and friends where everyone knew everyone else; enrolling them in conservative colleges; followed by renting apartments in safe neighborhoods when they were ready to fledge. Each knowing help was one phone call away. As young adults, they were already established in the continuum of upper-middle-class safety. Jade, the product of tough neighborhoods and tougher breaks, could turn on the don't-mess-with me attitude in a way that caused others to give her wide berth.

Before she had left, he found himself reciting the same litany he told his daughters about personal safety. Although she had indulged him with gritty impatience, she nevertheless appeared touched. Alone, he faced the grim reality. They could fail miserably. The killing could go on unabated. They could be harmed, or worse, not believed. Jonathan might never be safe. Robert Murdock could go to his grave without being cleared, his wife's death unavenged. "We are not going to fail!" he muttered angrily into the darkness. "We're sending that monster to hell."

ೞೞ

Night number one passed uneventfully. By one p.m. the following afternoon, Charlie fell asleep in a dayroom lounge chair where a gospel music video entertained the patients. At 3:15, following Mike's departure, Charlie hit the sack and didn't stir until Dietary presented his tray. He toyed with his dinner, without really tasting it, then slipped back to sleep. By the time Jade reappeared at ten-thirty, he was awake and alert. Dressed in pajamas, bible in place, he felt that he looked downright normal.

Jade glanced at the clock. "He can't possibly sneak in here until the shift changes. Third shift starts at eleven, but second shifters stay until eleven fifteen. Fresh staff is pretty busy, reviewing patients' status. Then things quiet down."

"Want to play cards for a while?" he asked.

"Never had time to learn." She shrugged. "Unless I can do something extremely well, I don't try."

"Why do you do that to yourself?"

She glanced up at him sheepishly. "That way I can't fail."

"When, and not if, this is all over, what would you like to do with your life, if you don't mind my asking? I mean, besides being a great mom, which you already are."

She smiled at his postscript then grew contemplative. "I think of myself as bound to one station in life. Guess you call that being a fatalist. That it's too late for possibilities. 'If this hadn't happened, I could have done this.' 'If I had chosen better, I could be that.' 'It's too late, I'm too dumb, I've got no training.' My life is one big brick wall. Jonathan is my grace note."

"But you're so young! Have you considered going back to school?"

"Well, yeah. I got good grades, even though I didn't study. But it's out of the question. It's a vicious circle. To get a good job, I need marketable skills. To get them, I need schooling. That takes money for which I need a better job. I couldn't get loans, 'cause I couldn't repay them. Every cent I earn is for Jonathan."

"Could you stay on in your parents' home?"

"That was put up as collateral to pay the money-grubbing attorneys. As soon as Dad's gone, that will have to be sold."

"Pretend the impediments didn't exist. What kind of job would you love doing?"

"When I was a little kid, teachers asked that—you know, where they have you draw a picture of yourself doing whatever—and they'd say you could be anything you want-ed. I'd imagine that I was a nurse. Like the lady in our doc-tor's office. She was sweet and smelled so good, and she made us kids feel so special. That's a big lie, you know. Telling a kid she can be anything she wants if she tries hard enough. An average kid can't be a brain surgeon. A color-blind kid won't be an artist. A tone-deaf kid won't sing opera. A clumsy skater or an awkward swimmer won't go to the Olympics. Hell, most great athletes can't make that team."

"A nurse. Yeah, I can see it. You'd be a good one."

"I'd get canned. I have no patience with idiots."

"You've got more brains and determination than any-one I've met in a long time." He glanced at the clock. "To be continued. Why don't you get some rest? I'm braced for whatever happens tonight. If he shows up, you'll hear me." He glanced at the digital numbers again. "If habit is any in-dicator, that shouldn't happen for hours. Go be with your dad while you can."

"You look pretty perky now."

He grinned. "I'm going to have jetlag for days when

it's over. How's my little buddy? I haven't seen him all day."

"This evening he's having a sleepover at a little friend's house."

"It sounds as if people are treating you better."

She sighed. "People do want to help. Know what one of my neighbors said? 'In order for someone to give, someone else has to receive.'"

"So maybe the whole world isn't out to get you?"

"Maybe."

"The plan for tonight—one more time."

"Are you very sure that you'll recognize him?"

"You bet!"

"Keep the gun under the covers. The closer you let him get, the more likely you'll be able to stun him and the more powerful the strike. You're going to have to—"

"See the whites of his eyes?"

"That would be nice. But, Charlie, watch his hands. I'm guessing he'll have that hypodermic ready, and you can't let him even graze you with it. Whatever poison he's using is bound to be lethal and fast, and we don't know what that will be."

"What if I miss? With the stun gun I mean?"

"You have five shots. Scream bloody murder. I'll tackle him from behind."

"How are you going to do that?"

"The room across the hall is empty—not even made up. No one will kick me out if I crash in there."

"What if—"

"If you're changing your mind—you're not? Then stop it. Nothing's going to go wrong. It can't. Your daughter Susan would have my head on a pike."

"Oh, yeah!"

"Did you tell either of your girls about your plan?"

"You have got to be kidding."

∽∾∽

Charlie riveted his eyes on his door. As time dragged inexorably toward the dying hour, he jumped with anticipation at every footfall that passed the adjacent room or from the stairwell door on his right. Jade had opened and closed that fire door several times until he memorized its machinations. From inside the stairwell, the doorknob made a small clunk as it engaged. Then the door whooshed when it opened into the stairwell, as if releasing a vacuum seal. Then the door would *ka-thunk* back into position when the airbrake pulled it shut. She had practiced trying to open and close it soundlessly, which Charlie's excellent ears could still hear.

Sometimes they played tricks as he picked up noises from way down the hall. Carts, elevators, late night visitors…

Footsteps! Charlie panicked, all trace of bravado gone. Street shoes, drawing closer and closer to his door. Clutching the sheet to his chin with his left hand, he positioned the armed gun with his right. Step. Step. Pause. Over the thrum of his heart, he realized the outsider had paused just to the left of his door. Silence. Then he heard muffled voices, the person responding and reversing direction. A soul in the adjacent room was actively dying, the comings, goings, tears and farewells, a continuum of grief. Death did not keep bankers' hours. Charlie wanted to run out the door and not stop until he reached his own home. He exhaled and, releasing his grip on gun, locked it.

If he could just turn on the TV or his reading light and distract himself with an absorbing book. But lights would disrupt the intricate plan and draw attention from staff. Mentally he practiced the motions of opening the bible, whipping out the stun gun, locking the handle and aiming the laser. The only light in the room came from the hall and the bathroom nightlight. Thank God, he did not have high blood pressure or heart disease, or he would be en route to the morgue.

Much later Jade slipped into his room wearing old

sneakers that made a distinctive squeak, which enabled her to announce herself or approach soundlessly. "You awake?"

"What if the killer targets your father?" Charlie asked without a preamble. "If you're down here, your dad's all alone."

"Not likely to happen. His door is cattycorner from the nurses' station. The killer would be in plain sight. And I did something sneaky—told them I'd spotted a photographer trying to position himself for a tabloid shot. I described a build like Jonathan's angel. I told them I would be out for a few hours and please don't let anybody into his room except staff whom they know. They'll be on the lookout and call the VA police if anyone approaches him."

༄༅༅

As day three melted into four, Charlie's routine got old. Bored and disoriented from his upside down schedule, he caught himself grousing at everyone, in spite of himself. Without proper rest, even routine activities such as PT were exhausting. Meal breaks and snacks took on new importance as the only antidote for lethargy and boredom. He gulped too much coffee, which made him jittery. By the fourth night, he found himself fighting complacency. Why did he ever think this would work? The perp could have moved on to fresh killing fields—out of state, or out of the country for that matter.

Two o'clock in the morning came and went uneventfully. Again. Finally, as the clock approached three and bored out of his skull, he rationalized that if nothing had happened by this time, it wouldn't. Even though he had slept so much during the daytime, he was exhausted. He took the stun gun out of the bible, and with it conveniently placed under the sheet, he slipped farther under the covers.

He'd close his eyes. Just for a minute. He would hear if anyone approached. His mind drifted to his father, his hero, that great hard-working guy who had taught him respect, patriotism, and family devotion. Not with words, but by his actions. Memories of his close-knit family paraded through his mind like a slide show. Soon he was dreaming. He and his dad were tearing apart his very first car's persnickety engine. He saw the old Ford, perched on cinder blocks, wheels somewhere else. Miscellaneous parts strewn about the cracked concrete floor. Along with the clatter of discarded wrenches and screwdrivers, his mind reinvented the grit. The feel. The sounds.

And the smell! His dad had been toiling to loosen a rusted nut from a bolt with—

Charlie's eyes flew open.

Penetrating oil! That was it—the oil that lingered on mechanics' hands. But he could still smell it. Right in his room. He froze, cutting his eyes without moving his body, and immediately saw him, not five feet beyond the foot of his bed. Huge—at least six feet tall. Big shoulders. Barrel chested. Silent as death. The apparition's left arm hung loosely at his side, but his right arm was bent behind his back as if to conceal—what? Charlie's heart leapt into double-time thuds while his body lay rigid, too frightened to move. Wait. He had to wait until the intruder got closer.

But what if? Could this visitor be staff? No! Instinct took over. Inching his hand beneath the voluminous folds of his covers, he felt for the gun. But his fingers touched nothing but sheet. He must have displacing it when he'd turned over. Where could it be?

Charlie jerked when a soothing voice incanted in a high-pitched whisper. "I've come to take you where you've been longing to go."

Panicked, fingers groping, Charlie widened the circles, hoping the intruder's eyes had not fully adjusted to the dark room. There! But the gun's handle was locked securely.

"Are you ready?"

"Who? Who are you?" Charlie stammered, trying to cover the scrambling noises his hands were making under the sheets. What had both he and Jonathan heard? How did it go?

"Are you my angel?"

A pregnant pause. "I am."

Two hands were required to arm the pistol. An idea—reposition himself. Pretend to prepare for that final journey. He groaned, as people will do when moving is painful. He shuffled himself onto his back. The apparition in white had inched even closer. Frightened, Charlie had to concentrate hard on what was supposed to come next. He glanced toward the hall, praying for intervention.

"Look. You must look at my eyes." The killer took baby steps around the foot of the bed on Charlie's right. If he sprang, he could grab Charlie's throat. The man was patient, however, hardly as impulsive as one might imagine a diabolical killer to be. He was enjoying the tableau he was creating—taking his time to savor the details.

With fierce concentration, Charlie moaned at the exact moment he pulled the gun's handle into position, praying that would muffle the click.

In one fluid motion, he threw back the quilt and bolted upright. But in his haste he had failed to take one precious moment to pinpoint that red laser light. He fired a round at the big target. The *bang!* startled him so badly, that he jerked, the weapon flying from his cold, stiff fingers, landing somewhere between the bed and the wall.

The attacker gave a high-pitched yelp as the acrid tear gas and pepper exploded around him. He staggered backward, but didn't go down. Raging in high-pitched curses, he lurched toward Charlie, a glistening object preceding his right hand. Charlie tore at the tangled covers that bound him to the bed. Nam flashed in his brain—the ambush, the scramble for cover, men screaming, men dying, trying desperately to save themselves and their comrades.

The disoriented figure, having regained his balance, shielded his face with his elbow as he groped around the foot of the bed. Charlie freed himself from his prison and plunged into the space by the wall, overturning his ankle. While the killer tried to correct his trajectory by circling the bed, Charlie burst into the hall, having no time to search for the stun gun.

"Help! He's going to kill me! Help!" Screaming, he hobbled down the corridor toward the nurses' station that seemed miles away. Dozens of people who he'd imagined would erupt from all over the ward, didn't. The corridor was dead-of-night silent. A hoard was not running to save him. Instead, a few curious heads popped into view. Way down the hall a nurse who had been on the phone bend over the counter, the receiver clamped to her ear.

"Help me! He's right behind me! I am not confused! Help me!"

Hide! But where? He could hear his attacker cursing and fumbling. A crash, as if he had tripped on the tangle of bedding. Then his high-pitched voice, approaching and raging through the door. A jerky look over Charlie's shoulder revealed the killer's hulking form, staggering in disoriented panic through the door. A few dozen steps would close the gap if his assailant could see him.

In a moment of clarity, Charlie remembered Hospice's intricate layout. He darted to his right into a short dead-end wing that momentarily hid him. He yanked at the first door he found. *EMPLOYEES ONLY.* Their bathroom. Of course, it was locked. He stumbled to the next door, a janitor's closet, which was supposed to be locked, but it yielded to his frantic twisting. Inside, he spent precious seconds easing the door shut, resisting the urge to slam it. Enveloped in darkness he fumbled to twist the knob lock, but it stuck halfway through the turn. Broken! That must be why it opened in the first place. There was no time to try forcing the lock to comply, which he feared would be futile anyway. A weapon. He needed one fast. But what?

The moment his groping hand found the light switch, he spotted the *golden plunger*, a brass contraption plumbers use to force clogs down, or in some instances up, through blocked pipes. No way could he club his way out. Not against an aggressor with size, age, strength, and health on his side, tear gas notwithstanding. One swing and the killer would grab it.

A white, ten-gallon plastic jug stood in the corner beside an empty metal bucket and mop. He grasped the jug's wide-mouth lid, and with enormous effort, pried. It opened so easily that he fell onto his butt, knocking mops off their wall hooks. Scrambling to regain position, he grabbed the jug, and realizing it had no handle, dumped its contents into the bucket. Fumes from the concentrated cleaner seared his nose and throat. Eyes running, lungs screaming, he fought through the pain, rehearsing his plan. Twist the lock. Fling the door open. Heft the bucket. Drench his attacker. Aim high. Get his eyes. Buy a few precious seconds for help to arrive.

Timing meant life or death.

Praying *please, please, please*, he cracked the door and, from a distance of twenty feet, locked eyes with the killer. Retreating into the closet was no longer an option. The caustic-smelling liquid gagged him as he muscled open the door while forcing his eyes to focus on the target. The mountain in white erupted into motion, rage in his eyes. His maniacal expression seemed to have lost all connection with where and what he was doing.

In that split second, Charlie wondered why the killer hadn't escaped through the stairwell. As the man surged forward, Charlie's brain flashed images of his girls, his comrades, his parents, and his life. With enormous concentration, he timed the distance that separated them. One thousand one…

Deliberately, he muscled the sloshing bucket, swinging it backward, then arcing it forward. The caustic fluid spewed toward the killer's face. His assailant backpedaled and howled as he slammed into the wall on his way to the floor. Rolling and moaning in agony, he tore at his face.

Chapter 14

From nowhere, Jade sprang toward the killer, cursing and screaming a torrent of threats. "Bastard! Murderer! I'll take out your eyes and your dick if you move one muscle!"

A dozen people edged toward the spectacle where Jade, legs planted, arms extended, arced the stun gun between the killer's face and his groin. The perp, reduced to whimpers, offered no resistance.

Minutes dragged unmercifully. Finally, a uniformed officer tore onto the scene, wearing a navy blue jacket that bore the yellow letters, *FEDERAL POLICE*, gun at the ready.

"Him! He tried to kill me!" Charlie wailed. The detective ordered the bystanders aside and trained his gun on the attacker. Jade backed away, having slipped the stun gun into her back waistband as soon as the officer entered the ward. He barked clipped instructions into his shoulder. Momentarily, additional police tore onto the ward to secure the area and ascertain what had happened and to whom.

Medical staff sprang into action as confused, panicked patients edged into the corridor. Hysterical visitors screamed. Charlie, shaking and exhausted, slid down the wall. The dripping bucket continued to rock back and forth somewhere between him and the killer. Charlie felt the pooling liquid seep into his pajamas, stinging his skin.

"His skin! He's melting!" somebody shrieked. The killer's skin began sloughing off in pinkish yellow globs that plopped onto his chest, his lap and the floor. His entire face became transformed into a garish mishmash of grotesque proportions. His very skull appeared to be splitting in two. An old woman fainted. A visitor threw up.

"Drench his face! STAT!" a nurse barked. Another snapped on blue vinyl gloves. With a large plastic sprayer that arched sterile solution, she saturated his face to minimize the caustic effect. Cream-colored droplets splattered everywhere. Onlookers gasped in horror as a ghastly scene continued unfolding.

Charlie, horrified by what he had done, sat transfixed as the macabre features of his attacker materialized. One brave nurse wedged herself into the chaos to gently probe the man's face. Backing away, she studied the swab and stared incredulously at the smear. "I'll be damned!" She turned to the others. "It's makeup! He's wearing thick makeup!"

"Check out that head wound." While a police officer stood guard, a doctor gingerly inched close enough to examine a possible gash in his skull. When the man didn't flinch, she carefully probed, then realized it couldn't be skin. She tweezed at the loose edge, its structure becoming obvious. "It's a wig! A bald wig! Or a swim cap!"

With swift, skillful motions, she removed the wig's remnants and dropped them into a vinyl bag proffered by the police. Without the wig, matted blonde hair came into view. At a doctor's insistence, the police stripped the man's contaminated clothing, revealing what was hidden beneath.

"Kevlar! He's wearing a vest. And shoulder pads." Charlie gaped as the killer's size diminished before his eyes, one layer at a time, realizing why the force of the stun gun had not stopped him.

"Everybody back!" the officer-in-charge barked, as the prisoner suddenly attempted to lunge in Charlie's direction. Panicked, Charlie shrank against the wall, pinned by his assailant's vicious eyes. Medical staff scurried for cover as the police barked orders for all onlookers to get out of the area. Quickly, they overpowered the suspect, securing him in a seated position against the far wall. He continued to struggle and curse. The prisoner reminded Charlie of a jointed wood doll as he pumped his flopping legs. Finally he relented, as further attempts to escape became futile.

Jade saw it before anyone noticed. "His hand!" she yelled, frantically trying to get their attention. "He's got a syringe! Get it before he sticks anyone!" Lunging forward, she trapped his hand against the floor with her foot. A gloved hand captured the weapon. Holding it gingerly away from his body, the officer dropped it into a plastic bag. "Secure the needle!" Jade yelled after him. "Don't let it prick anyone. It's poison! And it's evidence!"

From the far end of the hall, more VA personnel spilled into the hall. As the human perimeter of professionals grew, Charlie's view became blocked.

"Mr. Alderfer?"

He looked up at the charge nurse flanked by an aide. They had maneuvered a wheelchair into position. "We've got to get you into the shower then into fresh clothes. Doctor is coming to evaluate you."

"Wait," Charlie begged. "Just a minutes. There's somebody I've got to find. I need…" Scanning the crowd, he spotted Jade who was trying to squeeze through the knot of white coats and police who were clogging the hall. She looked exhausted yet triumphant. "I want her to be with me."

A commotion among the officers brought everyone's attention back to the perpetrator. They had wrestled him to a standing position, cuffed, and prepared him for transport. A nurse begun shrieking. "Hey! I know who that is! It's not a man. It's a *woman*! I recognize her. That's Les! Leslie Martin. She's the temp who works in the business office."

Charlie, like the others, stared in mute disbelief. Blazing with anger, the prisoner shot a murderous look directly at Charlie. How that gorgeous woman had been able to move undetected throughout the complex without arousing suspicion was instantly apparent to him.

ↄ⳼ↄ

Charlie, Jade, and the detective gathered in one of Hospice's private conference rooms. "Thanks for coming to us instead of the other way around," Charlie said. "Apparently, I can get around pretty well, but I still have medical issues. In wake of this incident, they're keeping me on a short leash." He rubbed his bruised head with a bandaged hand. "Guess they're sorting out liability issues, but they needn't bother. My injuries weren't the hospital's fault."

Jade jumped into the discussion. "I refuse to leave my father, even briefly. If he died while I was away, I'd never forgive myself. My mom died a terrible death, all alone. I won't let that happen to him.

"So—what did you learn?" Charlie asked.

The detective straightened in his chair and thumbed through a small spiral notebook. "You'll be interested in what the forensic toxicologist identified as being present in the hypodermic syringe. He determined that it contained a powerful toxic drug called Pavulon."

Jade flinched. He continued. "Its scientific name is Pancuronium Bromide. On a scale of one to six, with one being the least toxic and six being the most, Pavulon is a six. Just a few drops would be fatal. It is liquid, injectable, and can be administered intravenously, either directly into the body or via the victim's IV."

"How does it work? Is there an antidote? Was Charlie in any real danger?" she asked.

"The toxicologist says Pavulon is a neuromuscular blocking agent that can be used in the operating room—in correct amounts and concentrations, of course—to lessen the need for as much anesthetic. Sometimes it's imperative that the patient not twitch, even involuntarily, such as with delicate eye surgery. But Pancuronium Bromide also is one of the three drugs used for legal lethal injections. In plain words, it relaxes muscles. But you need your muscles to breathe. And your heart is a muscle. An antidote? Someone would need to be standing by."

Charlie's brain ricocheted with the horrid reality. War had been hard enough to fathom, even knowing that freedom wasn't free. But this? In a hospital devoted to healing? He forced himself to unclench his fists. "Why would even the most sadistic killer use a poison like that? And where would she even get it?"

"Why? Imagine a thrill-junkie who gets off on killing helpless people. This hideous weapon paralyzes the victim while enabling him to comprehend what is happening to him. Unable to move, speak, or summon help, he can still see, hear, or think. He understands exactly what the killer is doing to him. His eyes are frozen awake. Eyes from which the killer watches his power."

Jade jumped to her feet, tears streaming down her face. She shook her hands as if flinging water from them. "Oh, my poor mom! Jonathan's pictures—my mom's big, staring eyes. And those other victims. What did any of them do to deserve that?"

"Absolutely nothing. The problem with serial killers that makes them so hard to catch is that they don't need any connection to their victims. Ninety percent of murders are committed by someone the victim knows—a family member, neighbor, old lover, business associate, angry acquaintance—"

Charlie interrupted. "But veterans! They survived war, some struggling with disabilities for the rest of their lives. Amputees. Soldiers who never fully recovered from battle fatigue. Deafness. Blindness. What dreadful irony to have their final days snuffed in this caring place. How could anyone be that demented?"

"In some cases," the detective said, "the serial killer

feels compelled to put suffering patients out of their misery. Assisted suicide, euthanasia, whatever its label. Those people are typically medical personnel, like doctors, nurses, therapists, or technicians. People who treat patients in their day-to-day jobs. But, as in this case, there are sociopaths who get off on having the absolute power of life and death in their hands. It's an enormous high to watch as the light is extinguished. With a drug like Pancuronium, that experience can be heightened if the patient is awake and alert. And he can experience death by watching their eyes."

Jade frantically paced the small room. "No punishment could possibly be extreme enough. The killer should be sentenced to the same kind of death."

"That may actually happen. 'What goes around…' as they say."

"A question," Charlie raised a finger as if the teacher should call on him next. "Who is this person?"

The detective passed a three-by-five inch, color print across the coffee table. "Do you recognize her?"

Jade gasped. "Oh my god! She was one of our home health care providers. I used her so briefly that I didn't even recognize her the other evening. If I recall correctly, she was a substitute. Came only once after another nurse called off sick. Or so she said. She just showed up without notification from the service. She told me the woman we used— let me think—her name was Evelyn—couldn't come. Supposedly, the service hadn't had time to notify me. She did her job and then left. Beyond being pleasant and efficient, nothing else was memorable. I would have called the agency when their bill arrived, had they listed a stranger's name, but their statement was all about hours. And that was correct. So I paid without questioning her qualifications."

"Did she have access to house keys?"

"What Jonathan observed was correct. She didn't need one. During the day, especially in the summer, the sliding glass door was open, the unlocked screen in its place. Hospital rooms can have disagreeable odors, and the breeze was so pleasant. Mom loved it. We all did."

"Can she be convicted for the series of murders here at the VA?" Charlie asked. "My former roommates?"

"That is unlikely, although the possibility is being investigated. All three gentlemen were cremated. Even if the ashes were available for analysis and the families were willing, no trace of Pavulon would survive. And, as you may have observed, a deceased's room, equipment, and bedding are disinfected immediately. Within a few hours, unless foul play is suspected, all evidence is gone."

"But I saw all three murders. I even reported them."

"True, you did raise the issue. But you are on record as having seen a large man."

"And he/she came back to kill me, disguised as a man, and we caught her."

"Since the crimes took place at the VA, which is a governmental institution, it's the fed's jurisdiction. And their prosecutor can't take her to trial for triple homicide on your say-so and without physical evidence. A defense attorney would point out to the jury that a) you weren't wearing your glasses, b) the room was dark and c) you reported *a stranger* who appeared to be a large man. Granted the woman we arrested is tall—five feet ten in her sock feet—but without wads of clothes, she has no more girth than some fashion model. And if she's present in court in a skinny black suit, all blonde curls and feminine charm—"

"Can't she at least be tried for the attempt on my life?"

"She can. But if a defense attorney claims she was insane, she could be locked up only until she is 'cured.' She could be loose again."

"What—as long as she takes a few pills?"

"I can't answer that."

"And my mother. What about her?" Jade asked. "And my father. I want him exonerated before it's too late."

"That's a problem as well. Jonathan also referred to her killer as *he*. In fact, didn't you say he corrected you on that point, Mr. Alderfer, when you referred to his angel as *her*?"

"But he saw it! And we know what happened. That she wore a bald wig. Surely—"

"Ms. Kepley, all we can prove is that the same individual who attacked Mr. Alderfer performed nursing duties for your mother one time. And the day of that service was not the day that she died."

"What if the nursing service has no record of her?"

"Well, that's an entirely different issue— misrepresenting her credentials and showing up, that is. They may have no record of her at all. She might be guilty of something, but of what I couldn't speculate."

"But Jonathan saw her," Jade insisted.

"Would he recognize her in a lineup?" the detective asked.

Jade scrunched her face and looked helplessly at Charlie. "I don't know."

"Wait a minute," Charlie said. "When I asked him if he saw the angel's face, he said yes. The angel looked directly at the place where Jonathan was hiding. He said that the angel had 'mean eyes.' Even if she had been wearing all that makeup and all those bulky clothes—eyes can't be changed."

"Where was Jonathan the night she tried to kill Charlie?"

"At our minister's house."

"All evening? He couldn't have seen that woman here at the VA?"

"That's impossible. I dropped him off before dinner, and he spent the night. I didn't pick him up until the next morning. You see, I didn't want him anywhere near Hospice if the so-called angel of death reappeared. He could be killed."

The detective flipped his notebook shut. "It does seem unlikely that your son would have seen this woman any- where else. But she is—was—an employee. And I under- stand he did take an unauthorized tour throughout the complex, including the morgue. Still, we'll pursue it. I'll schedule a lineup."

After he left, Jade and Charlie huddled, comparing notes. "I've had a terrible thought," he said. "We know someone with expert computer skills got into my records and was responsible for my being drugged with those little green pills. If that person was able to walk into the VA during the daytime, hide out, then access a pharmacy computer, isn't it also possible that she might have seen Jonathan with you? When she took care of your mother that one day, was Jonathan at home? Remember, Jonathan told me the angel looked directly at the closet where he was hiding. That's how *he* saw *her* face. How motionless can a five-year-old be? Even if he tries very hard? Isn't it possible that's why someone pursued you that night on the highway?"

"Oh, dear lord. The stalker who followed me in that black SUV and tried to run me off the road. The same person I know shot and killed that patrolman. They've got to keep her locked up."

🙰🙰🙰

Jade and Jonathan waited on a bench in the VA's main lobby for their police escort. Having arrived too early, they killed time watching outpatients en route to their appointments. Jonathan swung his legs, restless and itchy, for the promised ride in a real police car.

"Will they turn on the lights and sirens?" he asked his mother again.

"If they're allowed. This is a hospital. People have to be very quiet so they don't disturb sleeping patients." She wondered if that still applied in this day of central air and sealed windows.

Precisely on time, the detective and a woman whom Jade didn't recognize inched through the automatic door. Jonathan hopped to his feet. Before the detective could make introductions, Jonathan blurted, "Can you turn on the siren?"

"Sure," he said. "But just for a minute and after we're away from the hospital's grounds. We don't want to startle anyone or scare other motorists."

"My son needs a booster seat suitable for a five-year-old."

The woman smiled and nodded. "Got one."

The ride to their destination seemed endless, traffic increasing exponentially as they approached the city limits. When the detective pulled into the vast parking lot, Jonathan scowled in disappointment at the plain brick building until he spotted the sea of police cars, including a SWAT vehicle.

"This way," the detective said, leading them through the visitor's entrance.

Several officers sat at desks located behind a glass barricade. Two wearing headphones engaged unknown people in lively conversation while others dealt with a mountain of paper. The closest one looked up and waved the detectives toward a connecting corridor.

"Don't we have to sign in or something?" Jade asked.

"We'll take care of that in due course."

To Jade, the place was like any other business office, except for the uniforms. Miles of flat-knap industrial carpet muffled their footsteps. Small offices flanking the wide hall housed employees either working the phones or dealing with paperwork. The overall ambience was hushed. Police stations, she guessed, were not like TV. They could just as easily have been in an insurance or real estate office. A uniformed officer approached with visitors' badges, which she helped Jonathan clip to his shirt.

The scene changed dramatically as the detective and his partner flashed their IDs at a sensor that activated double metal doors. Behind them unfolded the reality that Jade had expected. Phones, voices, clattering footsteps on industrial tile clamored competitively. "Down this hall," the detective motioned. Having made several turns, they arrived at another set of steel doors. A bench was positioned along the wall. "If you'll wait here for a few minutes with my partner, I'll see if they're ready for us."

They sat, the child flanked by the adults. "Is it just like TV?" she asked. "One-way mirror and all? Will someone who works with kids explain it to my son?"

"Of course."

The detective returned. "They're ready. This way, please."

Jade realized just how far they had traveled from the public area as they traversed the underbelly of law enforcement. She spotted what could only be described as a scruffy lowlife being hustled toward a perpendicular corridor. The prisoner in handcuffs sneered at Jonathan, bearing his teeth. Jonathan froze, eyes bugged, and keened like a trapped animal. He buried his face into Jade, clutching her body with brute force. "Nooo! Nooo!"

Jade pried his arms loose and stooped to his level. "Jonathan. That man can't hurt you. Nobody can. Not with all these police to protect us."

He jerked from her embrace, turned, and bolted haphazardly in the direction from which they had come. Quickly disoriented, he made several wrong turns. "Jonathan! Stop! Wait!"

A man in a suit jumped from a cubicle and grabbed the thrashing, kicking child. Jade caught up with him quickly. "Stop. Please. It's okay," she said to her son. Coaxing him from his renewed efforts to bolt, she hugged him tightly against her. "It's okay. You're okay. Tell Mommy what's wrong?"

Gradually his sobbing reduced to hiccups. He swiped his eyes and runny nose with the back of his sleeve. "Grandpa."

"Grandpa? What about him?"

"They took him away in those things."

"What things?"

Jonathan circled his wrist with his thumb and index finger and swiveled them in a revolving motion.

"Handcuffs?" He nodded. Jade sighed as if that would expel a world of evil from the depth of her soul. "Sometimes, when the police have to question someone and they don't know them very well, they're afraid they'll make the person very angry. And the angry person might hit them. They handcuff the person to make sure they aren't punched by the bad guy."

"Grandpa's not bad! He wouldn't hurt anyone. I hate you!"

Jade's eyes swept the ceiling in exasperation. "Honey, of course he's not…"

"You let them take Grandpa away."

"And I made them give him back. He came home again, didn't he?"

Furious and unrelenting, Jonathan glared and struggled, and only when his strength was exhausted, did he acquiesce.

The detective, who had kept his distance but stayed within earshot, interrupted. "Do you think we could proceed with the lineup?"

"We can try," Jade said. Gently she grasped the child's shoulders in an attempt to maneuver him in the direction from which he had fled. "Come on, Sweetie. The detective has a very special mirror to show you in a room down the hall."

Jonathan dug in his heels. "Nooo!" Thrashing and yelping, he gulped air while trying to squeeze behind Jade.

"I'm sorry," Jade said. "This ain't gonna fly." Although the detective kept his cool, palpable frustration radiated from him. "I can't force him to cooperate. Maybe another day…." Jade glanced at her denim skirt, blotched dark by her child's tears and runny nose. "I'll talk with him when he calms down."

He sighed. "We'll be in touch."

ↄ৴ↄ৴ↄ

"He freaked. It was as simple as that. There was no way to haul him farther down that hall."

Charlie listened intently to Jade's detailed description of the aborted lineup. "Would he have been okay in a more public area?"

"Not a possibility. They're not set up for that. The viewing area is not only secure from a prisoner transport perspective, but in a way that the prisoners can't pass the witness. It's just like TV."

Charlie rubbed the back of his neck. "Would you like me to talk to Jonathan? Find out what set him off? And what he might be willing to do?"

"That much we know. He blames both me and the police for taking his grandfather away in handcuffs."

"Can I at least try?"

She bobbed her head in agreement, the same way that was Jonathan's habit. Charlie smiled.

ↄ৴ↄ৴ↄ

"I hear you had a harrowing experience," Charlie said. The child was studying his left sneaker while he rubbed at it with his right.

He didn't look up immediately. "A hair...what?"

"Harrowing. Scary. Would you like to tell me about it?" Jonathan swayed his head *no*, eyes on the floor. "I got you something special," Charlie said. Jonathan looked up, brightening slightly. "Your mom's afraid if you keep eating chocolate, your teeth will decay. Go see what's in my bathroom."

Jonathan returned in a matter of seconds, clutching a toothbrush still in its wrapper and a tube of paste, both balanced inside a plastic cartoon character cup. "Think that will keep your mom off our backs?"

Jonathan grinned broadly, scurrying back into Charlie's bathroom. He returned after placing the cup next to Charlie's.

"I had another scary experience when I was your age. I never told anybody about it. But maybe you'd like to hear it."

Jonathan bobbed yes with the upper half of his body.

Charlie elevated the back of his bed, sat, and, positioning himself, patted the mattress. Jonathan scrambled aboard and nestled close to Charlie. With anxious eyes, Jonathan gave Charlie his undivided attention.

"When my great grandmother was a little girl in England, there was a huckster who used to bring his cart full of house wares down Grandmother's street."

"What's a huck…"

"A huckster is a peddler, like a door-to-door salesman. Anyway, his name was Billy Goose." Jonathan grinned at the sound. "Really, it was. To make their children behave, parents used to threaten to give them to Billy Goose if they were naughty."

The child's eyes widened. "Did they ever do that?"

"No. Of course not. But the children would stop their mischief immediately rather than find out."

"Was he a bad man?"

"After I grew up, my grandmother told me that he was a sweet old guy who never would have harmed anyone. By the time my mother was five, Billy Goose had become a family legend. Suppose somebody snitched cookies or broke something and no one would confess? My grandmother would say, 'Well, I guess Billy Goose did it.' He became my family's imaginary scapegoat.

"My family lived in an old farmhouse. You know—the one with the big black spider and the sewing machine? It had a basement, but not like the ones we have today that are a nice place to watch TV or play. Our basement had a dirt floor. It was damp and musty. I was forbidden to go down there because my dad stored dangerous stuff, like sharp tools and rat poison.

"One day, when everybody was outside, my curiosity got the best of me. I sneaked down, closing the cellar door behind me. The only light came from a dirty glass window, up high on the far wall. It was real spooky. There was a huge old chair with a big spring sticking out, right in the middle. I hurt, just thinking about sitting on it. Huge pieces of rusty metal were piled in the corner. I'd heard someone say they were old furnace parts. I was inching around, trying to take it all in, when I tripped and fell, face down in the dirt. As I looked up, there was Billy Goose! On a big wooden crate, inches away from my face. And he was blue. He was looking straight in my eyes!"

"What did you do?"

"Scrambled upstairs as fast as I could and slammed the basement door behind me."

"Did you get caught?"

"No. But I was too scared to ever go anywhere near that basement again."

Jonathan knit his eyebrows in concentration. Charlie let a few beats pass before continuing his story.

"Several years ago, I went to an orchard where you can pick your own peaches. Not knowing exactly which road to take, I stopped in the orchard's huge building where workers pack fruit for market. The cartons are then put on big trucks and driven to grocery stores. Guess what I saw?"

"What!"

"Billy Goose! Stamped on the side of every shipping carton were the words, 'Blue Goose Shipping Company.'" Jonathan sat stalk still, enchanted. "And the goose, my Billy Goose, was a drawing, no bigger than this." He held his hands eight inches apart. "He didn't even look like a goose—more like a cartoon character that was shaped like a gourd. Little head, big eyes, fat body, no wings, orange feet like a duck."

Jonathan giggled, hand cupping his mouth.

"You see, to a child, things look so much bigger and scarier than they really are."

"Did you tell your mommy or your grandma what you did?"

"I couldn't. I was doing something I was told not to do, and I didn't want to get into trouble. As a grownup, I know now that I could have asked my dad to take me down to the basement and point out the bad and dangerous stuff. He would have told me enough to satisfy my curiosity. Jonathan, when we have people we can trust, like you trust your mom, sometimes we just have to take their word that we will be safe."

"But Billy Goose. That guy—"

"That was a long time ago. Today parents understand that they shouldn't scare children to make them behave. My great grandma bought a lace tablecloth from Billy Goose. She wouldn't have done that if he were a bad man. She would have locked the door when she saw him coming. I think she really thought that the kids understood that it was a joke."

Charlie opened his little drawer and withdrew the cellophane bag. Jonathan grinned as he accepted the kiss. After eating it, he held out his chubby little hand to collect Charlie's wrapper. He scrunched both tightly together then trotted to the nearest waste paper basket. He gave them a toss. "Two points!" Charlie called. "Good man!"

Jonathan shrugged. "But I'm five."

"So—I told you my story. Now it's your turn. Tell me about *your* harrowing experience at the police station. Was it really that bad?"

Jonathan eyeballed the ceiling, remembering. "There was this really, really scary bad guy. He was all dirty. He smelled really bad."

"You were that close to him?" Head bob. "What happened next?"

"He looked at me, all mad, like I'd done something awful and he was going to come get me and eat me."

"Was he handcuffed?"

"Yeah, but he put up his arms, like he was going to grab me around my head. And he did this thing with his mouth." Jonathan opened his mouth wide, making a horrible face while baring his teeth. "Like he was going to bite my head off. Then he spit on the floor. His teeth were all yellow and brown." He shuddered involuntarily. "I ran away. Then this other guy grabbed me."

"Do you know who the second man was?"

"Just some big guy."

"What did he look like?"

"He looked angry. He was dressed up. Like when we go to church."

"Ah. He would have been a policeman or someone who worked there. Just like the detective who visits with us. Some police don't wear uniforms. Some wear church clothes. Some even wear jeans. He was probably trying to help. Is that possible?"

A shrug.

"If the police promise to have no scary people around, would it be okay to go back to the station to take a look through the magic glass window?" Panic overtook the child's face.

"Jonathan. Do you trust me?" The boy shrugged. "I promise, nothing bad can happen to you at the station."

Jonathan thought that over for a minute or two, then whispered. "Could you go with me?"

Charlie collected Jonathan into a hug. "Of course, if your mom agrees and my doctor says it's okay."

Chapter 15

The next day, Dr. Kaye met Charlie, Jade, and Jonathan outside the police station. She stooped to greet him. "You still drawing those wonderful pictures?" the child psychologist asked. "If you are, I'd love to see them sometime." Jonathan grinned, nodding affirmation, and took the hand that she offered. Together, the foursome walked into the station through a different entrance.

The detective, having coordinated the alternate route and clip-on visitor badges, led them into the room where lineups were held. No one else was around. Dr. Kaye pointed out a stepladder stool for Jonathan's use. "Here. Come look in the mirror."

While Jade held his hand, he climbed high enough to see over its frame and observe his own reflection. Turning, he grinned at the adults. "It's me!"

"What else do you see in the mirror?" she asked.

Jonathan swiveled his head, then looked into the mirror again. "I see Mommy, and Mr. Charlie, and that policeman."

"But can you see *through* the mirror?" She emphasized the word. "Can you see the hallway we walked through on the other side of this wall?" She tapped the glass for emphasis.

He frowned. "No."

The detective stepped forward. "Ms. Kepley and Mr.

Alderfer, will you please stand on that line in front of the back wall?" They complied. "And Jonathan, I'd like you go out in the hall with Dr. Kaye."

Jonathan darted a look at Charlie. "It's okay. You can trust them. Your mom and I will be right here."

Dr. Kaye steered the child the few dozen steps around the doorframe to the window side of the wall. "What do you see?"

He grinned. "Mommy, Mr. Charlie, the policeman."

"What do they see?"

He didn't respond, only looked puzzled. "Tell you what—you go stand between them and I'll stand right here. Then tell me if you can see me."

Jonathan did as he was asked, immediately seeing only their groups' reflections. He scampered back and peered out the door. Seeing Dr. Kaye, he scurried back into the viewing room and repeated the experiment. "We call this a one-way mirror. If you stand in the hall and look through the glass, you can see people who cannot see you. All they can see is themselves. Do you understand?"

"Yeah."

"Now. All of us are going to stand in the hall. The detective will close and lock the door to the room. Inside the room, there's another door. Six people will come in and stand back there, against the wall. Each one will be holding a number. Can you count to six?"

He bobbed his head. "One two three four five six seven eight nine ten eleven twelve thirteen…"

"Very, very good." Now, let's get your family out here to join us. Then we'll begin."

Jonathan sandwiched himself between Jade and Charlie, clutching each by their arm. He seemed satisfied that he wasn't going to see anything bad and waited, alert, for something to happen. The interior door in the viewing room opened. Six individuals, three men and three women, entered and filed to their places against the back wall. All six were about the same height, weight and age. The six wore white uniforms and held numbers against their chests. All six wore flesh-colored swim caps to cover their hair.

"Do you recognize any of these people?"

Jonathan beamed. He pointed.

"Which number?"

He held up his right index finger. "One."

"And where have you seen this person before?"

Jonathan shrugged as if he were humoring a really dumb person. "She helps Gram. Gram says she's a vam…vam something. She brings these little glass things and takes Gram's blood. She says it needs a test, but that's silly. Blood can't take tests."

"And you've seen her often?"

"Yeah. She comes on the day Mom lets me watch Sponge Bob Square Pants on TV. She's really nice. She gives me money for the hokey-pokey man."

"What's that?"

"That white truck that plays songs and brings ice cream. She's really nice."

"Did you see her the day the angel came?"

"Nooo!" Hand bob, palms up. "That's not Sponge Bob day." He waved at the woman.

"She can't see you, remember?"

He sighed.

The woman clicked an intercom button. "Number one may leave." And she did. "Okay. Do you recognize anyone else?"

Jonathan slid his eyes down the row, skipping over numbers two through five. "Him! I know him! He's a policeman at the hospital. He eats lunch when we do. He really, really, really likes hot dogs. He buys three! And do you know what else? Lots and lots of fries!" He made a mounding motion with his hands. "He lets me snitch one while we wait to pay. He's really nice."

"Have you ever seen him at your gram's house?"

"Nooo!" Exasperation. "He's at the hospital!"

Again the woman spoke through the intercom, dismissing number five. "Now, Jonathan, do you recognize anyone else?" He shrugged. "That guy looks like our mailman—sort of but not, and that lady, does she go to our church?" He looked up. "I—No.

"Do you recognize anyone else?"

He shook his head. "Can we go now?"

The detective wrapped on the glass and clicked on an intercom. "Let me have group number two." What was left of group number one turned like a well-practiced drill team and exited through the interior door. Shortly, six more people took their places along the back wall. Again, their size, age, and clothing were similar. Half were men and half women. Charlie noticed his attacker at once. He froze, statue-like, least he betray her. This was Jonathan's test.

A woman in a business suit, carrying a slender briefcase, had positioned herself in the hallway while everyone was focused on the viewing room.

"Do you recognize any of these people?"

Each held a number under his or her chin. Jonathan stared, sweeping his eyes right to left, then back again. He contemplated the scene for what seemed to Charlie like an excessive amount of time. Then he turned, looking puzzled, at Charlie.

"Take your time," the detective said.

"No coaching," the newcomer said.

Charlie stole a peek, immediately recognizing her as an attorney. Strange, he hadn't noticed her when the first group had entered. He returned his eyes to Jonathan, keeping his own face as neutral as possible, willing himself not to settle his glare on anyone in particular.

Slowly Jonathan's finger came up. He pointed. "Why does the death angel look like a *her*?" The angel is a *him*. But—but—" He swiveled his head to look at Charlie. "Why?"

The woman mouthed an admonishment to Charlie. "No coaching!"

The detective faced her. "Ma'am, if you interfere with

this lineup, I'll have to ask you to leave. We want to hear what the child has to say."

She glared, steel-eyed. "Go ahead. But remember, you can deal with me now or in court. Your choice."

The detective stooped to Jonathan's level and repeated her previous question. "Do you recognize any of these people? If so, what is the number?"

Jonathan pointed then, studying his hands, held up his splayed right, then tried to separate an extra digit from his left. "Six."

"And where do you recognize this person from?"

"He came to take Gram to heaven, but he wouldn't take her. He put Gram on the floor. Then he flew out the door." Tears spurted off Jonathan's thick lashes. "But—But—" He turned to Charlie. "Why does he look like a *her*?"

The detective persisted. "Why do you think number six is the person you saw?"

Jonathan patted his eyes with closed fingers, as if he were wearing mittens. "I saw his eyes. They looked right at me. He has really, really mean eyes."

"Did this person see you?"

Jonathan shook his head slowly, just once. "I was hiding. In the closet," he whispered.

"How did you see this person then?"

"There's this really big crack…"

❦❦❦

Dr. Kaye, the assistant district attorney, and the detective convened in the DA's conference room. The psychologist listened while the other two sparred. The assistant DA was shaking her head, having reached a decision. "At this time, we don't have enough evidence to prosecute her for more than the attempted attack on Mr. Alderfer."

"We've got a serial medical murderer on our hands, and thanks to two plucky people, we have her locked up without bail," the detective said harshly. "The attempted murder looked, at first, like a slam-dunk. But her attorney is pleading her *not guilty by reason of insanity or mental defect*. We'll be lucky to keep her locked up in a mental institution for a year and—"

"Trouble is," the ADA interrupted, "we have no solid evidence connecting her to those three deaths at the VA. Speedy cremation and a sterilized crime scene will do that for you. And, the only way to connect her to Clara Murdock's murder is the word of a five-year-old witness who insists the killer is an angel and a man."

"But she was dressed and bulked up with clothing when she attacked Mr. Alderfer at the VA, which sounds like the scenario at the Murdock house.

"Her attorney claims that Clara Murdock's murder was committed by her husband, a crime unrelated to her client. There's no known connection between her and Clara Murdock, other than that one home-health care incident, and she isn't wanted anywhere else. Presently, we can't prove otherwise."

"The c—child—" the detective stuttered.

"I spoke to witnesses at the police station about the first time they attempted a lineup. If he freaked when he saw an unsavory character or someone in handcuffs, what kind of witness would he make confronting his grandmother's killer in open court?"

"Can't they have him testify electronically from chambers?"

The ADA sighed. "Not in this state. He must be ten years old to testify. Even his lineup identification cannot be used, also because of his age. Her attorney is adamant about her client has a right to confront her accuser. Look, I'm sorry, but here's the reality. Suppose we take this to trial without insufficient evidence. We've lost our little star witness. Even if he could testify—what if he freaked? Or changed his story. The jury could acquit if the evidence is too weak. Then jeopardy applies. She's free to go on killing."

"Did I hear that her attorney is attempting to discredit Jonathan Kepley in order to get bail for that woman?"

The assistant DA leveled the detective with piercing determination. "Get us more. Re-interview all parties involved, including the child. If we can get enough to charge her with Clara Murdock's murder, we can try her for murder one. And that should generate a lot of press coverage. Perhaps other witnesses will come forward or other jurisdictions will take notice. This woman had no motive to kill a complete stranger except for the thrill. And that means *psychopath*. If we're lucky, others will recognize her."

The detective rubbed her neck. "That could take years. By that time, she could be free, have changed her appearance, and killed scores of people."

"Then we've got to get more." The ADA turned to the psychologist. "Dr. Kane, will you please take another run at the boy, pardon the expression? And talk to Mr. Alderfer. He seems to have the boy's confidence. There's got to be something we're missing."

✒✒✒

Sleep had not come easily to Charlie. At the detective's request, he had run mental tapes for what seemed like hours, for something he'd missed. Finally, he was almost asleep when something obvious hit him. Just as peripheral vision is sometimes sharper in near darkness, his near-sleeping brain had a flash.

What did Jonathan do with the bag? The one he took from the waste paper basket the day that Clara Murdock was murdered?

Charlie couldn't remember exactly how Jonathan had answered that question, except that he'd wanted to hide his own guilt. The child was so terribly upset when questioned about it that Charlie had lost his own train of thought. Now he questioned his own interpretation. Was other stuff dumped in the bag? Not just by Jonathan, but—who? He had added something like, "that thing that was dropped." Charlie had assumed that he'd meant whatever had rolled under his grandmother's equipment. Was there anything else?

The IV tube? Did the killer drop a piece of the IV tube into the waste paper basket? And why would she? Especially if the tube had a puncture hole in it. Could anyone who could plan such intricate crimes be that stupid?

Yeah. And some little thing *had* dropped. Had everyone, Charlie included, assumed that Jonathan ditched the bag? Outside or in some other trashcan as soon as the opportunity presented itself? He didn't say that he threw it away. He just said—what? In retrospect, Charlie assumed that he meant *until it was safe to dispose of it elsewhere*. Where could it be if the police didn't take it? In some landfill? But that would have been months ago. The entire property had been cordoned off as a crime scene, belatedly so. What had they missed?

Charlie hustled down the hall as fast as he could navigate his walker. Not seeing Jade in her father's room, he stopped at the desk. As if reading his mind, the night manager said, "She's not here. She had to go home."

Charlie double-timed back to his room. Frantically, he dug through the drawer to unearth the detective's card onto which he had scribbled his private phone numbers. Charlie stabbed it into his cell phone. A groggy voice answered.

"Detective, I think I've remembered something!" Charlie could sense the detective coming alive. "That knob or screw or whatever Jonathan thought he'd knocked off his grandmother's equipment—I *think* he said he retrieved the bag from the waste paper basket, which also might have contained the snippet of the IV tubing he described. I assumed that he threw the bag away. Perhaps in the kitchen or outside with the trash. Remember, he thought it was evidence that he'd killed his grandmother, and he didn't want his mother to know. When I asked him where he put the

bag, he started to tell me but was so terribly upset that I got
side tracked and never asked him again. He was mumbling
and crying and his wording was fuzzy. You can imagine his
state of mind. He was finally telling someone a horrible secret. When he mentioned his bear, I thought he was refer-
ring to a favorite stuffed animal that had been in the closet
with him. You know, his security thing. And then he'd di-
gressed.

"Tonight I was almost asleep and an unrelated memory
flashed through my mind. I was in the dentist's reception
room when a grandmother brought in a toddler and an old
lady in a wheelchair. The child wore a backpack that was
rigged with a leash. 'A two-year-old can outrun a car in a
parking lot,' the woman told me, as if she needed to justify
a kid on a leash. The child scrambled onto a chair, pulled
off the backpack, unzipped it, and pulled out a Sandra
Boynton book. You know—those cute little cardboard
books that all toddlers love. Sewn to the backpack was a
stuffed bear. What if Jonathan has a bear that started out as
something else? Like a pillow? The house was searched, but
I doubt if anyone looked at his toys. Why would they?" Silence. "Hello? Are you there?"

"We'll check it out."

"Please. Do that. If Jonathan needed to hide the bag
somewhere safe, what better place than among his toys?
Finding that bag could exonerate Robert Murdock, and that
would mean a lot to his family."

A yawn. "Yeah, we'll check it out."

"One more thing? Please don't tear the child's toys
apart. There's no way he could take out a seam, stuff something in, and sew it back up."

"As my kid would say, 'Duh!'"

೧೨೧

Charlie agonized over the least damaging way to take

Jonathan's memory back to that horrible day when he had witnessed his grandmother's murder. He had discussed it at length with Dr. Kaye after she and Jade had been unable to broach the subject. The child would clam up or have an anxiety attack whenever they skirted the topic's periphery. What if, suppose, that little plastic bag still existed somewhere? Might there be prints? Trace evidence? Something to link Jonathan's death angel to the woman in custody?

Deep in thought, Charlie strode the halls behind his walker, trying to shake his anxiety. As Charlie approached Robert Murdock's door, he stopped. Jade had briefed him that Jonathan was refusing to leave his grandfather's side. Charlie bore mute witness, as the child kept a vigil, his little face a wash of concern.

Charlie cleared his throat, not wishing to startle the pair. "I'm on my way to the kitchenette in search of a little snack. Would you like some ice cream? I know where they keep it. And it's for us. You know, if our bellies get hollow in between meals."

"I can't leave my grandpa," Jonathan mumbled then looked up at Charlie, almost beseechingly. "What if the angel won't take Grandpa either?"

Charlie hoped his sigh didn't sound as exasperated to Jonathan as it did to him. Jonathan's little mind still wasn't convinced. Charlie pushed his walker into the room, turned it, and then settled onto its built-in seat.

"Are you okay?"

Jonathan sighed again then returned his gaze to his grandfather. "Grandpa's going to die real soon."

Charlie waited. Finally, Jonathan focused sadly on Charlie. "They think I don't know 'cause I'm a little kid. They think I can't hear." He turned weary eyes toward his sleeping grandpa, his ragged breath keeping an irregular pattern. Their voices hadn't disturbed them. "He's really, really sick. They say he won't be around very much longer. Will he go to heaven?"

"Of course, he will. He's a good man who led a good

life. He took care of his family. And, if he felt he did anything wrong, God will forgive him. God is the biggest, best father there is. We are all his children, and He loves us. All of us. Especially your grandpa."

Tears welled in Jonathan's eyes. Charlie blinked back some of his own. "I want to help Grandpa. People hate him. That's why he's mad and he's sad."

Charlie's mind shot an idea. "There is something you can do that might make your grandpa happy, even though he's very sick. Would you like that?"

With a concerted bob of his head, Jonathan climbed from the oversized lounge chair and stood at Charlie's eye level, a foot from his face.

"Do you know what 'huge' means?"

Jonathan looked puzzled.

Charlie held his hands, palms facing each other, about one foot apart. "Is this huge or just big?"

Jonathan smiled. Taking Charlie's hands, he pushed them as far apart as his little-boy wingspan would allow.

"Good. Now we have huge. Now—do you know what tiny is?" Charlie continued to hold his hands far apart. Jonathan took one then the other, pushing them until they almost touched. Charlie made sure that only a little space remained.

"Do you know what a *detail* is?"

Jonathan shook his head.

Charlie curved his hand like a C, then positioned his thumb and finger together, nearly touching. "A detail is some tiny little thing that is so small we might not notice it. Like what you ate for dinner one week ago."

Jonathan grinned. "Macaroni and cheese, hot dog, green beans—"

"Wow! You have a great memory."

"I eat that every night. Except when Mommy makes me eat something else."

"Then let me think of another example of a tiny detail." Charlie paused. "I've got it. What color socks did I wear yesterday?"

Jonathan shrugged. "I don't know."

"But you were with me yesterday. For a long time. Can't you remember?" Charlie shook his head. "The color of my socks is a tiny detail that wasn't worth remembering. Maybe you didn't even look at my socks."

"What color were they?"

"They were green."

Jonathan laughed.

"See, sometimes we notice little things that don't seem important, so we don't remember." Charlie held out one arm in the familiar way that invited Jonathan to snuggle. The child nestled into its curve. "There's a tiny detail, a little bit of your story, that could make your grandfather very happy if you can tell me. That is, if you are willing to try to remember something about the day your gram died." He paused, letting his comment sink in. "I know—it's painful to think about that day. But you may know a detail that could help."

Jonathan hung his head.

"It's okay. Remember, everyone knows you didn't hurt Gram. *You* know you didn't hurt Gram. Will you try to remember something if I ask you a question?"

"They think—" Jonathan stole a glance at his grandfather. "—that *he* hurt my gram. But he didn't."

"That's right. But someone else did. Jonathan, this detail is very important. Are you willing to help if you can?"

Jonathan let out a deep breath and, eyes on the floor, nodded.

"Do you remember telling me that you took the plastic bag out of the waste paper basket?"

Jonathan hesitated then looked up, puzzled. "I don't understand."

"Try to remember. It was probably plastic, small enough to fit in the basket. Maybe you could see through it. Like that one over there in the corner." He pointed to the small trashcan in the corner of the room. "Can you picture the one in Gram's room?"

Slowly Jonathon bobbed his head.

"After the man left and you were able to leave the closet, what did you do with the bag?"

"I put that thing in it—you know—from Gram's 'quipment."

"Okay. Was there anything else in the bag?"

Jonathan shrugged. "Stuff." A guilty look betrayed his face. "And a little bottle. It was on the floor. The angel dropped it."

Charlie felt his eyebrows lift toward his hairline. "What did you do with the little bottle?"

A whisper. "Put it in the bag. So no one would know about the angel."

"Did you take the bag?" A nod. "Then where did you put the bag?"

The child said nothing for so long that Charlie's anxiety nearly crushed him. "Did you throw it away? Put it outside in the trash? Maybe hide it somewhere?"

Another whisper. "I hid it—in my bear."

"Your bear? How did you do that?"

Jonathan touched his thumb to his index finger and, squeezing them together, made a sweeping motion up and down his torso. "My bear has a zipper."

"Is the plastic bag still in your bear?"

He looked puzzled. "I don't know."

"Did you take the bag out of your bear?"

"No."

"Would it be okay if—" He almost said *the police* but stopped himself. While he needed someone official who could preserve the chain of evidence, he couldn't risk the child's balking. "Would it be all right if I looked inside your bear for the bag?"

Jonathan looked puzzled. "Why?"

"Because something inside the bag might help your grandpa."

Slowly Jonathan looked back and forth between his grandfather and Charlie. "But how?"

"So we can prove that your grandpa did not hurt your gram."

"I don't understand."

"Do you trust me?" Jonathan nodded slowly. "I have to be honest with you," Charlie said. "It's possible that the bag got thrown out a long time ago. But we need to look for it. We need to see what else was put the bag. Is that all right?" *(in)*

"Well. Okay."

"Where is your bear?"

"It used to go on my back, but the straps got too little. I'm a big boy. It's for a baby. But I hug my bear when no-body's looking."

Charlie struggled to remain patient. They were so close. "But Jonathan," he asked soothingly, "Where is your bear *now*?"

Chapter 16

Jade led the detective and a crime scene technician into Jonathan's room. She opened the closet door for their inspection. "There—that box in the corner. He had so few toys that I didn't have the heart to give any away when he outgrew them."

Without removing the box from the closet, the technician photographed it in position. With latex-gloved hands, he then removed the flimsy cardboard container and set it on the bedroom rug. He lifted the lid and photographed the contents without disturbing them. The trio nearly clunked heads peering into its depth. She pointed, and the technician extracted a fuzzy brown object. "Here—is this it?" He held up a matted, threadbare creature that had been extremely well loved.

She smiled. "That used to be one of those backpacks that a child can fill with his treasures. You know, to keep him entertained in the car or some waiting room."

The technician set the bear on the toy box lid and snapped its picture, right side up and upside down. He opened the zipper and took several more shots. "Why don't you use the kitchen table?" Jade suggested. When they agreed, she led them down the narrow hallway, through the dining room where her mother had died, and into the kitchen. She switched on the overhead light and the hurricane lamp that sat on the scared metal table.

The technician spread paper on the table then opened the bear's zipper. He looked in then up at the others, smiling. Carefully he extracted a clear plastic bag that appeared to be the two-gallon size. Tipping the bag onto the paper, he stared at the contents then grinned at Jade. One pair of extra-large white surgical latex gloves, an inch of thin plastic tubing, a small glass bottle, and a tiny metal object lay on the paper. The metal object was cylindrical, dime-size, and about one-eighth inch thick.

"Jackpot," said the detective.

"What's that?" Jade asked of the small metal cylinder.

"Looks like a battery to me—the kind you'd use in a watch, only bigger."

"That must be what Jonathan thought he'd knocked off his grandmother's equipment. Would a battery like that have been used on her medical equipment?"

"Wouldn't be much use if it were dead."

"Could you test it?"

"Sure. And we'll check it against the equipment to exclude it as having any need to be there. Maybe someone else dropped it and left a print."

The technician placed each item into a separate evidence bag onto which he wrote his name, the date, and what, when, and where each item had been collected. Before liberating his hands from his gloves, he placed all the evidence bags into his satchel.

"How long will this take? If we can link any findings to a woman who's already in custody, we need to do so before someone springs her."

"We'll put a rush on it."

⋯⋯

"What did you find?" the detective asked the evidence technician.

"First, the battery. And that's what it is. We found a

partial print that doesn't match anyone in AFIS—the Auto-
mated Fingerprint Identification System. If I were to guess,
it fell out of somebody's pocket at an undeterminable date
and time. Someone must have picked it up and set it nearby
where it subsequently caught the child's attention. You can
tell the little boy that such a battery was not part of his
grandmother's equipment. The kid's off the hook."

"He'll be relieved to hear that," Jade said.

"Now for the exciting news. That snip of IV line had a
small puncture hole. By the time we were able to do a tox
screen, a lot of time had gone by. That little bottle, however,
contained traces of a liquid, its label identifying it as Panduronium. That drug also was present in the hypodermic needle the police took from Mr. Alderfer's attacker at the hospital. Its rarity begs a connection."

"Were there any usable fingerprints on either Clara
Murdock's IV line or the bottle in Jonathan's plastic bag?
And what about the gloves? Anyone could have dropped
them since the last time garbage was collected."

"No usable prints were present on the IV or bottle, but
your perp, in an attempt to be clever, did something stupid
with the gloves. Criminals wear latex for the same reason
we do—not to leave trace on whatever they touch. Fingerprints, blood, saliva, seamen, epithelials, anything that could
co-mingle the victim's DNA with their own. Also important, in addition to biological trace, are minute particles
present in the room, such as lint and dust. So. While the vil-
lain is doing whatever to the victim, he wears gloves."

"What did she do that was stupid?" Jade asked.

"First, she didn't take them with her. Next, consider
this: when you wear latex gloves, how do you take them
off?"

"Like this." The detective stripped an imaginary pair
off his hands.

"They're inside out, right? Our perp figured on that and
apparently used a scrap of paper to grasp glove number two,
once hand number one was no longer protected. Ever notice

how these gloves tend to curl up at the wrist when you strip them? A fingerprint got rolled into the wrist edge of glove number two from the before-mentioned paper. It must have torn free, unnoticed. Then she used something abrasive to wipe the inside of each fingertip, supposedly to obliterate fingerprints there. Can you guess where else our killer went wrong?"

The detective repeated the imaginary motion, a sly smile overtaking his face. "In stripping off the gloves, they ended up inside out. What would appear to be the side against the fingertip that contacted his prints—wasn't. The killer wiped the fingernail side by mistake."

"As an added bonus, the gloves were a thin, cheap variety. We were able to raise fingerprints from the impression on the inside of the gloves. Your killer wouldn't have noticed that with the naked eye. And, if I may have a drum roll, the fingerprints match those of the perpetrator who attacked Mr. Alderfer at the VA."

"What about DNA? My wife keeps a box of latex gloves for gardening. 'Watch this,' she'd say when she stripped them off. Water flies everywhere."

"Right again. That's sweat. As in a source of the killer's DNA. Again, same perpetrator."

"Prints on the IV line or the bottle would be nice."

"No luck there. But we're trying to find the source of the Panduronium. Your friendly local pharmacist would not carry such an unusual drug. And the bottle is marked with a code."

"Who do you think could get hold of it?" Jade asked.

"Someone doing research in a university lab. Sign out four bottles, only use three, pocket one. Or someone with access to a hospital's leftover surgical supplies. Panduronium is a neuromuscular blocking agent used as an alternative to tubocurarine. It's used in the operating room."

"What if Jonathan had played with the bottle? Could that have killed him?"

The technician scrunched a skeptical face. "Anything's

possible, I suppose, depending upon how much he handled it, if the seal broke, dripped on an opening in his skin, and so on."

"Our time line could be a problem," the detective said, "placing our perp with Clara Murdock at the time of her death. If she had tended Mrs. Murdock one other time, her attorney could argue that the scene was staged or the items we tested were left during her previous visit. Furthermore, wouldn't even the stupidest criminal take his gloves with him?"

"Staging? That's a reach," Jade said. "How could my father possibly collect and stage the evidence if he didn't know that woman? Doesn't the evidence prove that he isn't guilty?"

"Seems unlikely now."

"It could be suggested that a third party killed her. Just playing devil's advocate here."

Jade paced, eyes unseeing on the industrial tile floor. "Wait a minute! An autopsy was performed on my mom. Toxicology tests would have been done on her blood. Wouldn't there be traces of Pandur...whatever you said?"

"Yes to the former, and probably no to the latter. In the body, Panduronium breaks down rapidly, hence the suitability for a knowledgeable killer. If the coroner knew to look for it, he'd have to have done it quickly," the technician said.

"Can you check the toxicology report?" Jade asked the detective.

"Of course."

"If there's no trace, can't you bluff? Let her killer think that the substance was identified at the time of her death but no significance seemed relevant until now? Until our witness informed us that he'd seen her drop the bottle onto the floor? Tell her that it had been preserved until now. That the bottle's number was traced to her. And that evidence, combined with her more recent crime, will identify her as a serial killer making the death penalty appropriate. On that basis, ask the DA to file murder one charges against her and ask for the death penalty. That might convince her to take a plea. That also could generate the kind of publicity we need to cast a much larger net," Jade suggested. "What about that oily smell? Was she a mechanic in her spare time?"

"We wondered about that too. We did find a container of penetrating oil, but it was in her bathroom vanity, along with bottles of high-end perfume. What we didn't find was mechanics' tools—not even a simple emergency kit. We suspect the she used the oil to reinforce her disguise as a man."

❦❦❦

Jade poked her head shyly into Charlie's room. "Hey!" he said. "Come on in! I could use a little company."

She entered, her large LL Bean tote slung over one shoulder. "Could you do me a favor?"

"Sure. Just name it."

"I got a packet of stuff from my in-laws. No way that could be anything but trouble. I'm thinking it's the first volley to get custody of Jonathan."

"Is that what it says?"

She shook her head in what Charlie could only describe as despair. "I'm exhausted. My poor dad, Jonathan's problems, the cops and DA, the press, nasty people. We didn't even have time to mourn my mom properly. I cannot face one more battle. I was wondering if you could possibly read through this stuff. Just give me the bottom line—how deep the water and how hot the hell."

"Jade, you're not alone, not as long as I'm around. Are these people really that bad?"

"What you saw the other day was a big act."

"How could they possibly have objected to you?"

"My father-in-law fantasized that he was like Joseph Kennedy but with a better pedigree. Supposedly a fine old family that came over on the Mayflower, mansions in New York and the Hamptons, a partner in a prestigious law firm. His son was supposed to follow him into law and then politics. Senator, ambassador, perhaps even president. Sound familiar? The only thing that interested my husband was photojournalism, even after he passed the bar. He hated man's inhumanity to man. Wanted to expose war for what it was really about—rubber, oil, diamonds, you name it."

"How did you meet him?"

"I was tending bar in a trendy restaurant. His date didn't show. After too many shots, he started grousing to me. Dad was running his life. Mom was auditioning Manhattan debutants and so on. I looked him in the eye and said, 'Just *how* old are you?' 'Twenty-six.' 'And you haven't cut the umbilicus, why?' He just looked at me as if it were a foreign concept. 'Is that the bulge in your pants?'" She laughed. Shook her head. "Talk about balls. I still can't believe that I said that to a customer. Next thing I knew, we were a very intense couple. He quit the law firm then struck out on his own. To pay the rent, he shot weddings."

"What did his parents do about that?"

"Went through the motions of cutting him off. But when he didn't run home for money and left Manhattan, they redirected their anger at me. To get their son back on a leash, they thought they could drive me away. Mysteriously, I was fired from one job then another. Drug allegations. Unsubstantiated bad rumors. Then one night he got a phone call. He left. Vanished. They won."

"Did he give you a reason?"

She shook her head. "I had no way to find him. No one to call. I just kept on keeping on, thinking he'd call or show up eventually. After three years, I filed. If it hadn't been for my parents, I don't know what I would have done. They were thrilled about the baby—held my hand through every step. Money isn't everything. They've given Jonathan and me all the love any daughter could want. Now she's gone, and he's going."

"Please. Sit down. Give me those papers."

Jade glanced over her shoulder as one more cart was wheeled down the hall, pushed by a man in green work clothes who was carrying some tools. "Can we go somewhere else?"

"That small private lounge down the hall. My daughters and I have never been disturbed there. Maybe you could give me a push. By the way, where's Jonathan?"

"He fell asleep in the recliner by Dad's bed. He's afraid to leave him alone. I think he knows Dad's time is near. He has overheard so much medical jargon. Grownups think children don't hear what they're not supposed to, but they do."

"If they're both okay for the moment..."

She nodded. "Let's go."

Jade didn't waste any time once they had relocated. She perched stiffly on the corner of the sofa near Charlie's armchair. From her bag she withdrew three envelopes, two slim and one very fat. "Open them. Please. I just can't look."

"If you're sure. They could contain very personal business." She handed him a stainless steel knife with which he slit the skinniest envelope. The embossed return address identified Jade's former in-laws. He scanned the first paragraphs of a two-page letter, then unfolded a third smaller paper. "Oh my god. This is an original death certificate." He paused to let that sink in. "It's for your husband." He handed it to her.

She studied the details, bug-eyed. "If this is accurate, why, he's been dead all along!"

Charlie waited while she absorbed it. When she finally looked up, he summarized the letter. "The first paragraph reads like another apology—more of the same from the other day. The second and subsequent paragraphs detail how the private detectives finally found his remains. Evidently, he was in a plane crash and was buried as the Italian version of a John Doe in a remote northern village. Investigators focused on unidentified passengers in private plane crashes whose flights originated in Rome. Evidently, they had dismissed the Greece lead."

"I don't get it. If a plane, private or commercial, takes off from Rome and doesn't reach its destination…"

"You're assuming they filed a flight plan. They may have used a private airstrip then headed for a clandestine destination. You know, under the radar. Sounds like they ran into the Alps."

"But if they were heading for the Middle East, what were they doing in northern Italy?"

"Concealing their true destination? Going elsewhere first? Picking up additional passengers or supplies? Who knows. Ultimately, he was identified by his dental records."

"That would have been easy if the Italians had known where to look. My husband had played ice hockey. He'd lost a few teeth. His parents sent him to a world-class periodontist for the best implants. They may have been scribed with a code."

Charlie continued to read until he came to a point that required him to open the second envelope. "This one's from an insurance company. Evidently, your in-laws filed death certificates for policies they took out when he was little. A newer policy that your husband bought lists you as his sole beneficiary. Your in-laws gave them your current address." Charlie read the details on a smaller piece of paper. "This is a check, made out to you."

He handed the letter to Jade, whose eyes filled with tears as she read the first page for herself. "He didn't dump me. And here, all these years, I've been hating him, cursing him every day, imagining him fulfilling his parents' dream with some debutant." Eyes streaming, she glanced at the check, which seemed of minor importance by comparison. "Twenty-five thousand dollars!" She smiled through her tears. "That will pay off some debts and buy Jonathan new clothes."

"Jade. Look again. There's one more zero."

"Nurse!" Charlie bellowed to anyone that might hear him. "We need some help here! Nurse! Somebody, please!"

Staffers came running. Jade, head between her knees, was gasping for air. Charlie watched helplessly as they ministered to her. Finally, the crises passed. "I'm sorry," she gasped. "So sorry," she kept repeating. "It's quite a shock."

Time passed. She sipped ginger ale that someone had brought while staring at the check. Finally she remembered the third envelope. "What does it say?"

Charlie extracted a blue-jacketed folder used to cover legal documents. Jade sagged. "Here it comes," she muttered. "What are they suing me for? The money? Jonathan's custody? What?"

Charlie opened the tri-fold documents then looked up at her in surprise. "Why, it seems to contain the details of a trust fund." He skimmed through the pages. "The trust is for Jonathan."

Jade slit her eyes. "I knew it. They give him a shit load of money with strings attached. Or, when he's sixteen he can buy his own sports car and wrap himself around a tree. Or maybe, as a condition, he has to come live with them. How's that for leverage? The best schools, toys, travel et cetera, ad nasium. They can't touch me, but they can force me to let him go—"

Charlie interrupted her with an outstretched palm. "Hold on. I'm still reading. There's more." He continued reading in silence then returned to their letter. "The trust fund is pretty straight forward. There's a specific sum to be held in trust. The interest and part of the principal won't be distributed until he's—get this—forty years old. Its intended purpose is for him or his heirs into perpetuity for education, housing, reliable transportation. Jade, sports cars are not reliable transportation. Oh! By age twenty-five he is supposed to be serving the community. There's more detail. Guess who they're naming as his trustee?"

"I can't wait."

"You!"

"And if I'm not around when he's forty?"

"You will be. But if ever you can't serve, you are to appoint the trust department of a bank."

"What's to stop them from canceling the trust if they disapprove of my decisions?"

"There's a lot of legalese here, but there's something about its being an irrevocable trust. You better read their letter yourself. It spells out their intentions."

"I guess this changes everything."

"You'll have homework to do. You'll need to talk to this lawyer, get one for your family, make a will, get an accountant…"

"I'd give every penny of that check to clear my dad's name."

eჂeჂ

Mike paid a second visit to his old friend in HR. "Should have put money on how long it would take you to show up again," she said, prying her bulky frame from her squeaky swivel chair. Circling her desk and then Mike, she shut the door to the corridor. "Sit."

He did. So did she. "Never, in my forty-odd years on the job, has anything come close to this episode in Hospice. Were you there? Did you see it?"

Mike shook his head. "I was off duty, but I'm intimately familiar with the situation."

"Then you've got no information to trade." She laughed heartily, underscoring that she was joking. "You want her background, right? Which I cannot give you, right again, because all HR information is confidential."

"And if you cough up personal details, you will be fired. Be honest, now—don't you have all the time in grade for maximum benefits? I suppose the perp could sue you—"

She pulled a folder from beneath a stack that covered her desk and gave him a wicked grin. "What do you want to know?"

"Who is she? What's in her background? How did such a person penetrate the VA?"

"Ground rules: You tell nobody. I mean *NObody*!"

"I owe Charlie an explanation."

She shoved the folder under another and laced her fingers on top of the pile. She grinned smugly at him. "My rules. My reputation. I repeat, *NO* one."

"I could agree, lying through my teeth. What's to stop me?"

"The content of your character."

He acquiesced with a nod.

She retrieved the file and palmed the rest of the stack to one side. She opened it. On top was a photo that could have graced *People*. "The original paperwork has been pulled already, but I kept copies. Name she used is Leslie Martin. I remember this gal rather well. She was—unusual."

"In what way?"

"First off, her demeanor didn't fit her scanty education and work record. I'd have taken her to be a high-level professional, rather than someone looking for entry-level clerical work. She was polished. Too mature for early thirties."

"Could she have been a downsized corporate type? Or been fired for some infraction she didn't want to disclose?"

"That would have come out in our background check. My sense ranged from divorced doctor's wife to a bored trust-fund type to witness protection. Maybe she was fleeing from an abusive husband, although she seemed like someone who could take care of herself."

"I assume, if you hired her, that she passed a criminal background check."

"Nary a blip. Another reason I remember her so vividly was how she answered this question here." She pointed to the bottom of page number two. "Under *person to contact in case of emergency*, she entered *none*. When I asked to list a family member or a friend, perhaps, she simply said no. She didn't try to fill in the awkward pause that followed. Most would. Parents are dead, no sibs, new in town, etc.

She just sat, perfectly poised. And speaking of which, she wasn't the least bit nervous. That's unusual in a job interview, especially when an overqualified applicant seems to be chasing last resorts."

"Did she, by any chance, have computer skills?"

"According to her supervisor, she was one of those people who could untangle complex problems without asking for help. On her application, she claimed to be self-taught. And she was young enough to be part of that fearless generation who cut their teeth on electronics."

"What did her co-workers say about her? Did she make friends? Play well with others?"

"Naturally, after what happened, those who knew her best couldn't stop talking. You know, basking in being an intimate expert. All have received a directive from upstairs to say nothing to the press, lest they be fired. I sense jealousy—she was a beauty—annoyance at her reserve, not wanting to socialize with anybody. Quiet. Aloof. Make that cold. No personal chatter. No interest in her fellow workers' lives. But she did excellent work. Preferred that solitary workstation that's located near the chapel."

Mike reacted. Of course! The woman all the guys were talking about. He had observed her himself when he and Charlie had talked in the chapel. Had she overheard them? That workstation made sense. A very private place to snoop into patients' records if she had the proper access codes. "Did her supervisor find any access-code cheat sheets? Did her job description even authorize her to have them?"

"It did not. She must have an excellent memory."

"I don't get it. Why would an ostensibly normal person kill strangers?"

"I think you've got that backward. What's normal for her is killing people. The rest is just cover. But my background is nursing and business, specifically what is germane to human resources. That question is better answered by a psychiatrist with a specialty in serial killers." She sighed. "This place will turn into a zoo—the fallout unprecedented. Every employee, every procedure, every record will be scrutinized. Fed will encamp. It's so unfair. Our beautiful hospital. Our wonderful people. Our excellent reputation compromised by one sociopath. I'm glad I announced my retirement before the shit hit the fan."

Mike rose to shake her hand, but when she circled the desk, they hugged instead. "There is nothing you could have done to prevent this. Don't even go there. Promise?"

She smiled, tears in her eyes, but nodded agreement as if for his benefit.

ೕೂೕ

Ben Tothero arrived for work as Elsabet Bentz was starting the coffee. She noticed immediately how uncomfortable he looked, squirming and twitching like a naughty child. "Ben—you're early this morning. Lose your watch?"

"I've got to talk to you and your husband."

Oh god, she thought. *Here it comes. He's going to quit. And just when I'm on the brink of several huge sales that will salvage our finances but hog lots of time.* "What is it, Ben?"

"Can we go back to his room? I'd like to speak to both of you together."

They gathered in the bedroom, Elsabet taking a chair and Ben, refusing to sit. He paced. Took deep breaths and squeezed his forehead with his thumb and index finger. She feared by his draining color that he would pass out. She waited.

"I've done a lot of soul searching, talked with my minister, and my support group, and I have a confession to make. It's about my background. You had to realize my references didn't check out. Most people wouldn't have hired me, or if they did, would have fired me. You guys have been great to me, trusting me, not making a fuss about my dubious background."

"Well, I have noticed that you sound well educated," Elsabet said. "Unless whatever's in your past impacts your work here, we don't need to know. You've been our angel."

Ben shook his head. "You do need to know. It's only fair. Then you can decide if you still want me working for you. That you're confident that you can trust me. That I won't endanger your husband." He took a deep breath. "Where to begin? My real name is Benjamin Samuel Clark, and I've been a recovering addict—clean and sober—since 1997. But I have a criminal record…"

స్చాస్చ

Jonathan held his *Go Fish* cards close to his face, concealing his mouth, his merry eyes peering over his hand. But Charlie caught the huge grin, given away by the child's crinkled eyes. If Charlie had been planning to let the boy win, he needn't have bothered. Jonathan forgot nothing, revealed little, could probably bluff any old soldier within a few years. Besides concentrating on every card played, he had a mind like a steel trap. Best rid his vocabulary of phrases like that before his vegetarian daughter lectured him on inhumane grounds.

Hopefully Charlie asked, "Got any sixes?"

"Go fish!" the child cackled. "Got any five's?"

Charlie did and handed them over. With a flourish, Jonathan set down his runs, victorious again. Charlie shook his head in dismay. "You got me! Want to make it best out of seven?"

As he watched Charlie shuffle, Jonathan bent his fingers to an imaginary deck. "How old do I have to be before I can shuffle?" he asked.

"It's not how old, but how coordinated your hands are and whether they're big enough to manage the deck. Here. Take them. I'll show you how. Doesn't always help just to watch. You've got to put your hands to the task."

Jade slipped into the room. Quietly, she smoothed her

son's back. "Jonathan?" He looked around at his mother. "The doctor says it's time to say goodbye to Grandpa." She paused, letting that sink in. The boy set down his cards. "His body is ready to die. He'll be going to heaven in a few minutes to be with Gram. Would you like to come say goodbye?"

Jonathan whipped a look from his mother to Charlie. "Can Mister Charlie come too?"

Charlie intervened. "Oh. I don't know if I should. The room is very small. I'm sure your family will want to be alone at this time."

Jonathan gave him sad, committed eyes. "But you're family."

"Could you?" Jade asked.

"Well. Sure. Of course." He pushed off the chair where he had been sitting, readied his walker to trail the pair down the hall. No sooner had they left Charlie's room than a nurse approached them. Rather than speak, she almost imperceptibly shook her head, eyes cast downward. Jade nodded, but proceeded down the hall as if nothing had been communicated.

As they approached Robert Murdock's room, an elegant volunteer with a vivacious smile nearly pranced as she approached them with a sleek little Sheltie. Jonathan laughed with delight. "This is Sophie," the volunteer said. "She's a pet therapy dog. You may pet her if you like. Sophie loves children."

Jonathan was so captivated by the delightful distraction that he forgot all about asking his mother's permission. Within seconds, he was down on the floor, nose to nose with the adorable creature. "I want a dog just like her for my birthday," he said.

The volunteer addressed the growing assembly with laughing eyes. "She's a Shetland Sheepdog. They make excellent pets. Even though they look it, Shelties are not miniature collies. They can herd, like Border Collies, but they aren't as hyper."

During the distraction, the nurse who had summoned Jade took her aside. "I am so sorry, Ms. Kepley. Your father's heart stopped while I was looking for you."

"Does he—still look all right? Like he's sleeping? I'd like my son to think he's had the opportunity to say goodbye. His grandmother's passing was—"

"Of course."

The volunteer and her little pet resumed their rounds, heading for patient rooms and lounges. Jonathan watched until they disappeared. Jade waited then took Jonathan's hand. They walked the final long steps together.

As they entered Murdock's room, Jade steadied Jonathan by his shoulders and looked at her father's face. She focused intently, swallowed hard, then calmly eased Jonathan to her father's bedside. The child looked up at his mother and whispered, "Is he asleep? Can he hear me? What do I say?"

"Just tell him you're here, that you love him, and…and…"

Jonathan inched to the old man's bedside and picked up his hand. Murdock's eyes fluttered open. "Hi, Grandpa. I love you. But—but—when you get to heaven will you tell Gram I'm sorry?"

Murdock made a small hand motion, beckoning Jonathan to come close to his face. He whispered something that made the child smile. Jonathan threw his arms around the man's chest. "Bye Grandpa. I love you." Then, beaming, he bypassed his mother and joined Charlie who was waiting at the door.

"He said something to you?"

Jonathan beckoned to Charlie, who crouched down to his level. Hand shielding his mouth, he whispered, "He says Gram loves me. She says I didn't hurt her. And heaven is great."

Charlie smothered a choke that tried to escape from his heart. Jade approached him. "Why don't you take him down to the dayroom. A volunteer says they're baking brownies."

Murdock's nurse drew Jade aside, aghast. "I am so sorry! His heart *did* stop. We thought—"

Jade squeezed her arm. "It's fine, believe me. Everything is all right. Thank you for finding us at just the right time."

As Charlie guided Jonathan toward the kitchenette, he was aware that the nurse and Jade had closed themselves into Murdock's room.

ℰ✷ℰ✷

Jonathan scarfed so many brownies and downed so much milk that Charlie feared the child would throw up. It wasn't as if they had missed lunch. Growing boys, he conceded, were not like little girls.

Much later, Jade appeared at the door and motioned Charlie into the hall. She looked drained but somehow at peace.

"Is he gone?" Charlie asked. She nodded in the affirmative. "Was there some kind of mix-up, back in the hall?"

"Strangest thing," she whispered. "It's as if he passed twice. After the nurse summoned me and before I could reach Jonathan, Dad's heart had stopped. You saw the nurse signal me in the hall. I didn't know what to do. I decided not to tell Jonathan or to say that he was asleep, to say goodbye anyway. But he must have rallied—you saw it."

"But he's really gone now?"

"Yeah. It's over."

"Could they have revived him? To give you time?"

"No way. He'd signed a DNR, and the staff respects that."

"Had he been dreaming about your mother? And what she would say?"

"Guess we won't know in our lifetime. But Jonathan has redemption. And that's good enough for me."

Chapter 17

The country church was elegant in its simplicity. The "new" structure bore a date stone that read 1885, but the congregation boasted its history to the earliest settlers who predated the Revolutionary War. On that site, two successive wooden structures had succumbed to fire and storms before the precisely cut limestone church rose on the hillside. Its towering white steeple with its four-sided bell tower supported a magnificent cross. Stained glass windows, memorial gifts to long-ago members that now slept in the adjoining graveyard, swirled pastel Christian themes.

Following the memorial service honoring both Robert and Clara Murdock, the great red doors stood ajar. The congregation dallied on the lush green lawn. Beyond a low limestone wall, graves aligned to a vanishing point into the countryside. Small children played tag among the tombstones while older ones read the earliest inscriptions, particularly fascinated by those that identified Revolutionary and Civil War veterans.

"Look at all these people," Jade murmured to Charlie. "I didn't know Mom and Dad knew so many people, or that we had so many friends. Seeing them all together blows my mind."

Charlie scanned the gathering, looking for telltale media cameras. There were none. Families appeared from a side door, carrying paper plates and white beverages cups. The church women had substituted a picnic lunch when the undercroft's air conditioner chose August's heat wave to die.

"Can I bring you something? Fix a plate for Jonathan?"

"In a bit. I need to circulate before anyone leaves. Thank them for everything they did."

Jonathan had wandered to the plot where his grandmother was buried, beside which a taut green tarp was encircled with myriad bouquets. He stared—his look vacant. Charlie watched him, wishing he could lessen his pain. He was too young to have suffered so much.

Ultimately, the child drifted to the edge of the graveyard and perched on the wall. In his hand, he clutched a drooping daisy, its stem bent in two places. Charlie approached him and sat down beside him.

"What are you thinking?" Charlie asked.

"Billy has two grandfathers. Nathan has three." Still absently twirling the daisy, he sought Charlie's face. "How come he has three?"

"Sometimes families grow bigger because someone special is added to the family. Some people are born into a family and others are chosen to be part of the family."

Jonathan hung his head, giving the daisy a little toss. "I don't have any grandpa now."

"You could adopt me. I could be your adopted grandpa."

"What's 'dopted'?"

"Ah-dopted. It means 'chosen.' Someone special you add to your family because you want to."

The child considered that for a moment, then brightened. "Megan's adopted. She is Chinese."

Jonathan drooped his head again, lost in thought for a few minutes. A gentle breeze riffled the leaves and waved the dense grass that was dotted with clover and daisies. Finally, he turned to face Charlie. "You need a new name if you're going to be my new grandpa. But I don't know what.

My Grandpa is Grandpa. Billy's are 'Pops' and 'Gramps.' I
don't like 'Gramps.' It sounds grumpy."

"What about Nathan's grandfathers? Do they have a
name that you'd like to call me?"

Jonathan shot him an exuberant smile. 'Papa!' Can I
call you 'Papa'?"

"I'd like that very much."

Jonathan gave Charlie's arm a rough squeeze then
hopped from the wall to go tell his mother.

ოჯო

Charlie said goodbye to his daughter Jeannette and
hung up the phone. He dropped his head against the back of
his chair and stared at the ceiling. Their conversation had
yielded nary a clue as to how to proceed. When did his
daughters become his parents? The concept had sneaked
into his life like gathering fog when he wasn't looking.
What decision would he and Emma have made if they
hadn't had children? They would have taken care of each
other until they were ancient. But one of them alone? And
still not yet seventy? Should he just give in, sell the house
and go into a retirement village? Goodness knows, attractive ones were popping up like toadstools.

He envisioned himself waiting, panic button in hand,
for some elder-age agency to respond. Rarely socializing
with anyone except his so-called peers, most conversation
about this ailment or that. Listening for ambulances summoned to cart away yet another new friend. He'd had quite
enough of that here. He hated the idea as much as moving in
with Susan or Jeannette. Just the thought of living on the
fringe of their lives depressed him. His daughters' local retirement villages seemed even worse. At least he knew people here. He'd seen the brochures. Places as lovely as five-
star hotels with their posh dining rooms, gyms, and pools
reminded him of an old joke that dated to the '60s.

Two hippies were dangling their feet in the water. One said, "Hey man. A barracuda just bit my foot off!" "Which one?" his companion asked. "How should I know—when you'd seen one, you've seen them all."

To him, retirement homes were elegant warehouses. Maybe he'd feel different when he was older—eighty or so—or in poor health. Home—that was the only solution that made any sense. Independence was key.

ᕗᓴᕗ

Charlie could feel the thuds in his chest and the blood pulsing through his arteries. When he closed his eyes and could feel the van turning, he knew their precise location. The miles counted down to a few blocks. Left here, left again, and now straight. He'd test it, but was afraid if he kept his eyes closed any longer, his companions might think he'd dozed off. No, he could not appear like an old timer who existed from nap to nap. He craned his eyes down the street. There! His house was still there!

The tiny caravan approached his driveway, his van pulling up to the double garage doors. A contractor's truck was already parked where the grass met the street. Charlie could have leapt from van like a child sprung for summer vacation. Instead, he waited patiently for the expected assistance.

Even with September's advance, the lawn looked as good as when he had left it. He longed to get down and roll on it, smell it, get grass stains all over his chinos. Instead, he accepted the proffered three-legged cane and proceeded with dignity to the front door. The others waited respectfully while he tried not to fumble with the keys. He pushed the door open then paused on the slate entryway to luxuriate in the sweet smell of home.

Obviously, his cleaning woman had outdone herself. He smelled the clean scent of the orange oil she used on the

kitchen cabinets. The draperies, as well as every flat surface, had been vacuumed to perfection. Fresh flowers he
recognized from his own garden graced the dining room
table. "Mr. Alderfer? Shall we get started?"

The transition specialist glanced at a clipboard then ex-
cused himself while he toured the main floor. "Do you use
your basement?" he asked when he returned.

"When my wife and I built the place over thirty years
ago, we imagined our parents, or some combination of
them, would spend a lot of time with us. There's a mother-
in-law suite with a living room, two bedrooms, and a full
bath. Over the years, we've used it for out-of-town guests,
but me? No. I don't use it myself."

The specialist turned to the contractor. "Can you install
a handicap chair to ensure access to the lower level?" Perhaps the specialist hadn't heard Charlie.

"Sure. Piece of cake."

"Now." The specialist glanced at his checklist onto
which he had already made a few marks. "Your bathrooms,
upstairs, are handicap accessible?"

Charlie nodded. Emma. He'd never removed her rails
and grab bars. "You'll need ramps, accommodations for
your kitchen, different toilets, and I recommend replacing
your bathtub with a handicap accessible shower. You'll
need to subscribe to a medic alert system whereby you can
speak directly into a personal device should you fall. I understand you have a cleaning woman and a gardener, but
you'll need to think about transportation. Doctor's appointments, groceries, errands, et cetera. Someone should check
on you every day, just in case. They'll need keys and your
emergency numbers."

"But—" Charlie scrambled to slip words in edgewise
before the specialist galloped farther down his page. "I
don't need a wheelchair anymore. I can walk. Use the walker or cane if I feel tired. Don't need a ramp or a babysitter."

"Mr. Alderfer. You've been away from your home a
long time. At the VA, meals and meds show up on schedule,

nurses and aids respond to your pages, and housekeeping duties just happen. If you want to live independently in your own home, plans must be made."

Charlie sighed, and batted his hand in dismissal. "Knock yourself out with that list. Just let me know when you're finished."

While the specialist invaded his private domain, making notes and discussing minutia, Charlie slipped from room to room, letting its comforting presence envelop him. He longed to throw out the intruders, make himself a sandwich, flip on CNN, then admire the garden. Slowly he pushed open his clothes closet door that still glided effortlessly on its smooth tracks. Emma's housecoat hung from its padded hanger. He picked up one sleeve and buried his face in its fleecy softness. Why did he feel so overwhelmed? *Emma—I need a plan.*

He sank into his reading chair that had been angled toward his side of the bed since the day they'd moved in. Closing his eyes, he concentrated, emptying his mind of all other distractions. From out of nowhere, the obvious answer burst forth.

෴෴

Surprisingly exhausted from his home visit, Charlie stretched out on his bed at the VA and rested his eyes. Suddenly, a happy distraction burst upon him as an exuberant Jonathan skipped into the room. He was clutching a large piece of construction paper onto which he had crayoned an elaborate drawing. He practically danced up to Charlie, arms extended, paper flapping, to give him a hug. Charlie beamed.

"Hey! You came to visit! Where's your mom?"

"Taking cookies to the nurses. I helped bake them, just like Gram and me. Look, Papa. I drew this *just* for you!" The paper, which was missing a corner where it had been torn from his tablet, was slightly wrinkled from being transported. It was covered with color. Hardly a square inch of white remained.

"Why that's beautiful! It looks like it's telling a story. Tell me all about it."

Jonathan snuggled close enough for Charlie to drape his arm around the child's skinny shoulders. He offered his artwork to Charlie, who tilted it for both to see.

"Who's this?" he asked, pointing to a large stick figure. The mouth, which occupied most of the face, was a large letter O.

Jonathan did an eye roll. "That's you, Papa!"

"And what's this big black thing?" Overlapping circles covered a sixth of the page. Two red discs were big as dimes.

"That's the spider!" Jonathan grinned all over himself. "See? There's that thing that sews, and there's you. You're really scared." Masses of brown rectangles, he explained, were the table and chairs. Blue sky, lollipop trees, V-shaped birds, and fluffy flowers back dropped the picture. Somehow, the house's exterior wall had disappeared into the child's imagination.

"That's the scariest spider I've ever seen. I don't think I'd want to meet him. Thank you so much. May I thumbtack this beautiful picture on the corkboard where I can see it?" Jonathan bobbed his head up and down. "I'll keep your older pictures to put in my happy box," Charlie said. "Then I can look at them whenever I need a smile."

"How come you looked sad when I came in?"

"Did I? Well, that must have been my thinking face." *No, don't lie to the child.* "That's not exactly true. I guess I was worrying. I have to make some very grownup decisions, and I don't want to make the wrong ones."

"De...what?"

"Decisions. That's when a person has to choose between one thing and another. Do you dress yourself in the morning?"

Jonathan nodded.

"You choose which shirt, which pants, which socks, right? We call that making a decision. Choosing one thing over another. Sometimes it's hard because we can't always tell which decision is best."

"Like when I wouldn't wear my jacket and it got really, really cold?"

"Exactly. Some decisions are small, like what we wear. Some are really big, like where we should live. I have big decisions to make."

"Like what?"

"They tell me I'm well enough to leave the hospital as soon as we can figure out where I should go. I have two daughters who live far away. Both of them want me to come live with them. That's right," Charlie said when Jonathan nodded. "You've met them. Anyway, both of them want me to come live with them."

"That would be fun. You could see them all the time."

"True. But I love my own house. My friends. Being my own boss. Do you know what a boss is?"

"I think so. He tells everyone else what to do."

"I want to be my own boss. Go back to my own house. My girls are afraid I can't take care of myself. There aren't any nurses at my house."

Jonathan scrunched his face in concentration, then radiated brightness. "I know. Take a nurse home with you. Take Mister Mike. He's really nice."

"Mister Mike has his own house and family. When he goes home, he has his wife and kids to look after."

"How about Miss Julie? She's always saying she's looking for some guy. She can't seem to find him."

Charlie chuckled. *Ah, yes, the too-much-information gal.* Yeah, he could see how her neediness scared men away. "That wouldn't work."

Jonathan flapped his arms at the elbows while bobbing with his whole body. "I got it! I'll come take care of you. I used to sit with Gram all the time."

"I'd love to have you come visit me when I go home. In fact, I'm counting on it. I've even talked with your mommy about that." The child beamed. "But I also need a grownup to help me. Someone who can drive a car, haul big stuff up and down steps, run the vacuum cleaner. Pick me up if I—" He froze the thought as Jonathan's face registered instant concern. "—stumble or drop something."

More excited gestures. "I know! I know! Mommy *and* I can take care of you."

Out of the mouths of babes…

Charlie reran Jade's dispassionate tick list of her insurmountable challenges and her new brave plan to achieve. What if he hired her? She and Jonathan could live in his mother-in-law apartment. He searched the child's earnest face.

"Suppose you got off the school bus, came into the house and found me lying on the floor. I'd be alone since your mom would be at work or at school. Perhaps I looked like I was asleep, but you couldn't wake me up. Do you think you could go to the phone and call nine-one-one?"

"Are you dead? Like Gram?"

"Probably not. I could be taking a nap. Or I could have fainted. Or fallen and hit my head. But you couldn't tell. But still. Knowing what to do without panicking is a big responsibility for a five-year-old child."

Jonathan's gaze was steady, his eyes never leaving Charlie's. He smiled with the pure love that only a child could give unconditionally. Finally he spoke. "But I'm almost six."

∽∾∽

"Did you know that your son is a genius?" Charlie asked Jade, who grinned at the obvious. "Yeah, of course you do," he continued. "My mother used to say, 'There's only one little white hen and every mother has it.' But in

Jonathan's case, it's true. Leave it to that smart little guy to state the obvious answer to one of our challenges."

She hadn't stopped grinning. "What did the little scamp say this time?"

"As simply as possible, I told him I wanted to return to my home when I'm discharged from the hospital. But that I couldn't live alone without some assistance. He said he could come take care of me. I explained that I also needed an adult. He volunteered you. A sweet gesture, but that got me thinking.

"I know you've inherited what must seem like a fortune, but if you go back to school full time for four years and have living expenses, much of that will be spent. My house has a complete suite in its lower level. Why don't you and Jonathan live there? Rather than pay rent, you could drive me to errands, appointments, and so on, and be in residence if I have an emergency. I can babysit for Jonathan while you're in class, lab, and the library. And you'd be free to entertain or hang out with your friends, go on dates, or field trips, and just take a break. That would be especially good during the summer."

"I don't know, Charlie. I'm so independent. I need my own space."

"You'd have it. The suite has its own private entrance. And the Buick's available. It needs to be run. Will you think about it?"

She smiled. She didn't say yes, but she didn't say no either.

"By the way, Jade. I understand Jonathan has a birthday coming up, and I don't want to miss it. Any suggestions for what a six-year-old might like?"

Jade grinned. "He'll be six on his birthday, all right. Next May. This being September, you have lots of time.

∽∾∽

Charlie nearly choked with emotion. Surrounding him

in the conference room was everyone he cared about, especially his team who had nursed him back to health. Their faith that Hospice meant transition had fresh meaning for him. Their dedication to his well-being, even near death, had made all the difference.

Jeannette, who had flown in from Atlanta, was doing her best to contain her toddler while Jonathan amused her four-year-old son. Jade, seated next to Susan, was engrossed in animated conversation about Jonathan's upcoming enrollment in kindergarten. Charlie's white coat team, including Mike, rounded out the assembly. After everyone was present and settled, Dr. Szish entered the room. The meeting came to order.

"Charlie asked that we all be together to share his decisions and to answer your questions about his future. As you know, he has been agonizing about what will become of him and how it will complicate your lives. He thinks that he's made the right choice. Charlie?"

He swallowed hard. "I took a hard look at my options, and how they would affect everybody I love. I cannot spend the rest of my life, be it brief or very protracted, as a ticking bomb. I've decided to have that second aneurysm surgically repaired."

"Dad!" Jeannette jumped to her feet. "That could kill you. The surgeon said last June that it was inoperable." She turned to her sister. "Didn't he, Susan?"

He held up his palm. "When I was home, I sat in our bedroom, asking—no listening—to what your mother used to say. 'Get the facts right.' Remember? She was meticulous about researching details. Sometimes it made me crazy because I made decisions too quickly, she said. Yes, the surgeon did say the second aneurysm was inoperable. I contacted him and asked him to clarify what he had said. What he meant was, 'It was inoperable *at that time*.' I was too fragile, had lost too much blood, had too many complications to pursue what, at the time, was an elective procedure."

"Even now, isn't that kind of surgery life threatening?"

"Well, I suppose it's not like a tonsillectomy."

"And if you survive the surgery, you'll be right back here for how many months?"

Charlie shook his head. "This time around, my surgery won't be an emergency. Pre-testing, blood work, X-rays, MRIs have already been done. The best surgical team will be in place. And happily, they won't have to break any ribs to get at the site."

"When are you planning to do this?" Jeannette asked as her toddler climbed onto her lap then changed his mind and slid off.

"Tomorrow." The women gasped. The white-coats remained grim-faced. "I wouldn't be doing this if I hadn't received some very good news." Opening a folder he passed copies of a report to his daughters they had not seen. "A blood sample was sent to Emory University for genetic testing, specifically for Marfan's Disorder. I am thrilled to report that I do not have it. That means you girls don't have to be tested. I would not have bothered with more surgery if I had Marfan's—if other vascular problems were likely. No, this is it."

"And the surgeon is all right with this?"

"Yep. I'm in my right mind, I've signed that I understand the risk and he thinks it's doable. Quality of life—that's what I told him I wanted, and that's what I'll be getting. But I'd appreciate your blessing. I want your approval and that you understand why I must do this. I have so much to live for, and for that, I need good health."

"And if it goes south?" Susan asked.

"At least you'll know it was what I wanted."

છબળ

September, 2009:

Charlie bent to deadhead a spent flower from his favorite addition to Emma's rose garden. The David Austin tag read *Pristine*, and truly, it was. He stood, his eyes sweeping the land from which he'd been carted sixteen months earlier. What a difference a year made! Roxie, his two year-old adopted Sheltie, swooped one more circle around Charlie's legs, then froze, ears perked.

Charlie looked at his watch—nearly three. Any minute now. He stood, focusing his excellent ears for that first indication. Aah, there it was. Right on time. The big yellow bus was turning the corner onto his rural road. Dropping his clippers into his bucket, he circled to the front of the house. How wonderful to be able to walk briskly, unassisted. The gamble to repair that other aneurysm had paid off big time. Guess God still had plans for him, right on this planet.

Way down the street, he glimpsed a yellow dot, which rapidly grew bigger. It stopped, red lights flashing, to free several other children before proceeding toward Charlie. Its brakes squealed as it halted. The minute the doors opened, Jonathan erupted, two-foot hopping the last step, already in midsentence. His backpack flopped as he ran, its straps loose at his elbows. Roxie herded him with joyful yelps.

"Papa! Papa!" He hurtled toward Charlie, the day's events already spilling forth.

Charlie squatted on the lawn to catch a hug and hear all the details—what he had learned, who brought in cupcakes, which child broke what rule, all in one sentence. Wistfully, thankfully, Charlie remembered his roommate Vincent De-Pasquali, the saint who had lured Jonathan into his life with a different kind of kiss. His words were prophetic: *Give a child your undivided attention and you can't shut him up.* Bless you. And thank you, God, for this precious gift.

Epilogue

Every day, Charlie gave thanks for his blessings. Jonathan was spared the agony of testifying at the killer's trial. The preponderance of evidence convinced the killer to take a plea to avoid the death penalty. For the killer, however, it wasn't over. Thanks to extensive national publicity, other victims' families were coming forward. Charlie heard that extradition procedures to death-penalty states were pending.

Unfortunately, Jade's tip about the black SUV led nowhere. The stolen vehicle was located in the airport's long-term parking lot, void of clues to the patrolman's killer. Jade told Charlie, however, that she believed justice was being done.

After a year of breezing through nursing courses with highest marks, Jade transferred to a local private college with a reputation for placing its best premed students in medical school. She quickly rose to the top of that class as well. Camped in Charlie's mother-in-law suite or attending classes while Jonathan was at school, she devoured life science with endless enthusiasm. She planned to specialize in pediatrics. Her first priority, however, was her whole family.

Jonathan's paternal grandparents had kept their word and had not forced their way into their lives. With civility, they followed Jade's lead in conducting a private memorial service for their son, Jade's late husband. When and how to include them into Jonathan's life, however, was an ongoing discussion between Jade and Charlie.

Charlie's doctors saw no reason why he couldn't live for decades—if he left crime fighting to the professionals.

That made Charlie smile.

About the Author

Nancy Hughes's family says of her work: "She murders people." On paper, that is. She made the leap from journalist, media, community relations and PR specialist to follow her heart and write mystery novels. She credits her love of writing to her parents, who were voracious readers. When Hughes was small, they spent hours reading to her, which fueled her lively imagination. Transplanted from Key West at age two, she never adjusted to the cold. While walking to grade school, then Penn State classes, she invented mystery stories to distract herself from the snow and ice. Now, nothing stirs the creative juices like a hot shower.

The view from her rural Pennsylvania home-office window is just as distracting as big city chaos when the deer munch her beloved azaleas. A three-hour commute to Manhattan connects Hughes to the Mystery Writers of America's New York chapter meetings. Their devoted leaders provide timely updates, inspiration, mentor programs, workshops, seminars, tours, legal tips, and boundless moral support. And friends! With whom she exchanges war stories and encouragement. Being published by Black Opal Books and working with their professionals is a prodigious opportunity. Her first BOB mystery is *The Dying Hour*, and a second mystery novel, A Matter of Trust, will follow.

CPSIA information can be obtained
at www.ICGtesting.com
Printed in the USA
BVHW040828300321
603707BV00012B/157